Welcome to GROOVE HOUSE

JILL MENIKETTI

Stanford Court Press

San Francisco

Published in the United States by Stanford Court Press, San Francisco, CA.
www.StanfordCourtPress.com

Library of Congress Cataloging-in-Publication Data has been applied for.

ISBN: 978-1-942828-01-3
Library of Congress Control Number: 2015900170

10 9 8 7 6 5 4 3 2 1

First Edition

Author Website:
www.JillMeniketti.com

Cover design: Adam Wayne
Interior design: Robin Krauss

"Dave Meniketti has been a dear friend, a great guitarist, and a great vocalist. We have grown up in different bands together. Who else knows the inside scoop better than Jill Meniketti, his longtime wife and manager?"
—**Sammy Hagar**

"*Welcome to Groove House* is a great rock 'n' roll read, clearly written by someone who knows and has lived the genre and its music. With so many rock-based autobiographies out there these days, it was fun to get lost in the fictional world of Mike Mays and company. A must read for any rock fan who loves a great story."
—**Eddie Trunk** (SiriusXM Radio / VH1 Classic TV host)

"This story rings true to 'all in the name of rock 'n' roll,' in a self-inflicted crash and burn lifestyle. It's never too late to redeem yourself. This is a movie waiting to happen."
—**Troy Luccketta** (Tesla)

"I've always thought if you're going to write a book about rock 'n' roll, it should be written by someone who has lived the life. Being that Jill Meniketti is the longtime wife of the legendary guitarist and singer of Y&T, Dave Meniketti, the characters in this book seem to come from real life experiences—the good, bad, and sometimes tragic side of rock, as well as a story of redemption. A good read for those who love all things rock 'n' roll."
—**Don Dokken** (Dokken)

"Jill has written a fictitious but uncanny portrait of the life of a rock star, the carnival of lost souls and innocent bystanders that come with it. I felt like I was looking into a mirror . . . yikes! Not only will you be bashing out the A chords, you'll be taking a look behind the rock 'n' roll fantasy curtain, wallowing through the blood, sweat, beer, and bullshit backstage, and into a heaping helping of R&R reality. But you've gotta love the ride!"
—**Eric Martin** (MR. BIG)

"This book **ROCKS!** I loved it! It's a totally cool journey through a rocker's world that most people don't get to experience until now. It's a blast!!"
—**Stef Burns** (Alice Cooper, Huey Lewis & the News, Vasco Rossi)

Acknowledgments

David Coverdale and Whitesnake—Immense thanks, as the 2003 Monsters of Rock tour with Y&T is where the idea for this novel struck me.

Dave Meniketti—My husband, soul mate, best friend, the greatest person with whom to share my dreams, and the best sounding board a girl could ever ask for. . . . Thanks for believing in me *always*.

Phil Kennemore—my friend, the consummate rock star. I'm gutted that I wasn't able to finish this book before he left this world. He was an inspiration for this novel, breathing some of his huge, rogue life into my characters. Sure miss ya, big guy.

Y&T band and crew, past and present—Thanks for giving me miles of laughter and decades of adventures, both on and off the road.

Y&T fans around the world—You truly are the best!

Joan Singleton—Your endless support, encouragement, and spot-on feedback have been incredibly invaluable throughout this fantastic journey. You rock!

August Tarrier—The most insightful editor a girl could ever desire. Thank you for always pushing my personal best. You are *the shit!*

Paula DiSante & Janna Wong Healey—Thanks for being the first sets of discerning eyes.

My early readers: Lauretta Kliest, Constance McKenzie, Sandra Squires, David McKinnon, Laura Bisceglia—*Mille grazie.* Thank you for your altruistic help and candor. An extra special shout out to my niece, Teresa Segura, PhD, for your enthusiasm and valuable feedback, and for always wanting to read more. And to her husband, Andy Hock, sommelier/rocket scientist, thanks for sharing your knowledge of vineyards.

Barbara Caporicci—*La mia professoressa vera. Attenzione! Grazie tante per tutto.*

Rob & Diana Jensen, and Bill Brosseau at Testarossa Vineyards—Thanks for all the fun times, countless bottles, and loads of insight on vines and wine.

Mikey Evans—One of my all-time favorite *geezers* . . . thanks for that!

Jeff Wallace and Christine Whitman of the Hollywood Bowl, and Tim Nielson of Los Gatos High School—Thanks loads for your time.

You don't stop laughing when you grow old,
you grow old when you stop laughing.

—George Bernard Shaw

Chapter 1

Mike Mays glared at Nick, the rhythm guitarist—his twenty-something, hired gun with tar-black hair veiling his dark eyes, and the shitload of hardware hanging off his face. *Poseur.*

"Face it, old man," Nick growled. "You left your chops in the '80s."

"I got jeans older than you, ya little pissant." Mike felt pressure rising in his chest. His breathing thickened. "Shoulda shipped your ass back to L.A. after the London gig."

"I'll be glad when this embarrassment of a tour is over." Nick scooped up his skull and bones McSwain guitar and began noodling.

Bones, the frizzy-haired guitar tech for the tour, straddled the dressing room doorway in his combat boots, plaid shorts, and a Judas Priest T-shirt. "Okay," he announced, "time to clear the dressing room."

Mike turned and ogled the chick's killer bod as she stood in her sexy red stilettos and her black lace skirt that barely covered her ass. One tug of the tie on her halter top, he thought, and her tits would come spilling out. He licked his lips. She'd be a tasty treat after the show.

She spun her back to him and he grinned as he ran his fingers over the bare skin above her ass. There it was: his own face staring back at him. He glanced down at the tattoo—the kid with pouting lips and long, puffy hair. Not bad, he thought, the jaw line looks pretty good and the eyes look okay. "Damn, they got my nose all wrong . . . too narrow."

He turned and caught sight of Nick in the mirror. He's about the same age as me in the tattoo, Mike thought, and then he glanced away from his own withered face and thinning hair. He turned back to the tat.

"I feel sorry for the poor bastard who has to stare at me when he screws her from behind." Mike grinned as his guitar tech and backing band laughed—all but Nick.

The chick shifted her head back to check Mike's expression, an auburn curl dropping to her shoulder. She handed him a black Sharpie. "Can you sign it?"

"I'd be delighted." Mike caressed the colors on her skin and then scribbled his name above the tat. "How 'bout you come back after the show and we'll see how great *your* ass looks on *my* face?"

The chick giggled and then hugged Mike as he planted a kiss on her cheek.

Then Bones ushered her out and poked his head back inside. "I'm off to the stage now. Need anything before I go?"

"A line of blow?"

Bones did a double-take.

Mike glanced at Dylan, the bleached-blond drummer. "Down boy. . . . No need to get on your AA soapbox." Even though Mike didn't believe in all that sobriety bullshit, he no longer did the hard stuff; it just took too much out of him anymore.

Mike felt a shiver when the roar of the festival crowd swelled into the dressing room. He glanced around the trailer—the same makeshift dressing room every band had that day, lined up side by side like an RV tailgate party at a Raiders game. He'd expected something more comfy, like the backstage at Shoreline Amphitheatre. . . . After all, it was his comeback tour.

He slipped to the back corner for some privacy and reached for the stage clothes hanging on a hook. He strained into his black leather pants and stretched into his charcoal tank top. On the floor next to his Harley-Davidson boots sat a jet-black eyeliner pencil and a plastic cup of Jack and Coke. He groaned as he bent over to get both, took a swig, and then grunted as he pulled on his boots. Guzzling the drink, he leaned in to the full-length mirror and pressed on the bags puffing out under his eyes. "Fuckin' hell." After trickling drops of Visine into each eye, he smudged on more eyeliner. His hair was looking so scraggly, so he fluffed it up and spritzed on another coat of hairspray. Taking a step from the mirror, Mike gave a final once-over.

He turned and then strutted through the dressing room casting a smirk at the three primping, half-naked, twenty-somethings who made up his backing band. He knew he was way better than these hired guns.

Dylan tapped a pair of drumsticks on his thighs. "Ready to rock, Mike?"

"Always. See you dudes up there."

"See ya onstage, man," said Lonnie, the bass player, spiking his blond streaks in the mirror.

Nick said nothing.

Mike flung the dressing room door wide open and paused, gazing at the surrounding mountains. He squinted toward the highest peak, which was crowned with a distant, medieval castle. "Sure ain't got shit like that in America." He looked back at Nick, but he had his head down, noodling on his guitar. *Poseur*, Mike thought, as he let the dressing room door slam.

Walking the backstage path past the artist catering tent, Mike fielded greetings from the other bands. When he felt an arm on his shoulder, he turned to face his manager, Bruce, in a white Panama hat and white button-down shirt, looking so outta place at a rock festival.

"How's the voice today?" Bruce asked, twisting his moustache as he glanced around the backstage area. Then he leaned in to Mike's ear and hissed, "I worked my ass off to get you back on the scene, bud . . . don't fuck it up."

"I got it covered," Mike crowed, as he dipped out from under Bruce's arm. He glanced around and then lowered his voice. "Dude, I, uh, could use another infusion of dough. Landlord's on my ass back home."

"I told you, give me three good songs to send the label. Remember, we only have an *option* for another recording. If they don't like what they hear, the deal's over."

Yeah, yeah. Mike couldn't look at Bruce. When he spotted a break in the chain-link fence where he could peer out at the festival crowd, he turned and changed course. "Worked his ass off," Mike muttered as he glanced back with a smirk to see Bruce herding his wife and two teenage sons toward the stage. He missed that hungry young Bruce who used to score hookers and blow, and could always squeeze an extra grand outta any promoter or record exec. Nowadays, he was pure business . . . that was, when Mike could even get him on the phone.

A crooked smile crossed Mike's face as he glanced out at the massive festival stage. Always a rush to play the big stages, he thought. Beneath the colossal lighting rig, a red and black banner rippled in the warm evening breeze: GERMANY ROCKS. Thirty-four thousand energetic rock fans were jam-packed on the field. From the crowd's center, thousands of rowdy fans—young and old—pushed forward, vying for closer range at the stage. Poor fuckers, Mike thought, meltin' in the sun all day. Sweaty bodies near the front shoved and swayed and pressed from every direction; the diehard fans stood their ground, pushing back to maintain their small parcel of dirt among the herd. So glad, he thought, I ain't out there with the masses.

At the chug of his guitar being checked through the sound system, Mike headed toward the stage, scoping out the untilled farmland and the mixing tower in its center. Onstage, the frantic changeover continued. Stagehands darted about, running cables, and swapping out amplifiers while a tech on the drum kit pounded out a line check for the sound man.

"Mike Mays!" a voice called out.

About to climb the tall stairs to the stage, Mike turned to see some dude with a buzz cut wearing faded jeans and a denim jacket covered with patches.

"Can you sign this?" The dude held out a silver Sharpie and a magazine featuring Mike, and then watched as he scrawled his signature.

Mike leafed through the magazine and paused at the festival advertisement. "Fuckin' hell." He was thrilled to get second billing, a position Bruce had miraculously finagled based on Mike's legacy alone. "They been beggin' me to come outta retirement for years. Got a killer band. . . . These cats kick ass, old school style. Ya won't see nothin' like *this* today."

He flipped a few more pages, scrutinizing the album ads, mainly newer bands. He didn't recognize the majority. Turning back to the feature, Mike winced at the photos. "Fuckin' hell. Don't nobody weed out the shitty shots no more?" He glanced at the German gobbledygook in the article and figured it was probably a rave, unlike the mixed European press reviews so far.

Mike's backing band breezed by him, kicking up dust before they headed up the stairs. His eyes focused on Nick, that ungrateful little prick in ripped jeans and a T-shirt.

"These fuckin' teenyboppers don't know how to dress for stage," Mike bitched as he readjusted his snugly tucked balls in his black leather pants. His gaze landed on the fan's patch-covered denim jacket. Iron Maiden. Mötley Crüe. AC/DC. KISS. Whitesnake. MM—Mike Mays. "Fuckin' hell." Mike traced a finger over the silver and red embroidery. "Haven't seen that patch since the '80s."

"You're an icon," the eager fan said in slight accent. "The best . . . lead guitar *and* lead vocals."

Mike nodded. After all, the little ass-wipes who called themselves musicians these days had cut their teeth on his chops, as did most of the '80s hair bands. Yeah, he knew his shit, alright.

The dude stood nervously wringing his hands. "Can't wait to see you play again."

Mike tossed him a nod. "Every interviewer on tour the last two weeks complained I been away too long." He grinned. "It's good to be back." Between drumming up an occasional gig and noodling every day in his San Francisco apartment, he'd kept up his chops . . . always.

Mike returned the pen and magazine. "Don't go sellin' this on eBay now." He leaned in to the window of a minibus parked nearby for a final glance. He fluffed his hair, tugging it forward to conceal the receding hairline. He angled closer, widened his eyes, and wiped a smudge of eyeliner. In the reflection he noticed the fan still standing behind him. He groaned. *How do these fuckers always get backstage?*

"It's been fifteen years. Too long, yeah?"

Mike squinted toward the setting sun. Even after countless interviews the past two weeks, he still felt unsure how to answer that one. He'd never intended to stay away so long.

"Mike!" Atop the stairs, Bones lifted a guitar and motioned for him.

"Have a good show!" the fan said, raising the two-finger metal salute, as Mike climbed the stairs to the stage.

Mike stopped on the platform to catch his breath from the long climb. He veered away from the stagehands darting about, moving road cases, until he found his spot stage right and out of view of the rowdy audience. Like a runner warming up for a marathon, he shook out his arms and legs and stretched his neck. Mike tried to ignore the house music blaring through the crowd; he didn't recognize the tunes.

The skinny tech held up Mike's prized 1960 Gibson Les Paul Custom "Black Beauty" guitar.

"Not yet, Bones."

Bones held the guitar, patiently waiting.

Mike belted out a few shrill vocal warm-ups, then calmed down, mentally preparing for the moment. Smoothing his hands over his tank top, he glanced down and sucked in his stomach. He inhaled deeply and slowly expelled the air. Yep, he was ready. . . . Ready to prove to Germany that he could still rock. Like a king commanding his court, he reached out for his guitar. "Okay. Now, Bones."

Bones lifted the flashlight hanging from his lanyard and aimed it out through the crowd to the mixing tower in the field. Flicking the light on and off, he signaled "show time" to the soundman. Then, for the final pre-show ritual, he adorned Mike with the guitar.

At Bones's signal, the subterranean low-end quaked through the sound system and into the audience. Mike grinned. His pre-recorded intro triggered the crowd every time.

As Mike inched closer to entering the stage, he spotted two hot chicks in ass-hugging shorts standing in his path. He wiped droplets of sweat from his unruly brows and gave them a cocky smile.

With one arm cradling the neck of his guitar, Mike sauntered toward the women. He reached out his right hand and grabbed the fine ass of the blonde as he passed. The women giggled.

As the thunderous fanfare faded, Mike watched his hired guns seize the festival stage and strike the opening chords to "Lucky Night," one of his hits from the '80s. A crooked smile spanned his face when the crowd roared. A chill streaked up his spine as the chanting mounted: "Mike, Mike, Mike!"

The crowd volume swelled when Mike chunked out the opening guitar lick from offstage, and the cheers amplified once he swaggered onstage.

He sauntered to the microphone, center stage, screeched, and then purred out the lyrics. Pummeling the audience with song, Mike pointed at three chicks near the front, each perched on shoulders, teetering above the festival crowd. His fingers moved subconsciously across the frets as he watched one of the girls remove her bikini top and fling it onto the stage. When he ducked, grinning, the crowd whooped. *Hell, yeah.*

After striking the last chord of the song, Mike leaned on the mic stand, absorbing the love. When the applause dissolved, he rested both hands on the mic and yelled, "Hell, yeah!" He cackled when the audience repeated his cry. Then he glanced at Nick, but he was fiddling with his pedal board, ignoring Mike. *Pansy ass.*

Giving in to the spontaneity of a live show, Mike raised a clenched fist and repeated, "Hell, yeah!" and the audience again echoed it back. Goddamn, he still had it.

As darkness fell on the field, lights bathed the stage in yellow and blue. Alone in the follow spot, Mike clutched the microphone. "The San Francisco Chronicle once called me the 'godfather of '80s hard rock.'" He waited as cheers rang out. "But ya know . . . I was around before all those '80s hair bands. . . . Here's one some of you old fuckers might remember from 1979."

The crowd howled.

Midway through the fifth song, Mike suppressed a powerful urge to cough. He pinched out a few lines and turned from the mic. But when he resumed singing, his voice cracked. *Fuck!* It cracked again. Between lines, Mike twisted from the mic and coughed up a glob of phlegm. As he spit, he spotted the two hot chicks mock-gagging on the side of the stage. Turning back to the mic, he continued singing, but the nagging urge to cough was hellbent on upstaging him.

From what he could see beyond the photo pit and the barricade that separated the audience from the stage, the first several rows of adoring fans cheered wildly, disregarding the few coughs and the wheezing that had started to plague his performance. The crowd sang along, pumping their fists in the air. As Mike screeched out the lyrics, he noticed several chicks in front clasping their hands, as though pulling for his voice to behave. But onstage to his left, the sentiment proved different as Nick glared, obviously bitter.

When the set entered the halfway point, though the cracking persisted, his voice full-out failing in spots, Mike's drive remained steadfast. At the end of "Slave Driver," he paused and muttered to the audience, "I must be allergic to Germany. I know . . . I need some of that kick-ass cough medicine you guys make—Jägermeister." He turned toward his tech and commanded into the mic, "Bones, get me a shotta Jäger."

Bones scrambled off.

"Hit it, dudes!" Mike barked to his band as they launched into the next tune.

He eked out the lyrics, focusing his eyes on his anchor point—the tits, still flopping to the beat in front. The hacking persisted. After coughing his way through a blistering guitar solo, Mike turned his back to the crowd and stepped toward Dylan. "Dr-u-u-u-um solo-o-o-o!"

"Now?" Dylan exchanged puzzled looks with the rest of the band.

"Do it!" Mike rasped.

Chunking away at rhythm guitar on the other side of the stage, Nick narrowed his stance before he bowed out of playing and yielded to the drummer.

Guitar dangling from his torso, Mike bolted to Bones's guitar tech station and out of view from most of the audience. He kicked a road case and bent forward, resting his hands on his thighs.

Bones rushed to Mike with a shot of Jäger.

"I don't want that shit!" Mike pushed it away. "I need a boost. Get me Gatorade."

"Gatorade?" Bones shrugged, set the cup of Jägermeister on a road case, and scrambled off again.

Mike's head reeled for a dizzy second. The chick with the tat hurtled into his thoughts. That fuckin' tattoo. He rubbed his temples as the cartoonish image haunted him.

Bones returned with a bottle. "All they got's Powerade."

Mike motioned for it. He slammed back the blue liquid and shook his head. He couldn't believe he was resorting to sports drinks. What a pussy.

Mike blotted his face with a towel. "After all these years," he said to Bones, "I'd better not be gettin' nodes." He lifted his hair and swiped the towel across the back of his neck. "More brew," he ordered.

Bones dashed to the thermos near his tech station, filled a plastic cup with the brownish-green liquid, and rushed the cup to Mike.

While Dylan battered the skins, Nick stormed across the stage and glared at Mike. "What the fuck?"

"Just gimme a minute." Mike lifted the concoction to his lips.

"That nasty potion ain't doin' shit."

"I been drinkin' this herbal brew since you were in diapers, shithead," Mike snapped. "A hot fuckin' groupie in Poughkeepsie turned me on to it. Done it every show since."

"It's bullshit. It reeks, dude, and it don't work. It's superstition."

Mike sipped the hideous elixir, but he suspected Nick was right—it didn't do shit for his voice. Maybe it never had.

Nick glanced at Dylan pounding out a solo, and Lonnie holding his bass, waiting on the other side of the stage. "Dude." He turned back to Mike and shook his head. "This is like the fifth time in two weeks. It's fucking embarrassing."

Mike looked around at the bystanders onstage.

"Drink up." Nick snatched the cup of Jäger from the road case and shoved it at Mike. "You need a miracle to get through this tour."

Mike batted the cup from Nick's hand. The nearby festival staff, other bands, and guests dodged the splashing booze, but watched the confrontation.

Nick leaned in close. "Butch up and get out there."

Mike watched Nick storm back across the stage. Disrespectful little prick. "This is bullshit," he yelled to Bones. "See if there's a festival medic who can shoot me with cortisone or somethin'."

Bones scrambled off again.

While the drum solo continued, Mike spotted a pack of smokes by the guitar rack. That'd knock that shit right out, he figured. Grabbing the lighter next to the pack, he lit up, planted his ass on a nearby road case, and hurriedly puffed smoke. He coughed again, spit up a hunk of phlegm, and wiped his mouth with the towel. *What the hell?* He stared at the blood dotting the white terrycloth. Then he glanced around.

Dylan locked eyes with him. Mike nodded, flicked the cigarette from his fingertips, and regained his composure. He stood up and sashayed back to center stage, damned determined to finish the song . . . and the show.

Mike soaked up the applause. Wiping the sweat from his brow, he glanced down at the set list. Three-quarters through. They were in the home stretch.

As the band rolled directly into the opening chords of the power ballad, fog flooded the stage, dancing in the colorful lights, swirling around the musicians.

Mike wailed through the first lines of "Love Gone Wrong" but his voice cracked again. The stage smoke choked off his vocal cords. He turned to cough and focused again on the chick's tits—his brass ring. Mike's fingers glided across the frets on the breakdown. Grateful for the vocal break, he sauntered toward Bones.

"No cortisone," Bones hollered.

Mike shook his head. "Cut the damn fog!"

Then he turned to the crowd and shredded a mournful guitar solo, as the band built to a climax. Adrenaline raced through his body. He dashed to the edge of the stage and lingered there, dancing his fingers across the fretboard, feeding the fans in front. He rocked his body to the beat, shaking the sweat from his hair. He spun in a circle and paused to headbang. He skipped toward the fans on stage left. Smack dab in the heart of his gut-wrenching guitar solo, Mike dropped unsteadily to his knees. The crowd cheered. Mike winced. He was gasping for air, and it spooked him. His fingers flailed across the frets until, mid-note, he drooped and teetered. As the weight of the guitar pulled him to the side, his vision blurred. He looked at the crowd. The tits were gone. He crumpled onto the stage, his guitar ringing out a melodic thud and landing with the neck pointing straight up. He thought he heard a groan from the audience.

The backing musicians stopped playing, abruptly ending the song. Mike could hear the distorted clang as Nick threw down his guitar. He lay on the dusty stage, conscious but weak, breathing uneasily. He could almost hear thirty-four thousand people catching their breath. In the front row he could make out a woman—about his daughter's age, he supposed—wearing his current tour shirt. Next to her, a man and his preteen son lowered their clenched fists. Behind them, three biker-looking dudes with long grey hair looked on, mouths open. Then Bones appeared, lunged for the strap locks, and removed the guitar.

Four stagehands rushed onstage. A security guard from the pit below handed up a bottle of water to them. Mike tried to roll away from the audience. He looked up at Bones.

"Can you stand up?" Bones wiped the sweat from Mike's face, and with it some of the bronzer smeared onto the towel. "Shit," Bones said, wide-eyed. "Medic!"

While Dylan and Lonnie encircled Mike, Nick lingered on the fringe.

"You gonna be alright, man?" Dylan asked, moving aside as Bruce stepped in.

Bruce stood there frowning at Mike. As he rubbed the back of his neck, an event medic pushed past him. In a thick German accent he asked slowly and loudly, "Sir, do you know where you are?"

"Yeah. Germany."

"Who's the president?"

"How the fuck would I know who the President of Germany is?"

The medic continued, slower and louder. "Do you know your name?"

"I ain't deaf."

"Okay, sir, where's your tour manager?"

Mike's eyes pointed to Bones.

"Guitar tech, tour manager," Bones explained. "We're a skeleton crew."

Mike grimaced when he heard a siren. The last thing he wanted was publicity that he'd gone down. He tried to push himself up but his muscles wobbled until his elbows finally caved to the stage. Within minutes an emergency medical team, armed with a stretcher, appeared on stage.

Nick tossed his arms up. "We'd better fuckin' get paid."

"Dude, have a heart," said Dylan. "He's sick."

Mike groaned as the medics lifted him onto the stretcher. As they strapped him in, he heard someone inform the crowd that Mike Mays would not be finishing his set. He cringed when the audience reacted with a collective "oh."

As the team hoisted the stretcher, the festival audience applauded. Eh, what the hell, Mike thought. He milked it and raised a weak metal salute to the crowd as the team transported him off the stage and toward the waiting ambulance.

On the ground he ignored the growing flock that had assembled backstage to catch a glimpse of a fallen rock star. Bones pushed through the onlookers and gripped Mike's arm before the gurney glided into the ambulance. Mike clutched his shirt sleeve and pulled him close.

"We played most of the set," Mike implored, "be sure ya get *all* of the dough."

"I'll take care of it, man."

As Bones stepped aside, Nick barged through. He placed his hand on Mike's shoulder and leaned in to his ear, glaring. "Metal Earth Records sure as shit ain't gonna save your ass if you cancel this tour. You'd *better* fuckin' pay me . . . or rest assured, I'll come after you."

As the ambulance doors closed, Mike overheard several bystanders.

"Dude should've stayed in retirement. . . . No way, he still rocks. . . . I hope he's okay."

Mike grimaced. Man, he thought . . . I am so fucked.

Chapter 2

"**L**imey teabag!" Gallo bellowed through the courtyard. "I'll get you for this."

Velvet Sabatino swung open the green shutters and flinched when they banged against the yellow stucco walls outside. A scruffy tabby cat darted from the lavatera shrub. Hmm, she thought, that stray is back. She scanned the courtyard and the surrounding complex. She didn't see anyone, but she recognized that bellowing voice. She closed both window halves and stared at the black 1984 Kramer Baretta guitar on the futon. Then she turned her nostalgic gaze to the eBay screen atop the antique mahogany desk in the corner.

She walked toward the computer, plopped into the black leather swivel chair, and fought back tears. When the office door blasted open, Velvet spun the chair around. "For chrissake, Harley, you scared the shit out of me!"

"Sorry, love."

Harley's posh London accent always seemed to tame any remnants of her badass '70s girl-guitar-pioneer past.

"Close the door," Velvet whispered with a swish of her hand. As Harley closed the door behind her, Velvet dabbed at a tear and wiped it on her khaki shorts.

Harley moseyed over to the futon and eyed the large plastic box and the guitar next to it. Her piercing, icy blue eyes looked so striking against her weathered, golden skin, and that gorgeous silver-blonde hair. For the first time, Velvet felt diminished by Harley's beauty, for how she still looked so damn cool at her age.

"What was Gallo yelling about?" Velvet asked. "Tank, I suppose."

"Naturally." Harley grinned. "He tossed Gallo's clean laundry into the pool. A bit of Blitz's, as well."

Velvet shook her head. "Those guys . . ."

"Perpetually twelve, I'm afraid." Harley picked up the guitar and started noodling. "Bloody hell, this is a cool guitar—"

"You're not helping any," Velvet chided. She could tell Harley was a little jealous that Vin had suddenly been working again—at first just a casual gig here and there around Italy and slightly beyond, but enough that Harley seemed a bit sullen about it. And now that Vin had returned to the States to temporarily fill the guitar spot for a buddy who had to duck out of his band's tour for knee surgery, Velvet sensed Harley missed being in the game. "Maybe *you*," she tested, "could tour again."

Harley released an edgy laugh. "I'd be lucky to get a hundred people out to a shitty little club in the States anymore. Couldn't even double that in the UK."

Velvet could feel herself pouting. "Vin and I should've just turned this place into a B&B like we'd planned . . . not a friggin' retirement home for rock stars."

"Hey, I resent that remark."

Velvet stared at the Kramer as Harley's fingers whizzed up and down the frets. "I can't do this," she moaned, glancing back at the computer monitor.

"He did say this one's just deadwood," Harley said as she stopped noodling. "Don't really have much choice, do you?"

No, she didn't. Velvet looked up at the wood-beamed ceiling, brushed a blonde wisp from her forehead, and spun the chair back around. With a hesitant move of the mouse, she clicked the button on the eBay window. Done. One of her husband's prized guitars would soon go to the highest bidder.

"If it makes you feel any better, love, I haven't seen him touch this thing in ages. It's so . . . '80s."

Velvet turned back to glance at Harley, who had moved to the window. Still cradling the guitar, she stood there staring out toward the Tuscan hills. Velvet turned back to the computer screen and reviewed her eBay ad.

"V?" Harley said from the window, and Velvet swiveled the chair to face her. "Why don't you sell one of your harps? You never play anymore." She turned and pointed toward the office door. "That gilded monstrosity in the living room would net you a fortune."

She shot Harley an incredulous stare. "My parents bought me that harp when I graduated from conservatory."

Harley slid a strand of hair from her eyes and then turned and peered through the window. "Well, it's no fault of yours. We're just plain broke. It's the fate we all chose long ago when we decided to become musicians." She turned back and looked Velvet in the eye. "If anything, you should blame that husband of yours for sinking so much into that bloody old vineyard."

True, Velvet thought. But Vin loved that vineyard. As a child, he had spent several summers in Italy visiting his grandmother, who taught him how to work the vines. But some fifty years later, Vin's efforts to restore his *nonna's* vineyard had become fruitless, nothing but a waste of money— which nobody at Groove House had any of, anyway. Well, Vin was a rock musician, not a winemaker, and it was too late to change that now.

Velvet pressed her lips. "I'll find a way. . . . I have to," she said, even though she had no idea how she could generate enough money to keep them afloat much longer.

"Wouldn't it be wild if some punter loved Vin so much . . . well, back in the day," Harley said as she rested the guitar on the futon, "that he'd pay twenty grand for this axe today?"

"Dream on."

"Aerosmith," Harley said with a grin. "Uh, 1976—ah, I remember it well. One point for me today."

Velvet tried to smile at their ongoing game, but it turned into more of a pout. "Right, fifteen thousand Euro—just what we need to pay our stupid fucking tax bill."

"Way out of line for what it should be." Harley tilted her head. "Do you think maybe Carlo?"

Velvet narrowed her eyes toward the hilltop across the way. "That prick had to have somehow convinced them to triple our reassessment—"

"But why would he? To force Vin to sell him that vineyard?"

Velvet cocked her head toward Harley. "Um, yeah."

"It must be a mistake—"

"I've checked like five times." Velvet stared off toward the hilltop again. "Maybe the guys are right and he really *is* mafia."

"Taxes did increase, love." Harley nodded toward the courtyard and the surrounding compound. "The reassessment . . . I mean, you do have loads of land . . . and farm buildings." She gave a heavy nod. "We are in Tuscany, after all."

"What good is that when we can't afford the tax hike?" Velvet sighed. "How am I going to pay that bill?" Velvet felt her lip quiver. "Vin's out there gigging his ass off, for what?"

"You're the most resourceful person I know," Harley said with a forced smile. "Meanwhile, your meatless Mondays and candlelight dinners will help keep us all above water."

Velvet sighed. "Sweet of you to try to cheer me up." She looked up at Harley. "They all hate me, don't they?"

"I don't know why you think they'd hate you in particular. We're *all* in the same leaky boat."

Velvet cast her eyes down and fought back tears. She seemed to always be fighting back tears these days. The old farmhouse had begun to fall apart, and with each unexpected expense Velvet could see her husband's optimism wane. She felt alone, over her head. It wasn't how she'd envisioned life when they had packed up their belongings, left their home in the San Francisco Bay Area, and moved for the promise of a simpler life in the Italian countryside. *Simpler, my ass,* she thought.

"Sorry to barge in, mates," Tank said as he flung open the office door.

Velvet squinted at Tank and his stubbly-bald head. The bristles were now a blend of ashen grey and coffee brown, but she remembered when Vin's former roadie sported a full head of hair back in the '80s. In fact, she remembered when Vin plucked Tank straight off the UK tour back in 1983; he and Tank had been buddies ever since.

"What is this, Grand fucking Central?" Velvet snuck a nervous glance back toward the computer screen.

"Have you heard the news?" Tank asked, straight-faced for a change.

"There's good rockin' tonight?" Harley replied, tossing out the next line to the rock song.

"Montrose," Velvet blurted, relishing the distraction. "Nineteen—I dunno. Mid-'70s. Whatever, still one point for me."

"Good one, V," said Harley. "Love that version."

"Right. I meant have you heard 'bout Mike Mays?" Tank continued, his Brummie accent thickening with excitement. "Bloody well took a tumble onstage, he did. Went down in front of thirty-thousand people. Just told Gallo and Blitz."

Velvet smirked. "Was that before or after you threw their clean laundry in the pool?" She stared at Tank, who grinned with delight over his prank. Then she noticed the concern on Harley's face.

"Mike Mays," Harley muttered. "Haven't seen him in ages. . . . Is he alright?" she asked, tucking a silver-blonde tuft behind her ear.

"Dunno." The more excited Tank got, the faster the idioms flowed. "Been tryin' like a rat up a drainpipe ta find out waz appen but so far nish."

Velvet looked to Harley for translation.

"Slow down, Tank," Harley suggested. "Your Brummie's taking off."

Mike Mays. Velvet shuddered. That was so long ago. He was always *on,* she thought, always playing the rock star to the hilt. She remembered all the press he once got for saying he'd pissed into David Lee Roth's classic red '51 Mercury custom convertible on Sunset Strip. She always figured it was just a PR stunt. Ugh. She shuddered again and then recalled that whenever Vin was off tour back in the day, Tank would roadie for Mike Mays.

"Got word through the ol' roadie grapevine. Should know more soon. . . . Shame, innit? Such a talent."

Velvet rolled her eyes. With her husband away, and the property tax debt due—or else—she couldn't be bothered thinking about a degenerate like Mike Mays. It was probably just another of Mike's tricks for attention, anyway. *Media whore.*

"Fuckin' 'ell! What's that?" Tank said, pointing to the plastic bin on the futon. He approached the box and leaned in. Rummaging through the photos, laminates, and handbills, he slid out an old tour program. "That's older than me teeth."

As Harley laughed, Velvet inched the chair closer to the computer.

Tank studied the front cover and then leafed through the pages. "I remember that tour. You was direct support for Vin on that one, Harl." He flipped to the end. "Fuckin' 'ell. Blitz Stryker, Golden Blonde . . . wankers."

"Bloody no-talent glam band," Harley growled. "Got lucky, is all." She turned toward the window. "All you had to do was open a show for *me* in L.A. back then and you'd surely skyrocket to fame. RATT, Poison, Mötley Crüe . . . hell, even Van Halen." She turned back with a glance at Velvet. "I should've opened up for myself, and perhaps *I* could've had some of that luck."

"Ooh," Tank cooed as he flipped back a page and flinched. "That hot pink jumpsuit looks straight outta the '80s. . . . Oh, wait, it *were* the '80s. . . . Harley Yeates, look at that Yamaha in your arms. SG2000. Aw, she were a beauty." Tank grinned and then looked up from the program, his gaze darting between Harley and Velvet. "You alright? Got a face as long as Livery Street."

"I just," Velvet said, "have so much to deal with here . . ."

"Fuckin' 'ell. Too bad the geezer had to travel so far this time." Tank arched a bushy eyebrow when he noticed the computer screen behind Velvet. "Is that my guitar . . . on eBay?"

"*Your* guitar?" Harley asked with a harrumph.

"Yes, that's right, Tom Thumb . . . *my* guitar."

"Vin told me to sell it," Velvet said as she stood and pushed the chair to the desk.

Tank stuck out his arm. "Ah, go on then . . . pull the other one, it's got bells on it."

Velvet tossed up her arms. "Think what you want but I was asked to sell it."

"You're jokin', right?"

As Velvet shook her head, Harley picked up Vin's guitar and began noodling.

"But Vin promised me that Kramer. . . . Promised it to me since 1987."

"Call him and ask him yourself," Velvet snapped. "He told me to sell it and that's what I'm doing. . . . You like food on your plate and wine on the table, don't you? Well, we're kind of desperate here, in case you hadn't noticed. I sure as shit don't see you doing anything about it."

Tank looked at Harley, as if he thought she might side with him.

"Don't look at me," Harley said, her silver jewelry glinting as her fingers danced across the frets. "I brought my money here same as everyone else."

Tank tapped the tour book on his hand and then tossed it into the box. He gritted his teeth and grabbed for the guitar. Harley turned, dodging Tank's swipe. "She manages our money and now we're fecked."

Velvet glared at him. "That's not fair."

Tank scratched his stubbly head. "Disaster. This was supposed to be paradise, retirement in Italy—"

"Oh for chrissake." Harley paused, cradling the guitar. "We *all* took the risk moving here. I gave all I had left from selling my Jag."

"That jalopy was shite," Tank snarled as he eyed the eBay window.

Velvet held her hand up. "Guys."

"I brought every bit of spondoolie I had," said Tank. "Same with Gallo and Blitz."

"Look, sheep-shagger," Harley retorted with a snide half-grin. "We've *all* got same as you—bugger all."

"Oy, that's a load of crap," said Tank. "You got record royalties. All but me, I'm skint."

Velvet snapped, "We don't *all* have royalties."

"Besides—" Harley scowled at Tank, as she rested the guitar on the futon. "They've dwindled to nothing over decades," she retorted, a vein in her forehead protruding as she broached the perpetually sore subject. "It's the musician's plight—no bloody pension. We're *all* skint now."

"Oy, no need to go mental." Tank fired a daggered glance at her. "Daft cow," he mumbled.

As Harley opened her mouth to fire back, Velvet interrupted. "Guys, stop, please?"

Harley nestled into the futon and began rooting through the box.

Tank paced the room, muttering, "If Vin hadn't poured so much money into that worthless vineyard—"

"My husband," Velvet defended, "never spent one dime of your money trying to restore those vines." She dabbed at the tears with the back of her hand. "It's our *own* money he's blown."

"Greedy feckin' bastid," Tank muttered.

"Fuck you, Tank. You have no right suggesting how Vin and I should spend our money. He had a dream. It just didn't work. And now that damn tax bill . . ."

"Disaster." Tank pouted toward the eBay window and folded his stubby arms. "I'm just a geezer with me pockets turned out, so what the hell do I know? But I do know one thing for sure." He paused, narrowed his eyes, and looked at the Kramer. "That's *my* bloody guitar. . . . Vin promised it to me since 1987."

Velvet sighed heavily. "I'll just have to get a job somehow."

"A job?" Tank snapped. "Which one of them eye-talian yokels is gonna hire a retired American Goth-pop-rock harpist? Maybe you could roll one of them things down the hill to the village and start buskin' for the tourists, eh?" He shook his head and resumed pacing.

Velvet glared at him.

"Better yet, why don't you sell one of them behemoths?" Tank pointed out the office door in the direction of the gilded symphony harp in the living room outside. "Never play no more, anyway."

Velvet fought back the frustration. "Because—"

"Christ on a bike!" Tank stopped pacing as his eyes widened. "We ain't gonna lose the house?"

"Not if I can help it," said Velvet.

"But you sayin' we might?"

Harley glared at Tank. "How 'bout you go get yourself a glassful of shut-the-fuck-up?"

"Disaster." Tank paced the room. "We're more fecked than I realized."

He shook his head. "I ain't got nowhere to go. You guys is all the family I got."

"Oh for chrissake," Harley chided. "Stop acting like a goddamn drama queen."

"Vin would never sell this place," Velvet assured him.

Harley stared into the distance. "I'm going to make that record."

"Good luck, mate," said Tank. "Nobody's gonna buy it. Nobody'll buy nothin' from anybody here no more."

Velvet looked at Harley. "You've been saying that for months. Have you even written anything new?"

"I've been noodling. . . . Just haven't been able to finish one bloody tune."

"New songs," Tank chided. "Oh, those downloads will make us all wealthy, won't they just?"

Harley cocked her head toward Tank. "And, remind me—what is it that *you're* doing to contribute?"

Tank folded his arms again. "What about all them bottles of olive oil?" he asked. "Just sittin' in the barn, growin' dust."

Velvet clenched her jaw. "You know damn well I've tried everywhere. The locals just won't buy from foreigners. . . . Even those Brits who own that little shop in Chiantishire stopped buying our oil." She shifted her glance between Harley and Tank. "It's a good oil . . . don't you think?"

"Aw, love, the olive oil is fab. It was a brilliant idea you had. Just the wrong continent, I suppose." Harley glared at Tank and then turned back to Velvet. "Vin's a lucky bugger to get some gigs. Should bring back a nice chunk of change this month."

Velvet rubbed her temples. "You know how much he's bringing home?" She hated sharing her personal finances. "After a month on tour in the States? . . . twenty-six hundred US."

"Fuckin' 'ell," Tank said.

Harley's eyes widened. "That's all?"

Velvet stared at Harley. It seemed her jealousy might have dipped for a moment. "Yep, that's it. Hardly worth the ass-kicking he's getting out there."

Tank counted on his fingers. "I made more than that as a roadie in the '80s."

As if in a trance, Harley picked up the guitar again and ran her fingers over the frets.

Tank eyed her and continued pacing. "Can't believe you're selling *my* guitar straight out from under me nose . . ."

Velvet stepped to the window and flicked a wave of hair from her shoulder. She sighed and stared out beyond the terracotta courtyard and across the Tuscan landscape. She thought of Harley's earlier comment: What if some fan *did* pay twenty grand for Vin's guitar? But she knew they'd be lucky if her husband's guitar fetched even a few thousand US. If only some ad agency would use one of Vin's old songs in a car commercial— that'd easily put them in the black. She sighed. Dream on. Aerosmith again—another point for her. She glanced out at the hill beyond. When her eyes landed on Carlo Moretti's house, she swallowed hard. It might be time for desperate measures.

Chapter 3

Mike Mays sloshed his boot onto the sidewalk and then stood there in the downpour. He glanced at the soggy, crumpled scratch paper he was holding and then up at the tree-lined street. "Los Gatos," he muttered. "My new fuckin' home."

He squinted through the drenching rain at the quaint Craftsman style house, hoping he'd made the right move. Mike sighed heavily and hustled toward the porch. He eyeballed the willow tree in the front yard. It must've been fifty feet high—so much taller since the last time he'd stood there. Light from the streetlamp washed an eerie glow over the branches, making them creak in the wind, as though a ghost had blown in to haunt him. He shivered, as if to shake the discomfort, sighed again and then stood tall. He swung his wet duffel bag over his shoulder and stepped onto the porch.

Mike took another deep breath before ringing the doorbell. As he bent over to set his duffel bag down, the door squeaked open. "Trick or fuckin' treat," Mike said with a nervous grin, even though it was late April.

When he straightened up, his eyes met the kid standing in the doorway. *Whoa.* Mike flinched. It was *him.* As the kid's blue eyes stared back from beneath the dark hood of his sweatshirt, Mike's lips formed a crooked smile. He glanced down at the kid's Converse Hi-Tops and then up at his face.

The kid looked puzzled.

Mike couldn't stop staring at him, and he couldn't stop smiling. He stabbed his hand into his jacket pocket, pulled out his pack of smokes, and bumped out a cig. He struggled to light it, but no matter which way he turned the wind seemed to whip around from every angle, killing the lighter flame. He glanced down at his shaky hands and then back up at the kid. "Damn . . . you're a helluva lot taller than the last time I saw ya."

The kid cocked his head and stared, eyes wide.

Mike huddled against the sheets of rain, still fumbling to light the cig. "Your mom home?"

The kid clung to the front door like it was a shield, and then turned to yell into the room behind him. "Mom. . . . Someone's at the door for you."

Hell, Mike thought, she's home.

"Who is it?" he heard her ask.

"Hell if I know." The kid inspected Mike standing there on the porch. "Just come here."

Mike continued to stare at the kid. Grinning with the cig between his lips, he gave up and shoved the lighter back into his pocket. He caught the kid sneaking glances at his ripped jeans, bullet belt, and black leather jacket, then up at his scraggly hair and the line of studs and hoops clinging to his ear.

The click-clack of her heels drew closer. And then she appeared in the doorway. She stood there, silent, frozen, staring at Mike, her mouth agape—the only loose part on her small, rigid frame.

Mike shifted away from her foreboding presence and chomped down on the soggy cigarette. Then he slid it from his lips and shoved it behind his ear. She looked horrified, as if the grim reaper were standing on her doorstep. Mike shivered as the willow tree creaked again and a chilly wind whipped onto the porch. He glanced down at the rain splatters, then back up at her. There he was, chilled with goosebumps tingling his arms and drenched from the freak storm, yet she just stood there, cold and distant, like she had no intention of letting him past the front door.

"Oh . . . my . . . God." She glared at him as she pulled a loose strand of bobbed, mousy brown hair from her mouth. Then she crossed her arms, damn near speechless.

He'd forgotten how tiny she was. He thought for sure she'd look older, but hell, she looked the same.

"Who is he?" the kid whispered to his mom.

She yanked the hood from the kid's head, gave him a nervous smile, and arranged his moppy brown hair. "Sweetheart—" She swallowed hard.

The kid swerved away from her touch.

"Fuckin' hell! The kid's even got my hair." Mike grinned and shifted his weight. "Well . . . mine ain't nothin' like it used to be—" He twirled the big hoop in his earlobe and looked at the kid. "But, hey, better mine than your mom's. . . . She got *her* mom's hair—that'd be your grandma." He shifted his weight to the other side. "Cute as a rat's ass."

The kid stared at Mike.

"Brayden, go to your room," she demanded, nudging him from the doorway.

The kid ignored his mom's command. "You told me to answer the door . . . remember?" He slid behind her and continued to stare at Mike.

She glared at Mike, seething, and then straightened her skirt. "The last time I saw you was at . . . my mother's—" She shook her head. "You showed up . . . disheveled, much like you look tonight, bragging about some new tattoo you got in Seattle—"

"As I recall," Mike said, still twisting the hoop, "you said then you never wanted to see me again." He shoved his hands in his pockets, waiting for her reaction.

"I didn't," she said coldly. "I don't."

In the folds of his pocket, his fingertip grazed the gift—his backstage pass back into her world . . . at least for the night. He curbed a grin. "Yep, I believe those were your exact words."

The kid squinted at Mike as he eavesdropped from behind his mom.

Mike stared at Lydia. "Damn, darlin'." He fingered the cold, tiny charm in his pocket and grinned. "You don't look any older than the day you graduated from high school."

She pressed her thin lips together. "Um . . . you weren't there that day."

"I wasn't?" Mike pondered. "Huh . . . well, on tour that summer I carried your graduation picture in my wallet."

Her expression seemed pained.

"Is he—?" the kid asked.

"He's nobody," she interrupted, pursing her lips, looking Mike square in the eye.

Mike jerked his hands from his pockets and held them up. *"Ouch."*

"I told you to go to your room."

The kid challenged her with a huff.

Mike sighed through the tension and glanced back at the stormy night behind him. He was fuckin' soaked and shivering and she didn't even have the heart to wave him inside. This was gonna be tougher than he imagined. Maybe he should just tell her the truth. . . . Well . . . maybe just some of it.

"Brayden," she ordered. "Go finish your homework."

"I'm not going anywhere until you tell me who the fuck he is." The kid glanced over at his mom. He didn't seem all that natural spitting out the word "fuck"—not the way Mike was—and he seemed to be checking his mom for her reaction.

She gasped. "Brayden Mays Wilson!"

Mays. Mike grinned. His name was the kid's middle name. He restrained an urge to laugh. Probably the reason the kid had turned out alright, despite his uptight mom.

"Who's at the door, Lydia?"

Mike grinned at Andy. He seemed so much taller standing next to Lydia. The kid moved back to make room for his dad.

"Mike?" Drying his hands on a dishtowel, Andy stepped onto the porch to shake Mike's hand. "What a surprise!" He pushed his wire-rimmed glasses up the bridge of his long, narrow nose. Mike recognized the frames as Berkshire Chase; he remembered when they were all the rage with his rock star comrades. "Well, how are you? Long time no see." Andy nodded.

"Um—" Mike knew why Andy seemed so nervous at that moment, but Lydia appeared too perturbed to notice.

"What's it been, ten years?" Andy continued, nodding.

"Right," Mike nodded, going along with him.

"Fourteen," Lydia barked, teeth clenched, arms still folded. ". . . actually."

The kid continued to stare at Mike with big blue suspicious eyes.

"Good to see ya, Andy."

"It's *Andrew*," Lydia corrected as she peered beyond the porch to the headlights shining up the driveway. She looked to her husband, who shrugged.

"Mike!" the chick called out as she hurried toward the porch. It was Diane and she had his wallet. She stepped onto the porch and reached it out to him.

"Uh, thanks." Mike glanced guiltily at Lydia before cramming the wet wallet into his jacket pocket. "Musta fell out when I got outta the car."

"Thanks, again." She smiled at Mike in admiration. "You're a gracious human being. . . . I truly mean it. Thank you for a wonderful day."

Mike snorted. He'd been called many things, but never *gracious*. He waved off the gratitude.

"Seriously. It meant the world to Ray."

He pitched her a wink.

"Thank you. . . . Good night," she said, waving as she beelined back to her car in the rain.

Lydia rubbernecked out the doorway at the departing car. "Who was that?"

"Oh, her? She gave me a ride here. Part of the deal for gettin' my Les Paul." Mike sloughed it off, but it had killed him to part with his old friend.

"You sold the *Les Paul?*" Andrew moaned as he ran a hand through his sandy blond hair. Then he wised up, and looked to Lydia, flustered. "That's right, I forgot about that one."

Lydia glared at Mike, her arms tightly folded.

"Well—" Mike coughed. "I didn't really sell it. . . . I gave it away."

"You *gave away* your guitar," Lydia said sarcastically. "What, in exchange for drugs?"

"The last one . . . my fave . . ." Mike checked the cig behind his ear. "She was a beauty."

"The *last* one?" Andrew asked.

"Yeah. It was for her ol' man. . . . *Huge* fan." Mike blinked at Lydia and thought about sparking the lighter again. "Followed my career for forty years."

She looked skeptical.

"What?" Mike asked her as he slid his hand back into his pocket and felt for the charm. "For chrissake, the dude's dyin' . . . so I spent the day at the hospital with a dyin' fan—"

"You?" she clarified. "*You* gave away a guitar . . ."

"Yeah. . . . To make him happy." He focused on Lydia and grinned. "My fans are the fuckin' greatest." His finger rubbed the smooth silver of the charm. "Here." Mike pulled it from his pocket. "I got ya somethin'."

Lydia's posture stiffened. Her gaze ping-ponged around the porch and then landed on Andrew.

Mike pressed the charm into her palm and grinned.

She glanced down at the silver horse frozen in a gallop. Then she flinched her head back slightly.

"You always dug horses."

She blew out a noisy breath. "When I was a *child*—"

"Wait." Brayden inched forward. "You play guitar?"

"Yeah, kid. . . . Of course." Mike beamed at the attention. "Hey, you still have that guitar I gave you?"

"What guitar?" Brayden's glance bounced to his mom, his dad, and then back to Mike.

"He was eleven months old!" Lydia said.

"I don't understand," Andrew interjected. "All your guitars are gone?"

Lydia shot her husband a cold glance.

Mike coughed and when he hawked up a hefty loogie and spit it off the porch into the pouring rain, Lydia cringed. He yanked a napkin from his jacket pocket and wiped his mouth. Glancing down at it, he noticed a smattering of blood. He quickly crumpled it up, hiding the bloody side, shoved it into his pocket, and cleared his throat.

"Mom," Brayden insisted. "What guitar?"

"It was a toy," Lydia said dismissively.

"I . . . would've remembered a toy like that."

"You were so young—"

"Sonofabitch!" Mike shook his head. "You never gave it to him . . . did ya?"

Brayden glared at his mom. "I'm not stupid, you know."

"Oh, sweetie." When Lydia reached out to the kid, he pulled away.

Mike kneaded his shaggy hair. "You never told him about me? . . . Your own fuckin' father?"

Lydia pursed her lips. She lowered her head and shifted her eyes to Andrew.

Andrew raised his hands. "I knew this would bite you in the ass one day."

She glanced guiltily at Mike. She looked beaten, he thought. Maybe he had a chance.

"*That's* your dad?" Brayden looked to his mother. "You said he was dead."

Lydia turned, as if she couldn't face her son.

"Ooh, now that's cold." Mike leaned back.

Lydia reached out to the kid. "I'm so sorry. . . . Sweetie . . . it's . . . complicated."

Brayden ducked and glared at his mother.

Mike stood silently on the porch. So much for barging in.

Brayden took a slight step back. "The man with a guitar standing next to grandma."

Lydia's expression softened. "You found the pictures."

"I can't believe you lied to me my *whole life*." Brayden shook his head, turned his back to his mom, and retreated down the hall. The house shook when he slammed a door inside.

Mike shuddered. "I'd say that kid needs a hug."

Lydia gave Mike what he read as a resigned look, before she turned to follow her son.

Andrew glanced toward the hallway, then back at Mike. "Wow. This is long overdue."

"Brayden." Mike heard Lydia in the distance as she knocked on a bedroom door. "Let me explain."

All Mike wanted was a place to sleep. He clutched his arms and shivered. "Fuckin' hell, it's cold out here."

"Come in," Andrew gestured.

Mike nabbed his duffel bag from the porch and stepped inside the house. He readjusted his balls as he sized up the place—the clean walls, crown molding, recessed lighting. Neat and orderly, just like his daughter. "Nice pad." He plopped his duffel bag onto the hardwood floor in the entryway.

"Have a seat." Andrew directed him down the steps to the living room.

When Mike swaggered into the room, he paused, not sure he should step on the Persian rug.

Andrew gestured toward the sofa. "Can I get you something to drink?"

"Jack and Coke?"

Andrew paused. "We don't have either. How about a glass of Port?"

"Hell, yeah." Mike settled into the starchy, upright sofa. "Some Port and a nice Cohiba!"

"Sorry, we don't have cigars in the house," he said, aiming his head toward the sound of Lydia's voice pleading down the hallway. He clasped his hands. "Seems like a perfect night for Port."

Lydia returned, teary-eyed. She gasped when she spotted Mike nestled into the sofa. "This is just great!" She pointed back toward the hallway, toward her son holed up in his room. "See how you just exude chaos?" She looked worn, exhausted, as she folded her arms. "What are you doing here?"

"I just . . . dropped by."

"Here you go, Mike." Andrew returned with a glass of Port.

Lydia's mouth dropped. "My Waterford Crystal *Powerscourt?* . . . Andrew!"

Mike licked his lips, slugged down the shot, and exhaled. "Good shit."

"Are you hungry, Mike?"

"What?" Lydia glared at her husband.

Mike thought she looked queasy.

"I'll warm up a plate of leftovers," Andrew offered.

Mike rubbed his hands together and sniffed the air. "Mmm, yeah, I'm fuckin' starved!"

"Hold it!" Lydia held up her hands. She stared Mike straight in the eye. "What do you want?"

Mike focused behind Lydia to the kid creeping into the room.

Lydia followed Mike's glance over her shoulder. "Sweetie." Reaching for her son, she noticed the duffel bag on the floor.

"Just leave me alone," the kid growled, shrugging away her touch. He loitered in the entry hall, eyeing Mike.

Lydia moved cautiously into the living room and propped herself on the edge of a chair. She stared across the room at Mike. "So, what do you want?"

Mike took a deep, exaggerated breath. "Lost the lease on my apartment. . . . Need a place to crash." He held out the Port glass toward Andrew in a plea for more. Then he lifted his feet and rested them on the coffee table.

Lydia's eyed widened. "Take your feet off the table . . . please."

"Just for tonight." He returned his feet to the floor. "I'll leave in the morning."

"You came all the way down here—" Lydia said, crossing her arms. "—from San Francisco . . . just to spend one night?"

"Yeah." Mike nodded.

"You've always had lots of friends—party, party, party." She crossed her legs and looked him squarely in the eye. "Surely, you have a girlfriend . . . or four."

"I'm . . . kinda between chicks right now." Mike coughed. "Certain individuals . . . I need to stay away from, if you catch my drift." He coughed again. "I—" He clenched his teeth and shrugged. "—can't . . . really impose on those people."

Lydia huffed. "And you don't think you're imposing on me?"

He shrugged. "You're family."

"Hardly."

The kid sized up Mike from a distance. "So are there any more grandparents I don't know about?"

Mike stared at Lydia and shook his head. "Can't believe you never told him about me."

Lydia huffed again. "I don't have a father, so he doesn't have a grandfather."

"For chrissake, he's a teenager now—"

Lydia rose, flitted up the steps, and snatched her purse from the entryway table. "How much do you need?"

"I ain't here for dough . . . just for the night." Mike slid the cigarette from behind his ear, flicked the lighter from his pocket, and sucked in the smoke.

"Mike!" Lydia said, darting into the living room. "No smoking in the house." She reached out her hand. "Give."

He took one more hit and then forked over the cig to his daughter.

She handed it to Andrew, who passed it to the kid and said, "Toss this out the front door."

Brayden stood on the threshold facing his parents. Glaring at his mom, he took a drag from the cigarette and choked out smoke.

"Brayden," said Lydia. "Get rid of that right now." She flailed her arms and turned to Mike. "That's just great. . . . You haven't even been here ten minutes and already you're corrupting my son."

"For chrissake." Mike shifted his ass on the stiff sofa. "I guarantee you he sees plenty of shit at high school."

The kid took another drag and coughed as he flung the cig out the door and into the stormy night.

Mike lifted a colorful bottle from the coffee table.

"No, no, no!" Lydia lunged for the object in his hands. "That's expensive, hand-blown Murano glass." She carefully returned the art to its precise spot.

He snickered, which made him cough.

"You can't stay here. You have to go. . . . Andrew will drive you to a hotel. I'll pay for it." She looked desperate.

Andrew shifted his stance. "It's late." He glanced toward the door. "And nasty weather out." He looked at Brayden loitering in the entryway. "And . . . it's a school night." He turned to Mike. "We've got a guest room—"

"What?" Lydia stepped toward her husband. "No . . . no."

"Why don't you stay the night?"

Lydia's jaw dropped. "Andrew."

"Yeah," the kid agreed. "Stay."

"I'll warm up a plate of food, and we'll talk more in the morning." Andrew gave a firm stare to his wife as he moved toward the hall closet. "Right, hon?" Lydia scowled at him. Andrew opened the closet door and pulled the extra blanket from the top shelf. "Right, Lydia?" He placed the blanket into her arms.

Clearly outnumbered, Lydia sullenly carried the blanket toward the hallway.

"C'mon, Mike," Andrew said. "Let's get you something to eat."

Mike struggled out of the uncomfortable sofa and then moseyed back across the Persian rug.

Brayden's blue eyes twinkled as he stared at Mike.

"Brayden," Andrew proposed. "Why don't you go help your mother get your grandpa's room ready?"

The kid looked peeved at the suggestion.

Andrew smiled and patted his son on the shoulder. "Go on."

The kid slowly scuffed his Hi-Tops down the hall.

Andrew leaned in to Mike and whispered, "And uh—" He winced. ". . . don't let on to Lydia that we've . . . you know . . . had any communication . . . these past years."

Mike cocked his head. Sure, he dug talkin' but he wasn't no snitch. Ah, Mike grasped—now Andrew is fucked.

Chapter 4

Lydia jumped when her son slinked into the guest bedroom. She dabbed at her eyes to hide the tears and then she turned from the edge of the bed and straightened her shirt. Patting the bed, she motioned to him to sit beside her.

Brayden's lip quivered as he glared at his mom. "Why do you hate him so much?"

"Sweetie." She glanced lovingly at her son. "It's rather complicated."

Brayden scratched his neck and tugged the hood up over his head, as if to seclude himself inside. He plopped onto the bed, not too near his mother, and shook his head. "What's so complicated about having a father?"

Lydia wished he had sat closer. When she reached out to brush the hair from his eyes, he ducked away. She sighed heavily. "Your grandpa and I . . . we've had a strained relationship . . . since . . . well, since the day I was born." She noticed her arms felt weak. "Actually, it's not a relationship at all."

"Duh." He wiped the sweatshirt cuff under his nose and glared at her.

"He's—" She swallowed hard as the queasy feeling returned. ". . . never been there for me." She took a deep breath and then said softly, "You see, I never really had a father. Grandpa Joe—your great grandpa—was kind of a surrogate father . . . since Mike was never there."

"Never?" Brayden looked skeptical.

Lydia shook her head. "Yes, mostly . . . never." She stared into the room, focusing on nothing in particular. "The few times he did come around it was always so . . . uncomfortable." She was silent for a moment. "Sweetie."

She hesitated, uncertain how to put it. "Just know . . . well . . . he's not a very nice man. . . . As your mother, it's my job to protect you."

Brayden rolled his eyes. "I suppose you're going to tell me he killed someone."

"Oh, heavens, no."

"Well, then how bad can he be?"

Lydia paused, uncomfortable with the new distance between her and Brayden, but equally uncomfortable with dredging up old skeletons.

"He's your dad." His blue eyes peered out from beneath the dark hood. "Isn't blood supposed to be . . . thicker?"

Lydia tilted her head. "You'll grow up to learn that saying doesn't always ring true."

He rolled his eyes. "I'm grown up enough. . . . I know friends are water, family's blood." He glanced down and picked at his sweatshirt sleeve, hesitating. "I drove the car the other day."

"What?"

"Dad let me drive the car."

They sat on the bed in silence. Lydia couldn't believe what she was hearing—they had all agreed to wait until he was sixteen. Why hadn't Andrew told her? She glanced at her son, wanting to take it all back, all fourteen of those deceitful years. She ached to hug him.

"I can't believe you lied." Avoiding her gaze, Brayden stared at the hardwood floor and shook his head.

Lydia felt her legs trembling. "Sweetie." She reached out to her son, wanting to swaddle him in her arms, but he inched away. "I was wrong. I should have told you. . . . But it was just so much easier not to—"

"I could've had a guitar." Brayden threw his arms in the air. He glared at her, his face flushed under the hood. He glowered for a moment and then returned to picking at his sweatshirt sleeve. "So . . . was he famous?"

Lydia pressed on her stomach as the knots and nausea overwhelmed her.

Brayden looked up at her from under his hood. "Maybe he's ready to be a father now."

Lydia snorted. "Not very likely. . . . Oh, Brayden." She sighed. "That man is self-centered and crass—the rudest person you'll ever meet."

"He seems like a cool guy—"

"*He* certainly thinks he is."

Andrew poked his head into the bedroom. "Everything okay?" Lydia and Brayden looked at him in silence. "He's okay. He's eating dinner."

"Thanks for the newsflash." She got up and set the extra blanket on the bed.

"Brayden." Andrew lifted Mike's duffel bag. "Set this on the dresser." As Brayden accepted the bag, Andrew reached out and caressed his arm. "I'm going back to Mike now." Andrew looked twitchy as he backed away.

Lydia glanced at her watch and then at her son. "Time for bed now, Brayden." As she watched him skulk down the hallway, she knew she was in for a sleepless night.

After settling Mike into the guest room, Andrew's footsteps drew closer down the hall. He entered their bedroom, closed the door, and gave Lydia an oblique glance. "He *is* your father."

Lydia drew down the comforter on her side of the bed. "After what he pulled at my mother's funeral?"

"Honey, shh," Andrew said as he slid off his shoes. "He'll hear you."

"I hope he *does* hear me!" She wriggled out of her grey flannel pencil skirt. "How can you forget? He showed up late . . . slobbering drunk . . . and he had the nerve to bring a guitar. What's an eleven-month-old supposed to do with a guitar?"

"He was probably hurting too, you know." Andrew slipped out of his trousers. "Maybe that was the only way he knew how to deal with it."

"I don't buy it for a second," she said as she removed her pearl earrings. "You know exactly how he is." She pulled a silky white nightgown over her head and felt her stomach knot up. "Do you know that he once bought a Ferrari and crashed it into a tree . . . the very same day? Totaled it. Of course, he was drunk or stoned or something. I was just a little girl but it made a big impression on me."

"It's in his DNA," Andrew said as he disappeared into the master bathroom.

"He's *completely* irresponsible—in every way—especially with money." Lydia walked around the bed and turned on Andrew's nightstand lamp. "He said he lost the lease on his apartment. Now, why do you suppose?" She noticed how tense her muscles were as she found herself slamming the dresser drawer.

Andrew poked his head from the bathroom door. "Slamming doors now, are we?"

"It was an accident." She heard the toilet flush and raised her hand to the light switch above the dresser. She stopped mid-motion and instead drifted to the standing photograph of her mother. Lydia caressed the frame. "What did she ever see in him?"

"I can't hear you, honey."

Lydia flicked off the light and closed the closet door as she made her way around the bed.

Brushing his teeth, Andrew leaned toward her from the bathroom doorway. "Know what he told me in the kitchen?"

Lydia rolled her eyes as she climbed into bed.

"He said he drove around with that woman tonight for two hours before coming here." Andrew stepped back. She heard him spit into the sink before he reappeared in the doorway. "He said the whole day in the hospital was one of the coolest days ever . . . or something like that."

"Mike tells tall tales, Andrew." She fluffed up her pillow. "The sooner he's out of here, the better."

"It's only for one . . . *night,*" he said, and disappeared into the bathroom.

She rubbed her eyes. "I don't see why he can't just go to a homeless shelter or something."

Andrew stepped out of the bathroom, wiping his mouth on a towel. "Sure. Maybe we should just roll him out into that monsoon right now, let him sleep in the gutter."

"We don't have *monsoons,*" she muttered with a smirk as Andrew slipped back into the bathroom. "He has no apartment. . . . He's homeless. . . . Works for me."

"I'm turning out the light now," Andrew announced as he climbed into bed.

The two of them lay there silently in the darkness.

Andrew turned on his side and said softly, "He's a little rough around the edges, but he's not a bad guy." He rustled the covers and then lay still. "Remember . . . before your mom died she asked you to look after your father—wherever he was. You know she had a crush on him until the day she died."

"Why couldn't he have been responsible and married my mom?" Lydia asked, tugging at the comforter. "Why couldn't I have had a normal, dependable father?" She could hear Andrew breathing . . . it sounded heavy, as if he was unsettled. The silence lasted so long she thought surely he had fallen asleep.

"Lydia." His voice sounded gravelly and unstable.

"Yes." She waited, but he didn't say anything. As she lay there listening to the pounding rain outside and the tick-tock of the grandfather clock from down the hallway, she could hear Mike bark out a muffled smoker's cough from the guest bedroom.

"Because of what you wanted," he said softly, "I ended up betraying Brayden, too."

Lydia felt an onslaught of tears. She lay there, gently sobbing as the rain gutters gurgled. She burrowed her head into the fluff of the pillow to muffle the sobs. Then she turned toward her husband. He lay soundless, except for his breathing. She dabbed her tears on the softness of the bed sheet. Glancing around in the darkness, she sighed heavily. The familiar queasy feeling had returned.

"He's not a stray dog, Andrew. . . . We don't *have* to take him in."

Chapter 5

Mike yawned, stretched his arms overhead, admiring his tats, and then farted—loud and proud. Stark naked, he started out of the bathroom, but there was Lydia in the hallway. *Shit!* He stepped back into the bathroom and slammed the door.

"Oh . . . my God," she said. "We don't prance around this house naked."

"You musta at some point," Mike fired back from behind the door. "Otherwise the kid woulda never been born." He followed his crack with a mild coughing fit, as he heard Lydia scurrying down the hallway.

Mike slipped back into the guest room and stood there inspecting a bruise on his forearm. He wondered why it hadn't healed yet. *Gettin' old sucks ass.* His tattoos camouflaged it enough, he figured, so probably no need to worry about being grilled by his uptight daughter. He certainly didn't need her meddling in his health issues. He tossed on a ragged Marshall T-shirt and ripped, faded jeans. Then he grabbed his smokes and cell phone and headed barefoot to the front porch.

He fired up a cig, inhaled, and coughed before resting his free hand on his phone. He glanced up at the clouds inching across the blue sky. Then he glanced down at the standing water in the front garden and the street still wet from last night's storm. Fuck it, he thought, and pressed his manager's speed dial.

"Dude," Mike said, surprised that Bruce would answer so early. "I, uh, just wanted to let ya know I moved . . . to Los Gatos." Mike sucked in more smoke, coughed, and surveyed the neighborhood. "Wanted to give you my new address."

"Nothing's changed since the last time you called," Bruce said, his voice low.

Mike watched two chatty teenage girls walk by the house, backpacks slung over their shoulders. When they glanced his way, he made a face and laughed as their pace quickened. Next door some square dude in a suit stared at him as he slid behind the wheel of some generic Japanese-whatever car. Mike made a face at him too. Then he gave a guarded glance back toward the house and lowered his voice. "I know I owe the record company another album—"

"Mike." Bruce blew his nose. "I—"

"I need you to get me an advance," Mike ordered. "Pronto."

"Mike . . . Bud . . . that deal's dead. The label dropped you months ago."

"But—" Mike glanced across the street. "You're gonna reschedule the cancelled gigs."

"Your shows last summer got shitty reviews—"

"I had a few health problems. That's all fixed now."

"It's a miracle I even finagled you into second billing on those European festivals." Bruce sighed. "Word's out, bud. . . . You're washed up."

"Bullshit."

"Well, sure, there are probably a few markets. But, honestly, there wouldn't be enough money in it for me to even bother picking up the phone."

"How 'bout an indie label? That one in Germany was hot to sign me—"

"That was years ago," said Bruce.

Mike tried to swallow the dry lump in his throat. "Well, call 'em again."

"I can't get anyone to bite," Bruce insisted. "Trust me, nobody'll take the risk. To put it bluntly, Mike . . . you're history."

Mike felt the muscles in his face droop as he stood there absorbing Bruce's words. He blinked at the perfectly straight mow lines in the lawn as he sucked in smoke and exhaled with full force. From the corner of his eye he could make out some lady across the street herding three rugrats into an oversized SUV, but he didn't have the juice for any more faces. He took a final drag, flicked the butt into the bushes, and then headed inside.

Fuckin' hell. He stood in the kitchen doorway, squinting from the brightness. In daylight the room looked puke yellow, like bile in the toilet after drinking too much Jack and Tequila and Crown Royal in the same night. He glanced over at Andrew, Brayden, and Lydia seated at the breakfast table. The death squad, he thought, his daughter at the helm.

"Are you hungry, Mike?" Andrew asked, wiping his glasses.

Lydia shot Andrew an icy glare.

"Here," Andrew pointed to the empty seat as he slid on his eyeglasses. "Have a bowl of cereal—"

"Before you go," Lydia interjected as she plunked a clean bowl onto the table in front of him.

"Listen," Mike said as he cautiously sat down and inspected the unfamiliar box of cereal. "About that—" He lifted the milk carton and noticed it was organic, nonfat. Fuckin' hell. "There's this thing—"

"Thing?" Lydia folded her arms. "No, there's no *thing*. I need to go to work. You need to go—now. I'm not leaving until you do."

"Uh, yeah . . . well, I can't leave . . . just yet." Mike shoveled a spoonful of cereal into his mouth. "Oh . . . fffuuu—" He looked around, wanting to spit it out. "Got any sugar to go with this?"

Brayden passed him a jar.

Mike inspected it. "Honey. Right. Save the bees."

"What do you mean?" Lydia asked. Her eyes widened as she fired a worried glance at Andrew.

"Well, see—" Mike sneered at the honeycomb inside the jar, which was fuckin' weird. Then he drizzled honey onto his cereal. "I gotta stay . . . just a little longer."

Lydia looked at Andrew and then at the kid. "Brayden," she ordered, "go get your things for school."

The kid ignored his mom and lingered at the breakfast table, scrutinizing Mike.

"I—" Mike admitted as he coughed, ". . . remember last night I mentioned there are certain, uh, individuals I gotta, um, avoid?"

Lydia looked panicked. "Drug dealers?"

"Oh, hell no." Mike slurped in another spoonful of cereal. "I'm sure jonesin' for some Froot Loops right about now." He glanced at the kid, who gave a slight shake of his head, as if he didn't like his mom's healthy shit either. "Some, uh . . . people . . . would, uh . . . very much like the pleasure of my company. But they'll never find me here. . . . Nobody even knows I have a daughter." Mike glanced over at Lydia and saw her face fall. Now he'd really fucked up; he could tell she was hurt. "I . . . didn't mean—"

"What people?" she uttered in a soft, firm tone.

"Well—" Mike watched his daughter brush crumbs from the puke yellow and green tablecloth that matched the puke yellow walls. "There's this young cat—" He scratched at the stubble on his face, and prayed for a Bloody Mary to materialize on the breakfast table. "He was in my backing band. . . . Fuckin' poseur—"

"Language." Lydia fixed her eyes on Mike and pointed her head toward Brayden.

Yeah, right, Mike thought, like a fourteen-year-old has never heard a fuckin' cuss word. He glanced at the kid, who glared back with that relentless stare of his. "Uh, let's just say it's in relation to my European tour last summer . . . awesome tour, but there's a downside to everything . . . if you know what I mean. But I'm gonna make things right with those dudes . . . just as soon as I get my shi—uh, *affairs* in order."

"I knew it." Lydia slapped her hand onto the table.

"Did someone threaten you, Mike?" Andrew looked concerned.

"You came here for money." Lydia pursed her thin lips.

"No. Just need a place to hang . . . ya know, where nobody knows me." He flinched again when he saw the torment in her face. He could do no right in her world.

"When are you going to take responsibility for yourself?" She rose and carried a stack of dirty dishes to the kitchen sink. "You're, like . . . perpetually twelve years old."

Mike sighed, wringing his hands. "This goddamn arthritis." He glanced at Lydia, fishing for a reaction. "Nobody wants to see some old fucker playin' hard rock. It's pretty much over for cats like me. . . . Ya know, I had to cancel my tour—"

"You said last night that you didn't need money." Lydia glanced down at her watch.

"Well, I didn't, last night." He coughed. "I don't. . . . I just need a place to crash . . . for a while . . . a few days."

"*Days?* No. You're leaving now." Lydia looked at her watch. "Come on. I refuse to be late for my meeting." She turned to Andrew. "I'll pick up Brayden from school today."

Mike snickered. "Ain't the high school just down the street? Kid's legs ain't broke. Why can't he walk?"

"Like you know anything about raising a child," Lydia snapped. She fired him a look of disgust and then turned to Andrew. "He has band practice today."

"Fuckin' hell!" Mike gloated and looked at the kid. "You're in a band?"

"Not that kind," Lydia quickly pointed out. "Marching band—"

"School orchestra," the kid clarified.

Mike laughed and then muttered, "Band geek."

"See?" the kid griped to his mom. "Marching band is *not* cool!"

Lydia forced an unconvincing smile. "Marching band is great."

"I hate that damn clarinet!"

"Clarinet?" Mike cackled. "Who plays that anymore?"

Lydia scowled. "It's a fine instrument." She tugged on her suit jacket. "Besides, Brayden wanted to play it."

"When I was *nine.*" The kid pushed his moppy hair from his eyes.

"You're a good-lookin' kid," Mike said. "I mean, for a dude. How come you ain't playin' somethin' with balls? . . . Like drums or bass."

The kid's face lit up.

"Or keyboards," Andrew interjected.

"Just whose side are you on?" Lydia squinted at Andrew. "He has eight new pieces to learn for the end of school year instrumental concert, and there's the talent show." She turned to her son. "Don't forget your clarinet today. You don't want to disappoint Mr. Whiteside again, do you?"

"I hate clarinet," the kid barked with a sheepish glance at Mike. "And I hate practicing."

"Brayden," Lydia scolded.

"He's already mastered the clarinet," Andrew softly boasted to Mike. "I swear, he looks at sheet music, runs through it once, and has memorized it. Used to take me about a hundred times of playing a piano piece before muscle memory would kick in."

"Andrew!" Lydia snapped. She glanced at her watch again and then pointed at her father. "I'm not leaving until he does."

Mike looked at Andrew, hoping to hell he still had an ally. He didn't want to have to throw Andrew's little secret out there as a stall tactic, but Mike held the ammo, ready if needed.

"Honey, I don't think it's a good idea for me to leave just yet." Andrew rose from the table. "Brayden, why don't you get your backpack ready for school."

"I'm not leaving. This is getting interesting . . . better than anything I'll learn at school today."

"Brayden," Lydia commanded. "Go get your things."

"No," the kid said and continued staring at Mike.

Mike held back a grin; he liked the kid's defiance.

Andrew glanced at his watch as he towered over the table. "Look. . . . Mike's obviously in trouble." He walked over to Lydia and rested his hands on hers arms, talking more to her than anyone else in the room. "Let's just go to work . . . and school. I'll leave the office early and we'll sort everything out this evening."

"But—"

"Now *I'm* running late for *my* meeting," Andrew interrupted his wife. "And you're not only late for work but you're now late getting Brayden to school."

Lydia leaned in to Andrew and hissed, "I can't leave him here . . . alone in my house."

"*Our* house." Andrew looked her firmly in the eye.

She looked at him, defeated.

"Lydia . . . it'll be fine." Andrew hugged her but she remained unresponsive.

"Come on, Brayden." She motioned her son from the table. At the doorway she stopped and scowled at Mike. "Do not touch *anything* while we're gone."

"She means it," Andrew said with a shrug. "See you when I get home."

Still seated at the table, Mike winked in gratitude.

"I swear, if you light a cigarette in this house," Lydia added, "the minute I get home I will call the fire department and have them drag your butt out of here."

Lydia turned off the Volvo ignition and swung open the driver door as Andrew carefully guided his BMW into the driveway beside her. She gripped her purse, dreading the thought of what her irresponsible father had been up to alone in her house all day. Brayden hopped out of the Volvo and slammed the passenger door. Lydia closed the car door and turned to Andrew.

"I agreed to *one* night," she hissed. "It's been two . . . miserable . . . days," she said, stressing each word. "He goes, now—"

"It hasn't been that bad." Andrew was defending him, again.

"He'd better not have ruined my Garnier-Thiebaut tablecloth."

Andrew looked across the driveway to his son. "How was orchestra practice?"

Brayden rolled his eyes.

Greg, their neighbor, came inching up the driveway, and Lydia greeted him halfheartedly. "Hey," he glanced at Lydia, then at Brayden and Andrew. "Is that . . ." he asked, pointing to the house. "Mike Mays I saw earlier?"

Brayden paused in the driveway.

"Sure is," Andrew offered. "We have a houseguest."

"A *famous* houseguest!" Greg beamed.

Oh, God. Lydia closed her eyes. *The neighbors had seen him.*

Greg whipped out a CD from behind his back. "Can you score me an autograph?"

Andrew smiled. "Sure—"

"Not now, Greg," Lydia interjected. As a blast of guitar-heavy music erupted from the living room window, Lydia clutched Andrew and Brayden and stormed up the driveway. Greg followed. "Not now!" Lydia commanded. Greg retreated as Lydia pushed open the front door and raised her voice above the volume. "I warned him ten times already about loud music."

She stepped into the entryway and then into the living room. There he was . . . sitting on the sofa in nothing but his briefs, a happy cigarette dangling from his mouth. Lydia felt queasy when her eyes landed on a woman standing in front of him. She glared at the woman, who was hastily buttoning up her blouse and fluffing up her bottle-blonde hair. When the woman turned around, Lydia could see her smeared red lipstick and thick black eyeliner smudged below her eyes. She couldn't make out the woman's age . . . fifties, maybe?

Mike grabbed his jeans and rose, stumbling into each leg. He stood there teetering and then he pointed at the woman. "Did you meet my new friend, Gina?" He giggled. "That's Gina. . . . Gina, that's my . . . family."

Lydia tugged at the bottom of her jacket and took a rigid stance. "Brayden, go to your room—"

"Me? What'd I do?" Brayden protested.

"You're too young for X-rated," Lydia said to her son. "Go to your room—now!" She made sure her tone signified that she meant business.

"Looks pretty PG-13 to me," Brayden sniped. He sloughed his backpack down to his hand and plodded to his bedroom down the hall.

Grinning, Mike hollered a string of slurred words above the blaring rock music. "That's my grandson." He looked at Andrew in the entryway. "What're you cats doin' home so early?"

"Mike, you too," Lydia demanded. "Go to your . . . room!" She stormed over to the stereo and turned it off.

Mike ignored her and extended a concerned hand to Gina as she struggled into her pumps. "You okay, darlin'?"

Lydia cringed. Watching her father feign chivalry disgusted her. She remembered as a teenager hating the thought of him out there on the road with the proverbial girl in every port.

Mike wobbled to a stand and planted a slobbery kiss onto Gina's red-smeared lips. "I'll walk ya out, babe."

"I got it," Gina assured him.

"Okay. Bye, doll." Mike teetered and fell back onto the sofa.

Lydia turned to her husband. "Andrew?" With Mike limp on the sofa, she watched Andrew escort the woman out of the house. She hoped the neighbors wouldn't see. God, she hoped the woman *wasn't* the neighbors.

Lydia scanned the room, the empty wine bottles scattered about dead-soldier style. She waved through the marijuana smoke and stormed over to Mike.

Aiming a crooked grin at Lydia, he pinched off the lit end of the joint and set it on the coffee table, as if he thought he'd save it for later. "God forbid," Mike squawked, "my daughter might inhale secondhand pot smoke and mellow out for a change."

"I told you . . . no smoking in my house! . . . And no drugs!"

She shoved the joint into a quarter-full wine bottle. Recognizing the label—Testarossa Diana's Chardonnay—she winced and began inspecting the empty bottles around the room. Chimney Rock Reserve Cabernet Sauvignon. Mike had tanked up on some of her best, most expensive wine. Caparzo La Casa Brunello di Montalcino. She felt woozy.

"You drank my *Brunello*?" Lydia said through clenched teeth. She thought she might strangle him had she not been cradling the pricey wine bottles. She closed her eyes and then opened them, ordering her father off the sofa. "Now!"

"Okay, mommy," Mike retorted as he wobbled to his feet once more. "Fuckin' hell." Giggling, his pants still unzipped, he stumbled past Lydia.

Lydia pursed her lips and trailed Mike as he staggered out of the living room and into the hallway. "I don't even want to know where you found that woman."

He paused at the guest room door, placed one unsteady hand on the door jam, and scratched his crotch with the other. Then he tossed a glance back at Lydia and grinned. "Sorry." She stood, clutching the wine bottles, as he turned clumsily toward Brayden, who was poking his head out of the doorway from across the hall. Mike smirked and drunkenly waved the kid on.

Lydia wanted to hurl one of the empty wine bottles at Mike's head. She turned and deposited them on the marble table in the entry hall, and then opened the closet door. Scanning the row of luggage, she spotted her Vera Bradley pullman. As she struggled to remove it, she could hear Mike and Brayden conversing in the hallway.

"What was that music you were playing?"

"That last tune?" Mike slurred.

"Yeah."

"'Velvet Sky' by Vin Sabatino." He let out a long, loud belch. "Coolest fuckin' tune. . . . Did you hear the nuances of harp? His wife, Velvet, played electric harp on that one. . . . Is that fuckin' cool or what? . . . He named it for her." Mike lowered his voice. "See, her name's Velvet and the song's called—eh, never mind." He belched again. "Vin . . . killer guitar player . . . . Dude was the shit!"

"He's dead?"

"I dunno, kid. Wouldn't be surprised. This is the age where we all start droppin' like fuckin' flies." Mike yawned loudly. "Fuckin' hell. I gotta go drop right now."

Lydia stomped past the guest room just as Mike passed out on the bed face first. She stomped into her bedroom and hurled the suitcase onto the bed.

As she packed, Andrew stepped into the doorway. "What are you doing?"

"From the minute he arrived you've been siding with him," she said as she jammed her nightgown into the suitcase and slammed the dresser drawer.

"I'm just . . ." he said, sighing heavily. "He's a human being."

"You have no idea what 48 hours with that man has done to me," she said through clenched teeth. "I refuse to endure another minute. You want him, you can have him."

"Put that away. You can't be serious."

"Well, then get rid of him."

"He's higher than a kite right now, we can't send him away. He needs to sleep it off."

Lydia glared at him. "I'm not even sure who's talking anymore, you or him. . . . He is *not* returning to my life. I mean it, Andrew. It's him or me."

"That's ridiculous."

"Is it?"

He reached for her. "Come on, let's be logical."

She shrugged him off, zipped up the suitcase, and flung it onto the floor.

"Lydia—"

"Just give me my space." She rolled the suitcase to the bedroom doorway. "You can call me at noon tomorrow . . . if he's gone."

She wheeled the suitcase down the hall and paused at the guest room doorway. The drunken, quavering snores grated on her last nerve. She clenched her teeth and inhaled slowly through her nose. Then she gave a long, deep exhale and closed her eyes tightly, hoping. But when she opened them, her worst nightmare hadn't ended. Her father was still there, back to trash her tidy little world.

Chapter 6

As the grandfather clock chimed nine, Mike shuffled into the kitchen. Andrew stood at the sink rinsing dishes. Brayden lifted his head from the pile of schoolbooks at the kitchen table.

"Hungry, Mike?" Andrew asked. Mike thought he sounded a little less sociable than normal.

"Fuckin' starved." He scratched his balls. "I musta slept right through the munchies."

As Mike sat down at the table, Andrew peeled the plastic wrap from a plate of food, dinner that must have sat waiting for him to sleep off the booze.

The kid stared. "Should I call you Grampa or Mike?"

Andrew set the plate on the table. "Brayden?" He motioned his son toward the bedroom. "Why don't you give us a few minutes? . . . This is grown-up business."

"This is family," Brayden said firmly, "and I'm part of it."

Mike held back a smile. Smart kid.

Andrew puffed out his lower lip, and nodded. "Fair enough."

Mike sucked in a huge forkful of pasta from the plate. He liked how Andrew didn't baby the kid the way Lydia did. "I'm hella thirsty," he said with a mouthful.

"So then drink something," Andrew replied in a stern tone. "There's water in the fridge."

"I'd prefer Jack and Coke."

"Hair of the dog?" Andrew asked, arching a brow.

Mike watched cautiously as Andrew pulled up a chair. The kid glanced up every so often, pretending, Mike thought, to be really engrossed in his homework.

"Mike." Andrew looked him squarely in the eye. "Lydia left."

"That ain't cool." Mike continued to scarf down the food as he listened.

"No, it's not cool at all. She went to the Toll House. She . . . gave me an ultimatum. Now, I can't have my wife unhappy and away from home . . . away from me, and our son."

"You two havin' marital problems?" Mike knew he usually had Andrew by the balls, but he felt that maybe his loyalty was slipping. "Eh." He waved it off with his hand. "You know what she's like. . . . Women. . . . She'll get over it—"

"Mike." Andrew pushed his eyeglasses up the bridge of his long, narrow nose. "You know that I love you—"

Brayden glanced up at his father.

"I've held my mug, ya know," Mike blurted. "Kept your secret."

"It's as much your secret as it is mine," Andrew said with a squinty glare.

Brayden looked at Mike and then his father. "What secret?"

Mike sighed. "I don't wanna have to tell her." He ran his fingers through his scraggly hair. "Dude, ya gotta help me out here."

"Mike." Andrew twisted in the kitchen chair. "It's her or you. I'm sorry but I have no choice. . . . You need to go—"

"I got creditors on my ass." Mike swallowed the food in his mouth. "Tour bus company, musicians—they know where I live . . . get it?" Mike thought Andrew's puppy dog eyes looked like he got it.

"I'm really sorry." Andrew adjusted his glasses. "Right now I need to go get my wife—"

"I'm, uh . . . not well," Mike blurted out, surprising even himself.

Brayden glanced up again.

"I got this thing . . . C-P-D . . . no, C-O-P . . ."

Brayden wrinkled his nose. "That spells *cop*."

"You mean COPD?" Andrew asked.

"Yeah, that's it. Doctor says I'm gonna die. . . . I can't smoke, tour, or even have sex. . . . Do you know how shitty that is for me? That'll kill me first."

Andrew shot him a suspicious glance. "You were just with that Gina woman, and look at you, you're not worse for the wear . . . except for the hangover." Andrew nudged his glasses. "Ask me, you'll live to"—he glanced over at his son—"be back in the saddle again."

"Fuckin' hell."

They sat in silence as Brayden glanced around the table at his dad and then at Mike. Mike watched Andrew's brows twitching, as if his brain had shifted into overdrive. "Tell ya what." Mike stood up and wiped his mouth. "I'll get her home."

"Absolutely not." Andrew shot up from his chair.

"Look," Mike assured, "I know how to handle her when she's pissed off."

"Uh, it's fairly evident that you don't."

"It's gotta be me," Mike insisted, placing a hand on Andrew's shoulder. "Trust me. . . . Leave it to her ol' man. I'll bring her home."

At the sight of Mike's face, Lydia slammed the hotel room door shut.

"Darlin'?" He knocked incessantly as he coughed.

"Don't patronize me with an empty term of endearment. Where's my husband?" she hollered through the closed door.

"He's waitin' for ya in the car. Can ya let me in . . . please?" He knocked again. "I'm tradin' places with you tonight. . . . You go on home to your family now."

Family? Lydia slumped against the door, relieved, and thawed long enough to open it. She turned, refusing to look him in the eye, as he gingerly entered the hotel room and set his duffel bag on the floor.

"Why?" She avoided looking at him. "Why did you really come to my house . . . after all these years? You could hide out anywhere—"

"Told ya . . . needed a place to stay."

She folded her arms, still averting his eyes. "I don't believe you."

"Hey, I'm not the one who lied for fourteen years."

She felt that familiar queasy feeling return.

"And," Mike said, "I wanted to see my grandkid."

That stung. He had never been interested in *her*, but now he suddenly expressed an interest in her son? She turned and glared at him. "Oh, don't give me that bullpucky."

"You can say *bullshit* around me, darlin'."

Looking at him reminded her of the dreadful scene in her living room earlier. She gathered up her belongings and stuffed them into the suitcase. "The sooner you're out of my life again, the better." She lifted the bag onto the floor and glared at him once more. "Enjoy your night . . . alone." But then she froze, immobilized, as if her mother had floated out of the grave to hold her back.

"Go on, then."

"Wait." She reached into her handbag and withdrew a pen. Then she walked over to the desk and scrawled on the hotel stationery. "I'll go as soon as you sign this." She handed the paper to Mike and then folded her arms as he read it aloud.

"I, Mike Mays, will never again try to contact my daughter, my son-in-law, or grandson." Still clutching the paper, Mike dropped his hand to the side. "Oh, that's fuckin' ridiculous."

She held out the pen. "Sign it."

"C'mon—"

"Sign." She glared at him and nudged the pen closer.

Mike lowered his eyes, snatched the pen from her grasp, stabbed it to the paper, and furiously scribbled his signature.

"Fine!" She yanked the pen from his hand, rolled the suitcase across the room, and flung open the door.

Mike stood there clutching the paper. "Fine."

Lydia slammed the door behind her and stood in the hallway, leaving him alone in the room. As she stood there, huffing, the hotel room door creaked open.

"There's no way in hell I'm promisin' *any* of this shit." He crumpled the paper, threw the wad at her, and then slammed the door shut.

She turned and stood there, as tears pooled in her eyes. With the back of her hand, she dabbed at them. Damn him, she thought, for always making her so emotional. Then she heard the hotel room door open behind her.

"Darlin'." Mike's voice was soft, calm. "You know, your mom woulda—"

"Don't you dare bring up my mother," Lydia choked out between sobs.

"I, uh . . . didn't wanna have to tell ya this . . . but . . . I ain't well."

Wiping her tears, she whipped her head around.

"I got this thing . . . C-D-P . . . it's . . . *real* bad," he said, forcing an overdramatized cough.

She looked him up and down, certain he was bluffing.

He humbly studied the floor and said softly, "I got nowhere to go."

Lydia studied his face. "Now that's the first honest thing you've said to me in forty-eight hours . . . maybe ever."

He hung his head and shifted his eyes up to her, overacting again.

"You don't seem sick to me." She scrutinized him in the doorway. "If you really had COPD you wouldn't smoke."

"Yeah, but—"

"Andrew's uncle had emphysema," she reasoned. "It's manageable, if you take care of yourself. But you need to . . . take care of yourself." She stepped into the doorway as several businessmen sauntered by.

"Come in," Mike suggested.

She took a deep breath. She didn't fully understand what possessed her to do it, but she followed her father into the hotel room.

"Don't tell nobody," Mike urged. "If word gets out, my career's toast." He coughed, prompting a fit, and then spit into the nearby wastebasket.

Lydia tilted her head. "You've had a smoker's cough for as long as I can remember."

Mike shuffled over to the plush hotel room chair and struggled into it. He looked up at her. "I can't smoke, or tour, or even have sex—"

"Oh, God. . . . Erase that last part." She perched on the edge of the bed, concerned, yet guarded. Then she squinted at him. "Wait a minute." She shot straight up, surprised she had let him bamboozle her into believing him. "Then what was that today . . . in my house?"

"Well, the *doctor* says I can't, but that don't mean—"

"You are such a liar!"

"You don't even know me," Mike raised his voice. "I bet you got no clue how old I am."

"I know *exactly* how old you are." She glared at her father. "I remember your thirtieth birthday. I bet you don't, but I sure do. . . . I was six." Lydia sat back on the edge of the bed. "Mom let me put the frosting on your birthday cake." Lydia felt her lip quiver. "You never showed up."

"I—I . . . was probably recordin' or somethin'," he speculated. "Yeah . . . I woulda been stuck in the studio . . . in Berkeley. Time slips away in the studio, but you'd never understand that. It's somethin' only musicians get."

She wiped her eyes. "I cried myself to sleep that night."

"Shit."

"I was six, Mike. . . . You disappointed a six-year-old—your own daughter." She just sat there on the edge of the bed, fighting back tears. "And you've never stopped disappointing me."

"Ouch." Mike reached toward her for an uncomfortable, hesitant moment and then retreated. He had never been one for affection.

He got up and disappeared into the bathroom. Then he returned moments later with a box of tissues, which Lydia accepted.

"Sorry, darlin'. . . . I just ain't very good with chicks cryin' 'n' shit."

She yanked a tissue from the box and soaked up the tears. "I'm not one of your *chicks*." She dabbed at her eyes. "I'm your daughter."

She watched him retreat toward his duffel bag. His back to her, he stood there for a long, silent while. There's no way he's crying, she thought. Mike Mays doesn't cry; he makes others cry.

"I know you don't like me so much, and I'm sorry I ain't so good at rememberin' shit. But, please, just let me—"

"Hide from the world at my house?"

"No." Eyes downcast, he said softly, "Be in your life."

Lydia sat stunned, speechless. He seemed desperate, she thought, the first time she had ever seen him look afraid. "Um." Stalling as thoughts raced through her mind, she suddenly recalled Andrew reminding her of her mother's dying request: to look after Mike. Lydia took a deep, shaky breath to clear the nervousness from her voice. "Okay." She noticed the instant relief in his expression. Then she straightened her blouse. "You can stay. . . . But you have to play by *my* rules."

"Rules—" He dropped the duffel bag at his feet as Lydia held up a hand to shush him.

"My house, my rules."

He half-nodded, waiting for her to lay down the law.

"No drinking, no smoking, no drugs in my house . . . and no women."

"You gonna whip out another piece of paper for me to sign?" He gave her a crooked grin, but that same cocky smile now seemed sheepish to her.

"I'm serious," she said, folding her arms, waiting for his agreement. "Oh, and no lying . . . or cussing."

Mike rolled his eyes. "Oh, *come on*. That's like askin' me not to fart. Ya know the average human farts like twenty times a day? It's involuntary . . . just like cussin'. Damn near impossible not to."

Lydia refused to smile. "I said you can stay . . . for a few more days." She shot him a challenging stare. "But you have to follow my rules."

Mike bent over and picked up the duffel bag. "I'll play by your rules." As he reached the door, he turned. "But just remember—you may be Brayden's mom," he said, raising a belligerent eyebrow. "But you ain't mine."

He stepped across the threshold, and she followed.

Chapter 7

"Cocksmokers!" Tank's howl resounded through the compound.

Velvet slid aside the beaded curtain and peered from the kitchen doorway. There, across the courtyard, stood Tank in the doorway of his quarters, arms outstretched and dripping wet. He wiped the water from his stubbly-bald head and looked up, inspecting the rigging. Then he bent forward, groaning as he reached beyond his rotund belly and lifted the empty bucket.

Blitz Stryker barged through the doorway, nearly knocking Velvet over. He rested his hand on the doorjamb and repetitively tapped out a beat; any surface, and Blitz would drum on it—he didn't even know he was doing it anymore. She glanced at his fingernails, painted royal blue this week to match the blue streak in his hair and his wrist sweatbands. So *drummer*, she thought; so *'80s*. He often wore a bandana to conceal the receding hairline, but today a yellow one was knotted loosely around his neck.

Gallo Lane lunged through the doorway, cackling, and grabbed ahold of Blitz's leopard print vest. "Dude's so pissed!"

Velvet shook her head at them. "It's not like he's gonna kill you."

Gallo looked at Blitz. "What'd she say?"

"How many times do I have to tell you?" Blitz said, "Put your fuckin' hearing aid in."

"Ah," Gallo grumbled with a dismissive wave. "Dude," he said, pointing to Blitz's belt. "The '80s are calling, they want your bullet belt back."

"Yeah," Blitz retorted, "and all that blow that went up your nose—they want that back, too."

Gallo tucked a peppered wave of hair under his black Borsalino cap. Velvet studied his lively face, his rippled hair, papery-dry skin, and the scar over his eyebrow. He was still gaunt, she thought, but much healthier looking than he'd been in decades.

"What?" Gallo shrugged. "I ain't even stoned—" He turned to Blitz and grinned. ". . . yet."

Tank ran into the courtyard, yelling like a lunatic, his Brummie accent thick. "Where ya tucked away, then?" He yelped when he spotted Blitz and Gallo, and then paused to catch his breath, the bucket still clenched between his stubby fingers. His soaked Fender logo T-shirt and denim shorts dripped onto the tile. "Come here, ya yampy yanks!"

Gallo grabbed Blitz's sleeve and the two men belly-laughed their way into the courtyard. Velvet followed and there was Tank, grinning.

"Bloody brilliant, that was," he conceded.

Gallo narrowed his eyes. "Payback."

Strange how life works, Velvet thought—how they had all come together one by one because they couldn't quite make it anywhere else. She folded her arms and leaned back against the doorjamb. "Maybe if you'd shower more often, they wouldn't have to rig a bucket."

"Touché," Blitz said as he grappled with Gallo for the remaining cushy lounge chair. They nearly toppled a geranium-filled urn in the heat of battle.

"What'd she say?" Gallo asked and then gloated when Blitz knuckled and retreated to a nearby chair.

Blitz smirked. "She said you should put your hearing aid in, dickhead."

"Trite prank," Harley muttered as she looked up from a chaise lounge, her fingers on the frets of her red Yamaha SG guitar. "Fucking juveniles." She slid a pencil out from behind her ear. "Acting like you're still on the road."

"Come now, southern fairy," Tank snapped. "Like you don't miss the glory days of tourin'."

Harley erased and scribbled on her notepad and then resumed working out a melody. "Unlike the rest of you, *I* have work to do—"

"Bugger that for a game of soldiers. You could write the world's greatest hit, but it ain't goin' nowhere today."

"At least she's trying," Velvet reminded him.

Gallo removed his cap and smoothed his hand over his hair. Then he crossed his legs and placed the cap over his eyes. "I'm just gonna lay here," he sighed as he tucked his hands behind head. "And contemplate the wide range of employment opportunities available to an American ex-rock bass player road dog living in a farmhouse in Italy with his friends."

"Ya forgot ex-druggie, geeze," Tank razzed as he wrung water from his T-shirt.

Gallo lifted his cap and raised his head. "Ah, yes . . . another important component for my résumé." He lowered his head and adjusted the cap back over his eyes.

His résumé, Velvet thought—and what would she put on hers? Den mother to a bunch of stone-broke geriatrics. And lately she had full custody of these guys, since Vin was away so often.

At the sound of a car topping the gravel driveway, all three men turned their focus to the edge of the courtyard by the old barn. Gallo lifted his cap for a better view as the three men froze, mesmerized. *Giulia.* All male life at Groove House screeched to a halt whenever she paid a visit. Harley let her pencil drop as she rested her guitar and then pushed herself up from the chaise.

Time seemed to move in slo-mo as the Italian goddess entered the courtyard. Her curvaceous body was as lovely as a Botticelli, Velvet thought, as she grimaced and looked down at her own sagging breasts. Giulia's petite Giuseppe Zanotti black pumps made the perfect capper to her tanned bare legs; Velvet glanced down at the cheap clogs on her own feet. Every waking hour Giulia looked like an Italian movie star—a severe contrast to the old farts who lived on Velvet's compound. Giulia gently whisked her long dark hair away from her face, unveiling her soft, pink, sexy lips.

"Ah, to be young again," Harley muttered as she stepped beside Velvet without taking her eyes off Giulia.

"And beautiful." Velvet sighed. "And wealthy."

"The chocolate princess," Harley said with a swish of jealousy.

Velvet eyed the large basket in Giulia's arms—filled to the brim with the usual bread, cheese, pasta, wine, fruit . . . and *La Principessa Cioccolato.* Perfect timing.

Giulia sure knew how to work her earthly delights. She lowered her eyes and shot a succulent smile at the men as she passed. *"Buongiorno, ragazzi."* She always referred to them as "boys" because, well, they acted the part—as Velvet, the den mother, knew all too well.

Gallo, Blitz, and Tank—the three amigos, as Harley had labeled them several years back—studied every sensuous move of Giulia's voluptuous body. Paralyzed with lust, the men replied, as if in a trance, *"Buongiorno."*

"Buongiorno, donne." Giulia greeted both women with an air kiss to each cheek. She smiled and blinked her big brown eyes as she withdrew her latest chocolate creations from the basket. "Wait until you taste these-uh." Even her Italian accent was exquisite. Her voice escalated an octave. "My new *cioccolato organico.* . . . Is Arriba, from the Nacional beans of Ecuador. *Settanta percento.*"

"Seventy percent," Velvet proudly translated an easy one to Harley.

"Did you say *organic*?" Blitz asked as he entered the patio.

"Right up yer street, ya tree huggin' lard 'ed," said Tank.

Velvet accepted a piece of chocolate from Giulia but before she could pop it into her mouth, Giulia reached up and stopped her.

"Is rich, the aroma," said Giulia, waving the scent toward her nose and inhaling, as though it was a fine wine. Then she stood, waiting for the reviews.

Velvet looked at Harley in her baggy shorts—the antithesis of Giulia's tight-fitting dress. Harley tucked her cropped, silver-blonde hair behind her ear, took a bite, and purred. Velvet closed her eyes and let the chocolate melt on her tongue. "Oh, Giulia . . . this is fantastic."

"*Grazie.* Is in my stores in the next days."

Harley handed a piece of chocolate to Blitz.

"Is it vegan?" Blitz asked.

"No, it's chock-full of *bufala* blood, you knob." Harley stepped away to share the samples with the men.

Velvet reached for the basket in Giulia's arms. Swishing her way through the doorway curtain, she carried it into the kitchen and set it on the counter. "Really, Giulia, you don't have to keep bringing us food. *Troppo gentile.*" Velvet seemed to say that a lot lately, as her neighbor in the fabulous house on the hill across the way consistently showered them with food, wine, and her delectable chocolates. *Santa Giulia,* Velvet mused as she withdrew cheese and fresh pasta from the basket.

Giulia flicked her gorgeous hair. "You are to me like parents. I enjoy to help. . . . Don't tell to my crazy husband." She parted her sumptuous lips. "Also because you are like me . . . *stranieri.*"

"You're not a foreigner," Velvet said as she took in the aroma of the pecorino cheese.

"*Io sono da Milano.* In this village, we are no one of them. *Hai capito?* They know we are no from here. Of course you know, the people in the village no go in my shop. Is all tourists."

"And me," Velvet said with a smile. Then she paused from unpacking the basket. "Do you think? . . . Maybe that's why our land reassessment was so high? Because Vin and I are not from here? You have land and a house, just like us."

"But the family of my Carlo is from this village." Giulia blinked her big brown eyes. "Anyway, you have also the barn and the buildings. All the things they add."

Carlo, Velvet contemplated as she removed two bottles of wine from the basket. "But it tripled . . . and our tax bill. . . . Do you think . . . maybe . . . Carlo?"

Giulia laughed. "My husband is a strong man, but has no that much power."

Velvet wanted to laugh but she could only manage a half-smile. "I think of all the money we would still have now," she said, removing the remaining chocolate from the basket. "If only Vin hadn't sunk all our savings into that vineyard." She paused as she thought about the old vineyard at the edge of the property. "And now . . . you've seen it—it's neglected and unruly, overtaken by weeds."

"For your Vincenzo, was a love of the labor." Giulia moved close to Velvet at the counter and put a hand on her shoulder. *"Tutto bene?"*

"We can't possibly pay that enormous tax bill." Velvet glanced toward the kitchen door and sighed heavily. "And I just can't keep watching Harley toil over writing new songs that she's never going to finish. And really, what's the point, anyway? . . . And Tank, Blitz, Gallo. . . . What can they do anymore? And nobody will even buy my olive oil. . . . And that stupid crumbling wall . . . and Vin away in the States . . ." She began chewing her thumbnail. "We can't lose the house—"

"*Carissima,* the house you will not to lose." She placed a caring hand on Velvet's arm. "You think . . . to sell the old vineyard—"

"I could never do that to my husband."

Giulia's cell phone rang and she gave Velvet a concerned glance as she spoke commandingly into her phone.

Velvet wondered how much *Giulia's* property tax had increased, but knew it would be rude to ask. She turned away, scanning the olive groves until her gaze fell on the old neglected vineyard far below. Pursing her lips, she took a deep breath.

Chapter 8

Lydia toyed with the food on her plate and then looked over at Andrew. "Greg has not stopped asking me for Mike's autograph."

"Why don't he just ask me," Mike growled. "I'd give it to him."

Brayden glanced around the table.

"Well, what do you expect?" asked Andrew. "He sees him out there smoking."

"And that's another thing—" Lydia started to say.

"How 'bout you talk *at* me instead of *about* me?" Mike blurted out. "I'm sittin' right here."

Andrew gave Lydia a look and then turned patiently to Mike. "It's okay, Mike," he said in a soothing tone. "The front yard is just fine."

Lydia shook her head. Andrew always sided with Mike. And why were they even allowing Mike to smoke at all if he was supposedly ill? She sighed and let it go, chalking it up to another of her father's lies.

"Um . . . Grampa?"

Mike stabbed a forkful of chicken and gnawed on it pirate-style. "I keep tellin' ya, you can call me Mike—"

"No," Lydia corrected. "It's disrespectful." She glanced at Mike and then smiled at Brayden. "You should call him *Grandpa*."

"Um," Brayden hesitated as he scanned the table. "Did you . . . really tour with Aerosmith?"

Mike grinned across the table at his grandson. "How do ya know 'bout Aerosmith, kid?"

"Don't call him *kid*," Lydia reprimanded. She glanced at Andrew, who was eagerly awaiting Mike's response. She took a deep breath. "Sweetheart, Grandpa doesn't want to talk about those days."

Mike snarled, "What's the fuckin' problem?" He looked down when his cell phone ringtone blared: *Have a drink on me.*

As he pulled his phone from his pocket, something tumbled out and clattered onto the wooden floor. Mike leaned down and scrambled to retrieve it. Then he shoved whatever it was back into his pocket and focused on the phone call. Lydia narrowed her eyes, thinking that he had better not be harboring drugs in her house.

"Hey, babe! Nah, I'm stuck in the South Bay." He turned from the table, shielded the phone with his hand, and failed at a miserable attempt to whisper. "But call me later," he said in a syrupy-sweet tone, followed by a revolting giggle.

Lydia glared at him. "We can all hear you." She motioned for him to hang up.

His eyes bounced to Lydia as he lowered the phone. Then he looked down at his plate and grinned crookedly before singing a few lines in a breathy twang. "I got a never endin' love for you. From now on you're all I wanna screw . . ."

Brayden giggled and Lydia glared at him, before turning to Mike. "I suppose that's your best George Jones imitation."

"Conway Twitty," Mike gloated. "I can do way better."

He took a huge breath and was preparing to bellow when Lydia put her hands over her ears and yelled, "Stop!"

Mike gave her his humble, hangdog look. "What—ya don't think I can—"

"What was that that fell out of your pocket a minute ago?" she snapped. "Drug paraphernalia? It had better not be a crack pipe."

"Crack?" Mike cackled. "That's for junkies 'n' shit. Don't ya know by now yer ol' man only smokes dope these days? My only vice . . . well, that and cigs . . . and booze . . . oh, and hookers."

Andrew put down his fork. "Mike, I don't suppose you spend much time around teenagers these days, but they can be"—he glanced over at Brayden—"impressionable."

"I was *jokin'*," Mike shouted. "Just messin' around, dudes!" He turned to Brayden. "The kid knows I was just jivin'. Right, kid?"

Lydia quickly lifted the bowl of kale and handed it to her son. "How was your day, sweetie?" She watched him rest the bowl next to his dinner plate as he shrugged and grunted. When she reached out to shift a long wisp of hair behind his ear, he recoiled.

Head down, eyes up, Brayden glanced around the table and returned his focus to Mike. "So, um . . . you toured with AC/DC?"

Lydia clanked her fork onto her plate and then smiled affectionately at her son. "Honey, please eat some vegetables. Put some kale on your plate. Grandpa doesn't want to talk about his past—"

"The hell I don't." Mike looked straight at Brayden and grinned. "Yeah, kid. One of my favorite fuckin' bands of all time."

Lydia pressed on the knots in her stomach.

Mike shoveled a huge glob of kale and gravy into his mouth. "You heard of Whitesnake?" Brayden shook his head and Mike said, "David Coverdale's one badass singer. One of my absolute faves. Played with them, too, in nineteen-eighty—"

"Must you talk with your mouth full? It's repulsive." Lydia looked at Andrew, who shook his head in nonverbal encouragement to let it go.

"Dad," Brayden asked. "Can Grampa . . . maybe . . . teach me guitar?"

Lydia glanced worriedly at Mike, who was smiling wickedly. "Sweetheart." With a doting smile, she gazed at Brayden and moved the wisp of hair from his eyes.

"I knew you had it in ya, kid!" Mike crowed. "Let me show you a few licks right now—ah, shit, I forgot, I ain't got no goddamn guitar—but I could always—"

"Brayden has a tremendous amount of important work to do these days," Lydia interrupted. "He has hours every day to spend on college prep—"

"Jeez, Lydia," Andrew interrupted, mid-chew. "He just asked about learning how to play guitar, not making a career out of it."

"I ain't stupid." Mike gave Lydia a hard-edged stare as he put his hands on the table and leaned in to her. "I know what you're doin' here." He coughed. "Look, I never went to college 'cause I didn't fuckin' need to. I knew I wanted to be a musician when I was eleven. You were still playin' with Barbie dolls at eleven—"

"How would you know?" Lydia snapped. She turned to her son. "You're only fourteen—"

"Fifteen on Saturday," Brayden interrupted.

"But you are going to do your college prep because *you are going to college*."

"What's the point in goin' to college just to learn how to drink lotsa beer and memorize a buncha shit you don't care about and you'll never use anyway?" Mike barked, leaning back in his chair. He was breathing heavily and seemed agitated.

"So he doesn't become a loser," Lydia said to no one in particular. She sat tall, refusing to be manipulated.

"So fuckin' what if I ain't rollin' in dough like you," Mike retaliated.

"Mike," Andrew stepped in. "That's not fair."

"You foolish man." Lydia shook her head at her father. "You wasted everything."

"Maybe so, but I had a helluva fuckin' life." Mike cracked a smile, which irritated Lydia even more. He coughed and then took on a serious tone. "Maybe one day—instead of bustin' your ol' man's balls about all the things *you* disapprove of in *my* life—maybe you'll realize that *you* were my goddamn investment."

Lydia blinked. Birthday cards, ice cream, and a day at the zoo, she thought, hardly constituted an investment.

"Yes . . . *you*," he said, pointing an index finger at her. "How do ya think you got that highbrow education?" Mike paused to take a breath. "Stanford ain't goddamn free to rock stars' kids, ya know."

Lydia looked at him suspiciously. "What do you mean, *investment?*" Then she glowered at him. "How . . . dare . . . you. My mother's hard work and the generosity of my grandparents put me through college. How dare you drag them in here, post mortem, to bolster your vainglorious fabrication." She took a righteous, ragged breath and stared him down.

Mike cocked his head. "I got no idea what the hell ya just said about that vain-whatever shit, but if yer mom and her parents told you they paid your college education, they're lyin' sonsabitches."

Lydia glared at him in silence.

"Look, I ain't never been one to brag about my goodwill efforts—" He broke off as his rant sent him into a coughing fit.

"Goodwill efforts? Are you suggesting that I was just some charity that you were tithing to?"

"Well, have at it, darlin'!" Mike sat at the table, open-armed, awaiting the retaliation. "I toured nine months a year to keep your ass at Stanford." He coughed. "Did that for twenty-five fuckin' years to pay off all the bills. Never once cancelled a show. . . . I played through hernias, broken bones, colds, flu, even pneumonia. . . . Do you know how hard it is to sing and play guitar with a hundred-and-fuckin'-four-degree fever?" He stood up, panting, and looked wildly around the room before landing on her La Pavoni espresso machine. "So you could just say that I paid for whatever the hell *that* is," he said, pointing a finger, "and all this fancy shit in your house." He leaned on the table, breathing heavily. "I'd say that's worth a helluva lot more than just a few lousy days of room and board—wouldn't you, little miss Ivy Leaguer?"

Lydia couldn't resist correcting him, as she murmured, "Stanford isn't actually in the Ivy League."

Mike pushed himself from the table and paced the dining room, raking his fingers through his shaggy hair.

Lydia sat staring at the food on her plate, unable to even take in what Mike had just said. She glanced up at him standing there, bobbing his head, cocksure and primed for combat. But she refused to engage him any further.

Brayden rustled in his seat before he spoke. "So, um . . . Dad?"

Lydia looked over at her son as he focused on Andrew, but he refused to look at her. She slumped in her chair, knowing that if she reached toward her son, he would just veer away again. She needed him to look, to see that she loved him above all—the love only a mother can give. Mike thought he had done so much for her, but he was never *there*. She prided herself on being a dependable parent, one who had been there every single day of her son's life. Mike had never taken her to her first day of kindergarten, or bandaged her skinned knees, or harangued her prom date. The only parent she had left had been no parent at all.

"Yes, Brayden," said Andrew.

"Can I . . . take guitar lessons?"

Chapter 9

Velvet gulped hard and slinked into the shade of the pergola—the imposing Carlo Moretti stood at the edge of her courtyard. *He never comes here*, she thought, as she felt prickles on her arms and neck. If Vin were home, Carlo wouldn't dare set foot on their property. She remembered how Giulia had suggested recently that she could always sell the old vineyard to Carlo to help alleviate their financial straits. Was he there to strong-arm her into selling since Vin was away? She took a step backward.

As the initial shock of seeing Carlo on her property began to dissipate, she could see that a woman was with him, and it wasn't Giulia. As they approached, her cropped raven black hair bounced with each step. Velvet clenched her clammy hands and took another step back. It was the girl from the *Catasto*—the land registry office—the very girl who had told her several times, quite stonily actually, that there was no mistake, that the property taxes had increased for *everyone* and that the outrageous tax hike was her balance due. *Oh God, they're probably in cahoots*, she thought. The day she had been dreading had arrived. They were coming to take their house—Vin's ancestral home.

She tensed and held her breath as they swaggered closer—Carlo wearing a designer suit and a smarmy grin, the girl in tight black stretch jeans.

"*Buongiorno, signora,*" Carlo said with bogus charm.

Velvet just stood there, stricken and unable to speak.

The girl looked at Carlo, parted her fuchsia-tinted lips, and uttered something in Italian that Velvet didn't catch.

Carlo gave Velvet a steely glare as he smoothed his hand over his slick, charcoal black hair. When he opened his mouth, she closed her eyes, certain he was about to shatter her world. He let out a hearty laugh and Velvet shriveled. Then he and the girl exchanged quips in rapid-fire Italian. Velvet opened her eyes and tried to recognize a few words, but they spoke too quickly for her to grasp anything but articles and conjunctions.

"*La chitarra*," Carlo spit out, as if he were tasting corked wine. Then he grinned. "My cousin is here for to buy the guitar."

Velvet slowly leaked out a huge breath. "Oh." She tempered her words with shaky laughter as she gasped for air. "The guitar. . . . Right." She stood there, wobbly-legged, trying to regain her composure. "*You're* . . . Angelina . . . from the eBay sale." She clasped her hands tightly to stop the trembling. *Breathe,* she told herself.

"She *non* speak English," Carlo said with a courtly smile. "She ask me to be the translating."

"Kray-mare-uh," said the girl. She was petite, with a smooth, pretty face, and yet there was something about her—a foreboding distance—that made Velvet want to flee.

Velvet thought she detected a slight smile but she couldn't be certain. "The Kramer." She nodded and relaxed a bit. "This way," she said, waving them to the house.

Velvet led them through the front door and into the great room. She pointed to the Anvil case by the door and felt a tug of sadness. The decades that beat-up old case had seen—all the tours and countries—it embodied Vin's life story. As Angelina lifted it, Velvet glanced down at the patchwork of '80s tour stickers blanketing the case—Aerosmith, RATT, Whitesnake, Mötley Crüe, UFO, Poison, Scorpions, Twisted Sister, AC/DC—and the "fragile" stickers, which always seemed a signal to airline employees to throw, drop on the tarmac, drive over, or damage the item in any manner they saw fit.

Angelina gently hoisted the guitar from its case and cradled it in her arms. She fumbled up and down the frets, as if the electric guitar felt foreign to her. Then she looked up, her dark eyes ringed with thick, smudged eyeliner. She pushed a wisp of bed-head hair off her cheekbone, said something in Italian, and then glanced at Carlo.

When Carlo fired back at Angelina, Velvet couldn't quite grasp his words, but she did catch *Vin Sabatino* and *non molto famoso*. It seemed that Vin's guitar wasn't going to a fan at all. The girl likely wasn't even familiar with his music, his history in the business.

"She like the guitar," Carlo rumbled, surveying the great room and then turning his ominous dark stare on Velvet. "But is too expensive."

Angelina continued noodling, her fingers haphazardly dashing across the neck of the guitar. Then she stopped, rested it in the case, and closed the lid.

That's it, Velvet thought. No sale. Another thousand Euro she could have put toward the property tax bill, gone. She looked at Angelina in her jeans and grey baby doll T-shirt. Well, this little pixie isn't a good fit for the guitar, anyway, she thought. Velvet would find another buyer, someone in the States who might better appreciate a relic, of sorts, from the '80s.

Angelina reached into her jeans pocket and pulled out a wad of Euro bills.

"Angelina," Carlo warned, his brows creased.

Velvet squinted at him. Was he trying to force Angelina to undercut the price she had already agreed to online? *Shifty bastard.*

"Is okay," Angelina said, handing the full thousand to Velvet. "I like." She aimed a slight, victorious grin in Carlo's direction.

Velvet smiled at Angelina before turning to escort them outside and into the courtyard. They all glanced back toward the sound of laughter wafting up from the terraces down below. Velvet hoped that Carlo would stay on course and get off her property before he had a chance to scope out any of her vineyards down below. And she hoped they would leave before Tank, Blitz, and Gallo made it to the courtyard. They turned again when Harley breezed past them and settled into the hammock.

Carlo scanned the courtyard and surrounding buildings. He grinned and said, deliberately, *"Il riso abbonda nella bocca degli stolti."* Then he turned his back.

Velvet watched him slither back across the courtyard, certain that he must have had something to do with their unreasonable property tax hike. Before he and Angelina rounded the gravel drive, Velvet took a final glance at the guitar case. What were the odds, she pondered, that someone from their little village would buy the guitar off eBay? She wished it had fetched more, but if she had to resort to selling off Vin's guitars to survive, she certainly had an armory full.

"Hey!" Tank scurried into the courtyard. "Was that my guitar?" he asked, goading her. "You know Vin promised that Kramer to me."

"In, like, nineteen-eighty-whatever." Here we go again, Velvet thought. "Times have changed, Tank. And now it's gone to the highest bidder."

"Disaster." Tank gazed out toward the driveway.

Velvet stepped away to fetch her gardening gloves from the patio table.

Tank flanked her like a sheepherding dog. "Who bought it, then?" he badgered. "Someone here in Tuscany? Were it a fan?"

"It was Carlo." Harley popped her head up from the hammock.

"Jesus wept." Tank scratched his stubbly-bald head. "What's that mongrel mob boss want with Vin's old guitar?"

"Not Carlo," said Velvet as she reached for the gloves. "His cousin. She doesn't speak English."

"A *bird?*" Tank checked. "Got *my* Kramer?"

"Sexy little minx, too," Harley baited him. "Hey, V . . . what'd Carlo say at the end there?"

"Not sure." Velvet glared toward the courtyard's edge. "All I got was *laugh* and *mouth.*"

"Was that *stolti* he said?" Harley pushed herself up from the hammock. "Doesn't that mean *fools?*"

Velvet shrugged. "He's an ass."

"He's Mafia," Tank assured them all.

"He's a businessman," Velvet insisted.

"Right. . . . The *family* business," Tank joked.

"What'd he say?" Gallo growled, adjusting his cap on approach with Blitz.

"Carlo," Blitz hollered toward his ear.

"Strange dude," Gallo barked.

"He's kinda cool," said Blitz, as he tightened the bright blue bandana twisted around his wrist. "Remember when he dropped off some firewood last winter?"

Velvet smirked. "I'm sure Giulia put him up to that. He usually ignores us."

"Mafioso," Tank taunted her.

"If he was," Velvet noted, "he wouldn't be bothering with us."

"I'm with Vin," said Tank. "Bet he used his special mafia powers to get the property reassessed so high that you can't afford the taxes."

"And why would he do that?" Velvet asked, even though she knew the answer.

"Drive us out," Blitz said, fluffing his bottle-blond hair. "It's no secret he hates foreigners. Then he could take your land and expand his vineyards."

"I wouldn't wanna fuck with that dude," Gallo admitted.

"Camorra," Tank hissed.

"That's in the south, Northern monkey," Harley argued. "Not Tuscany."

"Oh, and where does Giulia say Carlo travels often? What was that?" Tank goaded with a hand to his ear. "Napoli, you say?" He folded his arms and said with a presumptuous nod, "Mafialand."

The three amigos bobbed their heads and agreed in unison, "Mafia."

Velvet opened her mouth to respond but then stopped and glanced at her watch. "Oh, shit! Vin's Skyping me from the road in three minutes." She tossed her gloves onto the table and headed to the house. As she flitted through the great room toward the office, she caught a lingering musty trace of the old guitar case, and then the faint leathery-mossy scent of Carlo Moretti. She shuddered at the thought of his very presence in her sanctuary, and then wondered, what if he really *had* forced the local tax authorities to triple their property reassessment? What recourse could she possibly have?

Chapter 10

"See?" Lydia bent down toward the floor, kissed Brayden on the cheek, and whispered in his ear, "We didn't get you anything embarrassing."

Brayden dodged her and glanced at his two friends, as if checking the coolness factor with his peers. He looked at Andrew. "He's been gone since I woke up. You sure he's okay?"

"Your grandfather will be here," Andrew said with an easy smile.

Lydia shot Andrew an incredulous look. She turned to Brayden. "Sweetie, this is what I've been trying to protect you from. He was a no-show at practically every one of my birthdays when I was little. He's—"

"He's going to be here," Andrew insisted.

Lydia doubted it. She knew better than to say anything more, for fear of embarrassing her son in front of his friends; instead, she gave him a consoling smile. With the final birthday gift unwrapped, she began to gather up the torn wrapping paper piled high on the hardwood floor. Brayden's friends, Sanjay and Ryan, gathered around him on the floor to help unpack his new iMac computer from the box. "Thanks." He gave a quick glance at Lydia and then looked up at Andrew. "This is excellent."

"You scored," Andrew teased. "Not bad for a fifteen-year-old."

Lydia wanted to preserve that little boy, but he was growing up. She had been trying even harder to please him ever since Mike had arrived, even insisting to Andrew that they purchase the iMac so Brayden could sink into graphic design. Brayden had wanted it so badly, and she just wanted to see him happy instead of moping around.

While the three teenagers tore through the computer packaging, Andrew stepped close and hugged Lydia from behind. She shifted and returned the embrace. "See?" she whispered. "I was right. That was the perfect gift. Brayden said even Sanjay doesn't have an iMac." She smiled in Andrew's arms and gave a contented sigh.

The doorbell rang and Brayden hollered, "I'll get it," as he scrambled for the door.

"Wonder who that is," Andrew said, smiling slyly.

"Grampa!" Brayden yelled as Mike stepped into the entry hall.

"Happy birthday, kid," he said, holding a small gift-wrapped box.

Brayden hugged Mike emphatically, and Mike gave Lydia an uncomfortable glance as he ruffled the boy's hair.

"Nice of you to join the party," Lydia said coolly, as Mike croaked out a hearty laugh. She looked down and noticed that the computer hadn't quite made it out of the box.

When Mike attempted to speak again he ended up in a coughing fit.

"You know, if you'd quit smoking that cough would go away," Lydia said.

Sanjay and Ryan traded nervous glances, and Mike ignored her. Clearing his throat, he grabbed a tissue from the marble entryway table and raucously discharged a chunk of phlegm. The three boys looked on in awe.

Lydia's stomach churned.

"I got somethin'," he announced. "For the kid."

Lydia glanced at Andrew. He just shrugged but she was beginning to suspect he knew more than he had let on.

Mike held the package high and directed Brayden back into the living room. "This ain't the main one, though. Let me go get it." He shuffled out the front door and returned moments later with a long, oversized box wrapped in sparkly red paper and topped with a gigantic white bow. He bent down and placed the package on the floor in front of Brayden as the boys made way. "Here, kid. Happy birthday."

Brayden grinned broadly and looked to his father for approval.

"Open it," Mike said, and Brayden ripped open the wrapping.

Lydia glared at her father as he stood near the other end of the sofa. There he goes again, she thought—a grand entrance and a grandiose offering—so cocksure, so certain he was there to save the day. Claiming he's broke, yet he's out there conjuring up schemes to bribe his way into her life. Pathetic. Still gripping the pile of wrapping paper, she perched gingerly on the sofa and watched Brayden as he opened the present.

"Whoa!" Brayden beamed as he removed a metallic gold guitar from its case.

Sanjay's huge brown eyes and Ryan's open-mouthed smile put the Mac to shame, Lydia thought. As the boys handled the guitar, she closed her eyes.

"Wow, she's beautiful," Andrew exclaimed. "What kind of pickups are those?"

"I dunno," Mike said. "Just stock."

"Reminds me of that gold Strat you played at that radio gig at Shoreline," Andrew said as Lydia opened her eyes. He glanced over at her and said, "They had pictures . . . in the newspaper . . . I recall."

"Is this your guitar?" Brayden asked his grandfather.

"No, kid. It's yours."

Lydia turned and stared into the distance, suddenly aware that she was the only woman in the room. She looked at her son, her husband, and her father, all engaged in jovial camaraderie. As they laughed and gushed over the guitar, she felt distant . . . betrayed, and a little queasy.

"Mike," Andrew said, nodding his head. "This is truly . . . awesome—"

"How could you possibly afford it?" Lydia asked as she set the torn wrapping paper onto the sofa beside her.

"Ah." Mike waved it off. "It's a cheap axe . . . a good starter."

Brayden pushed himself from the floor and sprang over to Mike. "Thanks, Grampa!" He flung his arms around his grandfather and gave him a massive hug. "This is the best present—ever."

Sanjay and Ryan looked up at Mike in awe, then back at the guitar.

Mike smiled and uneasily returned the embrace.

Lydia squinted at him. "I thought you were broke."

Mike turned an unconvincing eye toward her. "I, uh . . . paid a visit to a friend who, uh . . . owed me a favor."

"You mean—" Lydia paused and glanced at the boys, but they were completely enthralled with the guitar. "A drug debt?" she hissed at him.

"Ain't nothin' like that." Mike laughed. "You should see how freaked out you look. Don't worry, it's legit."

He just sat there, dancing around Lydia's interrogation. She took a breath and scanned the room, her gaze settling on Andrew, who gave her a credulous look. Remaining calm, she leaned back into the sofa and said, "You didn't ask our permission."

Mike looked from Andrew to Brayden to Lydia. "I only want what's best for the kid." He glanced around the room. "He said he wanted to play guitar . . . remember? Ya gotta remember shit like that around birthdays."

Lydia sank a little lower into the sofa, and glared at Mike. If only he'd remembered her birthdays. Then she looked at her son, who was reveling in the gift.

"Mom." Brayden glanced up tentatively.

Lydia gave a hopeful look to her son.

"It's *my* gift—"

"Your grandma," Mike blurted as he glanced at Lydia, then at Brayden, "if she was here today . . . she woulda been damn proud to see her grandkid with a guitar. And she totally dug this color."

Sanjay and Ryan stole nervous glances at Mike.

Lydia sank deeper into the sofa. "But . . ." She glanced at Mike and then at Andrew. "We can't accept it. It's . . . much too expensive."

"Mom." Brayden scowled at her, and she knew she was embarrassing him in front of his friends.

She looked at her son. "But he plays clarinet—"

"And now he's gonna learn guitar," Mike said as he sat down at the other end of the sofa. "I'm gonna teach him." He motioned Brayden over with the guitar. "Here, kid. Let me show ya a few things to get started." He glanced at Lydia. "I got ya a little amp too, but uh, let's save that for later. Don't wanna drive yer mom up a wall on your first day."

As Brayden moved next to Mike on the sofa, Sanjay and Ryan arranged themselves at Mike's feet. Lydia pressed on her stomach as the queasiness returned.

"So the strings are numbered one through six," Mike explained. "The first string is the thinnest, and it has the highest pitch . . ."

Andrew inched forward, absorbed in the lesson. Of course, he's ecstatic, Lydia thought; he used to play keyboards in a garage band. She felt left out, as if she had nothing in common with the three of them.

"And these are frets."

Brayden grinned. "Uh-huh."

"He doesn't have time," Lydia tried. "He has orchestra . . . and the school talent show. He needs to practice. And study more, improve his grades."

Andrew smirked at her. "He's a straight-A student."

"And he needs to stay that way."

"And this is an easy chord . . . A minor seven." Mike looked at her, at Brayden, and then down at the guitar.

As Brayden beamed, Lydia glanced at the new Mac computer abandoned on the floor. She pressed deeper into the sofa. Mike had trumped her once again.

Chapter 11

"**R**eady for today's guitar lesson with yer gramps?" Mike asked from the kid's bedroom doorway. "Ya been kickin' ass these past few days."

"I Googled you," Brayden said, glancing at Mike and then back at the computer screen on his desk.

Mike stepped into the room, slid on his reading glasses, and looked down at the screen. "Whatchya got there?"

The kid turned a cautious glance to Mike and then started up a video on YouTube.

As Mike stepped closer he could see it was him, onstage. "Now, *that's* the shit." He puffed out his chest. A tingling crept up his neck and across his face. Then he felt his smile droop. Fuckin' hell, it was that apocalyptic gig in Germany. The chick's tits flashed in his mind and the view—lying on that stage with all those goddamn people staring at him. He suddenly felt woozy. He took a few short breaths. Then he lunged toward the screen, as if he could make the video stop. "You don't wanna see that, kid."

"I've already seen it." The kid stared at him, his blue eyes big and trusting. "It's okay. I won't tell anyone." He looked up at Mike. Then he cowered a little and turned back to the screen.

Mike whipped off his reading glasses. "Stop that thing," he barked, pointing at the monitor. The kid stopped the video, thankfully, before the dreaded crash. Mike sagged against the wall.

The kid did some maneuvers on the screen and then pulled up another video. "And here you are with—" He glanced back at Mike. "Harley Yeates." The kid ogled the monitor. "That shirt's hella cool! . . . Wow, you look so young."

Mike leaned in and slipped his reading glasses back on. As he stared at the grainy footage, warmth surged through his veins. "Fuckin' hell. That was the Slave Driver tour." He felt his eyebrow twitch as he rubbed a hand over his heart. *Harley Yeates.* He breathed in the memory of her scent—vanilla and sandalwood with a hint of patchouli . . .

"Those boots are rad! . . . Who is she?" the kid asked as he zipped to another page on the screen.

The chick who damn near stole my heart . . . twice—that's what Mike wanted to say. He coughed and stole glances at the screen. "Killer guitarist . . . ya know, for a chick." He winked at the kid. "And, man, what a red-hot lay." Mike laughed. "Remind me to play you some of her tracks . . . *'Darkest Hour'* . . . you'd dig that tune." He stared off into the room. "Harley Yeates," he purred. "Man, what I wouldn't give to fuck her again."

"Looks like all you need is a plane ticket to Tuscany." The kid shot Mike an innocent smile as Mike cocked his head. "Says so right here on Blabbermouth. Well, this is a few years old." The kid's voice squeaked out the headline, "Sex, Prescription Drugs, and Rock 'n' Roll." He glanced at Mike and then returned to the screen. "Eighties guitar hero, Vin Sabatino, and his wife, Velvet, had planned to retire to Italy and live *la dolce vita.* But over the years as the likes of Harley Yeates, Gallo Lane, and Blitz Stryker came knocking on their villa door, Vin and Velvet welcomed the washed-up rockers to the eighteenth-century farmhouse they call *Groove House.*"

"*Vin's* pad?" Mike jutted out his chin. "Man, I haven't seen or talked to those cats in, damn . . . twenty-some years." He fiddled with the hoops and studs that dotted his earlobe.

The kid fired up a new window on the screen. "Here's another one." As he read on, his voice crackled with excitement. "'80s Hair Band Has-Beens Find Retirement Paradise in Tuscany—"

"Ah, hell." Mike shuddered. "Will the media ever stop with that fuckin' '80s hair band shit? For chrissake, Harley had records out in the '70s . . . not just the '80s." His rant made him cough and he stole a glance at the kid. Then he scrunched his nose toward the screen and adjusted his reading glasses. "What's that shit down below?"

"Just stupid comments," the kid said, his voice rising as he leaned away from the screen. "You don't want to read those."

Mike nudged his reading glasses and scoped out the screen. "Masshole?" He grinned at the kid.

"That's his screen name." The kid swallowed hard. "People online can be . . . brutal. Let me show you this other thing instead—"

"Kid, I been lambasted my whole career. Every musician has. Ya just grow calloused to that shit. I can take it." Mike laughed and leaned in to read the screen. "Masshole6969 writes: *Die already, you old fuckers.*" Mike reeled back and winced at the kid. "Ouch."

"I told you," he said softly.

"They all like that?" He leaned closer to the screen. "JenRockLover writes: *A retirement home for old rock stars . . . cool!*" Mike grinned at the kid. "Well, that's uh . . . nice . . . kinda."

The kid nodded in half-hearted agreement.

"One more." Mike returned to the screen. "DeathMetalPsycho666 writes: *Good riddance, '80s hair bands. Worst music ever.*" Mike whipped off his reading glasses. "Motherfucker, I oughta rip—"

"Forget those losers, Grampa." The kid quickly closed the windows on the screen.

Mike drew back, turning away from the kid and the computer. "Retirement home," he grumbled as he rubbed his palms on his jeans and glanced around the room, groping for a distraction. His eyes landed on the kid's closet, neatly packed with all those boring duds that his mom, no doubt, had picked for him. "Damn, dude, are those *Dockers?*" Mike stepped to the closet and then turned back to the kid. "I wouldn't have been caught dead in that shit when I was your age."

The kid spun his desk chair around and looked uncomfortable. He rolled his neck and then aimed his big blue eyes at Mike.

Mike pointed at the kid's Polo shirt and casual slacks. "How can you wear that shit?"

The kid sized up the clothes on his body. "Mom-approved."

Mike shook his head. "What are you—*fifty* or fifteen?"

"School clothes." The kid rolled his eyes and swiveled the chair toward the desk.

"That's so square, dude." Mike laughed. "You ain't even gonna get to first base with a chick wearin' shit like that." He coughed and tapped his fingers against his thigh. "If you're gonna be a rocker, ya gotta dress like one."

Brayden swiveled the chair toward him. "You mean, like Slash?"

"Fuck *that* dude. I'll sort ya out." Mike lowered himself to the edge of the bed and pointed to the white louvered closet doors. "Whaddya got in there to represent?"

"Mom lets me wear my Converse Hi-Tops—"

"*Lets* you?" Mike shook his head.

The kid pushed himself from the chair and moved toward the closet. "Okay, but you have to promise you won't tell Mom."

Mike raised his hands. "Yer talkin' to the king of stealth."

The kid rummaged around the back of the closet and then held up a pair of Doc Martens. "I got these at a thrift shop with my allowance, but I have to hide them from her."

Mike smirked and mock-held a phone to his ear. "Skinhead O'Connor's callin'. She wants her boots back."

The kid turned back to the closet and snagged a black, hooded sweatshirt and a pair of jeans.

"Go ahead. . . . Try it on. I'll show ya what I'm talkin' 'bout."

Brayden undressed and then put on the jeans and boots before turning to face Mike.

"What are you—a rapper or a rocker?" With a frown and a pointed finger, Mike motioned the kid back to the rack. He watched him snatch tees from the closet and dresser drawers, trying on colored shirt after shirt, switching outfits as quickly as a scrawny runway model in a New York fashion show. Mike settled onto the bed, dismissing each wardrobe change with the shake of his head. *Fuckin' hell, this kid needs a lotta help.*

Arms out, Brayden stood in a burnt orange T-shirt with a duck on the front.

"Fuckin' hell, kid. Did you actually buy all those boring-ass shirts, or did your mom pick 'em out?"

"Trust me, it's living hell when Mom drags me to the mall. All the cool kids shop thrift, but I'm not allowed."

"Allowed? Dude, get with the program." Mike shook his head. "Got any scissors?"

Brayden gave him a sly smile as he handed over a pair from his desk.

"Got a plain ol' black tee? Not one with some lame-ass duck on the front."

"Maybe." Brayden rifled through his dresser drawers until he found one. Mike motioned him to hand it over.

"Got another pair of jeans?"

Brayden dug through his closet and tossed a pair to Mike.

"Cool." Mike grinned. He had all the tools of the trade. "Now take that shit off and get ready for some *real* duds." The kid stood in his white briefs while Mike artfully slashed and sliced and shredded the T-shirt and jeans into rocker chic. "Here. . . . Put these on."

Brayden stood at his bedroom mirror, eyeing the new outfit. He raised his brows. "It looks kind of '80s. I mean, that's cool and all, but . . . for, like, a Halloween costume."

"Yeah, I s'pose it's kinda '80s, but this style is still *the shit* to any *real* rocker," Mike said, grinning.

"The kids at school would laugh at me."

"Fuck 'em. Kids always laugh. You don't have to be a *sheep* like the rest of those little fuckers. Bein' like everyone else is boring . . . Dullsville."

Brayden turned to Mike. "There's this group of kids at school that are into the '80s thing. They shop at thrift stores and wear skinny jeans with zippers on the ankles and shirts with puffy sleeves and shoulder pads, and those fingerless gloves, and tons of big jewelry. But the cool kids all laugh at them."

"Ya gotta be your own man, dude, stand out in a crowd." Mike's eyes widened. "Hang tight . . . almost there." Holding up a finger, he left the room, and then returned with the icing on the cake—the accoutrements: a black leather jacket, a bullet belt, and some flashy costume jewelry.

"Here." He held out the jacket to the kid. "You're skinny like me . . . well, 'cept for this thing." Mike grinned and patted his little paunch. "These should fit, close enough."

Brayden slipped into Mike's leather jacket and bullet belt. A little big, Mike thought, but it'd give the right vibe. He strung several chains around the kid's neck, one with a Celtic cross and another with a silver dragon. As Mike struggled to fasten the studded bracelets onto his grandson's wrists, he noticed the kid smiling as he checked out the new garb in the mirror. When Mike reached over and tousled the kid's hair, Brayden gave him a massive grin.

Brayden twisted side-to-side admiring the shredded clothing in the mirror.

Mike smiled with pride. "Now *that's* cool."

"This jacket is sick! Makes me look like a badass."

The sound of jangling keys interrupted the rock 'n' roll designer fitting. "I'm home," Lydia announced from the entryway.

Mike and Brayden exchanged sly grins and knowing glances.

When Lydia reached the doorway to Brayden's bedroom, her smile faded. "What the—"

"Check out this jacket!" the kid yelped, beaming.

"Got that thing in London, 1984," Mike boasted. "Kensington Market."

Lydia scowled at Mike and then seemed super-peeved when she looked back at Brayden. "You are *not* wearing those clothes."

Mike dug how something as simple as ripped clothing could annoy the crap outta Lydia, and he could tell Brayden dug it too. He winked at the kid in a sort of private assurance.

Standing at the mirror, Brayden folded his arms and glared at his mother.

There's gonna be some changes, Mike suspected. He grinned. She'd get used to it . . . eventually.

✦✛✦

"Brayden, how many times do I have to ask you?" Lydia snapped as she paused in the living room, laundry basket in hand. "Please, turn that thing down. Can't you play with headphones or something?"

"It don't sound the same that way," Mike responded as Brayden bent over and adjusted the amp.

Lydia rolled her eyes, headed to the kitchen, and planted a kiss on her husband's cheek.

"Hi, hon." Andrew set his iPad on the kitchen table.

The guitar pandemonium continued, and Lydia let out a sigh. "The same notes over and over," she said as rudimentary guitar chord patterns crunched repeatedly from the living room.

"Okay, son," Andrew joked. "Your mother says it's time to learn a new song."

"Don't tease him like that," Lydia said, folding clothes at the kitchen table. "You're the one who went against my better judgment."

"Your judgment isn't really better than anyone else's. You just think it is."

Lydia glared at Andrew as she scooped up an armload of folded clothes and stomped down the hallway.

Brayden's plunking grew louder.

When Lydia returned to the kitchen, she pointed toward the living room. "You went against my wishes and let him keep that guitar when I had already told you *no*."

"Told *me* no?" Andrew raised his voice.

The volume of Brayden's guitar clatter increased as Mike's laughter boomed from the other room.

"Brayden, turn that down," Lydia demanded. The sound grated on her—a blatant reminder of just how much she had hated growing up virtually fatherless. There was no discernible difference in the volume. Lydia rested her hand on a stack of clean clothes, and closed her eyes.

"Brayden," Andrew hollered toward the living room. "You heard your mother. Turn it down, please." He turned to Lydia. "You *do* see his excitement, right? He loves that guitar. Maybe he'll give the whole thing up in another month, I don't know, but right now it's all he wants."

Lydia could feel her lip bunching up.

"We need to let him grow, give him some leeway to discover his own likes and dislikes." Andrew smiled. "I can't even remember the last time I saw him this excited. Can you? Before your dad came?"

"It's all of you against me," Lydia blurted. "I can't take it." She pushed away from him and blustered out of the kitchen, toward the bedroom. By the time she reached her bed, she was sobbing. She didn't think she'd cried that hard since her mother died—the only parent who was ever there for her. The screech of the guitar resounded from the other room, and Lydia thought that if Brayden turned out anything like Mike she would have to disown him. *What's wrong with me?* she wondered. In less than two weeks she had gone from confident woman to blubbering fool.

Andrew entered the bedroom and lay down next to her. She continued sobbing in the comfort of his arms. "Honey," he said softly. "He loves you."

"Certainly not Mike," she said, and buried her face in the pillow.

"We need to talk. About you . . . and your dad."

Lydia pushed herself from the bed and wiped her tears. "I need to make dinner—"

"Sit, please." Andrew pulled her back onto the bed.

She fidgeted with her blouse as she settled. She could feel the weight of Andrew's stare. "The thing that fell out of his pocket the other day—"

"An inhaler."

"Probably some ridiculous prop that he uses to get women into bed." She turned to Andrew. "If he were sick, we'd know it. Does he look sick to you? No."

Andrew wet his lips. "Well, he does cough a lot."

"The man smokes like a chimney," Lydia snapped. "Of course he coughs!" She sat there, fiddling with a strand of her hair. "He's had a smoker's cough since I was a child." She glanced at her husband. "Andrew, I wish I could change my feelings about Mike, but that man gets on my last nerve. And Brayden is spending way too much time with him . . . and that guitar."

"You won't like me saying this, but it needs to be said." He looked her in the eye. "You've been a total bitch since your father arrived."

Lydia's eyes widened—Andrew was rarely so candid.

"You've got to find a way to deal with this. When you're this unhappy, it affects Brayden . . . and me." He tilted his head. "Your animosity toward your dad is affecting the whole family." He scooted beside Lydia and put his arm around her. "Honey, just tell me. What can I do to make things easier?"

"Make him go away?"

Andrew gave her a look.

It was the memories—she knew that. Her childhood memories—and even adult memories—upheld a massive wall between her and Mike. She couldn't just knock it down overnight, and none of them understood that. As her lip quivered, she kept her eyes low. "For my eighth birthday, do you know what he gave me?"

"No," Andrew said softly as he brushed a wisp of hair from her face.

"An autographed UFO album."

"You mean, the *band* UFO?"

Lydia nodded.

Andrew smiled in spite of himself.

Lydia dabbed at the tears on her cheek. "He sucked down six margaritas at lunch that day and then gave me a UFO album. . . . What the hell is an eight-year-old supposed to do with an autographed UFO album?"

"You still have it?" Andrew asked eagerly, but then he immediately realized and replaced his smile with a concerned look.

"Yeah, right." She shook her head. "I suppose you'd want to sell it on eBay." She sat there, twirling a strand of hair.

He glanced at her. "I'm sorry. You're right, that was shitty. He was thinking only of himself." He embraced her. "But right now, it seems to me the best way to deal with Mike is to rise above his self-centeredness. . . . We should all do that. . . . For everyone's sake, including yours . . . try . . . please?"

Lydia sighed heavily. Andrew's request was a very tall order, a promise she didn't feel confident she could keep. "Um." She wiped a tear from her cheek. "I guess . . . I could . . . try."

She pushed herself from the bed, went into the kitchen to make dinner, and then called them all in to eat.

"Harley was one hot babe," Mike blustered to Andrew as they sauntered to the kitchen table.

"I used to love the Sex Kittens," said Andrew.

"Grampa turned me on to 'The Darkest Hour' today," Brayden added as he bounded in to the table. "*It was the darkest hour,*" he sang out, raising his fists in that devil-horned salute that everyone seemed to do nowadays. "Hey, can you teach me Whitesnake's 'Crying in the Rain'?"

"My boy has taste." Andrew proudly grinned, as Mike took a seat.

Lydia stared at the three of them, laughing and conversing about things that had no place in her world. The way Andrew and Brayden looked at Mike with such adoration gave her a slight chill. She was beginning to feel like an outcast in her own home. When she cleared her throat, Andrew glanced at her.

He aimed his smile back at Mike. "What do you want to drink, Dad?"

She could tell he got a kick out of calling an ex-rock star *Dad*.

"Ah, just gimme a beer," Mike replied.

Lydia bit her lip and stared at the ceiling.

"Sorry, we don't have any beer. How about a glass of wine?" he asked as he headed toward the new locked wine fridge in the garage.

Lydia clenched her teeth as she carried a plate of chicken to the table. Pausing, she sniffed the air. "Have you been smoking in here?" she asked, scowling at Mike, who ignored her. Andrew returned to the dinner table and poured Mike a glass of 7 Deadly Zins—thankfully, Lydia thought, not the most expensive wine from their collection. She watched in disgust as Mike swallowed the wine in one gulp and held out his glass to Andrew for a refill. Each time she glanced at Brayden, he was beaming with delight.

When a blast of music blared from the street outside, Lydia craned her neck toward the kitchen window.

Brayden's eyes widened. "Isn't that one of Grampa's songs?"

Lydia pushed back from the table and moved to the kitchen window. With one finger she lifted a slat from the blind and peered out. Brayden nudged Lydia from behind and jostled the slats open for a broader view.

The street light in front of the house poured down on the white Camaro like a spotlight bathing center stage. Two ladies maneuvered their torsos out of the car window. Like teenagers cruising the strip, they yelled, "Mike Mays, we love you! . . . Mike Mays is a guitar god! . . . You rock!"

Lydia looked at Brayden, who remained glued to the window. When his eyes grew wide, she moved in for a closer look. "Oh . . . God." There, outside her beautiful Craftsman-style house, in her upscale neighborhood, two women had lifted their blouses to bare their sixty- or maybe seventy-something sagging breasts for all to see. She reached to cover her son's eyes, but Brayden arched away from her. He laughed aloud and then grinned at his grandfather across the room. As the car screeched off, Lydia turned away from the blinds.

"My God," Lydia said. "They were flashing."

"Drive-by," Mike gloated and just sat there at the table with a smug grin. "Were they hot?"

"Um, they were . . . *old*," Brayden said, crinkling his nose.

"Old enough to know better," Lydia added.

"But that was pretty cool," Brayden admitted.

"I thought you were supposed to be *hiding out*," Lydia charged. "How do people even know you're here?"

Mike shrugged as he gulped more wine.

"Was it always like that?" Andrew asked with a boyish fascination.

"Andrew," Lydia reprimanded him, as she shook her head and returned to the table.

A crooked grin crept across Mike's face. "Fuckin' hell, I love rock 'n' roll."

Andrew laughed. "Having you here sure keeps things interesting."

Brayden sidled into his chair. "Tell me more about AC/DC."

Mike sucked down the next glass of wine and held it out for a refill.

"I think that's enough," Lydia said as Andrew replenished Mike's glass and gave her a warning stare. She bit her lip, annoyed that she was wasting her personal wine collection—finest or not—on someone who could never appreciate it. It was all just booze to him—a way to get a buzz.

"Last time I saw those cats was at the Oakland Coliseum . . . indoors."

Mike gnawed on a drumstick like a slovenly pirate—devouring it like he hadn't eaten in days. He turned to Brayden and said with his mouth full, "Did ya know your dad digs AC/DC? I got him backstage one night." He shot a guarded glance to Andrew.

Brayden glanced from Andrew to Mike and back again. Andrew stared nervously at his plate.

Lydia narrowed her eyes as she turned to her husband. "You told me you went to that concert with Bob."

Andrew and Mike exchanged nervous glances. Brayden looked around the table, as if trying to guess who might speak up next.

"We just . . . ran into each other," Mike explained as he ripped into another piece of chicken. "Ya know . . . there's like twenty-thousand people there. Ya always see someone ya know."

Lydia glared at Andrew. "And why didn't you ever tell me?"

Andrew flailed his arms, clearly flustered. "I didn't think you'd care to know."

"Running into my father is an odd thing to keep from me." She raised an eyebrow and glared at him.

Brayden divided his bright-eyed glances between Lydia and Andrew.

Andrew snuck a quick glance at Mike before turning to Lydia. "It's not like you think. It must have just slipped my mind."

"R-i-i-ight." She scowled at him.

Mike slurped his wine and turned to Brayden. "So we toured with 'em way back in the Bon Scott era."

Brayden shrugged.

"Do you know who that is, Brayden?" Andrew asked, avoiding Lydia's glare.

"You lied," Lydia charged.

Brayden smirked at his mother and then turned to his grandfather.

"Their original lead singer?" Mike tested. "'Highway to Hell'?" He coughed and then grinned when Brayden's eyes lit up with recognition. "We did several weeks in the States back in the '70s. . . . Bon totally dug partyin', so he rode with us in our motorhome for most of the tour . . . 'cause we had drugs 'n' groupies 'n' shit—"

Lydia clanked her fork onto the dinner plate. "Hello? Am I invisible?" She glowered at Andrew. "You keep playing peacemaker, and now I find out that you've been consorting with *him?*" She pointed to Mike. "Behind my back?" Exasperated, she pushed her chair from the table and stood. "I've been trying. . . . I really have." She threw her napkin onto the table. "Well, you three just go on and fraternize and talk about rock 'n' roll and flaunt your testosterone and make up some more lies. Don't worry about me. . . . I'll just . . . oh, I don't know. . . . Maybe I'll just go pack my suitcase."

She stewed in her bedroom for a while, but then eventually gave in— the mayor's reception was that evening and she didn't want to miss it. As she slipped into her silver cocktail dress and the squealing guitar clamor permeated the house, she still toyed with the idea that she might pack up and leave—just skip the event and go soak in a hotel bath with a nice glass of Chardonnay. Virtually every moment at home, she noted, Brayden seemed to cling to Mike and that damned guitar. Her son's growing adoration with Mike was . . . *unhealthy.* While fastening her diamond drop earrings in the bedroom mirror, she hollered down the hallway, "Brayden, put that thing down and get ready now. Please."

He paused from playing guitar long enough to shout back, "I *am* ready."

Andrew entered the bedroom with a tentative smile, as though painfully aware that he was still in trouble. "You have to admit that's pretty special."

"What, Mike teaching our son guitar?" Lydia snapped as she motioned her husband to zip up her dress. "No . . . it's my worst nightmare." She turned around and glared at him.

He looked at her and cowered just a little, as if he knew what was coming.

"One night a while back," she said as she narrowed her eyes, "you told me you were going to Oakland to see AC/DC with Bob."

Andrew struggled nervously with his bowtie.

"I didn't even know you liked AC/DC. Now, come to find out, you went with my dad?"

Andrew gave up battling the tie. "I—I *did* go with Bob. But . . . truth is . . . we met your dad there. . . . He got us *backstage.*"

Lydia moved close, nudged Andrew's hands away, and began tying the bow.

Relinquishing the chore to her, Andrew held his arms out. "I kept in touch with him . . . every so often . . . through the years."

She stopped fidgeting with the tie and glared up at him.

Sheepishly, he looked down at her. "I'm really sorry I never told you. But I felt I couldn't because you hate him so much. . . . I thought you'd find it hurtful."

She looked up into his eyes. "Then why do it at all? Why cultivate a relationship with him?"

"Because . . . well . . . I like him."

"I can't believe you lied to me." She shook her head. "For fourteen years."

Andrew looked away. "Not all fourteen . . . and I didn't really lie. . . . I just didn't tell you. For what it's worth, I don't feel very good about it." He glanced down at her, still finessing his tie. "You know how I feel about him. Sure, he's a little rough around the edges, but really he's a good guy."

She glowered up at him.

He sighed heavily. "Okay, do you want to know the real reason? . . . Yeah, I like hanging out with Mike, but I kept in touch with him for one hopeful reason—that one day you'd mend your relationship with him and let him back into your life. You know your mother wanted that more than anything. Hon, you only have one parent left."

She paused. "How do you think this makes me feel?" She looked up at him. "I'm hurt . . . and stunned that you betrayed me . . . for years."

"And what about the fact that you lied to your son for fourteen years?" He arched an eyebrow and then spoke more gently. "Look, you've got to understand—I did it for you, but I also did it for Brayden." When he reached a sincere hand out to touch her, she shoved it away. "I wanted to keep that channel open so that one day Brayden could know Mike."

Lydia gave a long, deep sigh, and with a firm tug, finished the bow.

Chapter 12

Mike lay on the bed with the light off. The family had left for some swanky charity event, and he found himself alone again. He laughed at the irony of a woman as bitter as his daughter running a charity. The things a college degree could buy, he thought. He lay there, naked, relaxing in the quiet hours. No bickerin', no yellin', no bullshit. As the sound of Procol Harum's "Whiter Shade of Pale" swirled through his headphones, he closed his eyes and submitted to the darkness. He thought back to when that song hit the charts in 1967, the young buck he was back then, playing the 45 over and over on the turntable in his bedroom, wearing out the vinyl grooves, smokin' dope and trippin' to the haunting melody—he was so eager back then, hellbent on making it in the biz.

Nighttime had always meant parties, hot chicks, sex, and endless quantities of drugs and booze. *Now look at me,* Mike mused. Fuckin' hell. He flashed on his 1984 headline tour—playing to sold out crowds around the States and Japan and Europe . . . those amazing fans in Paris singing every guitar lick so loud it brought him to his knees, the end-of-tour prank when the crew came out wearing masks and shook out feather pillows all over the stage. Fuckin' hell, he missed it all. As the downer of the present day overshadowed the buzz of his past, Mike slipped into a sinkhole of melancholy. His current life seemed so boring and one-dimensional, he thought, his very spirit asphyxiated by his bossy daughter who refused to let him have fun. He lifted his reading glasses and wiped his misty eyes. Then he looked down at the MP3 player. *Ballads.* Fuckin' ballads always grabbed him by the balls. He switched to *Favorites.* As the opening chords of the Scorpions "Rock You Like a Hurricane" torpedoed through his gloomy vibe, Mike pumped a fist in the air. Kick-ass rock remained his salvation. A crooked grin spanned his face.

He pushed himself from the bed and tiptoed over the clothes littered across his bedroom floor. He shuffled down the hallway to the shadowy living room. From the corner of his eye, he spotted the silhouette of the kid's guitar leaning against the sofa. He flicked on the light switch and tentatively stepped toward the axe.

When he had dropped off his last guitar—his prized possession— Mike thought he might be okay with never playing again. But when he looked at the gold axe leaning against the sofa, he realized how much the kid's enthusiasm brought back a yearning. But could he even act on it at this stage? With Lydia scowling at every turn, he hadn't even bothered to touch the kid's guitar for himself. What if he picked that damn thing up? Maybe he'd be right back in it. He ached to cradle it. He reached out his arm and then pulled back when he thought about Germany, and the chick's tits, and lying on that stage with thirty-thousand people staring at him. He forced himself to look away from the gold body. No point.

Brayden's question had brought back the tour with AC/DC, and the magic of playing live flooded right back in, making him higher than any spliff or Jack and Coke ever could. But then the specter of his daughter flashed before him; if she had her way he'd be in a nursing home wearing Depends.

Mike scanned the guitar, from the beautiful gold-finished alder body, up the rosewood fingerboard to the maple neck. He cocked his head. Like a mythical enchantress, the instrument lured him in. He picked up the guitar and pulled the strap over his neck. He cradled the body in his arms. Alone with the axe, an eerie scent awakened a memory—maybe it was the rosewood—and a magnificent vibe overtook him, one that had been absent for too long. The smell of resin and steel strings penetrated his nostrils. He breathed deeply as he thought of the killer tone he used to get from his trusty old Marshall rig. He held the guitar close and noodled a quick riff. Yeah, he thought, that's what he was meant to do.

He leaned over, flipped the switch on the little practice amp, and cranked the volume knob to 10. He adjusted the guitar around his naked body and then struck a power chord. Fuckin' hell! He paused to let the chord ring out. When the sound faded, he slammed out another and another. Hell yeah! He noodled on, stretching strings. Yeah, he still had more than a shred of talent.

Sustaining a note, he clutched the guitar and worked up a smoldering solo. His body felt loose as the music flowed through him, and he bravely tested a guitar player's kick. He crouched, wincing in pain, and caught his reflection in the entryway mirror. He stared at the naked man, belly bulging, with a guitar slung around his neck. Bruce's words echoed in his head: *You're washed up.* Who was he kiddin'? He removed the axe, leaned it upright against the sofa, and turned off the amp. He headed toward the hallway and then stopped, his hand on the light switch. Taking a final glimpse at the kid's guitar, he sighed, and turned off the light.

Chapter 13

As Lydia and Andrew carried bags of groceries through the garage and into the kitchen, the sound of Brayden's guitar playing emanated from the living room. Lydia noticed, though, that his playing seemed somehow vastly improved. Andrew shot her a curious yet proud smile. After she placed the final grocery bag on the kitchen counter, she trailed Andrew into the living room.

With Brayden next to him on the sofa, Mike was playing his grandson's electric guitar beautifully, flawlessly, it seemed—the best that guitar had sounded yet. From the grin on Andrew's face, Lydia assumed he recognized the melody. She stared at Andrew; she couldn't remember the last time she had seen him so struck with emotion. She noticed Brayden's hair was different—messy—and he was wearing a ripped T-shirt and those jeans Mike had ruined, and some biker-looking boots that she didn't even know he owned. She wanted to scold him and make him change his clothes, but Andrew gave her a look.

"That's 'Lucky Night'," Mike informed Brayden. "One of my hits from the '80s."

"I wanna learn it."

Mike slid the guitar over to him. He patiently began to show Brayden the fingering.

Lydia glanced between her husband and her son, both of whom were completely absorbed in Mike's lesson. Slowly, it began to dawn on her that Brayden was copying the way his grandfather cocked his head when he played, and now it seemed he wanted to dress like him, too.

Brayden glanced over at Mike. "Screw clarinet. I wanna play *this* in my school's talent show."

Lydia found her voice. "Over my dead body!"

Mike glanced at Lydia and then at Brayden. "Whoa, dude, you're good but you ain't ready for stage just yet—"

"It's not for another week," Brayden argued. "I'll have the song down by tomorrow."

Lydia opened her mouth to speak but Andrew's touch interrupted her.

"That's too soon, kid," Mike reasoned, and she was surprised that he was actually being logical. "Kids can be mean little sonsabitches." He watched Brayden struggling to reach the notes. "Spend time learnin' scales 'n' growin' yer chops."

"Okay," Lydia said as she stepped into the living room. "Enough of this *hobby*." Brayden brushed his hair out of his eyes and Lydia saw a glint of metal. "My God," she said, "Don't tell me you pierced your ear." A wave of nausea swept over her, and she turned to glare at Mike. "He's only a child. And he's *my* child, not yours."

"Mom," said Brayden. "Grandpa didn't do anything—"

"Don't try to cover up for him." Lydia folded her arms and stared Mike down. He shrugged and she turned to Brayden. "Besides, isn't that supposed to mean something . . . that you're gay or something?"

Brayden rolled his eyes. "Mom, mellow out. I have a girlfriend."

"Since when?" She turned on Mike. "Did you—?" He just sat with a noncommittal expression. Then she turned to Andrew. "Did you know about this?"

As she took another step, Andrew grasped her hand.

"I had Sanjay pierce it," Brayden explained. "We read how to do it on the Internet. You numb your earlobe with two ice cubes, then you take a potato—"

Lydia looked at Andrew and then at Brayden, who sat there with a defiant grin that he then flashed at his grandfather. She blinked at Mike. "I suppose all of you are in on this—"

"I ain't got nothin' to do with it." Mike locked eyes with her. "Dude's got a mind of his own."

Then she felt Andrew tugging her from the room. "Come on, hon," he said. "Let's put the groceries away."

"Here, kid," Mike said, "let me show ya this kick-ass part." He slid the guitar onto his lap and squealed away unremittingly.

"But—" Lydia felt an inertia overcoming her and she allowed Andrew to pull her into the kitchen. "He has a *piercing*, Andrew!" Lydia hissed at him, flailing her arms. "At *fifteen*! This is all Mike's influence—the clothes, the hair, the earrings. . . . Did you see those boots? Where on earth—"

"They're just clothes, Lydia, and it's only an ear."

"That you can *see*, anyway. What if there's more?"

Andrew shook his head. "Did you really completely miss what just happened in there?" He pointed toward the living room where the crunching guitar continued. "Didn't you get it?"

"Reliving your childhood memories?" Lydia snapped.

"What does that mean?"

"You're just smitten because *you* played keyboards in a garage band when *you* were in high school. Meanwhile, that man is ruining our child's life."

"Not *ruining*." Andrew shook his head. "You don't understand. Brayden is *really* good . . . light years ahead of where I was at that age."

Lydia pointed toward the living room and demanded, "I want you to take that guitar away from him. I want it out of this house."

"I'll do no such thing." Andrew stood firm, his hands on his hips.

"He absolutely will *not* play that guitar in the high school talent show. . . . He's playing his clarinet, and that's that." She turned to the grocery bags and began slamming bunches of celery and carrots onto the counter. Her stomach was grumbling and her blood sugar was low, so she felt especially on edge. She paused and just stood there for a few long moments. Her clenched jaw loosened. "Should he be that good so quickly?"

Andrew raised his arms and smiled. "He's a natural."

"I don't want him to be a *natural*," she whined. Gritting her teeth, she set the bananas on the kitchen counter and turned to Andrew. She glared at him and hissed, "I don't want him to turn out like his grandfather." When she glanced sideways she saw Mike standing in the kitchen doorway.

He just stood there, staring her down. "You're a real piece of work," Mike said before he turned and shuffled down the hallway.

Lydia stood silently in the kitchen.

"You'd be hella lucky," Mike's voice boomed from the hallway, "if that kid has even a shred of the talent I have. You ain't got no clue what it's like, the rush of havin' 20-thousand people hangin' on your every note!"

Lydia listened to his distant, hacking cough. He sounded as though he was truly having difficulty breathing. God, he sounded like he was dying. She glanced at Andrew, thinking maybe they should call an ambulance, but he was already heading into the living room. Then she heard the front door slam and Andrew calling out Mike's name.

She walked calmly into the living room. "Let him go," she said tersely. "I don't have time for this." She turned to her son, who was standing, still plunking away at the guitar. "Brayden, stop that caterwauling—right now."

Brayden paused and looked straight at her as he cranked the volume on his little amp and crunched out his grandfather's teachings, wailing on the steel strings full-bore.

Looking back at the house, Mike stopped to catch his breath at the edge of the driveway. "Fuck you," he muttered. "Fuck you, *fuck* you . . . fuck all of you . . . fuck her." He took a deep breath and then shuffled a few short blocks to the busy little main street.

Fuck this place, he thought. He shook his head as he walked and muttered. Fucking Pleasantville—a lily white community with no soul. Everything, everyone, was so *goddamn* perfect, or so the *bourgeois* thought. The little fairytale town was nothin' but a Disneyland for adults. It was *too* goddamn perfect, too sterile, too *Stepford*. He couldn't smell or feel the grit of the working class. He missed breathing in the life of a big city—San Francisco. He missed his little studio apartment where everything he needed was only a few blocks away. Mike longed for his old neighborhood, where *real* people knew how to live, to be alive in every moment.

He moseyed past the movie theater and the ice cream shop. People on the sidewalks, too occupied with their own lives, never once looked him in the eye. Even the wealthy housewives with their blown-out hair and freshly painted nails—who had nothin' better to do than stock up on flowery body lotions and hella-expensive shoes—didn't acknowledge his existence as he walked right past them on the street.

He shuffled down the sidewalk toward a bench, where he parked his ass and watched the passersby. Some young dude in a suit stopped and sparked his lighter several times, trying to light the cigarette dangling from his lips. A smoker, in this puritanical town? There's hope yet, Mike thought. He licked his lips. "Hey, dude, can I bum a smoke?"

The dude looked over at Mike on the bench and sized him up. He obliged, handed Mike a cigarette, and lit it for him before he walked on.

"Thanks, man." Mike took a drag. Fuck them, he thought, fuck this town. The smoke warmed his throat. He exhaled and let it out in a long "aah" followed by a cough. Sucking on his panhandled cig, he settled back into the bench to enjoy the freak show.

A chick in a miniskirt and fake tits traipsed by him. Fuckin' hell. He eyed a blonde heading the other way in skintight jeans, and wished he could peel 'em off that hot bod. Yeah, these chicks were plastic, alright, but the fake shit was okay too, worth every penny they'd paid their surgeons. Maybe the town ain't so bad. Hangin' downtown could easily become his new groove, he thought; well, maybe not daily, but definitely on warmer days when the sidewalks would be teeming with tits, high-creeping skirts, and smooth, young, golden-tanned thighs. But Los Gatos was no San Francisco. Damn, he missed the big city.

As Mike took a deep, shaky breath, Bruce's words echoed in his head: *You're history . . . the record label dropped you.* Fuck those guys, he thought. He flicked the ashes, pushed himself from the bench, and sauntered a little farther down the street. "Don't want my son to turn out like you," he mocked. Smokin', drinkin', fuckin', playin' guitar . . . damn straight, he thought, Brayden's gonna be like that. He took another drag as he dodged shoppers on the sidewalk. "I'm gonna see to it that kid has a great life. . . . She ain't gonna put him in a straightjacket and turn him into some pansy-ass yuppie." Mike sucked on the cigarette. "It'd be the best thing in the world if he turned out like me!" Mike nodded his head. "The kid's fifteen, for chrissake—he needs to get laid."

He peered through the window of a coffeehouse and stared at the plain-looking mountain mama playing acoustic guitar inside. Eyeing the chick and the little six-inch platform of a stage, Mike smirked. He'd played stages all over the world, for thousands of people; he'd never stoop that low. "Apple don't fall far from the tree," he muttered. The chick was fuckin' awful—pitchy, and her music hella boring. He glanced around at the ten or so people inside; not one of them ever looked at the stage. He glanced back down the main drag, toward the street that led to his daughter's house. Fuckin' clarinet, he thought. That kid's a natural. Maybe he *should* play guitar in that goddamn talent show. Then maybe she'd see the kid's got what it takes. Mike grinned and vowed to himself right there that he was gonna do whatever it took to keep a guitar in that kid's hands.

Chapter 14

Lydia tiptoed down the hallway as guitar notes saturated the house, rattling the walls, making it impossible for her to take a breath. It was Brayden's playing this time—she could tell. She paused halfway down and strained to hear the voices over the guitar clatter. My God, she realized, she had resorted to eavesdropping.

"So what's the difference between a spliff and a blunt?"

"That's just the package," Mike responded. "What really matters is the quality of the bud—"

Lydia stormed into the living room and glared at Mike. "Please tell me you are not instructing *my son* in the art of getting high."

She turned to Brayden, who just sat there plucking at the guitar in that ridiculous slashed shirt and those hideous ripped jeans that he'd worn for the past three days—even to school, against her authority. He looked like a hooligan, and he acted like one too: all he gave her was insolent backtalk when she demanded that he turn down the guitar.

They both stared up at her.

"Give me that guitar," she demanded.

"What?" Brayden snapped.

She glanced at Mike and did a double-take. "If I find out that you are getting Brayden stoned, I will make sure you burn in hell."

"I'm already in hell, just livin' here with you," Mike said, giving her one of his sardonic grins. "Besides, we were just talkin'. You don't think the kid ain't seen that shit at school?"

Brayden played harder, louder on the guitar.

"Brayden," Lydia warned. "I mean it."

Mike motioned to Brayden, who then rose from the sofa and stepped over to the amp. Instead of turning it down, though, Brayden cranked up the volume and wailed on the guitar. He looked at Mike and giggled.

"Hand over the guitar," she hollered. "Now."

"No," Brayden said defiantly. Then he danced around, taunting her as he kept playing.

She folded her arms. "If you don't hand over that guitar right now, I'll ban you from playing *any* instrument and—"

"Great," he shouted, "because I friggin' *hate* clarinet."

She turned toward him as he strutted around the room, strumming the guitar. "And your grandfather will have to find a new household . . . *tonight*. His butt will be on the street."

Andrew burst into the living room. "What's going on?"

Lydia pointed at Mike. "He was giving our son a lesson in the fine points of smoking marijuana."

"Bullshit," Mike croaked.

"We're just playing guitar." Brayden was all innocent and hurt feelings. "Dad," he said, moving toward Andrew. "She's trying to take my guitar away, and for *no reason*." He cradled the guitar and grumbled, "Nobody's allowed to have fun in this house."

Lydia stomped toward the amplifier and yanked the power cord from the socket. Brayden's final guitar chord dissolved. "I'm sorry, I tried, but I've reached my breaking point.

Andrew turned to her and held up a hand. "Okay, I'll soundproof the garage—"

"They're out of control . . . both of them." She paused and tried to breathe, but a wave of nausea crashed in her gut.

Andrew reached out to her but she pushed his arm away. He looked hurt, but then he turned to Mike and Brayden on the sofa. "Guys, let's give her some space."

Brayden's voice rose a full octave. "But I—"

"Set down the guitar and go to your room, please." Andrew looked at Mike. "You, too."

Mike looked up at him. "But we were just—"

Andrew held up a palm and calmly commanded, "Give it a rest."

"Dad," Brayden tried.

"Brayden," Andrew gave him a calm, unrelenting stare.

Brayden and Mike both stood without another word. Andrew motioned for Brayden to relinquish the guitar, and he did. Then Mike and Brayden quietly walked to their separate rooms and closed their bedroom doors.

Andrew handed the guitar to Lydia. "It's all yours."

Lydia held the guitar away from her body as if it were a venomous snake. Then she stormed down the hallway to her bedroom. After leaning the guitar against the wall, she flung herself onto the bed and buried her head in a pillow. She lay there, trying to quell the nausea, for a good fifteen minutes. When she finally lifted her head, the damned guitar caught her eye. She'd lock it away in her trunk, she thought, and take it to her office in the morning.

She slipped out of the bedroom and stole toward the garage, where she quickly deposited the guitar in her car's trunk. She dropped her car keys into her cardigan pocket and returned to the kitchen. The dirty dishes caught her eye but she didn't have the drive to tackle them. She could hear Andrew's voice from down the hall.

"This isn't like you, Brayden," Andrew was saying loudly. "Your mother and I are at our wit's end."

Lydia inched into the hallway to see Brayden step back and swerve around his father. She moved toward them and exchanged glances with Andrew.

Brayden skimmed past her and into the living room. He turned back, glaring. "Where's my guitar?"

Standing now at the edge of the living room, Lydia folded her arms. "Gone."

"What?" Brayden began a desperate search, looking under the sofa, the chairs, overturning pillows. "Where is it?" he demanded.

"None of you listen to me," Lydia said as she followed her son, and

Andrew trailed them. When Mike slinked into the living room, tying his bathrobe, she glared at him. Then she looked at Andrew and Brayden and folded her arms again. "Well, maybe now you will."

"But it's *my* guitar, not yours!" Brayden yelled.

"Ooh, that's cold," Mike said to Lydia as he shook his head.

She glared at Mike. "Your words mean nothing to me."

"Dad!" Brayden cried. "How can you let her do this?"

They all followed as Brayden carried his search to the garage.

Andrew threw his arms in the air. "Your mother did what she felt was best."

"You knew she was gonna take my guitar?" Brayden's voice escalated an octave. "And you let her?" As he stood there on the cold cement floor, his face flushed. "Where is it? . . . Dad?"

Andrew shrugged. "I have no idea."

Lydia pressed the car keys deeper into her pocket.

Brayden peered behind a stack of plywood that Andrew had leaned against the garage wall six months ago. Then he stopped and buried his head in his hands. "How could you do this to me?" He stared at the garage floor for a few seconds and then he raised his head and glared at Lydia. "You lied to me my whole life. And now you take my guitar? . . . the only thing in the whole world that I love?"

Lydia gazed at her son. "When you're older and more mature, you'll understand. . . . You'll see that I'm protecting you—"

"You're the worst mother ever!" Brayden yelled as he charged into the kitchen.

She stepped back inside the house and followed him. Then she whipped around to Mike. "This is all because of you." She glared at him with a quick nod. "So, Mr. Big Man. . . . You refuse to follow the rules? You're out—"

"What do you mean?" Brayden blustered from the hallway. "Dad," he implored Andrew. "He didn't do anything."

Lydia flailed her arms. "Oh, really? Where do I begin? Your grandfather has violated so many house rules." She turned to Mike. "You can pack your things and go stay at one of your . . . *fans'* houses."

"Mom!" Brayden yelled. "What are you doing?"

"Lydia . . ." Andrew called out.

"For chrissake," Mike roared.

As the cacophony of voices filled the hallway, Lydia closed her eyes, attempting to suppress the queasiness. "I've tried." She opened her eyes and faced her father. "But I cannot live in the same house with you." She tossed him a nod. "You knew the rules—"

"I ain't a fuckin' little kid," Mike said, adjusting the belt on his bathrobe.

"Then stop acting like one."

"I'm just tryin' to enjoy my life." Mike muttered, "What's left of it, anyway."

Lydia glared at him. "You've had *more* than your few days of safe haven. Now go."

"But Mom," Brayden pleaded. "You can't send him away. He's the coolest person I know."

Lydia stared at her son and tried to breathe. She stood silently for a moment and then turned to Mike. "Just as I said that fateful day fourteen years ago, I want you out of my life. Go get your things . . . and never set foot in this house again."

"Mom—"

"It's for your own good, Brayden." She turned to Andrew. "My responsibility is to raise my son in a healthy environment." She pointed at Mike. "And his behavior is . . . unwholesome." She couldn't even look at Brayden—the anguish on his face—but she couldn't look at Mike either.

"Honey." Andrew nudged the glasses up the bridge of his nose.

"He goes." She stared Andrew down. "Or I do."

He turned to Mike and shook his head. "I'm so sorry about all this."

"I don't even know what I did!" Mike barked.

"Dad," Brayden pleaded. "Are you just gonna stand there and let her kick him out?"

Mike crowed, "I'm just a do-what-I-want kinda guy."

"Yes, at the expense of others," Lydia snapped, gritting her teeth. "That's irresponsible, and that's what you've been every single day of your life." Tears started flowing, but she didn't care. "Why couldn't you have married my mother? You could have found a *real* job and stayed home and taken care of us."

Mike took a step back. "Oh, now that's a low blow. I had a *real* job. I traveled the world. You think it's easy bein' a rock star? I had to fight tooth and claw to get where I did. . . . I'm a musician, for chrissake, a bohemian. It ain't my nature to be tied down 'n' suffocated—"

"Suffocated?" Lydia pinched out. "So, to you, having a child—and a woman who loves you—is suffocating?"

"In a way." Mike scratched his scraggly hair. "Yeah."

"Family means nothing to you."

"The road was my family—my band, my crew."

"And where are they now?" She folded her arms. "This so-called family of yours . . . hmm?"

"He's your dad," Brayden pleaded. "You can't kick him out. This is wrong."

Mike shook his head. "Goddamn, you're heartless."

She glowered at him from the corner of her eye. "Consider it payback."

"Lydia," said Andrew. "Can't we just—"

"He goes. Now."

Mike shook his head as he looked Lydia in the eye. "I'm yer ol' man . . . but, obviously that don't mean shit to you." He shuffled toward the guest room. "So much for family values in this house."

"Family means everything to me," Lydia shouted. "And *this* is my family, right here." She pointed to Brayden and Andrew. "*My* family. You chose to abandon your family a long time ago." She choked on her tears. "You have no claim to my family, whatsoever."

"Comin' here was a bad idea," Mike hollered from the doorway. "It ain't workin' . . . too many goddamn rules. I'm happy to leave this puritanical prison."

Lydia shuddered when he slammed the guest room door.

"Who's gonna teach me guitar?" Brayden asked plaintively. Then he glared at her. "You just ruined my life. . . . I hate you!" He pushed past her, stomped toward his bedroom and, just like Mike, slammed his door.

Andrew moved miserably to Lydia's side and held her.

"Andrew . . . I—"

"I know," Andrew said, giving her a frightened glance. "I'm sure he didn't mean that last part."

Lydia looked up at him. "I want my son back . . . the one who'd never even touched a guitar."

Chapter 15

Mike climbed out of the taxi and sized up the joint. Damn, it looked so old. He'd imagined something more grandiose, not a shitload of crumbling stone buildings. He had a sudden urge to head back down the road, stick out his thumb, and hitchhike to the nearest metropolis. Instead, he sauntered into the tiled courtyard and plopped his duffel bag onto the long wooden table in the shade. He looked up at the stucco house. Fuckin' hell, he thought: three flights, a train, and a taxi later and here he was. His stomach rumbled and when he licked his lips he swore he could still taste the taco from San Fran and the Jack and Coke from the first leg.

"What the hell?" Velvet just stood there wearing gardening gloves and shorts, holding a basket of some leafy green shit, her eyes wide.

She looked damn good. Mike reckoned she'd aged better than most 60-something chicks he knew, hell, even some ten years younger. Looked like Vin was still tapping some fine ass.

"What're you doing here, how'd you even find us?"

Mike shrugged. "My son-in-law—very cool dude—used his frequent flyer miles."

Velvet tipped her head to the side—she didn't believe him.

"The kid read some story about you cats on the Internet, and, bam . . . here I am." He forced a grin.

Velvet pulled the basket tightly against her chest. She didn't exactly seem thrilled that he'd crashed her pad.

"Ah hell, we're buds, right?" He grinned again and then dialed in the charm. "Well, see, it all started when my uptight daughter kicked my ass out." Mike checked her reaction but she just stood there staring at him. "Can you believe that shit? Damn, she can be so friggin' cold. Don't know how I even put up with her bullshit." He gritted his teeth as he scanned the old buildings. "Wild pad." He scratched his cheek. "The music biz in America sucks now for rockers like us anyway. Europe's the shit." He coughed and spit a chunk of phlegm on the ground.

Velvet wasn't giving him anything—she just stood there. Then he heard someone yell, "You sonofabitch!" and from outta nowhere, some dude lunged at him and clipped him square in the jaw, knocking him flat onto the long patio table behind him.

Mike glanced up but he'd already tagged that ignorant, high-strung voice. *Blitz Stryker.* No-talent glam boy with his fake tan and blinding white teeth. Looked like it'd taken a whole can of Aqua Net to get his bleached-out hair so big.

"Hey!" Velvet jumped in to separate them but Blitz had already backed down.

Mike glanced up at Velvet and then Blitz as he reached for his jaw. "Oh, dude," he fake crooned, "that purple in your hair matches your purple nails." He eyeballed Blitz's shiny tiger-striped pants. "Are those spandex?"

Babying his fist, Blitz narrowed his eyes at Mike. "Call that payback."

"What the hell for?" Mike propped himself up on the table and held his jaw, wondering if it might be broken.

"Fucking my wife."

Mike laughed through aching teeth. "Dude, that was like a hundred years ago. . . . Besides, everybody fucked yer wife. Chick was bad news. Why you pissed at me? I ain't the one she left you for—"

"He was *your* producer—"

"I had nothin' to do with it." Mike laughed at the accusation. "Takes two to tango."

His breathing heavy, Blitz stared him down.

Mike tested his jaw action. "Man, you pack a gnarly punch for a pussy." He rubbed at his aching jawbone.

"Oh . . . my . . . God!" It was a voice Mike would've recognized on any continent. He turned to see *her* standing there holding a plate, looking as sexy as ever. It'd been fifteen years since he'd last seen her, when she'd come to see him play in L.A. in that shitty little dive in the Valley.

Harley Yeates. Even after living in the States her whole career, her British accent seemed stronger than ever. She squealed like a little girl, set her plate on the table, and stepped toward him with a warm, admiring smile. He set his feet on the ground and felt his knees wobble as he stared at her for a moment. Fuckin' hell, how'd he ever let her fall out of his life? Mike took Harley in his arms and squeezed her, reveling in Velvet's eye roll. "Feels awesome to hold ya again, doll," he whispered.

"Dahling, it's been ages! What are you doing here?" As Harley kissed him on the cheek, Mike turned and smothered her lips with a slobbery kiss. She reared back and let out a laugh. "Absolutely fab to see you. You in Italy on holiday?"

"Well, sorta. Thought I'd stay awhile." Mike saw Velvet exchange a nervous glance with Harley. "I'm hella hungry," he suggested, eyeing the food on Harley's plate. "Airplane food still sucks."

"Here, love," Harley offered, waving him to a bench at the table. "Help yourself to some *caprese.*"

"Wait," Velvet snarled.

Mike rubbed his hands together and dug in while Velvet just stood there with her mouth gaping open. "What's this shit?" he asked as he stabbed his fork into the soft, wet white stuff. He looked up to see Harley and Velvet watching his every move.

"Mozzarella di bufala," Velvet answered curtly.

"Don't look like no mozzarella cheese I ever ate." He scooped some tomatoes onto his plate.

"Wine?" Harley offered, lifting a bottle of red.

"Harley," Velvet snapped. "Mike, you can't stay—"

"Stay?" Blitz asked, exchanging glances with Velvet as he tried to run his fingers through his over-ratted hair.

"Fill 'er up." Mike winked at Harley and raised a wine glass from the table. He liked the way she looked at him, the same way she had the day they downed two bottles of Bordeaux on the grass near the Eiffel Tower when they'd stayed on in Paris after the tour that year. He wondered if she still dug him.

Harley stepped closer and filled the glass. Christ almighty, he thought, she was fawning over him like he was a god. He stabbed the food on his plate and shoveled a forkful into his mouth. "Fuckin' hell," he said. "This might be the best thing I ever tasted." He sighed, content, ready for a nap over in one of those shabby-looking rooms, and then later maybe one of those bottles of good Italian red . . . and Harley, naked, with those amazing tits she used to have.

"Still kissing Coverdale's ass?" Blitz snapped. He just stood there, arms folded, watching Mike eat.

"You can't stay," Velvet repeated. She seemed flustered.

"Bloody 'ell," a familiar British voice hollered. "Not another bleedin' guitar player."

Mike couldn't place the direction of the voice, so he scanned the courtyard for Tank. A big grin crossed his face when he spotted the old road dog. "Damn!" Tank approached and clutched him in a manly hug. "Been decades since this ol' tea bag roadied for me," Mike bellowed.

"Fuckin' 'ell, mate . . . indeed it has." Tank turned at the sound of a howl from behind him.

"What the hell is *that* prick doin' here?"

Gallo Lane. Mike turned to see him standing there, glaring. He looked like a scarecrow wearing a black cap. He stared at Gallo's stubbled face and papery skin.

"He's staying," Blitz hollered back.

"No, he's not," Velvet insisted, her expression pinched.

"He's still alive?" Mike laughed. "Dude snorted enough blow in the '80s to kill an army." Mike swallowed hard and sized up the zombie. Now *that* dude looked like an old fucker. Mike glanced around at all of them as Bruce's words came crashing into his thoughts: *washed-up, history.* Poor losers probably haven't been on a stage in over a decade.

Gallo inched closer and pressed his tongue against his false front teeth, removing and reinserting them—a creepy nervous habit. "If that asshole's stayin'," Gallo snarled, "then I'm outta here." He looked at Velvet.

"I'll max my credit card if I gotta, but I ain't stayin' on the same property as that prick." He looked straight at Harley. "Watch it, Harl. I won't be there to pick up the pieces this time." Then he turned and sauntered toward one of the buildings.

"What's up his ass?" Mike asked.

"Dude hates you," Blitz volunteered as he adjusted his bullet belt. He glared at Mike. "Says you stole his royalties—"

"What the hell?"

"'Lucky Night,' geeze," said Tank. "Says you stole his lick."

Mike glanced around the table, baffled. "But *I* wrote that lick." He stared at the somber faces. "Okay, maybe he came up with this one part but it was lightweight. . . . He thinks that was *his*? The version that made the record wasn't nothin' like Gallo's original lick, ain't even close." He studied everyone's doubtful expressions. "Are you guys serious?"

Velvet glared at Mike. "His recollection stands."

Moments later, Gallo reappeared with a duffel bag over his shoulder. "Fucker never paid me a dime. No songwritin', no publishin', no nothin'. He's still bankin' royalties while I'm stuck here with the rest of these broke dicks." He fired a daggered glance at Mike and then headed toward the gravel driveway.

Mike scratched his chin. They had no idea just how tapped out *he* was.

Harley stood up. "We can't just let him leave."

"I know Gallo," Mike assured them. "That dude'll be back."

"Well, he does got the least of us," Tank said, and Harley smacked him on the arm.

"Um, dude." Blitz started drumming his hands on the table as he directed to Tank, "*We* all get our penny royalties. What do *you* bring to this house?"

Tank looked toward the driveway and then sprinted after Gallo. "Grumplestiltskin, wait up!"

Harley sat back down, exchanging glances with Blitz and Velvet.

Blitz turned and glared at Mike. "You haven't even been here thirty minutes and you've already fucked things up." He hardened his glare before he dashed after Tank and Gallo.

Harley gave a pained stare toward the edge of the courtyard. Then she put a hand on Mike's arm as she stood up. "Sorry, love, got to help the boys." She backed away. "See you when I get back?"

"No," Velvet insisted.

Harley smiled at Mike and then turned to catch up with the others.

Mike looked at Velvet. "You mean he's held a grudge for, what, thirty—forty years? . . . Man, I never—" Mike looked down at the wooden table and rubbed his hand on the surface. "I had no idea."

"Mike," Velvet said as she sat down and removed her muddy gloves. "You can't stay."

"Ya can't turn me away. I just flew halfway around the world to see you."

"Me?" Velvet's brow twitched and she brushed a blonde strand from her face. She looked almost hopeful.

"Well, all of you." Damn, he thought, she was still kinda hot. "Ya know," he said, "the years've been good to ya."

"Yeah," she said sarcastically. She glanced at Mike and then straightened her posture. "Vin's away subbing on tour. He'd be pissed to find you here—"

"He's a hard worker, that Vin." He gave her a sideways glance.

Velvet tossed up her hands. "Who just shows up, unannounced?"

"I told ya." Mike half-shrugged. "I just happened into this ticket to Italy."

"I'm not following you."

"Free ride, babe." He grinned. "Gotta go where the wind blows."

Velvet gave him a crafty smile and a probing glare. "Wait, you were living with your daughter," she said in an accusing tone. "And she kicked your ass out."

Mike forced a laugh and then coughed.

"Why didn't you call?"

"It ain't like yer in the phone book." He shot her a grin but could tell by her tilted chin that she wasn't amused. "Ya won't even know I'm here." He glanced up at the clear blue sky and the warm, shining sun, and then down at the smirk on her face. "Can't turn me away, I don't speak a fuckin' word of Italian . . . 'cept *Chianti*, Ferrari, and Tony La Russa."

"We don't have room," she insisted and reached for the phone that began to ring on the table.

"Got a couch, don't ya?"

"Yeah, but . . . no, you can't," she said before turning her attention to the call. "Hey, you'll never guess who's here." Velvet shot Mike a flinty glare and then turned her back for privacy.

Mike could hear her, and judging from her end of the conversation, she was talking to Vin.

"Seriously?" she hissed, hand cupped to the phone. "Oh, I'm well aware of his reputation as the world's biggest hosebag." Then she turned and sized up Mike. "Trust me, you have nothing to worry about."

Mike noticed that his breathing was speeding up, like it did sometimes. Shit, he thought as he tried to inhale slowly; he needed to find a way to stay. He could see how flustered Velvet was, even with her back turned, and he considered how he might use that to his advantage.

"That was Vin," she said, hanging up the phone.

"No shit."

"He's freaked out that you're here . . . and he agrees that you can't stay."

"You still play harp?" Mike grinned, fishing for a reaction. "Man, the way your hands flew up and down those strings. So *sexy*. . . . You were always a killer musician."

She hesitated and he could see the beginnings of a weak smile playing on her lips.

"C'mon," Mike pleaded. "Just tonight, then I'll figure out where to go. . . . Ya gotta help me out. Just one night. That's all I'm askin'."

Velvet just stood there biting her lip. Mike hoped to hell she'd budge.

Chapter 16

"I made your favorite dinner." Lydia tested a smile as she dished manicotti onto Brayden's plate. He ignored her, avoiding eye contact. She served Andrew blindly, keeping her eyes on Brayden as he idly twisted the hoop in his ear. That stupid piercing—he *wanted* to remind her of it, of how much influence Mike had on him, even now that Mike was thousands of miles away. She could tell that he missed Mike. Even worse, he craved that guitar. She had lost her son the day she took it away; now he would barely speak to her, let alone look at her.

"Brayden," Andrew warned as he pushed his glasses up the bridge of his nose. "Don't ignore your mother."

"You're like, her accomplice," Brayden muttered.

She instinctively reached out to brush a wisp of hair from his eyes, and he pulled away. She stared at him, longing to have her son back—that innocent boy who wore slacks to school, who wasn't interested in girls, the boy who had never pierced an ear or played a guitar. But those days had passed. He was slowly slipping away from her, but maybe she could put a halt to that—if she returned the guitar. She fantasized for a moment about having the old happy Brayden back. He'd be thrilled and grateful—just the thought of it filled her with hope.

"May I be excused?" Brayden asked, and before she could answer he stood up from the table.

Lydia eyed his ragged jeans as he headed toward his room. She turned to Andrew. "How did *I* become the bad guy?"

Andrew blinked at her from across the table. "Don't you think you've made your point?"

"I suppose," she said, toying with the food on her plate. "It's been hard to focus on anything else." She glanced at Andrew. "All he wears are those ripped jeans and those hideous boots—"

"What concerns me is that he won't do his homework." Andrew scooted his chair closer to the table. "Playing guitar isn't the worst hobby he could have." He glanced over, as if testing her expression. "You know, in high school I played keyboards in a garage band, and *I* turned out alright."

Lydia lowered her eyes. "You're right." She looked up at Andrew. "And that's exactly why I put it in the trunk before I left work today." She stared at the uneaten food on her plate and sighed. "I pushed him farther away by taking that guitar."

Andrew shot her an "I told you so" look.

She got up from the table, went out to the garage, and retrieved the guitar. Then she placed it in the hallway outside Brayden's bedroom. She poked her head into his room. "Sweetie?"

Brayden spun his desk chair around to avoid her. "I'm busy," he said, his back to the door.

When Lydia entered the room and sat on his bed, Brayden spun the desk chair in the opposite direction. He resisted when she pulled the chair around toward her. "Sweetie, I know you're mad at me."

Forced to face her, he rolled his eyes.

"I'm sorry I took your guitar—"

"And sent Grampa away."

"Well, your father—"

"*You* were the mastermind," Brayden snapped.

"It was *both* of us," she said smugly, reveling in the thought of her husband's bold move in using his frequent flyer miles to send Mike away. "And it was a wise move . . ." She stood up and reached for him but he dodged her touch. So she set a foot outside the door, lifted the guitar case, and placed it on his bed. She noticed his eyes light up, but once she opened the case and looked back at him he had rearranged his face into the usual blank stare. Lydia sat next to the guitar and caressed the plaid bedspread. "I want you to have it back."

His face hardened. "I don't want it."

"What do you mean?" She tilted her head and forced a smile. "Of course you do. Maybe you could"—she took an apprehensive breath—"take video lessons from Mike over the Internet—"

"Grampa's a way better parent than you'll ever be." He faced her down, glowering at her.

Lydia reeled from his comment, and she could barely form words.

"You ruined *everything*," he said, and his tone frightened her. "Too bad Dad doesn't have any frequent flyer miles for me."

She stared at him, wishing she could rub the pinched expression off his face.

"I said I was busy," he muttered through clenched teeth. "Please leave."

Lydia stared at her son and then got up from the bed. When she reached the door, he spoke.

"How do I know you won't just take it again?" he said, his voice rising. "Any time you damn well please?" He reached over and slammed the guitar case shut.

"I'm," Lydia said softly, "your mother." She swallowed hard and just stared at him, as she realized that she might never regain her son's trust.

"Take it with you," Brayden ordered.

Lydia turned and straightened her blouse. "No. It's *your* guitar. If you're done with it, sell it, or give it to a friend . . . or ship it to your grandfather in Italy. I won't take it from you again."

Chapter 17

Mike lifted his head from the couch, rubbed his eyes, and then glanced at his phone. Two o'clock. Fuckin' hell, that Ambien Harley had given him last night had knocked him out cold for sixteen straight hours. He scratched his balls and glanced around the room. An old gilded symphony harp peeked out of a corner, behind the baby grand. He recalled how Velvet used to play like a sexy angel, with her cascading blonde hair. *One night only*, she'd said when she caved last night and tossed him a blanket for the couch. He could hear voices outside, and struggled to sit upright. Then it really hit him. . . . The other side of the planet. . . . What the hell was he thinkin', buyin' into Lydia's bullshit and Andrew's itinerary? Then Brayden crossed his mind. Mike pressed his lips tight as he traced the speed-dial on his cell phone. With conviction, he pressed it.

"Hey, is the kid around? I gotta talk—"

"It's five o'clock in the morning," Lydia hissed through the phone. "Did you not think of the time difference? No, of course, you didn't."

"Can ya wake him up?"

"I'll do no such thing," she snapped. "Honestly, I think . . . it's better if you just stay away from him."

Ouch. Mike felt the sting drive straight through his gut. "Well, maybe you could—"

"You've done enough damage around here."

He just sat there listening to the silence on the other end of the phone.

"I'm hanging up now." And she did.

Mike dropped his phone onto the couch. The pang in his gut felt razor sharp. He'd figure out a way to reach the kid.

The sound of sappy opera music melded with the voices outside and Mike turned toward the window. He could make out Blitz's annoying squeal.

"Mays has gotta go, or else Gallo will never come back. Harley, we all know you *especially* want Gallo . . ."

Mike wondered what that meant—was Harley sleepin' with that fucked up dude? He pushed himself from the couch and pulled on his jeans. Then he slipped into his shoes and blew out of the front door and into the courtyard.

He scanned the old buildings to the long patio dining table where Blitz had clocked him yesterday. There he sat with Velvet and Harley. Mike grinned when his eyes landed on Harley. He didn't care about the history of the place or the Tuscan bullshit vibe; it was just too freakin' cool to be hangin' with his own kind again . . . and the chicks were a bonus. As he approached the table, he sneered at the opera swirling through the courtyard. "What's that shit?"

"Are you kidding me?" Velvet asked with a righteous stare. "Puccini's most beloved aria? . . . 'Sì, Mi Chiamano Mimì'? . . . La Bohème?"

Mike shuddered at the shrill sound of some diva screeching out a high note. "Sounds like Blitz."

Harley laughed. "He should be so lucky to sing like that."

"Piss off," Blitz snapped.

Velvet gave Mike a harsh stare. "Are you *completely* passionless? You just hurled an insult at the most beautiful, climactic note of the aria—the long-held "è"—the emotionally-charged, goosebump-delivering note that's sent shivers down the spines of listeners around the world for over a century." Lost in a musical orgasm, she closed her eyes and swayed her head to the melody.

Not my sturdy spine, he thought. Mike Mays was 100 percent rock 'n' roll, baby. He hated opera with a passion—it was for snobs and pussies and yuppies. Hard rock was the only music that filled Mike's world—*real* music, chock-full of testosterone. "Whatever." As he reached for a cig, he could see Velvet rolling her eyes.

"Smoke over there, please." She pointed to the other side of the patio. "Near the ashtray. Never inside any of our buildings."

"Dudes." Blitz glanced around the table. "We gotta bring him back."

Mike tucked the cig behind his ear.

Harley gave Mike a slow nod. "Gallo never came home last night."

"Where is he?" Mike asked, shoving his hands in his pockets.

Velvet frowned. "Village bar, probably."

"Where's this bar? I'll go get him."

Blitz smirked at him. "Bad idea."

"I'll bring him back," Mike insisted. "C'mon, let's go."

"I'll go with you," Harley said and started to get up from the table.

"No," Velvet commanded, placing a hand on Harley's shoulder. "*I'll* go."

Tank loped toward them with a huge grin. "Jawanna gew fora pint down the pub?"

"Of course, he appears when there's booze involved," Blitz said, adjusting the yellow bandana that hardly hid his receding hairline. "Looks like we're all going."

"Let's go get pasted, then." Tank smiled, revealing his tea-stained teeth.

Dude probably hadn't seen a dentist ever, Mike thought, but he was always up for a drink. Mike grinned at Tank and then swung his grin toward Harley and took a breath; there was still somethin' about her. He rubbed his sore neck and found himself squinting at Velvet. Pain-in-the-ass couch or not, he needed to find a way to stay.

The village streets were dotted with Fiats and Alfa Romeos and compact Fords that Mike had never seen in the States. He cackled when he spotted some other make that was so puny he thought a shitload of clowns might come spilling out. Mike squinted at a worn-down plaque placed high in the mustard-colored wall of a crumbling corner building. *Via Dante Alighieri*—they'd parked on the village's main street, he noted. A breeze brushed his face as he glanced up at the open shutters above the ramshackle storefronts; from opposite sides, two old broads bantered in melodious Italian. So this was *la dolce vita*, Mike mused.

"Look." Blitz pointed to the window up ahead. "Gallo's in the bar."

Mike glanced at the bar window and then at the shop beside them— some sorta candy store lined with display cases loaded with chocolates, and some crusty old dude hunching over a cup at a table near the window. "Gimme me fifteen minutes with Gallo. You guys duck in here."

Velvet stepped in front of him. "But—"

"He thinks I fucked him over. Ya gotta let me sort this out." Mike glanced at each of them and motioned for them to stay put. "Fifteen minutes."

Mike paraded through the doorway and sized up the bar, from the plaster walls to the wood beam ceilings overhead—just like Velvet's house. All the buildings in Italy, he figured, must be like that. He spotted Gallo seated by the window. He was amazed at how lanky the dude still was, after all these years. Slinking up from behind, Mike put his arm on Gallo's shoulder. "Can I buy ya a drink?"

"Huh?" Startled, Gallo turned and squinted up at Mike.

Mike grinned at him, noting his wrinkled face and deep laugh lines. Dude looked *old*. Gallo turned his back on Mike. "So how long's it been?" Mike said as he pulled up a chair.

"I got nothin' to say to you," Gallo said, turning away.

"I—" Mike scratched his head and slid his chair closer so Gallo would hear. Fuck it, he thought, head first. "So you think *you* wrote 'Lucky Night'?"

Gallo took a swig of his drink and answered without looking. "That's *my* lick, *my* fuckin' hook. You outright stole it."

"Dude, I never knew . . . I swear." Mike sighed heavily. "My hook was nothin' like yer idea. Your lick *inspired* what I came up with." He looked at Gallo's stubbled face, but Gallo just stared out the window.

"That weekend back in '84," Gallo growled without even a glance at Mike. "When you came to my pad in L.A. 'Cause *your* label forced us to write together." He took another swig. "I came up with this cool lick but we never finished the tune. Next thing I know, that lick *I* wrote is all over *your* hit single on AOR. You fucked me over, Mays. Never paid me a dime."

"I remember you were pissed off at Rousseau. You said you gave that lick to *him* but when he canned your ass, you said *I* could use it. Don't ya remember?" He looked at Gallo but the dude didn't flinch. "I didn't even use it . . . I *changed* it." Mike leaned in closer. "Dude, if I had any money, I'd give it to ya right now. Wish I could make it up to ya but I ain't got shit."

Gallo took another hit of his drink.

Mike knew Gallo was nearly deaf, but he suspected he'd heard him. He hears what he *wants* to hear, Mike figured. "I got . . . this album I still owe the record company . . . I'll cut ya in . . . let ya write a tune for my new album—"

"You think I'm a moron?" Gallo blurted. "None of us is worth shit anymore. . . . You know that. Not you, not Vin, not Harley. Nobody gives a shit about Blitz's drumming these days. And nobody wants to hire me. They want young bass players. You can't bullshit me, Mays. It's over for us old dudes; we're just waitin' to die."

Mike forced a hopeful smile. "Vin seems to be gettin' some work—"

"You shoulda gave me a percentage."

"Like I said, I owe the label another album." Mike looked down and rubbed his hand across the slick table. "We can write together—"

"You gypped me outta dough that was rightfully mine."

"Dude." Mike found it hard to look Gallo in the eye. "I . . . I really didn't know."

Gallo turned his back to Mike. "I got nothin' more to say to you."

"Dude." Mike put his hand on Gallo's shoulder, but Gallo shrugged it off. "Come on back to the house . . . come home." Mike grinned.

"Home?" Gallo growled, "It ain't *your* home."

"I saw the barn. Let's jam tonight. It'll be like old times." Mike smiled, hopeful, when Gallo turned toward him.

"Listen, Mays." Gallo took another swig. "The others might buy into your bullshit, but I don't want nothin' to do with you." He took a final swig and slammed the glass onto the table. "Fuck . . . off." Then he stood up and strutted out the door.

So much for being the hero who'd bring Gallo home. Mike squinted at the floor. He needed to find another way to worm his way in to Groove House.

Velvet spotted Mike near the window staring down at the floor. "Well?" she asked, as Tank, Harley, and Blitz flocked around her.

"I'm sortin' it," Mike said with a half-shrug. "That dude's one stubborn sonofabitch. . . . Man, he couldn't hear a train if it was right in front of him." He sighed and then forced a grin. "Hell, we're in a bar, let's drink and I'll fill you cats in." He handed Tank a wad of Euro bills, as if he expected Tank to roadie his booze.

Tank grinned. "Let's go get our little eyes on, then. . . ."

Velvet knew Tank would try to wheedle a bottle of some horrid alcohol from the barista; it was like her friends always tried to see who could stomach the worst-tasting drink. He and Blitz spent money like they had it—they all did. None of them ever seemed to think twice about spending the last few Euro for the month on alcohol. She felt relieved that Mike had paid for the afternoon's round.

As they moved toward a table in the back, Velvet noticed Mike rubbernecking the Italian beauty who had just walked in. It was Angelina. Velvet narrowed her eyes and imagined Angelina with Carlo at the *Catasto*, plotting to jack up their property taxes. She realized Angelina had an acoustic guitar slung over her shoulder, and breathed a sigh that it wasn't the Kramer; she didn't need another earful from Tank.

Mike grinned and swallowed hard. Angelina's dark brown eyes, olive skin, and cropped, messy, raven black hair seemed to command his full attention. She was way too young for him—that was obvious to all, including Harley, who was aiming a pained expression at Mike.

Tank returned from the bar clutching shot glasses and a bottle of Fernet-Branca.

Mike licked his lips and Velvet couldn't tell if he was thirsting for Angelina or the booze—probably both.

Velvet looked at the round of drinks that nobody at the table but Mike could really afford. She scrunched up her nose. "Not that dirt and pine cleaner crap." When a flash of light caught her eye, she glanced toward the door. "Ah, shit," she mumbled and downed the nasty-tasting liquid in her glass.

Mike pried his eyes from Angelina long enough to follow Velvet's glances. "Who's that?"

Harley leaned in. "Carlo Moretti."

"Local mob boss," Tank hissed from the other side.

"Isn't," Harley snapped. "He's our *neighbor*. Lives in that fab house on the hill across."

As they all continued to drink, Angelina settled into the corner. Velvet could see that she was setting up to perform. Mike grinned at Angelina and she gave him an entrancing smile.

"Still have a knack for picking up birds, I see," said Harley. "How does she even sit in those jeans?"

"Mays is the master," Tank insisted. He seemed delighted to be around Mike again.

Mike raised a playful eyebrow toward Angelina and she returned an engaging smile. Velvet turned to see that Carlo was glaring in Mike's direction.

"Uh-oh," Blitz warned Mike. "*Il Duce's* givin' you the evil eye."

Tank knocked back another shot of Fernet. "I'd like to beat seven shades of shit outta him."

"Do that," Blitz said in a mock mobster tone, "and you'll be sleepin' with the fishes."

"Why do you idiots think he's mafia?" Harley asked.

"Well, 'cause he is," Tank insisted.

Velvet glared at Carlo. "If Vin was here, he'd kick that bastard's ass straight back to Naples. That's where he was raised, you know. The house on the hill is his grandfather's."

Mike ignored the banter and swaggered toward Angelina like a peacock with feathers fully plumed. She faced him off with an inviting stare. When Angelina rose, Mike's cocky stance blocked Velvet's view of her. For a good few minutes, all she could see was Mike's back. Then he stepped sideways and glanced over at their table. He grinned crookedly as he scrawled on a napkin and then reached forward to tuck it into her cleavage.

Velvet smirked. "Classy."

"His mobile number, no doubt," Harley said, also smirking.

"Un-fuckin'-believable!" Tank exclaimed. "We can't get any birds in this town 'cept hookers, and he lands one first try. Smooth as shit, he is."

Harley huffed. "She's got to be, what, fifty years his junior?"

Carlo threw back the last drop and slammed his glass onto the bar. *"Angelina!"* he commanded.

Angelina put down her guitar to go over to Carlo, and the two exchanged words in explosive Italian. Then she turned to smile at Mike and he made a face. Behind Carlo's back, she flicked her hand under her chin before picking up her guitar.

Carlo stopped cold and headed over to their table. He focused his glare on Mike. *"Non* to touch your hand on my cousin," he warned in a thick accent. He pointed a finger at Mike. "I am watching you." Then he changed course and tramped toward the door.

Mike shrugged. "What's the big fuckin' deal?"

"That's one badass dude," Blitz said, "that you *don't* wanna fuck with."

"Eh." Mike waved them off. "I ain't afraid of him."

"Just ignore him," Velvet said as she slammed back another shot of Fernet and shuddered. "He's an ass."

"Yer probably on his hit list now, geeze," Tank offered.

"Hit list or shit list?" Mike laughed, unfazed. He glanced at the somber faces around the table and laughed again, as if to shatter the serious vibe. "You guys are yankin' my chain."

"No, we ain't," Tank insisted.

"Don't believe these dumbasses," Harley said with a dismissive wave.

"Enough of your folklore." She pushed her chair from the table. "We came for Gallo. And I'm off to find him."

"I'll go too," Blitz said and scrambled to his feet.

As Velvet started to get up, Mike rested a hand on her arm. "Stay a minute, doll," he said with a wink. "Ya know, we haven't . . . really caught up."

Velvet felt heat surging from her toes up to her face. She hadn't had a hot flash in nearly a decade so the sensation surprised her. She snuck a glance at Mike. She'd never liked him much, yet she'd slept with him. It was just that one time, like, a million years ago—before she even knew Vin. She shuddered at the memory of his shriveled dick when he'd climbed, naked, out of the hotel pool that one ridiculous night so long ago. She took a deep breath and reasoned that Mike probably had no recollection of that night, anyway. When she glanced up, Harley shoved a wave of hair behind her ear and shot Velvet a pissed-off look before she headed toward the door with Blitz.

Tank cleared his throat and bounced a glance between Velvet and Mike. He began humming under his breath as he eyed the nearly empty bottle of Fernet. Then he downed the final shot and swiveled his attention toward the door. "Wait up, geezers," he said and chased after them.

"I hear the Italians make some killer red," Mike said to Velvet with a wink as he flashed more Euro bills. "Order up a bottle. My treat."

Velvet hesitated. "I should really go see about Gallo."

"Shit, didn't ya see 'em all go chasin' outta here after him? Sit here awhile and keep me company. When's the last time ya just relaxed?"

Mike had a way of getting to her, or maybe it was just that he knew exactly what to say. In fact, she couldn't remember the last time she had just relaxed. "Um, okay," she said. "A glass of Sangiovese."

"San—what?"

"San-gee-oh-vay-zay."

Mike shrugged and shuffled up to the bar, and then returned with an entire bottle of Fonterutoli. Velvet sat there listening to Angelina strum her guitar from the little performance area that she had created in the corner. She began to sing in Italian, and Velvet couldn't really follow the lyrics, but her voice was surprisingly lush and sultry. Maybe it wasn't so bad after all, she considered, that Angelina now owned Vin's guitar. Maybe she'd do it justice.

Velvet was starting to relax and savor the wine, but then Angelina—this woman who barely seemed to speak English—began a sultry rendition of the Whitesnake ballad, "Is This Love" . . . in English. It sounded like she was casting a spell, and of course it was Mike she was bewitching. He could hardly take his eyes off her. Velvet wobbled to her feet. "I'm gonna take off."

Mike laughed and grasped Velvet's arm. He pulled her back down, and tuned in to her in that legendary Mays fashion, gracing her with that famous crooked grin. "You were so hot."

"Me?" Velvet could feel her cheeks flushing and she avoided his stare. "You can't possibly remember . . . that night. . . . I think you passed out before . . ."

He leaned in. "Still got that hot bod."

She rolled her eyes at his cheap line, but held his grin.

Mike glanced at Angelina and then back at Velvet. They politely applauded at the end of the song. Then he whispered, "You got a birthmark on your ass in the shape of a heart."

He was so close Velvet could feel the tickle of his breath as he spoke. She let out a slight gasp and then laughed to stop her mouth from dropping all the way open. "You mean to tell me that of the hundreds—probably thousands by now—of women you've screwed, you actually remember *my* ass from, what, some forty years ago?"

He looked over at Angelina as she started her next song but quickly returned his focus to Velvet. "Change had spilled outta my pockets," he said with a wink. "And when I rolled ya over, coins were stuck to your cute little ass." He started laughing. "Quarters, nickels, dimes."

Velvet laughed so hard she had to put her hand to her mouth to stop from snorting. She stared at Mike, who was still laughing. He seemed so genuine, almost vulnerable.

"You weren't only a hot lay, babe," he said with a salacious grin. He snuck a glance at Angelina. "You were a killer musician, too . . . so sexy, the way you used to move on stage."

Velvet grimaced but it turned into a smile. "You never saw me play live."

"Shoreline. When ya played with Heart. Damn near moved me to tears." His eyes were soft and he seemed lost in the memory. "You were an amazing harpist."

Velvet rubbed the back of her neck and glanced toward the door. The others, she considered, never complimented her musicianship. "Since we moved to Italy," she muttered, "I hardly touch my harps anymore."

"And that little strap-on Vin made for ya?" Mike poured the last of the wine into her glass. "Strap-on electric harp, I mean. The way you used to prance around stage with that thing . . . in your sexy Goth clothes . . . mmm. Way, way ahead of yer time."

Velvet closed her eyes and let the memories come flooding back. Shoreline Amphitheatre, 1990. On the same stage as her idols, Ann and Nancy. Most people had never seen an electric harp back then . . . she used to play it in a black and red velvet bustier with black gossamer sleeves . . . so Goth, so badass. When she opened her eyes, Mike was staring at her, absorbed, as if he was sharing in her fantasy. He hadn't even glanced at Angelina.

"So why'd you name the place 'Groove House' anyway?" Mike asked, his hand skimming her shoulder.

Velvet glanced at the door. She was so sick of playing den mother to a bunch of slovenly geriatrics—when was the last time she'd had a single uninhibited hour away from all of them? She took another sip of wine.

Mike held his grin.

"Years ago, Vin and I were vacationing in the UK. Driving through Stratford-upon-Avon, I misread a sign for 'Grove House' as *Groove*. We laughed and decided right then and there it was the perfect name for the property."

When Mike placed his hand on her arm, she could feel the heat of his touch. He looked into her eyes.

"Velvet, ya gotta help me out. I can't go back to the States. I'm in some shit there—"

"With the law?"

"No, that ain't it. Look, I just gotta stay at your place."

"I can't. . . . I . . ." Velvet reached for the wine glass and took another sip. If Vin ever found out. . . . Mike was giving her the pleading eyes, and it was as if he had forgotten that Angelina even existed. He was another stray and it crushed her to turn down a cry for help. She tried to muster a convincing explanation, but every time he looked at her, her mind got hazy. "Truth is . . . I . . ." She glanced around the bar and then let out a sigh. "We're broke. We can barely pay the bills." After shooting a quick glance at Mike, she focused her eyes on the table. "I keep selling old tour memorabilia, but . . . we have this huge property tax bill, thanks to the new property *re*assessment." She fired a glare in Angelina's direction, but then softened when she turned back to Mike. "We can't pay it. . . . The ridiculous penalties keep adding up. We're so behind. . . . I just don't see how we could possibly take on another mouth to feed, more electricity to pay."

"Look, doll—"

"And Vin." Velvet squeezed her eyes closed and then opened them. "God, Vin's been working so hard subbing on these shitty little tours for nothing. I'm so worried." She rubbed her chin, trying to enunciate. "He's working twenty-three days straight and barely clearing two grand US. . . . that's not going to help. We need fifteen thousand *Euro* . . . that's like twenty thousand dollars. He thinks he's doing the best he can and he won't quit. He's killing himself. I'm really worried about him. He's not twenty anymore." *Oh God,* she whispered to herself, as she realized she was weepy-drunk. She swiped a tear from her cheek and snuck a glance at Angelina, who was still wailing out her Italian songs from the corner. "If we don't pay this property tax bill by Thursday, they'll add another delinquent fee—it could be 200 percent of the amount due. Can you believe that?" She leaned close to him and hissed, "Vin thinks that bastard Carlo has something to do with all this."

Mike glided her wine glass toward her. "You mean that mafia dude who was just here?"

Velvet couldn't help but start giggling at the mention of mafia. "He's not . . ." she began, but then she dissolved into giggles. She put her head down on the table and laughed to stave off the tears. "I have no idea how to get that kind of money by then. We could lose the house." She gripped the sides of the table and raised her head. She knew there was a silly smile on her face but she couldn't figure how to wipe it off. "We'll have to sell the land."

Mike leaned in closer. "What land?"

"Land," Velvet said with a single hiccup, fanning herself. "There's land."

Mike cocked his head. "Yeah, ya said that. Spill it, babe. . . . Land?"

She closed her eyes and let the words pour out. "Damned old vineyard. Carlo's wanted it forever, but Vin would never," she said between hiccups. "Seventy thousand Euro . . ." It was her favorite fantasy, how far that kind of money would go. They could pay off the property tax and then some.

"Only seventy thou?"

Another hiccup shook Velvet back to reality. "He only wants this one little bit that borders our property line." She glanced at Mike and pushed the wine glass away. Then she sat there and clutched her arms. "Mike Mays, you are one sorry dude, but you can't stay." She reached behind for her purse strap on the chair. "This has been . . . I need to go home—"

"What if," Mike said, grasping her arm, "ya sold the land to that dude so you could pay the tax bill before the deadline?"

"I could never do that to Vin. That's his grand—" A hiccup jolted her entire body. "It would kill him if I sold that old vineyard—"

"But what if it was just *temporary*, and you could get the land back in a few weeks?"

She squinted at him.

"Ya know, like a stop-gap measure—"

"Whoa." Velvet raked her fingers through her hair. "I'm drunk, right?"

she said, smiling up at Mike. "I was just hallucinating that you suggested I go sell a piece of my husband's land to our creepy neighbor."

"What if Vin would never know?"

She reached for her purse again and he stopped her.

"Would you do it?"

The room was spinning a little and she gripped the table again. "Speak English—Ennngglish."

"Creative financin'. I been doin' it for years, doll. It's all about jugglin'. Ya just borrow money from one place till ya can pay it back from another—"

"Got to pay it back."

"That's where I come in." Mike licked his lips and glided into an easy, crooked grin. "Ya see, I got this dough comin' . . ."

Mike was prattling and she could almost hear him over the buzzing in her ears and Angelina's crooning. "Wait a minute. What *dough*?"

"Record advance. Should have it in two weeks, three tops. I'll give it all to you cats."

Velvet tried forming her mouth but words escaped her. She sat there, numb, as she tried to sort through her foggy brain for some clarity. "You mean, you have real money? Not just bullshit promises?"

He just stared at her. "It's comin' . . . and it's all yours, babe."

She settled back into her chair and looked at him through bleary eyes.

"I'll have the dough in three weeks. You'll get the land back then, and Vin will never even know."

"Wait, you're confusing me." Velvet shook her head, which made her dizzy. "How am I going to get the land back?"

"Oh, that's easy." He shot her another lopsided grin. "Don't worry your pretty little head. I got that one covered. Trust me."

Velvet sat there waiting for her head to clear as Mike's voice cut through the music, jabbering on. She thought about Vin, slaving away, and worried again about his health, his blood pressure. *Just three weeks*, Mike kept repeating. *Vin will never know.* With Mike's infusion of cash, Vin could quit that crappy tour and come home.

She looked at Mike. "But I don't understand how . . . you'll get the land back."

"You don't need to know," he assured her. "Leave it to me."

"And you swear you can? . . . Get the land back—"

"But we gotta do it now."

"Now?"

"Right now." He stabbed a pointed finger on the table. "Trick is, we gotta get *cash*."

"I'm in no shape to go groveling to Carlo." She stared at Mike, unsure.

"You wanna keep the house, right? You gotta pay the tax bill. This is the only way. Trust me. I do this shit all the time. I got yer back, doll. Gimme yer car keys. I'll drive."

Velvet swallowed hard and hesitantly withdrew the keys from her purse. "Can you drive a stick?" she asked with a hiccup.

Mike slid the keys from her grasp. "Babe, I was born drivin' stick."

Chapter 18

"Turn here," Velvet said and then pressed one hand to her mouth. She knew what the sour taste on her tongue meant. With her other hand, she directed Mike the rest of the way up the hill. As the old Fiat rolled to a stop, she opened the door and slid from the passenger seat onto her knees in the gravel before she hurled. Then she drew in a slow breath as she looked up at the salmon-pink walls in the dusk.

"Oh my God," she hissed at Mike. "I just vomited in their driveway."

"Here." Mike shoved a bottled water in her direction. "Guzzle this. You'll feel better."

She staggered to her feet, gulped the water, and reached in her purse for a mint. "I can't go in there now—"

Mike clutched her by the arm and marched her up the stone steps toward the front door.

Velvet glanced up at the stone archway and the wrought iron lamps affixed to either side. Each step seemed more daunting than the last. The planked door stared back at her, dark and almost too ominous to approach. She stood there on the landing, twisting the hem of her shirt as Mike stabbed at the doorbell. She wanted to turn, hurdle the balustrade, and run like hell. "I've never been inside before," she whispered.

"How many years you lived here, and ya never once set foot in this dude's house?"

"Not inside." Her hands felt clammy. She could see movement through the glass. "His wife is lovely," she hissed, "but Vin and I aren't exactly on friendly terms with *him* . . . in case you haven't gathered." She glanced at Mike and felt another wave of nausea.

He winked at her. "Just introduce me to this cat. I got it covered."

A frail old woman opened the door. Velvet's eyes shifted from the white apron to her black dotted housedress and the silver chain and pendant of some saint hanging from her neck. She looked like somebody's *nonna* but Velvet knew she was no relation to Carlo. "Housekeeper," Velvet whispered to Mike. Then she cleared her throat. "Carlo? *A casa?*"

The woman rattled off something in Italian, her voice soft yet husky. Then she motioned them inside and ushered them into a grand living room. *"Minuto,"* she said and then shuffled away.

Velvet pressed on her stomach and noticed the nausea had subsided, though her head still felt murky. She scanned the lavish interior—from the marbled floors and arched doorways, to the silk curtains and chandeliers. The room started to spin and she teetered, thrusting her hand out to catch herself. She glanced at Mike, who seemed unfazed by the opulence. My God, she thought, calling the place a farmhouse was a joke—it was more like a palace. Modern and old world—no doubt Giulia's taste prevailing over Carlo's. She noticed the dining room wall, where Renaissance figures caroused through the countryside in a fresco so splendid it looked as though Michelangelo himself could have painted it. Of course it would be impeccably designed, she thought. "Just like Giulia," she blurted to no one in particular, and then found herself hoping that Giulia might be home too.

Mike made himself right at home as he examined sculptures and vases. "Why does this dude want your land so badly, anyway?" He dove his hand into a Murano glass bowl on a marble table and stuffed candy into the pockets of his ripped jeans.

Velvet shushed him. "Expand his vineyard," she mumbled, and then let out a loud belch that tasted of vomit. She wanted desperately to run away, but she forced herself to stay. Cold sweat trickled down the small of her back. Feeling dizzy, she lurched toward a gleaming mahogany side table. Mike still looked like he was casing the house. "Holy shit!" she said, and she knew she was speaking too loudly, but she didn't seem to be in control. A stately, neo-gothic-style harp stood in the corner. "Gorgeous," she whispered, as she approached the treasure. She blinked, trying to focus as she read the decorative etching on the front action plate: WURLITZER ORCHESTRAL GRAND. "Giulia once mentioned they owned an old harp," she hissed at Mike, "but I never . . ." Tracing a finger down the heavily carved, gilded column, she pondered the worth of such a low serial number, guessing it might date back to 1900. She traced the honey-toned soundboard, its gold leaf design intertwined with faded red and green floral vines that rambled up the length. As she stroked the beautifully staved soundbox, she fantasized about all the decades the ancient harp might have seen. She giggled and slinked her finger up the strings in a ghastly out-of-tune glissando. "Must be worth a friggin' for—"

"Is *un'antichità*, no for to play." It was Carlo approaching from behind to scold her. "Is the harp of my grandfather, Sergio."

Velvet flinched and felt a chill. She turned and clutched her arms to her chest as Carlo swept into the room, imposing in a finely tailored dark suit, as if he might be going out to a formal event or having important people over for dinner. He began circling her and the harp. Velvet gulped. "Your grandfather?" she stammered. "Played harp?" She wished she could just fast-forward to driving home.

"*Sì,*" Carlo replied. His pompous nod told her that any cultured person certainly would have known such a thing. "For Giacomo Puccini. Is very special, this *arpa.*"

Velvet gulped again but she could scarcely look at Carlo. "Do *you* play?"

"No," he said with a disgusted snort. "Is just for to keep." He squinted in her direction. "Ah, yes. My wife she say you play *l'arpa*. She is no here now. She is at one of her shops. Pienza, Greve, or Firenze, I do not know."

Velvet nodded and began to turn away, but Mike stepped forward and gave her a nudge.

Carlo's posture stiffened as he noticed Mike. "You, *signora*, are welcome here, but this *Americano* is no invite as a guest at my house."

"This is Mike Mays," Velvet stammered an awkward introduction as she eyed the path to the front door.

"*Ciao*, dude," Mike said with a crooked grin.

Velvet cringed. This was the worst idea ever. She took several steps backward, toward the entrance, until Mike reached back and grasped her arm.

Carlo angled toward Mike. "Respect we have always for *la signora.* But the American way is no respect. I tell to Angelina I no allow her to make company with you."

Mike let go of Velvet's arm and began to cruise around the room, touching the drapery, the polished wood. "It's cool, I'm cool," he said, nodding at Carlo.

Carlo ignored him and turned to Velvet. "You are here, so late in the evening. *Tutto bene?* Your husband is okay?"

"Yes, *bene,* Vin is fine. I, uh . . ." Velvet glanced at Mike. "He wants to talk to you."

Carlo gave Mike an icy stare.

Mike shot him that stupid grin. "What she's tryin' to say is . . ."

Carlo stood there, stone-faced, his glance shifting between Velvet and Mike.

"Ya know that little piece of land you been askin' to buy? Well, she wants to sell it to ya, and I'm here to, uh, help." Mike gave him a confident nod.

Oh, God, Velvet thought. What the hell was she doing?

"Think of me as," Mike said with a quick glance at Velvet, "her . . . broker."

Carlo narrowed his eyes. "Broker."

"But ya only got one chance, dude," Mike blustered. "Right here, right now . . . in *cash.*"

Carlo placed a hand on the harp and gave a dubious glance. He seemed surprised, or maybe a little disgusted . . . but not so much, Velvet suspected, that he wouldn't take advantage of the hasty offer. He glanced at her, as if for confirmation, and she gave him a rickety nod that she hoped conveyed something like consent.

"Why you do this now, eh?" Carlo asked.

Velvet looked at Mike for guidance.

"Tick, tock," Mike crowed. "We're gonna walk, dude. It's now or never."

Carlo clenched his hands, clearly annoyed by Mike, and then set his glare on Velvet. "You have *permesso* . . . from your husband?"

"Permission?" Velvet turned away from his stare. "I'm not a child."

Carlo removed his hand from the harp and said coolly, "Fifty thousand—"

"Seventy," Velvet blurted out. "Your last offer was *seventy*." Her head was still hazy from the alcohol, but she still had her negotiation skills.

"Seventy thousand." Carlo repeated, as if considering it. He stood there, tapping on the harp.

"Cash," Mike reminded him. "Clams, one-spots, *dinnneeeero.*"

Carlo glared at Mike and then at Velvet. "I no have American dollars," he said with disdain.

"Oh," Velvet said, forcing a laugh. "He means Euro."

"*Euros,* dude," Mike added.

Carlo lowered his dark brows and stared hard at Mike for a few long moments. "Is a big difference, American dollars or Euro." He raised his chin toward Velvet, who stood firmly, holding her ground. "And your husband, he agree?"

Velvet nodded and uncomfortably folded her arms.

Mike began to pace around the room. "Offer expires in ten, nine, eight . . ."

"Allora," Carlo said, ignoring Mike. He gave Velvet a knowing grin. "If I give to you the cash—"

"Dude," Mike barked. "Take the deal. You don't want her changin' her mind, do ya?"

Carlo clenched his jaw and then forced a smile. "I must hear the words from the mouth of *la signora.*"

Velvet gulped. She wished Mike would get the hell out, but she knew she never would have been able to do this without him.

"You tell to me," Carlo said, his chin high. "That you want to sell the land."

Velvet turned away from both men. God, she wished Giulia was there; she'd know how to handle Carlo.

"Don't blow it, babe," Mike said under his breath.

Her gut told her to run, but her whole body was flooded with the immense relief she would feel as she stood at the office paying off the tax bill. Mike would get his record advance and Vin would never know about the sneaky deal. And if Mike didn't come through, last resort, Giulia would undo the whole thing. Lovely Giulia, she didn't deserve a friend like her. Slowly, reluctantly, Velvet turned.

"Yes . . . I—" She swallowed hard. "Want to . . . sell you the land."

Carlo blew out a long, slow sigh and bowed his head. With a slight smile, he took a step back and said in a soothing voice, *"Minuto,"* as he slipped from the room.

Velvet spun around to Mike and took a step forward. "What if he's calling *his* broker?" she hissed. "Or his lawyer?" She stumbled, catching herself on the harp. "Vin can't know," she pleaded. "Promise me."

"What are you, Saint fuckin' Velvet?" Mike snapped. "He's gonna burn you at the stake? I'm busy makin' a deal with the devil, and you're trippin' about who might find out?" He shook his head. "He wants that land. Trust me, dude's gonna keep his mouth shut."

Velvet found herself standing in front of the harp and she stepped forward, embracing it. "Do you think he'd let me play it?" she asked, turning to Mike.

"Now ain't the time." Mike spun her around just as Carlo reappeared in the room holding a brown leather messenger bag.

"Seventy thousand Euro," Carlo said as he patted the bag. She stepped toward it but Carlo pulled back. "But first."

Velvet took a step back and glanced at Mike.

Carlo glided to the marble table and withdrew some papers and a pen from the drawer. He stepped toward Velvet and presented what looked to be a contract. "You must to sign."

What the hell? Velvet felt her knees begin to shake. *He had a contract? Ready to go?* How many years, she wondered, had he been waiting for this very moment?

"*Allora*, you sign and is also your husband signing . . . is the same."

Carlo grinned at her. "You and the one you love so much, is the same for to sign. *Ha capito?*"

Velvet felt her stomach knotting up. Carlo was practically rubbing it in her face that she was betraying Vin.

"And is the same for me. I sign without my wife. Tonight is only the two of us." He gave a courtly nod in Mike's direction. "And your . . ."

"Broker," Mike blurted out with a crooked grin. "I'm her broker."

Velvet glanced at Mike. When he gave her a coaxing nod, she gulped and accepted the pen from Carlo.

Carlo glared at Mike. "For the American, also a contract. But is only the words, not on the paper. If you go with Angelina . . . *romperò i coglioni.*"

That was one phrase Velvet recognized, but Mike just stood there with a blank stare.

"I will break . . ." Carlo gestured toward the zipper on his trousers. "The balls."

Mike gave him a smarmy grin.

Carlo placed the messenger bag in Velvet's hand. "You count."

Velvet gave a probing glance at Mike. "No, that's okay—"

"I insist," Carlo said with a smug smile.

Velvet glanced between the two men, and then took a seat on the white divan and opened the bag.

"Tonight we are with friends, no?"

She looked up and when she saw Carlo grinning, she gave a hesitant nod. He gave her a crisp bow. Then he uttered something in Italian to the old woman who had just entered, and moments later she rolled a cart into the room.

Velvet impulsively closed the bag. Clutching it, she rose. Another knot twisted in her stomach, a painful reminder that she'd just made a terrible mistake. Mike shot her a wink.

Carlo uncorked a bottle of wine and filled three glasses. He offered a glass to Velvet and to Mike, who rushed to it like the lush he was.

Velvet stepped forward. Even the smell of alcohol sickened her, but then she noticed the label on the bottle. It was a 2002 Case Basse di

Gianfranco Soldera Brunello di Montalcino Riserva, worth probably 300 US, she guessed.

"To the land," Carlo said raising his glass in a toast. *"Chi la dura, la vince."* He gave a spirited laugh as he savored the wine.

Velvet could barely swallow a sip of the pricey vintage.

"Allora, I am a busy man," Carlo announced. "Is a pleasure to do the business with you." He set down his glass and reached out his hand.

Velvet looked down at his outstretched hand, waiting there for her to shake. Then she glanced at Mike, who tossed her a nod. Her stomach bubbled when Carlo firmly gripped her hand, and then she pulled hers away, tucking it under the messenger bag.

Carlo said something in Italian to the older woman and then looked at Velvet. "Carmella will take you to the door."

"Guess we oughta leave that bottle with you," Mike ventured, eyeing the mostly full wine bottle. "Don't want no DUI on the way home," he said, laughing at his own joke.

Carlo stared blankly at him, and Velvet gave him a warning glare before grabbing his arm and heading to the door. She couldn't wait to get home and shower off the sleazy deal.

Carefully stepping around her vomit, she climbed into the passenger seat of her old clunker. Mike slid into the driver's seat and started to drive away. Her legs bounced nervously.

"Who has that kinda dough?" Mike asked, eyeing the bag in her lap. "Just sittin' around his pad?" He shot her a glance. "Maybe that dude *is* mafia."

Velvet's stomach twisted tighter. She noticed her hands were trembling. She stared at Mike, the creepy one night stand dude who had come back to haunt her . . . or maybe to save her.

"Hey, how do we get home?" Mike asked, as if he had just assumed he was *in* now.

And he was right—he was *in.* She couldn't exactly send him away now, not until he had followed through with the rest of the deal: his record company advance.

"Take the next dirt road," she said, pointing up ahead.

"What'd he say, anyway?" Mike nodded to her. "At the end there, in Italian?"

"He said, *veen-chay*," she said, stressing the syllables. "From the verb *vincere*. It means *to win*."

Chapter 19

Velvet gulped down a couple more aspirin and returned to the Skype window. Dark circles sagged under Vin's brown eyes and his olive skin looked a little sallow. The grueling tour schedule was wearing on him, she knew, and all for barely anything. Her head throbbed a little harder—a painful reminder of yesterday's piss-up at the bar. She adjusted the screen and closed her eyes. No way she'd allowed Mike to fuck her again, let alone fuck her over. But now she had let him stay in Gallo's room. Just as she felt her shoulders slump, Vin's voice rattled her back to the conversation.

"I can't believe you sold the Kramer for that much." Vin smiled broadly, dabbing a towel under his jaw.

She could see he was on the tour bus, still sweating even though he'd likely been offstage for an hour. "Yeah, how about that?" She swallowed the lump in her throat and glanced toward the window and the courtyard. If Vin ever found out she'd sold a piece of his precious land, he'd never forgive her. What had she done? Sure, she'd paid off the delinquent tax bill that morning, hangover and all, and saved Groove House . . . but until Mike made good on his promise, Velvet knew she was in for some sleepless nights.

Vin swiped the towel over the damp waves in his hair. "So, babe—" She heard a commotion on the tour bus and he leaned out of frame. "Keep it down," he hollered. "I'm Skyping with my wife."

"Groupies?" Velvet teased him. She trusted her husband and knew he trusted her. Hell, in the '80s he used to call her from the road, alone in his hotel room after each gig, and give her blow-by-blow accounts of what he could hear through the walls of his bandmates' rooms next door. The two of them would crack up over the moans and groans and then talk until one of them fell asleep.

"*Vin, sign my tits,*" he teased back in his best girlie voice. "Only nowadays the fans have tits sagging down to their knees."

She laughed and then winced at her pounding headache. "I miss you so much."

"Then you'll love my surprise." He smiled and tossed the towel out of view. "Paul's recovered from surgery well enough to play the rest of the tour. So I'm done, catching a flight home after the Seattle show."

Velvet held her breath as a rush of panic tingled through her body. That meant he'd be home in two days. *Shit,* she thought, way too soon.

Vin's smile waned. "I thought you'd be happy."

"Well, of course," she said, her voice cracking. "I am. . . . It's just that . . . wow."

He lowered his voice. "After tomorrow's show, I'm done with this 'sub gig from hell' and—"

"You were *on fire* yesterday, babe," Mike roared as he came thundering into the office. "I dig a chick with balls."

Velvet cringed. "Mike, I'm on Skype."

Vin's pale olive complexion suddenly reddened. "What the hell is *he* still doing there?"

"I'm Skyping with Vin," Velvet clarified, and when Mike cocked his head, she could tell he was clueless.

"No shit?" Mike lumbered over and bent down to inspect the computer screen. "Fuckin' hell." He grinned and positioned his head next to Velvet's so he could see himself in the caller window. "How's it hangin', dude?"

Velvet glanced at Mike, his face dangerously close to hers. When he turned and grinned at her, his nose grazed her cheek.

"According to Mays," Vin said, "you were on fire."

Velvet swallowed hard and tried to wipe any emotion from her face. "Oh, that." She forced a giggle with an uneasy glance at Mike. "Well . . . I, uh—"

"Killed a spider," Mike blasted, sporting a Cheshire grin, as though he thought his stupid outburst had saved the day. "In my room."

"No, *Gallo's* room." Velvet turned away from Vin's onscreen grimace. She could feel sweat trickling down her forehead and she tried to keep her shoulders from slouching. "You know how much I hate spiders. . . . Turns out Mike hates them even more." She let out a nervous giggle.

"Hate them little bastards." Mike nodded.

Velvet nudged Mike away from the screen. "You'd be proud of me. It was above eye level and I scooped it into a—"

"Wine glass," Mike interjected from above her head.

Velvet cringed. God, she hated herself for being in cahoots with Mike Mays, of all people. "Vin . . . you know he just showed up here from San Francisco. So I put him up for the night—"

"You mean, *two* nights," Vin corrected her, as his posture stiffened. He just sat there, staring, unusually quiet, his body lurching from the motion of the tour bus.

We're here, Velvet heard a male voice announce from inside the bus.

"We're at the hotel now," Vin said, soberly. "I gotta go." Then he leaned in close. "By the time I get home, Mays had better be gone."

Velvet touched the computer screen. "I love you." But he had already disconnected the call. She pressed on her stomach. The queasiness she felt was definitely *not* hangover-related. She closed the window on-screen and placed a trembling hand on her throat. Then she swiveled the chair toward Mike. "Killed a spider?"

Mike shrugged.

She rubbed her throbbing head and said in a shaky voice, "I need that record advance—"

"It's comin'," Mike said, blinking calmly at her.

"You don't understand. Vin's coming home. He'll be here in two days." She gasped for air. "You've got to call—"

"It's like, three a.m. in L.A. . . . Don't worry. I got it covered." Then he fired a crooked grin in her direction and strutted out of the office.

Velvet stood up and stepped toward the window, focusing on the easel out in the courtyard and her unfinished painting. She spotted Harley lounging in the hammock, and so wanted to tell her friend about the stupid deal she'd gotten herself into—but Mike had warned her not to tell anyone. God, she couldn't admit that she'd gotten drunk and taken in by Mike Mays . . . again. And Harley had seemed so snippy toward her lately . . . since Mike had arrived, she realized. She never should've let him stay. She had only herself to blame.

She took a deep, shaky breath, straightened her posture, and headed out of the house. She shot past Mike, who was now leaning back on a chaise with Vin's Yamaha acoustic guitar in his lap . . . so footloose, so comfortable, like he owned the place.

She stumbled when she heard Blitz say, "You can't just hijack Gallo's room."

"Dude's gone," Mike crowed. "What's the big deal?"

"But he'll be back, geeze," Tank insisted.

Harley climbed out of the hammock and stepped toward Tank and Blitz, who were playing cards at the little patio table. Painting always calmed Velvet, so she headed to the easel she'd set up at the edge of the courtyard, lifted the rigger brush, and examined the roofline she had painted on the canvas. Then she dabbed the brush into the Burnt Umber pigment that she'd mixed earlier with the perfect amount of Ultramarine.

"Where can a dude get some pussy around here?" Mike burst out.

Velvet paused, mid-stroke, and glared across the courtyard. She rolled her eyes and returned her attention to the easel, trying not to stress.

"Any Asian massage parlors nearby?" Mike prodded.

Velvet held her breath, snuck a glance toward him, and then applied a precise stroke of pigment to canvas.

"They's some scrubbas down the road a bit," Tank said, slapping his cards onto the table.

"Where else am I gonna get laid?" Mike asked with a cough. "All the way out here in Bumfuck?"

Bumfuck? Velvet lowered her brush. What a moron, she thought. Mike couldn't appreciate beauty unless there was a piece of ass involved. He'd had a stable of groupies in every city on every tour, and now he had to resort to roadside tarts. If he so much as laid a hand on her ass, she'd clobber him. Just try me, she thought; she relished the thought of punching the shit out of him—payback for all the women he'd used over the years. One well-landed roundhouse punch and then she'd send him packing, as Vin had ordered. She focused back on the canvas and found herself brushing the word *dickhead* into the roof. The blaring AC/DC ringtone shook her from her thoughts.

Have a drink on me. Mike glanced down at his cell phone and rested the guitar on the chaise. "Duuuude. How's tricks in Tucson?" He pushed himself up and then swaggered past Velvet and down the terraces toward the pool, blustering into his phone the whole way.

Harley sauntered over to Velvet and stared in Mike's direction, and then did a double-take when she saw the word Velvet had painted on the canvas. She glanced back at the terraced land below. "Flirting with disaster now, are we?"

Velvet held her breath to steady her brushstroke. Surely Mike hadn't told Harley, she thought as she daubed paint over the word.

Harley nodded toward Mike, who was down by the pool. "Mike, a phone, and a body of water."

Velvet let out a shaky laugh.

"Either the pool or the toilet—how much you want to bet he'll have drowned that mobile before the sun goes down?"

"God, he's a disaster."

"I'm surprised you let him stay."

Velvet stopped mid-stroke. "I know, but . . . it's just . . ." She glanced guiltily at Harley.

"*Seriously?* . . . *I'm* the one who has a history with him." Harley seemed to be goading Velvet. She lowered her voice. "You only screwed him that once."

Velvet glanced around, set the brush onto the easel, and hissed, "Are you kidding me?"

They both turned when Mike cackled. Then his voice boomed up from the terrace below.

Dude, I tapped that ass so good, she's payin' homage to the almighty Mays . . .

Velvet shuddered. "You're trying to start a fight over *that* dirt bag?"

Harley's jaw slackened and then she began to laugh.

Velvet gazed out beyond the terraces and then scrunched her nose at Harley. "That little thing he does with his tongue and your—"

"You mean the—" Harley broke into a belly-laugh.

Velvet nodded and shuddered.

"I used to *love* that."

"Really?" Velvet gave her a credulous stare. "Oh, God, I hated that." She smiled and focused her attention on outlining a cartoon of a huge cock on the roofline.

Harley laughed but a moment later she sighed and turned to Velvet with a frown. "That cock makes me miss . . ."

Velvet shrugged. "Tank has his hookers, and you have . . ."

Harley gave a rueful laugh. "She stoops to conquer."

"Gallo's not so bad."

Harley shook her head. "If he just wouldn't kiss me," she said with a shudder. "Those nasty false teeth." She leaned toward the pool. "With Mike here . . . I guess I realize . . ."

"You could do better," Velvet said flatly. She glanced at Harley. "If Gallo can't get along, then maybe he *should* max his credit card and have a timeout."

"V, we can't just leave him—I mean, Gallo's part of the family."

"We can't force him to come back—" Velvet turned when she heard Mike's voice again, closer now, and obviously on a different phone call. He sounded almost . . . pleading.

"He's my grandkid," they heard from the terraces below. "You can't keep him from me. That ain't right."

"Brayden," Harley whispered.

Velvet hissed, "Isn't it like, four in the morning in California?"

Mike shuffled into the courtyard and gave them a look, as if he were accusing them of eavesdropping, and then held up his phone. "My, uh, daughter." Then he feigned a grin and muttered, "Chick's got issues."

Mike returned to the chaise, cradled the acoustic guitar in his lap, and noodled for awhile. Harley stepped over to him, rested her hand on his arm, and whispered something in his ear. Velvet noted that Mike responded with a huge grin.

Then Harley strolled over to the patio table and shot a glance at Velvet. When Mike began strumming a ballad, Harley turned back toward him. "Always loved that tune."

"Classic," Tank said, smiling up from his hand of cards.

"You gonna throw down a card, or what?" Blitz bitched as he filed his nails, which Velvet could see were pink today, matching the streak in his hair, as usual.

As Mike strummed, Velvet didn't recognize the ballad—one of his, she supposed. She washed over the cartoon outline and returned her attention to the painting she'd intended in the first place. She concentrated on comparing the main house to the watercolor house. The missing red tiles near the left corner of the roof, the chipped stucco—her painting seemed a fair representation. She scrutinized the green shutters, debating a darker shade on canvas.

Then Mike began to sing: *Love gone wrong, it's all too clear . . .*

Velvet had forgotten how compelling his singing voice was—a gorgeous resonant tenor that filled the courtyard. The crackle of a car topping the gravel driveway halted the card game as Blitz and Tank turned their heads. Giulia stepped out of her white Alfa Romeo sedan, and the men froze in their usual lustful stupor.

Still playing, Mike turned toward the driveway. "Hellooo, Betty," he said with a lecherous grin and then snuck in a lick from Hendrix's "Foxy Lady." He shifted his weight in the lounge chair and choked on the chords when he tried returning to the ballad. "Who's that?"

"Giulia," Tank and Blitz droned in unison, hypnotized by her beauty.

Velvet swallowed hard as she watched Giulia approach. Had Carlo told his wife what had happened the night before?

Giulia clip-clopped into the courtyard in her dainty heels and body-hugging dress—probably a Donatella Versace, Velvet guessed. Oh, to be the beneficiary of her hand-me-downs; too bad they'd never fit. Even Harley, who took a seat next to Tank at the table, looked frumpy in her Capri cargo pants and cotton tank top.

"Buongiorno, ragazzi." Giulia puffed out her luscious lips and flicked her long dark hair. "So this must be Mike-uh Mays-uh."

Velvet thought his name sounded ethereal flowing from Giulia's lips—she could even make the word *shit* sound divine. Drawn to her like a john to a hooker, Mike stood and rested the guitar on the chaise. Velvet rolled her eyes. What power there is in beauty, she mused. But then it hit her: how did Giulia know who Mike was?

The Italian goddess extended her hand to him. "I am Giulia, your neighbor. From the hill across." She pointed beyond the courtyard toward the fabulous house. Velvet closed her eyes and prayed that even if Giulia knew, she wouldn't broadcast Mike's bogus deal to the entire courtyard.

Mike broke into his famous crooked grin. "Charmed to meet you." He kissed the back of her hand.

Giulia slipped her hand out of his and turned to nod at Blitz and Tank, who were still gawking at her.

Velvet nearly knocked over her painting when Mike reached down and brazenly parked his palms on Giulia's ass. From behind her easel, Velvet could see Blitz and Tank look down at their cards, as if pretending they hadn't seen; even they were embarrassed at Mike's crass move. Jesus, didn't he know he was hitting on Carlo's wife? She tried to flag his attention, but it was hopeless. Giulia turned with a smile and a flick of her hair, as if almost . . . flattered. Velvet waited; was Mike playing along, pretending he had no idea who Giulia was, or was his horniness blinding him to the events of last night? Velvet set down the brush and hurried toward them.

Mike nestled close to Giulia and said in a syrupy voice, "How 'bout you and me blow this joint, babe?"

The idiom obviously didn't translate well, as Giulia smiled and placed her hand on his arm. "My husband tells me of you."

Velvet froze and held her breath, fearing what Giulia might say next. She glanced at Mike, who just stood there with a self-righteous grin.

"Carlo," Velvet said with a forced smile. "Her husband is *Carlo*." Her eyes widened as she shot Mike a covert glance.

"He say he meet you yesterday," said Giulia.

Velvet swallowed hard. "Right, in the *bar*." She shot Mike a stealth glare. His eyes darted around the courtyard before meeting hers. Velvet squeezed her eyes shut for a moment, hoping Giulia didn't yet know about the vineyard.

"I play you on the YouTube yesterday night," Giulia explained as she sized him up. "Please . . . is no for me to be the interrupting." She pointed to the guitar on the chaise. "Continue. Your voice, *la chitarra* . . . is . . . *bellissima.*"

Good God, Velvet thought; Giulia was flirting with the biggest male slut on the planet.

"Is a pleasure to meet you." Giulia grinned at Mike like a giddy teen. Then she clasped her hands together and looked at Velvet. "*Allora.* You must to try my new *cioccolato* . . . organic extra dark with organic *vaniglia di Mananara*, and on the top is Trapani sea salt . . . also *organico.*"

Mike wiped the sweat from his face and lowered himself onto the chaise. He picked up Vin's guitar and his fingers fluttered across the fretboard.

"Tell me what you think, eh?" Giulia held out the chocolates and everyone descended on them like vultures. Mike just continued strumming the guitar.

Velvet fired a look at him. Then she clutched Giulia's arm and escorted her across the courtyard to the terraces, safe from any loose tongues.

"Beautiful man," Giulia cooed and nudged Velvet's arm. "Why you don't tell me before about Mike-uh?"

Velvet paused at the vegetable garden. "Why is everyone so gaga over Mike Mays?"

"*Non ho capito,*" Giulia said inquisitively.

Velvet shook her head and stepped into the dappled shade of the walkway. "He's a player . . . he's . . . disgusting." She looked up at the wisteria vines clutching the blossoming lavender cascades.

"You no like him?" Giulia flicked the long hair from her shoulder. "He is sexy . . . for *un* . . . *anziano.* And so talent."

Velvet grinned at Giulia. "You have a crush on him."

Giulia gave a sly smile. "The new *cioccolato* is good, no? The sweet and the salt in the same bite . . ."

Velvet tuned out Giulia's words, wondering if Giulia would think as highly of Mike once he managed to finagle the land back from her husband. Or would she side with Carlo? Velvet didn't like the thought of the latter.

"... is just right," Giulia said as Velvet tuned back in. "No?" she asked, tilting her head.

Velvet shrugged and forced a smile. She looked out at the vineyards with their first blooms of the season, the sprinkles of red poppies scattered with pink and yellow wildflowers. Then Mike's cackle wafted down from the courtyard.

"... *sessantacinque percento,*" Giulia was saying.

As Giulia came into focus, Velvet looked away from her. Oh God, she thought; last night she'd puked in Giulia's driveway. She squinted up at the terrace and felt the nausea return. Then she looked back at Giulia, still gushing on about her chocolate. Velvet felt a tinge of panic. Would Mike's shady scheme cost her a friend?

Chapter 20

At the far end of the complex, Mike pushed open the door leading to Gallo's room. Velvet had said he could sleep on the couch, but why risk a stiff neck, he figured, when there was a whole room just sitting there, empty? He fumbled for the light switch and then skirted the cluttered tile floor, sidestepping stacks of boxes and clothes and Gallo's random shit piled high, until he reached the nightstand. Spotting his pack of smokes, he pulled out a cig. When he shoved it between his lips, Velvet's lame-ass no-smoking rule echoed in his head. He hesitated for a sec and then flicked the lighter anyway.

Meet me in the office at eight o'clock, Harley had whispered. She was gonna *sort him out.* Oh, yeah, he thought as he blew out smoke and coughed, she still dug him. He licked his lips and grinned, ready for some hot sex. Shit, he'd be happy with a blowjob.

He coughed as he rummaged through his duffel bag and pulled out the bottle of musk and orange oil that some redheaded hippie chick in San Fran had mixed for him. After smearing it on his neck, he grabbed his jeans and stepped around the storage boxes to the mirror.

He tugged at his Marshall T-shirt and eyeballed his bloated calves. *What the fuck?* He'd never had fat legs before. He coughed as he changed out of his shorts and into his jeans, making a mental note to just wear jeans from now on.

"You're not supposed to smoke inside."

He turned to see Blitz standing in the doorway, holding a stack of folded towels. "I'm allergic to rules," Mike said, as he took a gutsy hit on the cig and stepped toward him, glaring right at Blitz's eyeliner-smudged eyes. "What, ya gonna rat me out, glam boy?"

Blitz glared at Mike. Then he tossed the towels onto the bed, flipped him off, and left the room.

"Pussy," Mike muttered. He glanced at his phone. *7:45*. He eyed the wooden ceiling beams and wondered if any big-ass spiders might be lurking up there. He fuckin' hated spiders. He glanced at the armoire across the room and his bag on the floor. One of these days he'd unpack his shit. The baggage tag reminded him of the puritanical prison he'd left behind, and his poor grandkid, who still had a few more years under Lydia's thumb. Maybe tomorrow he'd unpack his shit, shove Gallo's crap aside, and then look into his songwriter royalties. The amounts were much smaller now, but he could always fork over some of that to Velvet whenever the next payment landed in his bank account.

He glanced at his phone again. *7:47*. His jetlagged brain bounced to Harley, waiting for him—not the Harley who'd whispered in his ear today, but the young Harley of decades ago, with her teased blonde hair and long legs for days. Man, he'd sure fucked up that one.

Mike took a final drag, flicked the cig outside, and closed the door to his new digs. As he crossed the courtyard he noticed his breathing seemed heavy. Damn, the thought of sex with Harley was gettin' to him. He pushed through the main house, and then puffed up his chest when he reached the office door.

"Come on in," said Harley.

Mike's grin drooped. She wasn't naked. Hell, she wasn't even dressed in a sexy negligee. Instead, she sat at the desk, waving him over.

"Sit here." She patted the chair beside her.

He stepped into the room and took a seat. Maybe she's got some kinky geek fantasy, he wondered, or maybe they were gonna watch some Internet porn. He gave her a hopeful smile.

"Dahling, I know you've had . . . issues . . . reaching your grandson— don't deny it," she said, holding up a hand before he could react. "I've heard you try five times already."

"My ball-bustin' daughter," Mike muttered, rubbing the back of his neck. "Ya know." He couldn't tell what was up, except that he wasn't likely to get laid tonight.

"Got me thinking. Wouldn't it be fab to give him guitar lessons via Skype?" She put her hand on his and said softly, "It's sort of a video phone, over the Internet."

"I know," Mike snapped. He whisked his hand out from under hers even though he really wanted to keep it there.

She looked at him sideways. "You're computer illiterate."

"I'm an analog kinda guy," Mike barked. "Old school all the way, babe. Hell, I ain't even into that manscapin' bullshit." He laughed.

"Right." Harley scratched at her cheek.

He glanced at the monitor. "I saw Velvet talkin' to Vin on that thing."

"It's easy, I'll teach you." She pointed to a list on the screen. "I've already saved the number here."

"Wait, my grandkid's?" he asked and she nodded. "Good luck gettin' past Cruella Deville."

"Direct connection."

"Serious?" Mike sat there, stunned. She'd gotten through to the kid, he thought, when he couldn't even pull it off himself. He cocked his head. "What's in it for you?"

"Mike." Harley smirked. "Not everyone in this world is looking for reciprocity." She rolled the desk chair close and put her hands on his thighs. "I remember how devastated you were when Lydia banned you from seeing Brayden. He was just a baby. What was it, twelve, thirteen years ago?"

Fourteen. Mike remembered exactly.

She stopped talking and looked him in the eye. "What happened?" She just stared at him. "I mean . . . with us. . . . I thought we were good mates and then . . . you just seemed to fall off the planet."

When Mike looked away, she spun his chair and held him captive, face to face. He didn't dig bein' interrogated, but of all people, he owed Harley Yeates an explanation. He glanced back at the door. It seemed as safe a place as any. He sighed and the dryness in his throat made him cough. Harley just sat there, staring at him, waiting.

"We have a history, you and me."

Mike cleared his throat. "And that's why I'm gonna tell ya somethin' very few people know." He snuck another glance toward the door.

"Don't worry about them," Harley urged.

"After grunge wiped out melodic rock in the '90s, I couldn't get arrested—"

"You think it was easy for *me*, or *any* of us?"

"Then later when my daughter turned on me . . . I got into this weird space . . . sunk into a kinda depression . . . well, not kinda, I did—"

"Why didn't you ring me?" Harley interrupted. "I worried about you, tried to reach you for ages."

Mike thought her piercing blue eyes looked a little misty. "I didn't see or talk to no one for years." He glanced away and hoped she wouldn't cry. He hated it when chicks cried. But Harley wasn't just any chick. She was like one of the dudes, and a killer musician, and the only chick he could hang with on the road—or anywhere, for that matter. "And then . . . the dough ran dry."

"Hence, your comeback tour." Harley nodded, and stared at him like she really cared. "I'd given up on you—"

"Yeah, well, me too—"

"I figured you no longer valued our friendship."

"Quite the opposite, babe. You're the only chick I could ever just . . . talk to." Mike cleared his throat. "I'm a hopeless old fucker, ya know—"

"Rubbish. You should see yourself. You light up when you talk about Brayden, your body language totally changes." Harley smiled that same warm smile that always made Mike feel comfortable. "Call me a sentimental old fool, but that looks like love to me."

Mike laughed. "You're a good chick, Harl. I shoulda never fucked up—"

"Then . . . why? . . ." She stared at him, unable to finish the sentence.

He did *not* want to go there, so he pointed at the screen. "You gonna show me this thing, or what?"

Harley gave a wry smile—she knew him too well, Mike thought. She turned toward the screen and focused. "So you use the mouse to open this window here . . ."

As Harley schooled him on Skype, Mike studied her face. She'd aged pretty damn well, he thought. Her silver hair looked cool, her skin color looked good, and she didn't have nearly as many deep lines as he had. When he inched his chair closer he could feel her warmth—a different feeling than he got from other chicks. With pretty much any chick he was always seconds away from a hard-on, but with Harley there was something more. Maybe it was the killer wine at dinner, but he just couldn't help himself. He was used to gettin' what he wanted, when he wanted it, so he zeroed in for a kiss.

And she kissed him back. For a second he was right back in Houston with her, that last night of the tour. When the hotel electricity went out, and they'd braved the storm by candlelight in bed and watched the lightning. That awesome night flooded in, but then ebbed right back out when Harley pushed him away.

"Once upon a time," she said with a kind smile. "Believe me, I wanted nothing more—"

Mike shushed her by planting another kiss on her lips. Harley melted into the kiss and then pulled away.

"I'm not doing this," she said, palm out.

"But," Mike whispered, "what if?"

"As fantastic as it feels to relive—" Harley touched her fingers to her lips. "I'm not that young, dumb bird anymore." She blinked at him and then straightened up, as if snapping back to current day. Then she reached out, caressed his cheek, and smiled. "There's a boy waiting for our call."

Mike sat there, dejected. He could count on one hand—okay, maybe two—the number of times he'd been rejected by a woman.

"Shall we?"

He groaned. His interest in technology stopped at a guitar, an amp, and a few effects pedals. But he dug the idea of seein' the kid. When he nodded to Harley, she turned to the monitor.

She fiddled with some settings on the screen. "Since I've already added Brayden to the contact list, all you have to do is double-click his name. Then press here."

A crooked smile crossed Mike's face when she touched his hand. He liked the feel of her guiding him on the mouse.

"Hear that? It's dialing. Just like a phone. Simple." Harley glanced at Mike. "He's quite special, isn't he?"

Mike stared at Harley and imagined her calling up this kid she didn't even know. When Brayden's face popped up on the screen, Mike's grin widened. He turned to Harley. "Now, that's some cool shit."

"Remember, the camera's right here." She pointed to the webcam on top of the monitor. "And there's the mic. Hello again, Brayden."

Mike giggled. "Hey, kid—"

"Hi, Gramps, er, Mike. . . . Hi, Harley." He seemed peppier when he spoke to her.

Harley moved into view and waved at Brayden. "I'll leave you two alone now—"

"You're leaving?" Brayden whined. "But you were gonna show me the lead on 'Spellbound.'"

"Another time." She winked at Mike, and he wondered how long they'd talked. "Here's your grandfather." Harley grabbed her red Yamaha SG from the futon and placed it in Mike's hands.

When Harley left the room, the kid leaned in to the webcam and smiled. "She's cool . . . I mean, for an older lady. I like her."

"Me too, kid." Mike glanced back toward the empty doorway. Being alone with Harley had seemed to spark something he hadn't even known still existed. Nah, he brushed it off; he was just horny.

The kid shifted and Mike could see he was holding his guitar.

"Got your guitar back."

Brayden started noodling. "Mom only kept it from me a few days."

"Huh." Mike shrugged. "Hey, about that . . . maybe we should keep this Skype thing on the sly from yer mom." He fidgeted with all the gadgets around him, trying to position the guitar into view on-screen.

"Harley showed me how to do harmonics."

"No shit?" Mike glanced again toward the doorway, surprised. "So you two are best buds now?" Then he turned back to the screen. The kid's hair seemed longer. Maybe he was finally grasping the vibe of cool. "Hey, shouldn't you be in school?"

"I cut class and came home for lunch," the kid said as he kept noodling.

"Dude, that ain't cool. If yer mom finds out—"

"She won't. But so what if she does? I can handle her."

Mike stifled a laugh.

"I have a surprise." Still noodling, the kid giggled. "But I'll tell you later. I've been wanting to call you but Mom doesn't have your number."

Bullshit. Mike smirked. "Yeah, I, uh . . ." He considered draggin' Lydia's ass through the mud. "I, uh, lost the house number . . . never had yer cell number."

The kid stopped noodling. "There, I just sent you my cell number. See it on the screen?"

Mike leaned in close and squinted at the box that had popped up on-screen. He looked down at Harley's guitar and started riffing on the "Lucky Night" melody, grinning when the kid echoed back on-screen from thousands of miles away.

"I was wondering . . . how do I get that awesome tone you were getting out of my amp? I have the knobs all turned how you had them, but it doesn't sound the same."

Mike grinned. The kid had lots to learn, and Mike aimed to teach him every trick. "Tone ain't entirely about yer settings. You can mess with that all ya want, but it's really in the touch."

The kid quickly glanced away. Then he leaned forward and said softly, "I gotta go. Gotta get back to, um, school."

"Dude," Mike boasted as he clutched Harley's guitar. "This place is way cool. Ya gotta come here, check it out. You'd totally dig it."

"I'm so there," Brayden said, closing his eyes and slowly shaking his head. "But . . . living with *her* . . . you know."

The kid's face looked funny on the screen, Mike thought. But he dug seein' his grandkid and the guitar back in his arms . . . so cool.

"Someone's here. I really gotta go now," the kid said, turning his head away. "Text me from your cell phone as soon as we hang up, okay? Then I'll call you later. This is gonna be great. See ya."

Mike squinted again at the numbers in the box on-screen. "Got it."

"Mike," Velvet said from the doorway. Her hair was wet, slicked back, and she stood there wrapped in a pool towel. She glanced back toward the great room. Then she looked down on him with a condescending vibe and hissed, "Vin will be home in less than—"

"For chrissake, it ain't even been twenty-four hours. I'll get the dough." He got up from the chair and avoided her stare. "You need to chill, babe." He started for the door. "Lemme see if Tank's got some weed."

Velvet flung her arm across the doorway and blocked him. "How can you live with yourself? . . . I'm going to march that messenger bag over to Carlo right now," she said, lowering her voice to a hiss, "tell him I made a terrible mistake and I need the land back. I'll give him what money's left from paying the tax bill, and tell him that *you'll* be paying him the balance due."

"Whoa, doll," Mike said, grasping her arm. "Cool yer jets. You don't wanna fuck up the plan."

"Plan." She shook free of his grasp and stared him down. "I'm beginning to think you don't even have one."

Mike gave a sharp nod. "It's already in gear." He said with a wink, "I told ya, don't worry—"

"I *am* worried," she hissed, her face reddening. "We're out of time," she said through clenched teeth. "Do you understand?"

"Relax. It's comin'." It was the best he could come up with on such short notice. He shifted in the doorway and glanced at her. She looked hella stressed, almost shaking. He hoped she wasn't gonna cry. He couldn't call Bruce again. That slick-as-shit L.A. cockhead wasn't gonna do fuck-all for him. Mike tapped his finger on his chin. If he could just figure out a way to get some dough . . . fast.

"Are you still in love with him?" Velvet stared hard at her friend.

"Why? What does it matter?" Harley missed the counter and dropped a glass on the floor.

They were in the kitchen, and the others had stayed in the courtyard since dinner, polishing off another bottle of ten Euro wine and passing around a spliff.

"You know what I mean," Velvet muttered as she filled the sink with soapy water.

"Um," Harley said as she knelt and picked up the shattered pieces from the floor. "I'm not *in love* with him. It's just that he's—" She turned a reverent glance toward the courtyard. "He's—"

"Got a big cock?" Velvet teased, plunging her soapy hands into the water. "Or rather, *is* a big cock."

Harley let out a belly laugh. She was sitting on the floor amid the shards and it took a moment before she could compose herself. Then she got up and tossed the fragments into the trash bin. "That's not it at all." She continued grinning, as if she held a secret. "It's just that . . . Mike and I go way back." Her eyes focused on nothing in particular as she trailed off. "I'd just arrived in L.A., young, knew not a soul . . . I headed out to the Starwood one night . . ."

Velvet stepped to the drawer for a towel and could hear the guys talking outside.

"What meds you takin', geeze?"

The voices seemed to blend and she wasn't completely sure who was asking the questions and giving the answers.

"Blood Pressure? Tell me somethin' I don't know. Cholesterol? Yep. GERD? Who ain't? Arthritis? Oh, yeah. Prostate? Thought I'd have ya beat on that one."

Harley rested a hand on the counter and blinked at Velvet as she returned to the sink. "You don't know him like I do." Her grin was smug. "He's a rebel, a bad boy. And that's what makes him so appealing. He's just . . ."

Velvet heard Mike talking outside.

"Ever hear of . . . CD . . . C . . . P? . . ."

"What's that, geeze? Some new shite kids are sniffin' in the States?"

"Nah. . . . Just wonderin'."

Velvet swished the wine glasses around in the soapy water and opened her mouth to speak but then paused. As much as she wanted to bash Mike, she didn't dare—Harley might side with him. And he could so easily make her life an even bigger living hell.

"It's a pure love." Harley stepped over to the sink, her posture relaxed. "An admiration I don't think anyone else could ever understand. On the surface, sure, he's a bit rough, bit of a loaf, but he's a gem . . . he's . . . the consummate rock star."

Velvet swallowed hard and began to towel-dry the glasses while Harley gushed about Mike. She was so tempted to tell her how she'd fallen under Mike's influence and made a mistake.

"We've been through a lot together," Harley reminded her. "We were kids, in our twenties, struggling to make it in the music biz. You ride this rock 'n' roll rollercoaster and when you connect with someone—*really* connect—it's for life . . . even if you haven't spoken for years. It's like the time doesn't matter."

Velvet suppressed an uncomfortable lump in her throat as she shoved the kitchen towel inside another wine glass.

"You all right?" Harley asked, tilting her head. "You look . . . well, more than a little peaked."

No, she wasn't. She had betrayed Vin, and he'd be home in thirty-some hours. She couldn't keep it to herself any longer. She glanced at the kitchen door and then lowered her voice. "If I tell you something, will you swear to me you won't repeat it?"

"What is it, V?"

"And most importantly, you *cannot* go to Mike." Velvet noticed her hands were trembling. "You have to promise me."

Harley wrinkled her forehead. "Okay."

"I did something stupid, Harley." Velvet tossed the towel onto the counter. "Mike got me drunk and somehow convinced me to sell part of that old vineyard to Carlo."

"What?" Harley had to steady herself against the counter.

"It was only supposed to be temporary," Velvet said, rushing her words. ". . . so I could pay off the tax bill and we wouldn't lose the house, and Mike has a plan to get the land back but first he needs his advance, and he said three weeks but now Vin will be on a flight home way sooner than I ever expected, and—"

"Take a breath, dahling. I'm not sure I'm catching all this. . . . Plan? . . . I can't believe—"

"I know, I know. I've been stuck playing den mother for so long . . . and for those few hours with Mike. . . . He made me feel so . . . comfortable. . . . The wine and . . . he saw me play—God, that was like, 25 years ago . . . Oh, I don't know what came over me. I really believed that Vin would never know—"

"Vin'll go absolutely mental." Harley pinched her lips together. "Wait." She squinted at Velvet. "Back up. . . . What advance?"

"Mike has a record advance coming. . . . In three weeks."

Harley rolled her eyes in the direction of the courtyard. "Does he, now?"

"Vin never even goes down to that old vineyard anymore. I really thought . . ." She whispered, "I need Mike . . . to . . ."

Harley gave Velvet a sad stare. "Dahling, I so wish I could help here, but Mike is Mike, you know?" She leaned back against the counter and folded her arms. "I could have a word with him. Find out about this *plan* of his."

"No." Velvet released a sigh.

Harley looked across the kitchen, toward the courtyard. "I know how to manage Mike. I'll do some sleuthing. He won't even know what hit him."

"I can't believe I let him talk me into this—I am so screwed!"

"He can be awfully persuasive." Harley turned her attention back to Velvet and placed a warm hand on her shoulder. "It could have been me, love, honestly. I can only imagine how many hundreds of women made the same mistake you did—trusting Mike."

"Hundreds?" Velvet said as she stepped into Harley's embrace. "Probably *thousands*," she moaned, a testament to the legions of women who, like her, had said yes to Mike Mays.

Chapter 21

Lydia and Andrew slinked unnoticed into the back row of the school auditorium.

"You know, he's in big trouble with Mr. Whiteside for missing orchestra practice," she whispered as she settled into her seat. "He should be practicing clarinet for the graduation ceremony." She looked down at the program in her hand. "It even *says* he's playing clarinet—"

"Did you really expect—"

"He only just started playing guitar," she hissed. "Why would he risk playing it in the talent contest?"

"It's high school," Andrew whispered, "not the Grammy Awards." He shook his head. "They're *all* inexperienced." He glanced around the auditorium and pushed his glasses up the bridge of his nose. "And it's a *show*, not a contest."

"But what if he fails?" Lydia said in a soft tone. "He'll be crushed."

"He'll never learn anything if you keep him in a protective bubble. Let him take chances, grow from his mistakes."

"But—"

"Quit coddling him." Andrew's voice grew a little louder. "You wouldn't let the poor kid play sports because he might get hurt; you wouldn't let him play outside because he might get kidnapped. Let him explore, have his own adventures, break an arm. Those are the things that help a person develop."

Glancing around at the students and parents, Lydia lifted her finger to her lips, urging Andrew to whisper. "As I recall," she said, lowering her voice. "You agreed to the same parenting methods." She tried to calm herself by focusing on the honeyed tones of the stage flooring and layers of brown and black curtains. Onstage, kids scrambled to remove the last act's props as they set up for the next performer.

"He's been practicing like there's no tomorrow," Andrew whispered. "He'll do fine. And if he screws up, he screws up. He'll bounce back."

Lydia couldn't shake her motherly instinct. She leaned into Andrew's ear. "But kids can be so cruel."

"He's a teenager. Besides, this will be good for his shyness."

The lights dimmed, and the students applauded and catcalled at the introduction of the next performer, Ashley Something-or-other. Lydia fidgeted in her seat as an impeccably dressed teen with California blonde ringlets took the stage. As Ashley started to sing, Lydia smiled at Andrew and whispered, "She's good." But then the Mariah Carey copycat warbled through her performance with so many vocal acrobatics that she lost track of the melody. Lydia leaned toward Andrew and hissed, "Have you noticed he has a bullet belt?"

"What?" Andrew asked, focusing on the stage.

"Where would he get such a thing . . . and why? . . . I should have never returned that guitar." Lydia realized it hadn't brought her son back the way she'd hoped it might. "He's Mike Lite, if you ask me. What's next, black nail polish?"

Andrew whispered in her ear. "Mike doesn't wear nail polish." He focused straight ahead and then leaned toward Lydia again. "It's just teenage rebellion. I know what he's going through. . . . I've already warned him about his grades. The way I figure it, as long as he's still in school, we're ahead of the game."

Lydia leaned in to Andrew again. "What is it with this Coverdale fellow that he's so hung up on?"

"Whitesnake?" he whispered and she just shrugged. "I bet you remember, 'Is This Love,' 1987."

She did a double-take. "What are you, the Rain Man of rock music?" He was right, though, she did vaguely recall the title.

Andrew straightened in his seat when a woman to their left shushed them.

At the end of her performance, Ashley bowed to feverish applause. Lydia sat upright when she spotted Brayden in the wings. "There he is!" Ashley pushed past Brayden as she exited stage right. The girl snubbed him and turned back with a demeaning, snooty glance. "How rude," Lydia said, glowering toward the stage.

The prom-queen-wannabe strutted to her seat, front row center, among what appeared to be popular girls and cheerleaders. The girls in her row and the obvious jocks in the row behind smiled, launching plaudits and high-fives.

"You have to swear," Lydia whispered to Andrew, "you'll never let him know we were here."

Keeping his focus on the stage, Andrew muttered, "Just give him a chance—"

"He forbade me to come, you know. Can you imagine? His own mother."

The applause faded as a teacher took center stage and announced, "And last, we have a change in the program. Brayden Wilson will be playing guitar."

To boost the scant applause and encourage her son, Lydia began clapping, but then thought better of revealing her presence. She gripped Andrew's arm as their son pushed his little amp-speaker combo onto the stage. Her heart pounded as he plugged in and fiddled with the settings.

"Loser!" The jocks in the front row began heckling as Brayden fumbled through his setup. "*Gay*-den!" the bullies' voices echoed. The girls turned and giggled at the insolent boys. Lydia pushed forward in her seat, but Andrew restrained her. She wanted nothing more at that moment than to rush the stage and rescue her son from those ignorant teenagers.

Brayden looked sheepish as he took center stage, his electric guitar cradled in his arms like a security blanket. Lydia tensed up as her son tapped the microphone like he'd seen in movies—fortunately, without feedback; only the sound of his tapping finger reverberated from the PA. She thought she could hear his nervous breathing, or maybe it was hers. She peered through the sea of heads as her son inched toward the microphone.

His squeaky voice resounded through the theatre. "My grampa wrote this tune."

Lydia felt a pang of jealousy.

Brayden timidly launched into a musical introduction with darn near perfection. The familiar notes of "Lucky Night" surprised her. Watching Brayden onstage reminded her of the countless hours that Mike had spent on the sofa teaching Brayden that damn song. She tilted her head and hated to admit it but "Lucky Night" was kind of catchy.

She gasped when Brayden began to sing. She clasped her hands and her eyes widened as she glanced at Andrew. So those were the muted sounds she had heard from his bedroom; he had been too shy to sing in front of his own parents. She felt nervous, yet proud to see him make such a bold move. His voice wasn't half bad, she thought. She remained tense, the protective mother, as her son powered through the song—not terribly sophisticated, but quite confident in his guitar playing.

Lydia noticed that the snooty little bitches in the front row began to tone down their ridicule. They grew quiet, as if Brayden's performance had charmed them into submission. The passion pouring from his guitar was gripping. His playing appeared flawless, and his voice—earnest and pure—somehow fit the song. By the end, the girls were shushing the jocks in the row behind them.

As Lydia watched her son up there performing, so brave, so mature, a wave of pride washed over her. She marveled at the way he cocked his head and swiveled his foot, the same way his grandfather did when he played. When Brayden struck the last chord, Lydia clapped so hard her palms stung. Automatically, she began to stand, but Andrew pulled her back to her seat. From the back row, she watched her son bashfully accept the applause and then look down at his feet. She could tell he felt nervous with all those people staring at him. She ached to run up there and hug him.

Andrew beamed during the applause as Lydia dabbed at her tears.

"Not bad. . . .Well, for his level," she clarified.

"Not bad? He was superb," Andrew said as the applause faded. He nudged Lydia. "We'd better duck out before he sees us."

As the audience members began to head for the exits, a swarm of girls waited at the front of the stage . . . for Brayden, Lydia assumed. Caught in the mass exodus of students, Lydia and Andrew found themselves stalled in the crowd at the auditorium doors. They both turned to see a group of girls flock to Brayden, flirting and showering him with praise.

Lydia moaned. "Dammit, Andrew. This is how it all starts."

Brayden clutched his guitar and soaked up the attention from the girls—he was Mike Lite indeed. She gripped Andrew's arm to steady herself as the reek of cigarettes and Jack Daniels came crashing into her world; Mike, his wheezy laugh and slurred "fuckin' hell" when he bounced her on his knee, that Kathy-floozy with the mile-high bangs whom he had the nerve to bring along on their father-daughter trip to the zoo, the day he stumbled up the front steps and blubbered to her mother that he'd just wrapped a Ferrari around a tree only hours after driving it off the lot.

Yes, Brayden was pulling away from her, but she'd be damned if she let him head down the same doomed highway as Mike. Lydia shook her head to purge the thought and then tugged at the bottom of her jacket. Music had stolen her father from a once longing little girl. And she wasn't about to let rock 'n' roll abscond with her only child.

Chapter 22

Mike grinned at Harley as he chunked away at chords on Vin's blue Ibanez. "Hell, yeah," he hollered and stretched a string on "Rock Bottom," the classic UFO tune. Then he ripped the lead from her and opened fire on a blistering guitar solo. When the song wound down to hoots and high-fives, Harley forced a grin but said nothing.

He glanced around the old barn that Vin had converted to a music room, complete with PA system. Man, it felt killer to rock out with these cats, although Tank standing in on bass was the worst idea, and he couldn't restrain himself from asking, "How can you fuck it up so badly?"

Blitz laughed and leaned over his drum kit. "That was *crushing!*" he blurted in a bubbly tone.

"Mike!" Velvet hollered from the barn door, frantically waving him over. Chick looked freaked out.

Mike set down the guitar and hustled over to her.

"Hide it!" she said in a shaky voice as she shoved the messenger bag at him. "Vin's early. His taxi's at the bottom of the driveway!"

Mike snatched the bag and then hightailed it to his quarters. He hurled the bag inside and rushed back to the barn before the taxi had reached the top of the gravel drive. Fuckin' hell, he thought, he needed to walk more or start doin' laps in the pool. Panting, he strapped on the guitar again.

Blitz tinkered around the kit before launching into some crap that Mike thought barely resembled "Love Gun."

Mike dissed him with a wave of his hand. His heart was still pounding, his breathing still rough. He leaned over to Harley and patted her on the shoulder. "You're still the shit," he said between breaths. "It's good to keep your chops up."

"What ever for?" she mumbled and forced a smile.

Mike shot her a wink. "You oughta play on my new album, babe. It'd be killer."

"Right," she said sharply and then turned away.

"But not you, dude," he razzed Tank. "I need a *real* bass player."

"Feck off," Tank replied.

Mike grabbed onto the Marshall amp as his breathing started to mellow. He saw Blitz lean forward over his kit and Harley strain toward the barn door. Mike turned to see Vin Sabatino storming into the barn with Velvet trailing. He sized up Vin's shoulder-length brown hair. Damn, he thought, dude still had most of it. And his distressed leather jacket with silver chains wasn't *too* much of a stretch.

Tank rested the bass against the speaker cab.

Mike pulled the Ibanez off as Vin headed straight for him. His eyes looked cold and hard. "Dude." Mike grinned. "Long time no—"

Vin ripped the Ibanez from Mike's grasp and handed it to Tank, who set it in the stand. "What the fuck are you doing?"

Mike stole a glance at Blitz seated behind the drum kit fiddling with his hardware, twisting and tightening bits. "Jammin', dude." Mike grinned again. "Killer pad ya got here. Man, I wish I had a—"

"Who gave you permission to play my guitar?"

Mike glanced over his shoulder at Velvet, who closed her eyes as if she wanted to disappear.

"Don't look at her," Vin snapped. "She wouldn't dare." He just stood there, his nostrils flaring. "Why are you still here?"

Popular question lately, Mike thought. He glanced at Blitz, who brushed past him and hotfooted out of the barn. *Pussy.*

Harley set her red SG in the guitar stand and exchanged glances with Tank before they split too.

"What, did you run out of people to fuck over?"

"Vin," Velvet pleaded.

"Whoa, that ain't cool." Mike raked his fingers through his hair.

"Pack your shit and get out—"

"No," Velvet blurted out and stepped beside her husband. She shot Mike a nervous glance. "He has nowhere to go."

"You think I give a shit?"

Velvet looked at him and pleaded, "He's still jetlagged—"

"Uh, who just got off a plane here? Three fucking flights in twenty-four hours?"

Velvet stared at the floor.

"So Gallo calls me." Vin flailed his hands in the air. "For chrissake, Velvet, we can't have Gallo gone and Mike here. What the hell?"

"Mike will go . . . tomorrow." She gave Mike a half-shrug and then put her hand on Vin's shoulder. "Come on, have something to eat. I have dinner ready." She started to tug him away.

"Pack your shit," Vin demanded and then walked toward the other end of the barn as Velvet inched him away.

Mike growled out a cough, and said under his breath, "Nice way to treat the dude who paid your tax bill."

Vin stopped and turned back. "I must be hella jetlagged 'cause I swear I just heard that douchebag say something about paying *my* tax bill."

Velvet stopped and swung around toward Mike, her eyes blazing. Grabbing a tighter hold on Vin, she pulled him back. "No, it was nothing." She glared at Mike and then tugged at Vin again.

Vin shook his arm from her grasp. "What the hell, V?"

"I, um . . ." She fired a desperate glance at Mike and struggled for words. "I . . . I have a surprise," she said to Vin with forced enthusiasm. When she glanced back at Mike she looked like she'd rather crawl in a hole. "It's . . . paid off."

Vin's ears turned pink.

"Well . . . Mike . . ." Velvet began.

Mike shuffled his feet and hoped to hell she wasn't about to throw his ass under the bus.

"He, um . . . secured a loan," she said, glancing at Mike. "And paid our taxes."

Mike tried to maintain a blank expression but then shrugged.

Vin turned quiet as he scanned their faces. Then he sighed and stared down at his hands. He looked almost defeated, or maybe humbled, by the words Velvet had just pulled out of her ass.

Velvet gingerly touched Vin's arm. Dude didn't flinch.

After an uncomfortable silence, Vin tilted his head at his wife. "So you *didn't* sell the Kramer."

"I did, but not for that amount." Velvet parted her lips and muttered, "Not even close."

Vin angled toward Mike and narrowed his eyes. "I know Mays well enough to know he doesn't do shit like that unless . . . there's something in it for him."

"He was just trying to help," Velvet pleaded.

Vin angled toward her. "He's trying to buy himself a stay here, Velvet, but you're too kind to even realize that."

Velvet bowed her head.

"I oughta kick your ass out right now," Vin said, and Mike took a slight step back. "But I'm beat—jetlagged and hungry for *real* food. So I'm gonna let you slide for tonight."

Velvet avoided eye contact with Mike and gave Vin an admiring smile as she nudged him away. Vin fired a nasty glance at Mike and then let Velvet lead him from the barn.

Mike stood there, rubbing the back of his neck. He stared at the instruments stowed in their stands. Damn, having Vin home was fuckin' up everything. He needed to find a way to stay, regardless. He felt woozy for a second and then shook his head. Man, he really needed a smoke. He snatched his smokes off the amp and shoved a cig between his lips, turning when he heard the barn door slam. He grinned as Harley headed toward him, but she wasn't smiling.

She stopped in front of him and flung out her arms. "You got her drunk?" She just stood there, shaking her head, staring him down. "What were you thinking?"

Mike lit the cigarette dangling from his mouth. "I didn't fuck her—"

"Oh, here we go." She clenched her fists and turned away and then back again. "But you've fucked her over. You've fucked us *all* over."

Mike stood there puffing smoke, staring at her. He could feel the pinch of his brows. "That explains the cold shoulder." He took a drag and swayed away from her. "Ya don't understand, I got this record deal—"

"Don't bullshit me, Mike Mays."

"It ain't that, it's . . ." Somehow an excuse escaped him.

"You're not supposed to smoke inside."

Mike hated rules, but he turned and headed out of the barn.

"She told me everything," Harley shouted as the barn door slammed.

Mike exhaled and coughed, and then Harley appeared in front of him. *"Everything,"* he muttered. He could see Velvet in the distance as she lit the lanterns hanging above the table, then flitted like a little bird back inside the main house. She returned seconds later and handed the phone to Vin at the courtyard dining table.

"So what's this plan of yours?" Harley hissed.

"Babe." He cocked his head at her. "You know me—"

"That's what I'm afraid of," she mumbled. Her chin dipped to her chest and she scuffed her shoe on the gravel. "I'd been so happy to see you again. And now . . . oh, you've put Velvet in a real muddle."

Mike let out a booming laugh and then took another puff on his cigarette. "I got that shit covered."

She raised her chin. "What, were you thinking you'd sleep with her and she'd let you stay?"

"Trust me, bangin' Velvet is the farthest thing from my mind." He sucked on the cigarette and noticed the cherry glowing more brightly now in the dusk. "See, I got this dough comin'—"

"Don't bore me with bullshit."

"It ain't like that." Mike sagged against the barn and exhaled a cloud of smoke, followed by a cough. "Actually . . . thing is . . . it's . . . *you.*"

"Typical Mike Mays." She shook her head. "Only care about a shag."

"I mean it. When I saw ya the other day for the first time in . . . I just . . . somehow, well . . ." He sensed that she was softening a bit. "I dunno, Harl. I guess . . . I still dig ya—" Her laugh interrupted his thought. "It ain't funny. It's just that . . . after all these years . . . well, you're the only chick that—" The gleam in her eye made him pause.

"Falling for you again, love—" She crinkled her nose. "Not gonna happen."

Mike lowered his head and scuffed his shoe in the gravel before glancing back up at her.

"I love you, Mike. I really do." She brushed a strand of silvery hair from her eyes. "But just not in the way you think." She gave him a flat glance. "Nice try, but how are you going to get Velvet, all of us, out of this before—" She motioned toward the others and then hissed, "Before Vin finds out?"

He opened his mouth, but before he could respond he heard Velvet calling out their names with urgency. "Guys, come here!"

Mike flicked his cigarette into the courtyard and the two of them high-tailed it to the patio table. His eyes widened at the huge bowl of pasta and the spread of bread, cheese, tomatoes, and grilled asparagus. Fuckin' hell, he thought, rubbing his hands together, always a killer spread at Groove House. Then he noticed Velvet's shoulders had drooped, and he hoped it wasn't going to be the abrupt end to his residency.

She swallowed hard and glanced at Vin, who was still on the phone, before glancing at each person around the table. "We lost another. . . . Toby Blaine just died."

As chatter filled the courtyard, Mike stepped back a little and watched the different reactions.

"What happened?" Harley asked.

"Heart attack," Velvet said with a fleeting look at Vin. "He was having dinner with his family and just keeled over."

"'at's how I wanna go for a Burton," Tank noted. "Like shit off a shovel."

"He was such a love," Harley said, twisting a strand of hair.

"*Crushing* guitar player," Blitz said.

"About *your* age, I suspect," Harley noted to Blitz and then sighed. "Too young to go."

Mike stepped back a little farther, and looked at Harley—she was dry-eyed. That was another thing he dug about her: she didn't bawl, like most chicks, over every goddamn little thing.

"Well then," Harley calmly said and looked at Velvet. "Have everything we need?"

Velvet paused, as if taking mental inventory. "More wine."

Mike liked the sound of that, even though he had no clue what was goin' on.

Blitz slapped his hands on his thighs and pushed himself from the table. "I got it."

"I just now got back home," Vin said into the phone, and then glared coldly at Mike. "I'd need a few minutes to think about going back out on the road again so soon . . ." Velvet's gaze snapped toward Vin, who gave her a half-shrug. "Give me a few hours to think about it before you confirm anyone else. I'll call you back."

Mike slipped further away from the group and squinted at the commotion in the growing darkness. He shoved a cigarette between his lips and watched everyone dashing around. He flinched when his ass cheek began vibrating. Keeping his eyes fixed on the courtyard, he dug into his jeans pocket.

"C'mon!" Harley shouted, gesturing for Mike to join them.

He tugged the phone from his pocket, wondering why it didn't ring. Right, he'd set it to vibrate while jammin' in the barn. Mike peeled his stare off Harley and glanced down at the display: *Brayden*. Damn, he was supposed to Skype with the kid.

"Mike!" He looked up to see Harley impatiently waving him over.

Chewing his lip, he let out a heavy sigh and lifted the phone to his ear. "Hey, kid."

"Hey, Gramps, remember we're supposed to—"

"There's some real heavy shit goin' down right now," Mike interrupted as he glanced around the courtyard. "I gotta call ya back."

"Mike!" Harley called out, still waving him forward. *"Forget-Me-Not Forest* . . ."

"But I just wanted to—"

"This is real important, kid." The commotion in the courtyard made him anxious.

"But you'll never guess what—"

"I gotta split. I'll call ya right back. I swear."

Mike switched off his phone and wondered why he should give a fuck about Toby Blaine anyway. He stood there in the dusk, jaw clenched, watching the others.

Velvet trailed the line of friends through the rugged darkness, toward the silhouette of the hill near the property's edge. As she glanced ahead at everyone, goods in tow, the candles they held glimmering under the Tuscan night sky, she felt as though their ritual seemed to be happening more often lately . . . too often. She struggled not to be so damned emotional. Nerves, she suspected. So much had happened the past few days and it had left her exhausted. She looked up at the rising full moon and then glanced at Vin, the man she loved so much; she hated herself for what she had let Mike talk her into doing in a moment of weakness. It gnawed at her gut. She would tell Vin everything, she decided with a sigh . . . tonight.

On the hilltop, Vin reached toward Blitz for the shovel. Mike coughed and just stood there, watching Vin as he began to dig. Velvet smiled weakly at her husband as he pitched the dirt; she knew how much he loved the land. Tank stepped in with the bag of soil, eager to please. Velvet knelt and placed the slender sapling into the ground, whispering, "For Toby."

"*Forget-Me-Not*," Blitz said to Mike. "Get it?"

As Vin rose and dusted off his jeans, Velvet looked up at him admiringly. It hurt, keeping the land deal from him. She would tell him straight away, she vowed to herself. But as the group meandered to the other end of the plateau, and Vin and Tank began building a fire in the brick pit, she waffled. *Maybe not tonight*, she thought as she spread a blanket on the ground. He had barely been home a few hours.

She missed the days when it was just the two of them . . . when they were renovating the old farmhouse together, working long hours past sundown even though every muscle ached—and they had loved every grueling minute. The sound of Tank popping the cork from the Sangiovese snapped Velvet from her thoughts, as Harley began to play Toby Blaine's "Blink of an Eye" on the acoustic guitar and the brightest of stars twinkled above.

Vin scooted next to Velvet on the blanket and rubbed her arm. She grasped his hand, closed her eyes, and enjoyed the warmth of his touch. It felt so good to have him home. A distant drone lulled her, like the purr of a neighbor's lawnmower on a lazy summer afternoon . . . or maybe it was cicadas. She just lay there and for once didn't feel guilty for indulging in a moment of relaxation. She felt Vin get up, but she just lay there and began to doze. All the trees they had planted to honor fallen rock heroes— Ronnie James Dio, Kevin DuBrow, Gary Moore, Ronnie Montrose, Phil Kennemore. . . .

Then she heard Vin shouting. "What the fuck? . . . Who the hell is on my land?"

Velvet sat up and traced the sound of Vin's voice. In the moonlight, she could see him at the edge of the plateau. Those weren't cicadas, she realized. That was the distant sound of machinery.

"What is it?" Tank asked, moving toward Vin.

"Motherfucker has a bulldozer!" Vin exclaimed. "In my *nonna's* vineyard!"

Velvet gulped hard. As Vin bolted down the hill, she sprang to her feet and ran to the edge of the hilltop. "Vin!" she shouted. "Wait, let me explain." But with the distance growing between them, he didn't appear to hear her and he never looked back. Knocking Tank aside, Velvet cleared a path to chase after her husband. If he got to Carlo first—before she had a chance to explain—there would surely be blood. Under the light of the full moon, she sprinted down the hill, trying like hell to catch him.

Her thighs burned with every jogging step, and the dirt felt spongy as she struggled to maintain her footing. As the roar of the bulldozer grew closer, she heard Vin yelling: *Basta! Basta! Che sta facendo?* Her heart throbbed in her throat.

"Vin!" Velvet hollered. Then Carlo came into focus, at the helm of the bulldozer, sneering at the fast-approaching Vin. She lost her footing and her ankle twisted sideways. She winced and slowed to an aching hop. She doubled over, hands on her thighs, as the others barreled past her. For chrissake, she thought, why do they have to stick their noses in everything? She limped toward the property line, where the two men at the boundary glowered at each other—Carlo on the bulldozer and Vin in front of it. Giulia's white Alfa Romeo zoomed into the vineyard, leaving a trail of dust.

"What the hell are you doing?" Vin screamed.

Carlo ignored him and revved the bulldozer engine.

"Vin!" Velvet cried out, panting as she staggered closer, past the others. Giulia jaunted to Carlo and rattled off something in rapid-fire Italian but Velvet couldn't make out a single word.

Carlo cut the engine and wiped his hands on his button-down shirt. He turned and ordered Vin, "Go home. Talk to your wife."

"What's my wife got to do with this?"

"Vin!" Velvet winced, as the pain in her ankle flared.

As Carlo climbed down from the bulldozer, Giulia grasped his arm. He shook his head at Vin and said, *"Tra moglie e marito non mettere il dito."*

Velvet inched closer but then turned at the sound of Blitz's voice behind her.

"What's going on?"

"Not now, Blitz." The rest of them came up and stood beside her, except for Mike, who kept his distance.

"What'd he say?" Tank asked.

"Something about putting a finger between husband and wife."

She limped over to her husband and he turned to her, the vein in his temple pulsing in the moonlight.

"When were you planning to tell me that you *sold my fucking land?*"

She shrunk from him, unable to even wipe the beads of sweat she felt trickling down her forehead.

He clenched his jaw. "Huh?"

In the four decades they'd been married, she had never seen Vin like this. She could feel her lips trembling. She pressed on the knot in her stomach and felt dizzy, nauseated. "Please." She looked past Vin and pleaded to Carlo. "Please don't bulldoze the land. Giulia—"

Carlo belly-laughed, and said, "A fool bulldozer at night." He shot a smug glance around the group standing in the old vineyard. "Tonight I only check. See if this run good."

"No bulldozer tonight," Giulia assured.

Carlo stood at the boundary, hands on hips. "I bulldozer tomorrow."

Vin lunged forward. "Motherfu—"

"Steady past yer granny's," Tank warned as he and Blitz grabbed Vin's arms, stopping him from tackling Carlo. Tank hissed into Vin's ear, "Don't mess with the mob, geeze."

"This is *my* land," Vin shouted as he shook free from their hold.

"Please," Velvet pleaded to Carlo. "I was wrong. I'll give you back the money. Just please don't—" Desperate, she turned to Vin. "The taxes. We're so broke," she reasoned. "And you'd wasted so much trying to revive this old vineyard—"

"*Wasted?*" Vin challenged, his face contorted.

"Spent . . . whatever . . . it's gone. And *you* were gone." She knew she sounded whiny. "And the money was running out, and Carlo's been wanting this land for so long, and—"

"Now is my land," Carlo boasted.

"Please," Velvet repeated her plea. When she reached out to Vin, he pushed her hand away. She closed her eyes and felt the tears trickling onto her cheeks. "Vin," she whispered. She glanced at Mike but he stepped back. Of course—this was Mike, he wasn't going to admit any blame. She looked at Harley, who gave her a concerned nod. "Vin," Velvet whispered between sobs as she clutched her arms close against her stomach. "I'm so sorry."

"This is *my* land!" Vin insisted. He turned to Velvet. "How could you? *Nonna's* vineyard means everything to me. You knew that, Velvet." Vin's eyes watered as he choked up. "You fucking *knew* that."

Mike took another step backward.

"I know," Velvet said softly. Her eyes welled up as she watched Vin fight back tears. She hadn't seen him cry since his grandmother had died. "I'm so sorry. I don't know what I was thinking—"

"My entire heritage has just been sold out from under me!" Vin sputtered.

"Only a small piece," she moaned. She took a deep, pained breath and pressed her arms against her stomach. "I'll get the land back. I promise—"

"I'm busting my ass for peanuts just to make ends meet," Vin shouted, his voice breaking. "Traipsing all over Europe and the States, subbing for guitarists whose tunes I don't even like, in shitty little clubs, trying to bring money to this household . . . and you do *this* behind my back?" He stood there, scowling, his brows drawn together and his breathing heavy. Then he nodded to his friends standing behind Velvet. "You guys knew about this?"

"No . . . hell no," Tank and Blitz muttered as they shook their heads.

Velvet dipped her chin. She could barely glance at the others. How humiliating for Vin, she thought, to bare his soul in front of everyone . . . especially Carlo and Giulia.

Vin glowered at Mike and then her. "I take it there was no loan, then."

Velvet stood withering as Vin's cold eyes burned into her, his fists clenched, his breathing raspy. She felt helpless, unable to move except to just blink at him. He turned away from her and stared up the hill. Mike just stood there, scuffing his feet in the dirt, and didn't offer up one word. Tears streamed down Velvet's cheeks, and she felt so ashamed that she couldn't bring herself to point blame at Mike and admit that she'd been coerced by him and a bottle of Sangiovese.

"You want the land?" Carlo asked with a sneer. He folded his arms. "Okay. You can have . . . for two times the price."

"Che palle!" Vin turned and lunged for Carlo again, but Tank and Blitz held him back.

What balls, is right, Velvet thought.

Carlo sneered at Mike. "Because this . . . *uomo galante*. . . . He touch my beautiful wife so the price is now double."

Velvet glowered at Mike.

"Oh, that fucking figures," Vin snarled.

Giulia flung her hands as she spit out words at breakneck speed. She shouted so fast at Carlo that, once again, Velvet couldn't understand. Carlo seemed indifferent to Giulia's words, yet he then stepped away with her.

Vin shook himself from Tank's and Blitz's grasp. He glared at Mike and then fired a final, cutting look toward Carlo's back. *"Vaffanculo."* Then he turned and stomped through the vineyard in the direction of home.

Velvet reached out to him. "Vin!"

"I can't even look at you," he yelled without turning back. "Don't come after me. Just . . . don't."

Velvet stood there in the moonlit vineyard that, thanks to her, no longer belonged to Vin. As her husband climbed the hill, she watched the distance grow between them. She felt a chill as it dawned on her that he might just accept that new offer to sub on tour, and once again leave her solo to deal with everything.

"Have a heart, dude," Mike hollered out to Carlo. "Don't bulldoze. Give Vin a chance to swallow all this first."

Carlo turned and snickered while Giulia ushered him away.

Tank crossed his arms and squinted. "So you wasn't sellin' them guitars to pay off the taxes?"

Velvet knew that he specifically meant the Kramer, but she just stood there, utterly despondent as tears streamed down both cheeks and dripped onto the vineyard soil. She didn't even have the strength to reply. As she looked up toward Forget-Me-Not Forest, she saw Vin's silhouette crest the hill and disappear into the shitty night.

Chapter 23

Mike lay on the bed having a smoke, watching the cherry glow brighter in the darkness as he sucked in. As he tossed around ways to get some dough and ensure a roof over his head, a knock at the door startled him. He coughed and fumbled around the nightstand for the water glass—his makeshift ashtray. He snuffed out the cig and flicked on the light. Moving toward the door, he fanned the air, hoping to kill the smoke. "Who is it?" he asked, placing his hand on the doorknob.

"Who do you think, at this hour?" said Harley through the closed door. "Open up, old man."

Mike grinned. Fuckin' hell, he figured, finally sex with Harley again after all these years. When he opened the door, his shoulders slumped. She was wearing black pants and a pullover sweater, about as revealing as a ninja. Most of the women who'd knocked on his door through the years arrived wearing almost nothin' at all. At least she'd brought an enticing haul: two bottles of wine, a corkscrew, and two glasses. "Ah, red, my fave. Doll, you rock."

"Anything that gives a buzz is *your* favorite," Harley teased as she entered Mike's room. "Ooh, naughty boy, smoking inside." With an impish grin, she added, "Give us a fag, then."

Mike laughed—she still had that rebellious spirit he used to dig. He grabbed the pack of smokes from the nightstand and lit a cig while Harley popped the cork and filled both glasses. Then he wondered: she'd shut him down the other day, so why the sudden change of heart? He shrugged it off and decided to roll with it. The two rebels settled onto the bed, disobeying house rules as they shared a cigarette and a bottle of wine.

"Car's still gone," Harley said as she slid the cig from Mike's fingers. She inhaled the smoke and then let it out as she spoke. "You don't suppose he'll take Toby's sub gig, do you?"

"Dunno." Mike guzzled the wine.

"So," Harley said with a forced smile. "Record advance, eh?"

Mike choked down the wine, tempted to just tell her there was no deal. She held the cigarette out in front of his face, breaking his thought.

"How many songs have you written so far?" She swigged the wine from her glass. "For your . . . new album."

Mike took the cig and a drag and looked at Harley again. He knew her well enough, and suspected she might be testing him. Or maybe she was startin' to believe him. "This gettin' old shit sucks . . . not knowin' how we're gonna make it, money-wise, till we croak." He gulped the last drop and then reached out his glass for a refill. "More numbin' meds," he teased.

Harley leaned forward, lifted the bottle from the floor, and eyeballed the contents. She poured wine into each glass and then inspected the last bit in the bottle. "Oh, what the hell," she said and then drained it, filling both glasses nearly to the top. "Dead soldier." She rolled the empty bottle across the tiles. "So, Velvet said you have a plan?"

Mike examined the tile floor as he took a drag. "What's the big deal with that gnarly old vineyard, anyway?" he asked, blowing smoke rings.

"Sentimental." She reached out and smashed the rings, just like she always used to do. "Vin spent summers here as a boy, helped his grandmother tend that vineyard. Means everything to him."

"Fuck." Mike leaned forward and sat on the edge of the bed. "I had no idea."

"So what's this plan?" She reached into her pocket, held up a joint, and winked. Then she lounged back onto the bed, propping a pillow behind her.

"Now yer talkin'." Mike snuffed the cigarette into the water glass on the nightstand and then reached over to light the joint in Harley's hand. He stared at her and smiled. He was twenty-four again and he and Harley were taking on the world—one tour date at a time. "Remember how you and I used to get high and jam till the sun came up?" he asked, sliding the joint from her fingers and happy to change the subject. He inhaled the sweet leaf, held it in, and then coughed out smoke. "In hotel rooms, my apartment, your pad." He took another hit and spoke as he held in the smoke. "Yer the only chick who could drink me under the table," he said, passing the joint back to Harley. He could tell by her lingering smile that she dug the memories they shared.

She took a hit, a gulp of wine, and then lay back smiling. She laughed and gave him a playful nudge. "We had a good life, didn't we?"

He couldn't tell if she was playin' him. "Yeah, we were great together." He turned and snuggled close to her, but she gave him a gentle push.

"Not *us* us. Our careers. I mean, we didn't make loads like AC/DC or Ozzy—"

"Not even close," Mike interrupted as he handed her the joint and then guzzled more wine. "You still rock, Harl. Still a killer guitarist . . . for a chick."

"Bloody wanker." She smacked his arm, took another hit off the joint and then the wine. "In the end, I'd say it was a decent career. Hard as hell, but good. We had a great time . . . even though we struggled." She handed him the joint. "Can't imagine trying to have a go at it now. How a musician can make a living these days when everyone just downloads music for free is beyond me. Damn near pointless, really." She gulped from her glass. "It's here, you know. The day the music died."

"Not *everyone* downloads." Mike sucked in the smoke and then chugged his wine. "The *real* fans support the artists they like, buy the music."

"Too hard to survive anymore. . . . Don't know how you could release another album in this musical climate. I mean, who the hell would buy it?"

Babes had a way of tryin' to reel him in. Mike grinned—man, he dug her. He knocked back the last drops in his glass and then cleared his throat. "Oh man, too much blood in my alcohol stream." He handed her the corkscrew and what was left of the joint.

Harley giggled. "You finish it," she said, as she reached for the second bottle. "Given the situation," she paused with a smile. "Couldn't you just ring Bruce to put pressure on the label? If anyone can get them to rush the advance, he can."

Mike took a final toke before snuffing the joint. He didn't have the heart, or maybe it was the balls, to tell her the truth. What would he say? That Bruce had basically canned his ass, told him his career was toast? What artist ever wants to admit to that shit? He held his wine glass out to Harley. She obliged and then settled back onto the bed. When she gave Mike that sexy smile, he couldn't help himself. He leaned in and pressed his lips against hers. She caved and they lingered in a deep kiss. Her lips felt amazing. His pulse raced. God, he missed her touch . . . or maybe he was just horny. Just as his skin began tingling, she gently pushed him back.

"That felt . . . bloody brilliant," she said, touching her lips before taking another swig of wine. "But I won't go there again." She sat up a little. "We tried it decades ago and then again later, but not now. It means a lot to me to have you back in my life, and I don't want to ruin our friendship . . . ever again."

Mike rubbed his chin. "So what are we doin' here?"

"Getting high. Talking. Enjoying each other's company. If you could keep your cock in your pants for once you'd realize it's what friends do." She let out a frustrated sigh and then looked into his eyes. "I adore you, Mike Mays. I love just being near you again. Isn't that enough?" She snuggled up next to him and closed her eyes for a moment.

No, Mike thought, that wasn't enough. He held her close and rubbed her arm. His body pulsated, aching to be with her. But her signals seemed mixed. He twisted a strand of her silvery blonde hair and wondered if they could still be good together again. "Ya know, there wasn't a single chick I ever slept with that I loved—"

"Thanks a lot," she said, straining to look up at him before settling back into his arms.

"I mean, we were young back then . . . and now, well, ya know, I think—"

"You're high and horny, that's all." She giggled and took another gulp of wine. "Maybe I shouldn't sit so close to you," she teased, inching away before he pulled her back. She sank into him and turned reflective again. "So . . . not even the mother of your daughter?"

Mike loosened his grip and leaned over to the nightstand. He could feel the scrunch of his brows as he slid a cig from the pack and slipped it between his lips. Harley took the lighter from his hand and flicked it as Mike puffed. "You know damn well—" He blew the smoke from his mouth and coughed. "I didn't plan on that."

"No skirt chaser ever does." She turned away from him. "Sorry, that was mean." She took a gulp of wine. "Mmm, but you gained a lovely daughter—"

Mike grunted. "Lovely, my ass. She tried to put me out to pasture. . . . Can you believe that shit?"

"Well, she gave you a brilliant grandson."

"Shit! The kid! . . . He rang me earlier tonight. I'm too fucked up to call him back now."

"He reminds me of you, in a way . . . only he's a right little angel."

Mike laughed and then dropped his smile. "She never got me, ya know . . . Lydia . . . especially after Em died. . . . Told my grandkid I was dead, for chrissake. Imagine lyin' to yer own kid all them years." He glanced at her and then smiled as he thought about the other day in the office. "Thanks . . . for sortin' me out with the kid . . . on that Skype thing."

Harley smiled and reached for the cig. "Give us a drag." She took several slow, long hits and then returned it to him, making a point to touch his hand. "I remember the day she cut you from his life. You called me from their driveway, hammered and raging—"

"I did?"

"Yeah." She reached the cig toward him.

He rubbed his chin. "I remember talkin' to ya later, but not—"

"You'd gone mental. You were all gakked up, wanted more blow, said you'd find a way to take the baby from her." She took a drag off the cig. "The thought of losing Lydia and that little baby was unbearable. I was quite touched you'd reached out to me."

Mike slid the cig from her fingers. He'd reached out to her alright, just before he fell into a downward spiral and outta touch with everyone who'd played any part in his life.

Harley pushed herself upright, set her glass on the floor, and turned to Mike. "I think I loved you still . . . even then, hurt as I was." She let out a lengthy sigh. "You've never had a stomach for commitment." Then she stared out into the room.

Mike lay there, silent, numb. Harley was the only chick who accepted him for who he was, the full fucked up package.

"Ooh." Harley shook her head and held her hand to her forehead. "I'm bloody smashed."

Mike reached up and played with her hair. "Me too."

"I've got to have a lie-down." She cozied up to him, settled in, and sighed. "She trusted you, you know. . . . Velvet."

Mike raked his fingers through her silvery hair. He didn't want to think about anything but Harley.

"You're a hard-lovin' man, Mike Mays. . . . I hope to hell you know what you're doing. . . . Your . . . plan . . ."

He pulled her close and kissed the top of her head. As he held her, he felt her body relax. "We've been through a lot together, Harl." They lay there in silence. At one point he thought she might've been cryin' . . . just a little. But thankfully, that thought split once he heard snoring. When she turned and pressed herself into the mattress, he smiled, lifted her head, and propped it onto the pillow. When he rubbed her arm, she moved it away. He pulled the bed sheet over her, kissed her cheek, and whispered, "I think you might just be the best friend I have, Harley Yeates." She let out a drunken coo as she snuggled deeper under the sheet.

The room began to spin. Mike rolled his body toward the pack of smokes on the nightstand and withdrew another cigarette. He wedged it between his lips, flicked the lighter, and inhaled deeply, which made him cough. He looked at Harley passed out beside him—fully clothed, dammit. That's not how he'd expected the night would go when she showed up at his door armed with two bottles of booze. He took a drag and slid a strand of hair from her face. It'd been kinda cool to just lay there and talk. He took another drag and then turned off the light and sank into the bed.

The room didn't seem to spin as much in darkness. With each puff he watched the cherry glow and listened to the soft crackle of the burning paper and tobacco. He heard Harley rustling under the sheet as she turned toward him, still out. He turned and snuggled up to her. It kinda felt like they had just fucked. He pressed against her warm body, noticing her tits were still pretty damn firm. He held her close but she stayed zonked out. She smacked her lips a few times and pulled away, turning her back to him and taking the sheet with her. Mike took a drag off the cig and grinned. He dangled his arm off the bed and thought of the young, blonde Harley, strutting across the stage, wailing on her favorite red Yamaha SG guitar—the way she stooped and then arched when she stretched a note, the killer tone she got out of that old Marshall JMP 2203. She was always hot, so . . . damn . . . hot . . .

Then he was opening his eyes, choking as someone pulled at him. "What the hell?" A figure came into focus. It was Blitz yanking on his arm. What kinda weird dream was this, he wondered. "Stop. Yer killin' my buzz."

"Wake up!" Blitz screeched in that annoying high-strung tone.

The sting of the slap on Mike's cheek was no dream. Man, the room seemed hot and smoky. He rolled his tongue around his dry mouth. Then he looked right and saw flames. "Oh, fuck!" He knew he had to get outta bed, but he couldn't move. He felt woozy. He looked to his left but Harley was gone.

"I got it," Blitz yelled, waving Tank from the room. "Move!" He yanked Mike's arm. "Or I'll leave your sorry ass here to suffocate," Blitz grunted as he heaved so hard Mike thought he might just pull his arm straight out of its socket.

Mike lunged for the door but the bed sheet tripped him up and he toppled to the floor. His body trembling, he glanced around, gave himself an unsteady push upward and then bolted out the door. Once outside, he coughed and felt wobbly. Before he could take another step, Blitz grabbed his arm again and ushered him into the courtyard.

"Let me in there," Velvet cried, as Tank held her arms and sat her on the bench at the patio dining table. She struggled to break free. "I have to get—"

"The armoire's in flames," Blitz said as he led Mike to a chaise lounge next to Harley. "I'm so sorry, Velvet."

Mike watched Velvet sob as he passed. "Fuckin' hell—"

"Fuckin' 'ell's right, geeze," Tank said to Mike as he held Velvet close. "Look what you done."

Fuck off, Mike started to say but decided to curb it at the "F." He exchanged glances with Tank, who held a bawling Velvet in his arms. He noticed Harley balled up in a lounge chair, hunched over her knees, cradling her legs.

"The money!" Velvet moaned as she rocked back and forth, head in her hands. "What am I going to do? I'll never get the land back now." Her wails filled the dim courtyard.

Mike's head swirled in the chaos. He rubbed at his throbbing temples and squinted out toward the faint hint of rising sunlight. *"The money?"*

"I gave it to you," Velvet sobbed. "Right as Vin came home." She glared at him and then bawled, "You knew that cash was in your room!"

Shit, he'd forgotten all about that messenger bag. He set a foot forward, intending to backtrack across the courtyard, but Blitz held him back.

"Them bucks is nothin' but ashes now," Blitz informed him.

"Euros," Velvet said in a flat voice. Then she aimed her puffy eyes at Mike. "You did it on purpose. . . . I know you did!"

Tank cradled her. "I know Mike well enough to know he wouldn't do that, V."

Blitz leaned in to Mike's ear and hissed, "I know you started the fire, asshole."

"Fuck off," Mike said, shaking his arm loose from Blitz's grip. "I ain't no arsonist."

Blitz angled toward him and lowered his voice. "Dude, I saw you smoking in that room—Gallo's room. I saw your cigarette butts just minutes ago." He leaned in and hissed, "Buncha butts right under the burned curtains. . . . Face up, man, it's *your* fault." He glanced at Velvet when she let out another wail, then he pulled away and nudged Mike toward a lounge chair. "Now sit down, shut up, and be happy I smelled smoke and saved your raggedy ass."

Mike lowered himself into the lounge chair. *Washed-up. History.* Of all the lame-ass times, Mike thought, for Bruce's words to pop into his head.

Harley was still curled up in the lounge chair.

"For chrissake, Harl." Blitz said to her. "Stop trying to relive your past with this dude. You're not a rock star anymore. . . . Get over yourself. . . . If Gallo were here he'd kick your ass." He glared at Mike. "And yours."

"I told you," Harley barked. "It was purely a reconnaissance mission . . . for Velvet. I was trying to get the truth out of him." She pointed at Mike but averted her eyes. "About the money he has coming, and his plan to get the vineyard back."

Mike's chest felt tight and he couldn't breathe. He could swear he felt his heartbeat stop for a moment. Shit, he wondered, Harley's visit to his room wasn't even legit? Or was she just trying to redeem herself to them?

He glanced at Velvet, sobbing, her head still buried in her hands. At the sound of a vehicle driving up the gravel road, he saw her lift her head, and look hopefully toward the edge of the courtyard. But it wasn't Vin.

As the truck turned in, Mike could see the words across the front: VIGILI DEL FUOCO. He didn't need to understand Italian to recognize a fire truck. Mike watched the firemen scramble toward his smoky quarters as Harley cradled her knees in the lounge, and Velvet still sobbed—not only about the fire damage, or her missing husband, but, Mike figured, all that dough from Carlo now burned to ashes. Damn, why'd she have to give him all that cash to stash, anyway?

As he watched the chaos, he felt woozy, nauseated even. Hell, he hadn't thrown up since his dark days, after Lydia banned him from her life all those years ago. He felt his phone vibrating in his pants, and as he pulled it out he recognized the ringtone. *Brayden.*

The puke rose in his throat and he rocketed from the lounge chair and pushed through the door of the main house, running, hand over his mouth until he reached the bathroom. The toilet was too low for his aching muscles, so he let loose and blew chunks into the basin. Steadying himself after the last hurl, he turned on the faucet and sloshed the sink clean. Then he splashed water onto his face and looked in the mirror. He swiped at a puke-covered strand of hair and then leaned on the sink for a rest and listened to his heavy breathing. The commotion outside seemed to fill the bathroom and he felt woozy again. As he stared at the weathered face in the mirror, his ass vibrated again, followed by the familiar ringtone. He reached into his pocket for the cell phone and squinted at the display. Fuckin' hell, he mused, the kid's got rotten timing. As another wave of nausea struck, the bedlam outside swelled, and the relentless ringtone echoed, Mike dropped to his knees and hugged the toilet for the next round.

Chapter 24

Mike woke up staring at blue sky. The damn birds circling above made him dizzy and their high-pitched screeching made his head ache; he thought he might hurl. Some flowery scent in the air made his nose tingle. Shit, he was on a bench on one of the terraces. He pushed himself upright and shook his head to try clearing the fog. He glanced at his phone—it was 10:00 a.m. He remembered Velvet's wailing had kept him awake for hours, but it was quiet now. Then Harley's voice wafted down from the courtyard above.

"She's called Vin's cell a hundred times, but he won't answer."

"A perfectly good life," Blitz griped. "Now ruined."

"They'll be forced to sell the house," Tank said.

"Then what?" Blitz asked, his voice strained. "We have to return to the States? Move in with relatives? Live in government housing? This is fucked up."

"I'm skint," Tank said. "I ain't got nowhere to go."

Tank sounded rattled. Mike knew that this was his only home . . . apparently, *everyone's* only home.

The talk soon fizzled and Mike got up from the bench and trudged up the path to the empty courtyard. He glanced around but saw no one. When he eyeballed the scorched building, he wondered where he'd sleep now that his charred quarters reeked of smoke. His head throbbed and he shuffled forward, nearly tripping over a box of clothes. The lounge chair looked appealing, so he settled in. As the haze overtook him, he dozed off.

"Gee, let me guess which lame-ass burned down the house."

Mike opened his eyes to see Gallo standing there, duffel bag in hand.

"Dahling," Harley said as she rushed to him. "You back to stay?"

"I'm not letting that prick," he said, nodding toward Mike, "kick me outta my home."

Blitz smiled ruefully from the kitchen doorway and then sneered over at Mike before he turned back to Gallo. "Uh, dude, here's the thing. . . . All your shit's burned." The colored bangles on Blitz's wrist clanked as he fluffed up his ratted hair and headed for a patio chair.

Gallo slowly cocked his head, and his eyes cut toward his burned quarters and then over at Mike.

Tank stepped into the courtyard. "All's left is that box, geeze." He pointed at the box of clothes on the patio and then eased into the chair beside Blitz.

"Motherfucker!" Gallo tossed his bag on the table and lunged for Mike, but Harley held him back.

Grasping his arm, she nodded toward his duffel. "I know the things you most care for are in there."

Gallo glanced at her and then shook himself free, going straight for the box. He rooted through it, tossing one piece of clothing after another. "My concert shirts!" he yelled. "Where are they?"

"Burned, geeze." Tank grimaced and slid his chair into the shade of the overhang.

Gallo practically bared his teeth at Mike. "I had T-shirts from as far back as 1975 . . . Purple, Sabbath, Queen, Boston, ELO, Lizzy—Jesus, I even had an Allman Brothers shirt from the Whisky just weeks before Duane died."

"October '71," Mike said. "They played Winterland *two* weeks before he died. I partied with Duane that weekend—"

"Fuck you and your bullshit stories," Gallo snapped.

"Where ya gonna sleep, geeze?" Tank asked Gallo and then looked at Mike. "And where *you* gonna sleep?"

"I'll shack up with Harley," Mike suggested with a glance at Gallo.

"Not going to happen," Harley said, and turned to stare at the charred building.

"Gallo should room with her," Tank suggested. "He's the one shagging her every night."

Harley fired a daggered glance at Tank. "Not *every* night."

Whoa. Mike felt his hands go limp. He thought about last night with Harley before the fire and all that *just friends* bullshit.

"The bed didn't burn," Harley said, clearing her throat, as if deflecting her *thing* with Gallo. She turned to Blitz. "Why not drag the mattress into *your* room?"

Blitz sneered at Mike. "I'm not rooming with that . . . Neanderthal."

"I'd rather sleep on the couch," Mike crowed, even though he recalled how uncomfortable it'd been his first night.

"Velvet won't stand for that," Harley said, staring flatly at Mike. "Anyway, I meant Gallo and Blitz."

"Why not Gallo and Mike?" Blitz lamely suggested.

"If I'm in the same room with that asshole," Gallo snarled, "sure as shit one of us'll land in an Italian jail." He glared at Mike. "You burned my shit. *I* get the couch."

"Tank's got the bigger room," Blitz tried to bargain. "Drag the bed in there."

"No way," Mike said with a laugh. "I've roomed with that dude on the road and he snores at like, 120 dB."

Harley turned toward the edge of the courtyard as Velvet appeared, pushing an old bike up from the driveway. "Velvet," she called out.

Velvet looked up and spotted Gallo in the courtyard. Mike watched as she dropped the bike and rushed over to embrace him. "We've been worried sick about you."

"Yeah, so much so," Gallo snapped with a glower at Mike, "that you let Mays kipe my room. . . . We—I—heard about the fire." Gallo stared at the ground.

"I'm sorry," she said, putting a hand on his arm. "I know how hard—"

"Everything," he said miserably. "Except some shit I got here in this box. And what I had in my duffel." He sighed, shaking his head. "Velvet," he said earnestly. "My t-shirt collection." He turned to stare at Mike, his eyes misty. *"What the fuck?"*

Velvet pulled back and looked him in the eye. "Have you seen Vin? I've been on that bicycle looking everywhere."

"He was just—" Blitz started to say. As he pointed halfheartedly toward the driveway, Tank smacked him on the arm.

"You mean he was here?" Velvet hugged her shoulders and craned her neck toward the gravel drive.

"You just missed him," Harley admitted. "Shortly after you left. He got some . . . things."

"Things?" Velvet said with a pained stare.

"He's so pissed off right now," Gallo said as he grabbed a chair next to Blitz at the patio table. "He can't even speak to you."

"He don't want you callin'," Tank added.

"Probably needs his space," Mike said, but everyone just sort of ignored him.

Velvet chewed on her lip.

"Dahling," Harley said, as she placed a comforting hand on Velvet's arm. "He took the tour. He's going to sub for Toby."

"You mean . . ." Velvet frowned. "Did he already leave?"

Mike shuddered at the thought of subbing for someone else on a tour. No way he'd ever play anyone else's shit, no matter how desperate.

"I've got to go find him. I'll try the village again," Velvet uttered.

"No, love—please. He's really gone," Harley pleaded.

But Velvet lifted the bike as if in a trance and pedaled out of the courtyard and down the gravel drive.

"This is our home, asshole," Gallo barked. "That was *my* room." He lowered himself into the chair and stared at Mike. "Why'd you have to come here and fuck it all up?"

"How do you know *I* did anything?" Mike defended. "This dump's got bad wiring."

Blitz leaned forward, his elbows on the table. "The fire department said it was a cigarette."

Mike glared at Blitz, who shook his head. "They dunno everything." He coughed and crossed his knees in the lounge chair. He reached for a cigarette and then thought better of it . . . for the moment.

Tank got up from the chair and scratched his bristly head. "Geezers, we got to muck in and help Vin and Velvet . . . or we *all* lose this place."

"I could look for a job," Blitz offered.

Harley smacked him on the head. "What the bloody hell are you going to do, dumbass?"

"Make that fucker pay," Gallo blustered, pointing across the table and over at Mike.

Mike felt the weight of the cold, uncomfortable stares from around the courtyard. He glanced down at his chest, which felt tight again. Fuck, they were all blaming him. He wasn't the one who'd sold the land, or forced someone to stash the cash in a hurry. That was the real problem and it was Velvet's fault. He coughed and looked up to see them still staring. "I got this thing. CO . . . DC."

"What'd he say? *DC?*" Gallo smirked. "Still got a boner for Coverdale, I see."

Mike shook his head. "No, I got this . . ." He coughed again. "The smoke from the fire fucked up my lungs."

"*You* fucked up." Gallo's eyes seemed like they could cut right through him.

"Dude." Mike dragged his fingers down his cheeks, tracking fake tears. "I saved your life. Remember that night in '85? I gave you mouth-to-mouth? I tasted your vomit, man. I'm the one who got the paramedics out to save your ass."

"Fuck you, Mays," Gallo snapped.

Blitz narrowed his eyes. "I shoulda kicked your ass when I had the chance."

Mike fidgeted in the lounge chair. He tightened his fists and glanced around the courtyard before turning back to Blitz. "Get over it, dude. Yeah, I fucked yer wife, but I ain't the one she split with. You should be after Mick Johnson, not me."

Blitz glowered at Mike and shook his head.

Mike forced a grin. "And now *you* saved *my* life. See? That's what friends do."

"Friends don't drive everyone away," Blitz said.

Mike felt uneasy. "I'm gonna get this record advance." He looked down at his pack of smokes. "I'll call about it again today—soon as those record label cats wake up in America."

Mike didn't look up again. Instead, he tuned out all the bitching and lit a cigarette. He thought about the last thing he remembered from the night before—that cig and his arm dangling off the bed. Maybe the firemen were right, and maybe they weren't, but shit, he oughta do something to help these guys. He wondered how he could get ahold of some quick cash. Two solutions crashed in . . . and he hated them both. But he had to try. He gave a lengthy sigh, snuffed out his cig in the patio ashtray, and headed to the edge of the courtyard.

He walked down past the garden and the bench where he'd crashed last night, to the pool below, and pulled the cell phone from his pocket. Those fuckin' annoying birds circled above, chirping as they swirled around and around in the blue sky. As he parked his ass on the low stone wall, he flinched when he saw a small scorpion between the stones. "Fuckin' hell!" he blurted. Close but guarded inspection with a twig proved it was dead. Safe from a scorpion sting, he settled back onto the wall and looked down at his phone. Before he could dial, he felt a cramp in his calf. Damn, he thought, a shotta whisky would be perfect right about now; it wasn't quite noon but that had never stopped him. Fuck it. He took a deep breath and braced himself for the last thing he ever wanted to do. "Here goes nothin'," he muttered as he pressed the speed dial button.

"Hey. . . . It's yer ol' man."

"What are you, drunk?" Lydia snapped. "You seem to have a penchant for calling at ungodly hours," she hissed. "Your grandson tried to reach you all day yesterday. Where have you been?"

"Darlin'," Mike confessed. "Some people here . . . well . . . there was this fire last night. And my shit got burned. . . . And, ya know, I gotta . . . poor Vin and Velvet, man. I gotta help 'em. And I need cash to do it." He could tell it probably sounded like bullshit to his groggy daughter on the other side of the planet, but he couldn't think of any better way to put it. "I need to borrow some money to fix things . . . get the land back and repair the shit that burned."

"Borrow?" Lydia said loudly.

Mike heard Andrew's muffled voice in the background and then Lydia order him back to sleep. "I knew I shoulda called Andy's phone," he said, "but I was tryin' to do the right thing by callin' the house, talkin' to you."

"Don't you think Andrew has done enough for you?" The way she spoke, it seemed like she had her teeth clenched. "Whatever's happened, no doubt it's all *your* fault."

"What the hell was I thinkin'?" He rubbed his forehead. "Sorry I woke you for my own bullshit problems. Go on back to your perfect life." Before she could respond, he hung up.

He looked out toward the vineyard, gearing up for his next dreaded move.

"Bruce?" He could tell by the gruff voice on the other end that he'd woken up his old manager. "Dude . . . it's Mays."

"Mike?" There was a bit of silence. "You need bail money?"

"No. But I need yer help. I'm in Italy—"

"Italy? As in Europe? For God's sake, what're you doing there?"

Mike gave a quick recounting of how he'd sold his guitars, moved in with his daughter, and ended up at Groove House.

Bruce listened for a minute or two before interrupting with, "And I care, because? . . ."

"Because I fucked up and caught the place on fire. Can't ya scrounge up some sorta deal that'll make me some dough? Another 'greatest hits' package or somethin'?"

"Look, bud." Bruce yawned. "I already told you. There's nothing more I can do—"

"What about royalties from the last record? Maybe you could—"

"You took a massive advance back then." Bruce blew his nose. "You're nowhere close to recouped. Maybe next year's statement you'll be a few bucks out of the red."

"Next year?" Mike wanted to throw the friggin' phone in the pool and drown out the sound of Bruce's voice. "I swear this time, I'm writin' for a new album—"

"No label is interested in only a few hundred sales—"

"Thousands."

"Okay, maybe a thousand—"

"Thousands. Plural," Mike corrected him. "C'mon, you know there are indie labels that'd kill to sell even a thousand albums off one artist."

Bruce's heavy sigh whooshed across continents. "Listen, Mike, you're no longer on my roster. I can't help you. You're on your own, bud."

Mike hung up and scuffed his shoe in the dirt, glancing up at those noisy fuckin' birds. His shoulders slumped as he lowered his phone and plopped his ass onto the stone wall. His mind churned as the landscape turned to a blur. *Finished, my ass,* he thought, and kicked the dirt. He had to do something. But what the hell was he good at besides playin' guitar and bein' a front man and orderin' people around? Mike sat there for awhile, pondering. He stared up at the relentless birds circling overhead, swirling and chirping. Fuckin' hell, he thought, they never give up. If only he had his Les Paul and a Marshall stack . . . that'd blow 'em away. Then he stood up and grinned.

Chapter 25

Has-been . . . screw him, Mike thought, and brushed Bruce's words from his mind. He loitered around the patio table, marveling at the spread he'd prepared all by himself—bread, cheese, tomatoes, olives, and wine . . . lots of wine. Though he'd never sampled Giulia's chocolates, everyone seemed to dig them, so he topped off the table with the fancy black and purple box from the kitchen. Not the best fuckin' lunch, he thought, but it'd do. And sure enough, nobody missed lunch, although they all pouted and pussyfooted to the table.

"Have a seat," he encouraged, clapping his hands with a forced grin. "I know it ain't much, but it's the best I could do . . . short notice 'n' all." He watched as they took seats . . . except for Velvet, who was still out searching for Vin. He took a deep breath. "Look, this ain't easy for me to say." He noticed Harley glance up at him. "I, uh . . ." He looked around but everyone else just stared at the table or their laps, anything to avoid eye contact with him. "I . . . I been tryin' all day to find a way to fix this."

Harley eyeballed the others. "I, for one, appreciate the attempt . . ." Her words trickled off with a weak smile, as she stared down at her empty plate.

"I figure . . ." Mike said with a quick glance at the charred building. "Well . . . what the hell. *I'll* do the repairs." He glanced around the table but all he got was faraway stares. "Shit, it's a start."

"Fuck me," Gallo blurted.

Mike couldn't tell whether his outburst was sarcastic or supportive. And judging by the others all eyeing Gallo, neither could they.

"How generous," Gallo snapped.

"You and tools, geeze?" Tank asked, giving Mike a cockeyed stare. "Fuckin' 'ell, you'll be blartin' first swing of the hammer." He gave a halfhearted shrug and then grunted. "Awright, I'll 'elp."

Mike winked at Tank. "Now we're talkin'." He rubbed his hands together and looked around the table. "C'mon, guys, it's for Vin and Velvet."

Damn, he thought, what the hell did he know about construction? He needed more bodies so he could just kick back and supervise the whole operation. Mike figured Blitz would be the easiest sell. Dude smiled when he played drums, for chrissake. Back during the tour when Golden Blonde had opened for him, it had taken him barely ten seconds to convince Blitz to kick a chandelier off a Chicago hotel room ceiling.

Sure enough, the dumbass stuck out his chin. "I'll help too."

Mike gave him a quick "Namaste" and then shot him a ceasefire glance.

"But not for you." Blitz glared at him. "For Vin and Velvet."

"Cool," Mike said, "that makes three of us." He looked at Harley's sagging shoulders and expressionless stare. He didn't expect her to jump in. Hell, she was a chick. He hoped Gallo would sign on, but he just sat there with a sour face and crossed arms.

"*You* fucked up," Gallo charged. "*You* fix it. I ain't liftin' a goddamn finger." He stuck his lip out, which made him look more ape-like than usual. "I'm gonna sue your ass, Mays. For loss, theft of property. Gonna land your skanky ass in court—don't underestimate me, prick."

"We ain't got time for this shit." Mike said, dismissing Gallo's crappy attitude. "Anyone got any ideas what we can do to raise some dough so Velvet can get the land back?"

Harley squinted at him. "No plan, then." She pursed her lips and turned away.

Blitz raised his hand like an over-enthusiastic schoolboy. "A friend of a friend works in TV in L.A. and I bet we could get them to do a reality show of us."

"Dude." Mike could feel his face scrunch up. "Are you serious? It'd be like the Osbournes meets the Golden Girls." He pointed around the table. "Ya think we want people to see us all old and fucked up 'n' shit? See that your drugs of choice are now blood pressure, cholesterol, and prostate meds? Ya think Gallo wants people to see him all deaf and crotchety? Screw that reality TV bullshit. That idea sucks ass." Mike turned, realizing he'd just gone a little ballistic.

"Hey, it ain't my problem if you're older than Ozzy," Blitz charged, scanning the other faces for confirmation.

Mike checked the rotten expressions around the table. "That dude's ancient."

"Mays is right," Gallo agreed, looking at Blitz and not Mike. "Your idea does suck ass."

When Harley poured herself some wine, the others followed her cue and began helping themselves to the food.

Mike grinned as they seemed to be coming around. "So . . . I been thinkin'—" His ass cheek began to vibrate. When the familiar ringtone sounded, he held up a finger. "Gotta take this," he said as he stepped away from the table.

"Hey, kid. How's tricks?" Mike smiled, happy to welcome a friendly voice amid the sea of animosity he'd stirred up. But, shit, he'd blown the kid off yesterday . . . twice. "Sorry I didn't answer your calls earlier. Had a really shitty night."

"Mom told me."

"Told ya what?" Mike scratched his chin and kept heading toward the edge of the courtyard. "What time is it there?"

"I guess it wasn't really your fault for ignoring me—"

"I wasn't ignorin' ya, kid."

"Mom knew how mad I was yesterday and when you called just a little while ago, I heard the phone ring and she could hear that I was awake . . . so she sat me down and told me you had some problems . . ."

"Yeah." Mike stole a glance back toward the others. "Got myself in a fix—"

"She said I should call you today."

Mike felt a thickness in his throat.

"Is Harley there?" Brayden seemed excited, his words rushed. "I've been dying to tell you two something since yesterday."

Mike glanced back at the others sitting around the patio dining table. Then he turned and scuffed his foot at the ground. "She's, uh, kinda busy right now. What's up?"

"Well, I played in the talent show at school and it was totally rad!"

"Guitar? Or clarinet?"

"Guitar, duh."

Mike's eyes grew wide. "Ya did it. That's hella cool, dude."

"I played 'Lucky Night' . . . and sang it too."

My tune, Mike thought. Fuckin' hell. He could feel the pull of his open-mouthed grin. His eyes turned misty as he closed them for a moment to soak in the kid's words.

"I wasn't that scared, except . . . all those people staring at me . . . so I just focused on playing . . . and then it was such a rush."

Mike's legs felt weak and he glanced around but there was nothing to sit on. He stood, unsteadily, listening to the kid lifting his spirits from thousands of miles away.

"I wanted to tell Harley, 'cause she helped me on Skype with that chord change, you know, that one part that goes from E minor to C? Gets me every time. And she gave me some tips on how to handle the twin guitar melodies on one guitar. She liked my . . . arrangement . . . said I'd nailed it."

"No shit . . ." Mike found himself blinking away tears.

"There was this lame girl who was like a Shakira wannabe. Mom said I was really good—"

"Wait . . . yer *mom* was there?"

"Yeah, she and dad snuck into the show. That pissed me off 'cause I didn't want them there. You know, Mom can be kinda negative. But she actually liked it. She said I was *really* good."

Mike scratched his cheek. "Shit, you're pretty ballsy to do that after only playin' a few weeks." He smiled and shook his head. "That's . . . fuckin' great."

"I gotta hang up . . . but just wanted you to know that I'm much cooler now. By the way."

Mike cleared his throat. "I sure miss ya, kid."

"Tell Harley I said hi. Thanks for teaching me that song, Gra—Mike."

Mike choked as tears spilled onto his cheeks. He slipped the phone back into his pocket and then quivered as he wiped his tears. He couldn't remember the last time he'd cried like a little pansy. He stared out at the fields, sprinkled with red poppies and pink and yellow wildflowers, as they turned to a colorful blur. "Fuckin' hell," he said, turning to glance back toward the table. "That's *it.*" His heart raced and his whole body warmed as he laughed out loud. With a huge grin, he drummed his fingers against his thigh and strutted back to the table.

"You alright?" Harley asked.

"My grandkid." As he took a seat next took Blitz, he wiped the last tear from his cheek. With a satisfied grin he said, "Fuckin' little kid played 'Lucky Night' in his school talent show."

"*Your* tune?" Blitz asked and then glanced at Gallo, who sneered at the mere mention of that title.

"Brilliant!" Harley clasped her hands, momentarily lifted from her funk.

"Ya done him right, geeze," Tank said as he gave Mike a high-five.

"Yeah, guess I did somethin' right." Mike grinned, thinking of the day he'd presented the kid's birthday gift. "Damn." He snickered. "His mom must be pissin' her pants right about now."

He cleared his throat and glanced around the table. "So I got this idea. . . . What's the one thing we're all good at?" Mike felt a glimmer of his old genius returning. "All we know's music, right? So what if we did a gig?"

He watched as they pivoted their heads in his direction, horrified.

"What," Gallo growled, "and call it Viagrapalooza? Cialis Fest?"

"Trust me," Mike confessed, squeezing his fingers. "It's hella painful to bend strings these days—"

"They got drugs for that, geeze," Tank teased.

"You suggesting we do a benefit for ourselves?" Harley scowled. "That's rather self-serving."

"Consider the source," Gallo mumbled.

Mike knew his idea rocked, plus he figured it would get him off the hook and get everyone focused on planning a show. Yeah, he liked it, alright. "I'm willin' to try."

"Are you fucking kidding me?" Gallo asked. "It'd be an embarrassment."

Harley hung with the resistance. "Don't think enough people really care about us anymore."

"Well, they came out to *my* shows last year." Thoughts crashed in of being sprawled out on that stage last summer, the fans' expressions in the front row, but Mike couldn't let anyone—anything—bash his idea. "At least a few people gave a shit about *me*. And people still go see Vin—"

"Not him in particular," Harley noted. "He's just a sub now, a generic hired gun in *other* people's bands."

The more they resisted, the more Mike believed it could work. He knew he had to force the issue. "I'll get someplace in Rome. . . . Or somewhere in London," Mike blustered. "Hammersmith."

"If anyone can, you could probably do it, geeze," Tank said.

"I have a friend who's the production manager at the Hollywood Bowl," Blitz said. "Remember Gunner?"

"We're here in Italy, dumbass," Mike snapped at him. "The Bowl's all the way across the planet in California. Besides, that venue's way too big for any of you cats."

Blitz leaned in to Mike's ear and hissed, "I could've just let you burn." Then he shot Mike a look, as if to remind him—*you owe me big-time*.

Mike's throat felt uncomfortably dry. He coughed as he stalled for time. "Fuck it, we should play the States," he said, thinking grandly and out loud. "L.A. . . . Someplace on Sunset. Nah, it's gotta be somewhere free of them corporate conglomerate promoters." He kept talking but nobody seemed to be buying into it.

"Jamming in the barn with you dudes is one thing," Blitz wavered. "But playing live again, that's for real. I'm not so sure we could cut it anymore."

Mike looked at Blitz, knowing his rusty joints didn't react as fluidly on drums as they had even just ten years ago. He studied the faces of his colleagues around the table. Fuck, he thought, he didn't really wanna do it either. But he had to do something. It was all his goddamn fault. He got up from the table and lit a cigarette. Stalling for courage, he inhaled and then slowly released the smoke. "C'mon, we sounded pretty good jammin' those old classics yesterday."

"Yeah," Tank agreed. "We did."

Gallo glared at Tank. "Did you touch my bass?"

"Think about how good that feels." Mike looked down at the burning cigarette in his hand. God, he hated being the cheerleader, but a concert seemed their best hope . . . and his out. He gave a hopeful glance around the table. "I'm gonna get the Hollywood Bowl."

Gallo howled. "Go ahead, windbag, keep on dreamin' big."

Harley scowled. "It's not exactly affordable—not to mention embarrassing when only 70 people turn up."

"One show. I'll rent it out myself if I have to, keep those conglomerate paws off our dough," Mike blustered.

Gallo shook his head. "Wow, the bullshit's gettin' thick out here."

"How come *now* this dude can hear?" Mike asked, pointing at Gallo and glancing around the table. "Ya haven't missed a single word I said, ya deaf motherfucker!" Nobody laughed. Mike took a deep breath and then exhaled loudly. "This is the only way, man. Ya know it is."

"You know what?" said Blitz. "I haven't played live in years, but for Velvet and Vin, I'd do it . . . I'm in."

"Then you'll sound just as shitty as you used to," Harley said as Blitz gave her a hard stare.

Of all people, Mike figured Harley would jump at the chance to play live again. He looked at Gallo and figured he'd be into anything that might spice up his monotonous life. "Fuck it, I'll get my other friends to help out," Mike boasted. "Call on some big names, dudes who owe me."

"I could call up Sheehan," Blitz suggested.

Mike grinned. "Good one, dude." He cupped Blitz's shoulder. "I was thinkin' Mendoza."

Tank leaned forward. "I'd be honored to hump your gear again, geeze." He looked around the table. "I'll tech for the lot of you—"

"Get me Gunner's number," Mike ordered Blitz.

"Sure, I'll hook you up."

Harley threw her arms in the air. "Have you all gone completely mental?"

Gallo sat with his arms folded. "Delusions of grandeur."

Mike stood tall and spoke as passionately as a pro football coach priming his team in the locker room before the big game. "Hey, we've all had moments throughout our careers where we whored ourselves out and did something that our hearts weren't 100 percent into—just because management or the record company said it was the right move for our careers."

He watched as every one of them nodded in accord.

Fuck it, Mike thought, Velvet's usually a goddamn peppy cheerleader, so he could amp it up too. "Look—" He pointed around the table and the property. "I know I just got here, but just like you, this is all we got now . . . right here. We're damn lucky to have Vin and Velvet . . . and all this."

"That's right," Blitz concurred.

Mike listened to his heart pounding. Shit, what they had at Groove House was pretty damn cool. "I got nowhere to go, and there's no way I'm gonna lose this cool vibe . . . with all of you."

He noticed they were all nodding in unison. All eyes were fixed on him as he stood shakily on his soapbox. Blitz stared up at him, captivated with the sell, sucked right into the sermon.

Mike rubbed at his aching knees. "If there was ever a time to put our collective talent together, this is it. Don't let puny little egos get in the way. Now's the time for every one of us to step up to the plate."

He paused to catch his breath and inhale the energy in the air. He couldn't believe he was actually rallying the troops—he might be the fuck-up, but he was also the savior. "We might never have another chance in our lives to put our musical talents to such good use. I don't care how old we all are, sittin' at this table today. *I've* heard you. I heard ya thirty years ago, and I hear you now. I heard ya when we jammed yesterday. And I know we could *all* still wipe the floor with some of these young punks who play what they call music today. Let's show 'em what we got. Some of the most talented musicians that ever graced the stages of rock 'n' roll live *right here!*" He stabbed his pointer finger on the tabletop. "Age don't mean shit. Let's show 'em . . . let's show the world we still got it."

Drained, he snuffed his wasted cig in a patio ashtray and returned to his seat at the table. He looked up to see Velvet walking into the courtyard, head down.

"Glad yer back," Mike said as she approached the table. "Any luck findin' Vin?" He felt bad for her as she shook her head.

"What am I going to do?" Velvet's lip bunched up.

"We're gonna get yer land back," Mike said with confidence. "I got a plan."

She looked at him and took a deep, shaky breath. "Record advance," she said, her voice barely a whisper.

"Shit." Mike hated to own up to it. "I, uh . . ." He dipped his chin and glanced up at her. "That money ain't comin'."

She collapsed onto the chair at the end of the table, dropped her head, and closed her puffy eyes. Chick looked completely spent, like maybe she hadn't the energy to bitch him out. Everyone watched as she slowly opened her eyes and then wiped her nose with a crumpled tissue.

"We're gonna do a gig," Mike announced. "For Groove House."

She turned to him with an empty stare.

"To raise the money, get your land back, repair the fire damage."

Velvet gave a hopeful glance around the table. Her eyes landed on Blitz and Tank, who each gave her a slight grin. "You guys would do that for me?" She perked up just a little and a slow smile began to form. "For Vin?"

Mike stared down Gallo and Harley—the naysayers—sending a daggered glance that dared them to sabotage Velvet's newfound hope. "I'm thinkin' Hollywood Bowl."

"Hollywood Bowl?" Velvet stared off as she fiddled with her wedding ring.

Gallo swatted at the air. "Don't listen to—"

"Don't worry, V," Tank interrupted as he snatched one of Giulia's chocolates off the table. He let out an ecstatic moan as he munched. "Mike'll find the right club."

"Club?" Mike smirked at Tank. "What I'm talkin' 'bout's bigger than some shitty little club gig."

"You're talkin' out your ass," Gallo snapped.

"No," Velvet said as she leaned in. "A concert is . . . a good idea." She nodded, almost as if she was trying to convince herself.

Mike glanced from Velvet's hopeful face to the others, staring them down.

"It's brilliant," Tank assured her.

Velvet hooked a finger through the purple ribbon, dragged the snazzy chocolate box over to her, and rummaged among the frou-frou papers before popping a chocolate into her mouth. She closed her eyes and seemed to slip into a trance.

Mike lowered his eyelids and shot her a crooked grin. "Just think of the spin-off products," he said, and she opened her eyes. "We could easily unload all them bottles of olive oil ya got stockpiled in the barn, just collectin' dust."

He reached for the box of chocolates, pushed aside all the confetti and doilies and dumb shit, and then popped a square into his mouth and started to chew. *Holy shit.* The silky smoothness gave him pause. As the creamy chocolate melted onto his tongue, he caught a burst of salt— sweet and salty in one bite. It was . . . the best fucking chocolate he'd ever tasted.

Velvet's smile got bigger. "We could even sell our limoncello . . . with a cool Groove House label—"

"Yeah," Gallo mocked her, "and maybe Carlo will give you the grapes from that vineyard he just bought, and you can sell that too."

Mike glared at him. Couldn't the bastard see that Velvet was happy once again, just dreaming of the possibilities?

Velvet began tapping her fingers on the table. "Mike's onto something." She turned to him. "But . . . how could we possibly pay for it?"

Mike felt his breathing speed up. He winked at her and stole a glance across the courtyard before he squinted around the table. The salty sweet chocolate lingered on his tongue. He glanced at the box—the artisan chocolates, the tarted up label—and then looked over at Velvet.

"Sponsors." He grinned and stared out toward the vineyard. "And I think I got that one covered."

Velvet gave Mike a knowing glance. "Giulia."

Chapter 26

Velvet stared at Mike's road-worn face as he scribbled on a notepad. An unlikely alliance, she considered. She glanced up at the sunset's pink cast filtering in through the little window in the living room and her thoughts drifted to Vin: he still wouldn't take her calls.

"That room's got electrical issues, ya know, bad wiring," Mike said. He hadn't stopped trying to convince her of his innocence. "I ain't gonna room with Blitz—"

"You can room with the barn owls for all I care," she said, rolling her eyes. "For chrissake, my husband's gone. I really should kick your ass out."

Aaaoooogah. Mike snapped his attention to his phone and giggled.

"What the hell is that?" Velvet asked.

"Submarine dive." He glanced up at her and grinned. "Get it? Chicks? Deep sea dive?" He laughed and focused back on the phone. "Chick from the bar," he said with a nod. "She digs me."

Velvet stared at him, unsure whether she was amazed or disgusted. "How do you text with someone who doesn't speak English?"

At the sound of another incoming text, he looked at his phone and laughed. Then he half-grinned at her. "Oh, and leave Giulia to me—"

"You're texting Giulia?"

"What's it to ya? She digs me, ya know. Man, that chick has *killer* chocolate. Never tasted nothin' like it. I bet she'd do anything to get 'em into the States—"

"But Carlo said—"

"Fuck that guy. I'll get Giulia's help. Boobs, bucks, brains, and branding—what more could ya want from a first sponsor?" He grinned and then focused back on the notepad. "So then we'll close the show with 'Lucky Night.'" He tapped the pencil on the coffee table and turned to Velvet.

"I practically gave that vineyard away," she said, and took a deep, pained breath. "What if we never get the land back? What if this concert ..." She stared across the room until it blurred.

"I'll get it back," Mike assured her. "And don't worry what anyone else says. We don't need no promoter. *I'll* do it. *I'll* rent the Hollywood Bowl. We'll do it all ourselves, and *we'll* get all the dough," he assured. "I'm gonna make it happen. Trust me."

"Trust *you?*" Velvet let out a snide laugh. "Already tried that and got burned ... pardon the convenient pun."

Mike glanced down at the notepad and then over at her. "We gotta add you in there somewhere."

"Me?"

"You were killer, doll," Mike said with a crooked grin. "Ya gotta play."

Velvet imagined herself onstage again—young and sexy, so different from her daily routine. The ringing phone startled her. Hopeful, she grabbed the cordless, but was surprised to hear Giulia's voice.

"Vin is on the vineyard ... drunk and yelling and raking the havoc."

Velvet dropped the phone and ran to the door. "Stay here," she ordered Mike.

She raced to the barn and hopped onto the yellow Vespa, but the scooter sputtered on start and then croaked, the needle hovering on empty. "Dammit! Can't anyone ever fill this thing but me?"

She grabbed the rickety bicycle leaning against the barn—the old silver three-speed that Vin had always threatened to toss out if she wasn't ever going to ride it. And now she'd ridden it three times in twelve hours. Without another thought, she vaulted a leg over the seat and began pedaling. The saddle felt hard on her ass, but she pushed the pedals with every ounce of adrenaline. The rusty suspension springs squeaked beneath her as she wobbled across the dirt and drifted into a bumpy downhill coast. The bike skidded as she hit flatter land. She raced along in the dusk, under the rising full moon, out of breath and legs burning, until she reached the edge of the old vineyard. There sat the old blue Fiat *Cinquecento*, haphazardly parked near the bulldozer. The driver door was open, but she didn't see Vin. She stopped and pulled a flashlight from the glove box. Then she saw him, bottle in hand, staggering up toward the Moretti house on the hill.

"Come out," he hollered and took an unsteady swig from the bottle. "Chickenshit motherfucker."

"Vin!" Velvet beamed the flashlight at him and he stumbled back, surprised, and shielded his eyes. She rushed over to him, catching his fall as he teetered to one side. "Aw, baby." She took the near empty bottle from his grasp and inspected the label. *Mirto.* She reeled from the odor, remembering how nasty it had tasted when Vin had coaxed her to try it at that restaurant on the little *piazza* back on their first trip to Como.

"Go off my land," Carlo bellowed as he stalked into the vineyard. Giulia was with him.

"There you are." Vin pushed himself away from Velvet. "Thievin' bastard." He wobbled toward Carlo and threw an erratic swing that never landed.

Velvet rushed to Vin's side. The men stood, defiant, shouting at each other, Carlo in Italian, Vin in sloshy English. Velvet shot a helpless look at Giulia.

Giulia jumped between the two men and blustered at Carlo in rapid-fire Italian. She grasped his arm and encouraged him to retreat.

Velvet stared at Carlo and felt the resentment rise. She had to stand up to him so Vin could respect her again. "You increased our property taxes," she blurted out, surprising herself.

Carlo belly-laughed as he turned toward her. "You, lady, must think I am the mayor of the whole village." He gave a cocky shrug. "I am a businessman. I do not have this type of power." He took a couple steps toward her. "You complain always the taxes. . . . I pay. Do *you* pay?"

Velvet cowered, blinking at him.

Then Carlo narrowed his eyes at Vin. "I bulldozer the rest," he said, raising a finger. *"Subito."* Giulia muscled in, ushering him back up the dark hill toward home, but he turned back with a final scowl.

"Motherfucker," Vin shouted.

As Velvet steered him toward the car, Vin clenched his teeth and muttered incoherently about Carlo's "straightaway" threat. She could see a few new scratches and dents on the open driver door. The skid tracks in the dirt told the story: he'd been spinning donuts in the vineyard in a drunken fury. Vin staggered, dropped to his knees, and began to sob.

"Fucker's rippin' up my vineyard," he slurred. "Mine," he moaned and began pounding his chest before resting a clenched fist over his heart. *"Nonna*... Helped her work the land. . . . *Nonna* taught me everything." He rocked back and forth, sobbing. *"Mia nonna."*

"I know, baby." Velvet knelt in the dirt beside him, reaching over to rub his head.

"Bastard . . . fuckin' steal my land . . . got some balls bulldozin'." He reached for the Mirto bottle but Velvet moved it behind her. "Wasshisname . . . yeah, Sergio," Vin muttered. "That fucker."

"Who?" Velvet asked. "Oh, *Sergio*," she said. Carlo's grandfather.

"Helped us work the vineyard. Asshole's betrayin' him too." His head wobbled toward her as he cried. "Tearin' up my vineyard."

"I know, baby, but we're going to stop him." She smiled at him with an amazing sense of calm. "Mike came up with a great plan."

"Mays?" He looked at her, cross-eyed, and blinked, as if attempting to focus. "Can't believe anything that fucker . . ."

"I'm so sorry, Vin," she said, leaning toward him. "I was too embarrassed to admit it, even to you, but Mike, he was the one. He . . . he got me drunk and then he just took over."

Vin shot her a darting glance.

"Not like that, but . . . the Fernet-Branca and Sangiovese . . . all that talk . . . the property tax bill . . . I don't know why I let him convince me to sell the vineyard to Carlo."

"Bullshitter like Mays? . . . Thought you were smarter than that."

Velvet reached out to touch his cheek but he pulled back.

"Dude's gotta go . . . tomorrow."

Velvet relished the idea of kicking Mike out, but now she needed him and his connections. And Vin didn't seem anywhere close to forgiving her. "We're going to do a concert—"

Vin cackled. "Nobody wants to see old fogies tryin' to rock . . . 'specially here in Italy. Pathetic." He swatted at the air. "Fuckin' lemonade stand would make more money."

"Mike's going to get the Hollywood Bowl."

Vin let out a dry, squeaky laugh. "Lamest thing I ever heard." He licked his lips and rolled his tongue around his mouth in slow motion. "Gallo? Harley? Blitz?" He cackled at the full moon, teetered, and then sat in the dirt. "Can't even get arrested these days."

She felt her shoulders sag. "You'll play too."

"Mays playin' live again? . . . Sucked so bad his last tour." He wobbled and Velvet reached out to steady him. "All over the Internet . . . his sorry ass. And Gallo . . . dude's got issues."

She looked straight ahead, out into the moonlit vineyard, past the small chunk that Carlo had already bulldozed. "But you'll—"

Vin held up a shaky palm. "Count me outta this bullshit."

Velvet lifted a twig and swirled it around in the dirt. "And we can film the concert for a DVD and—"

"With what, buncha Euro ashes?" Vin asked, his voice rising. He raked his fingers through his hair.

"And we can sell our olive oil—" His dismissive laughter gave her pause.

"Of all your lame ideas . . ." Vin lifted a finger. "That one . . ."

Vin had predicted their olive oil wouldn't sell, not only due to the glut in the local marketplace but also because they were foreigners, expats. He'd been right and now they were stuck with it. She glanced around and wanted to say that at least the oil hadn't sucked as much of their savings as the vineyard had. But now she had a real chance to put things right.

"Fuck Mays, fuckin' bullshit." He swatted at the air again. "Fuck everybody. . . . *Vaffanculo.*" He grabbed onto the car and pulled himself up to a shaky stance.

She glanced at his square jaw, contoured by the moonlight. "We'll get Giulia as a sponsor."

"Mob money?" He began staggering around the vines, teetering and then trying to correct his wobbly steps.

"No—it's—"

"Right. Giulia's gonna go against that bastard . . ." He took a breath and shook his head, as if he thought it might steady his slurred words. "And *give* you money so *you* can get *my* land back from *him*?" He teetered forward until a vine caught his fall. "Mob money, babe. . . . All in *la famiglia.*"

"Not *giving* us money, she'll be a sponsor." Velvet got up and then stepped toward Vin, who was now circling the bulldozer. "It's *her* company, not Carlo's."

"Buncha crooks. Loan you dough then jack up the price."

"But Carlo won't be involved."

Vin quivered and careened to the side. "Fuckin' bulldozer," he said, kicking the machine. He turned and stared at her, all pouty and wobbly. "Nothin' ever gets you down," he blubbered and swallowed hard three times as she steadied him. "God, I love you so much." He pawed at her and then pulled away.

Velvet could see what was about to happen, as Vin's face went grey. But before she could react, he leaned onto the bulldozer and retched intense ruby red vomit. Goddamn Mirto. She cringed and then reached over and rubbed his back as he retched again.

"Let me take you home. You're going to have a nasty hangover."

"Wouldn't be the first time," he said before the next hurl. "And don't think I'm still talking to you." He wiped his mouth and looked back at her. "I'm taking Toby's gig . . . leave tomorrow."

"What?" She leaned away from him and stared down at the dirt. "I'm going to get it all back. I promise you." Velvet looked out at the vineyard and then back to the moonlit bulldozer. She hoped to hell Mike Mays wasn't bullshitting this time.

Chapter 27

Velvet settled into her place at the breakfast table.

"Peaceful courtyard this morning without that asshole around," Blitz said as he reached for the pitcher of orange juice. "He shoots me a B.A. from the office window and pretends his ass cheeks are talking to me when I'm in Anjali Mudra."

"What the hell is that, geeze?" Tank asked as he offered the pitcher around the table.

"Salutation seal?" Blitz said sarcastically, as if yoga poses were a standard wake-up routine for everyone on the planet.

"Just do your yoga in the barn," Velvet suggested, as she toyed with the pancake on her plate.

Harley cradled a cup of coffee, but her plate sat void of food. "So Mike vanished in the night. Why am I not surprised?"

"Hopefully, that moron's on the next flight outta here," Gallo grumbled.

"We need him," Velvet said and then rolled her eyes when Gallo smirked.

"Shoulda been *him* on that airport shuttle last week," said Blitz. "Instead of Vin."

Vin had been gone a week, subbing on tour again for next to no pay, but at least this time he was on the same continent. Velvet leaned in slightly to Harley. "Still won't take my calls."

"He's got what, seven more weeks to go?" Harley reached over and gave a soothing rub to Velvet's back. "Surely he won't hold out that long."

"Here comes our conquering hero," Gallo blurted.

Velvet turned and looked toward the barn, surprised that through all the mealtime chatter she hadn't heard the car on the gravel drive. No one took a bite of breakfast as they all watched Mike get out of a car. Then Velvet recognized the Alfa Romeo and noticed Giulia waving.

"Bloody 'ell." Tank dropped his fork. "Thought he done brung a scrubba to the house."

Harley uncrossed her legs and sat upright, her eyes fixed on Mike in the distance. "Not unless Giulia's resorted to turning tricks."

Gallo shot Harley an I-told-ya-so look. "If you're goin' for that self-absorbed bastard again, then you ain't learned much since your twenties."

"I'm not *going* for him." Harley glowered at Gallo before returning her attention to Mike. She said half-aloud, "I would've never written 'The Darkest Hour' if not for him."

"Careful, Harl. I can't watch him fuck you over again . . . and you know he will."

At the sound of the car crunching gravel back down the drive, Mike came whistling across the courtyard toward breakfast. He looked down at the incoming message on his phone and laughed. "Hey, how do you say *blowjob* in Italian?" When he glanced up he noticed the stunned expressions around the table. "What?" he asked with a nonchalant toss of his head. He grinned, snatched a pancake from the platter, and began munching. "Stayed up all night, eatin' chocolate, drinkin' unbelievably killer wine."

Harley knocked over a glass of water and muttered a sullen "sorry" to the table. Velvet snuck a glance at her. My God, she wondered, was Harley actually jealous?

"Her ol' man's outta town so we—"

"What ya doin', geeze?" Tank asked, stroking a wiry brow. "Carlo'll kick your bleedin' arse."

Mike laughed. "I couldn't sleep." He rubbed at his back. "That futon in the office is rank—"

"You're not even supposed to be here," Blitz charged. "Vin kicked you out a week ago."

"Where'm I gonna go? *My* shit's burned, too." Mike grabbed a plate and heaped on food as he took a seat. "So I figured now's as good a time as any to sweet-talk Giulia—"

"You were supposed to wait for me," Velvet said sharply.

Mike grinned. "I'm a lot more charmin' one-on-one—"

"Yeah, a real fuckin' stud," Gallo growled.

"She digs me," Mike boasted, lifting his chin. "Ya gotta use that shit. Anyway, she's key to gettin' the Hollywood Bowl."

Harley and Gallo groaned, shaking their heads. Their dissent had begun to wear thin, Velvet thought, as she scowled at them.

"Bullshit," Gallo grunted.

"I'm workin' on it. Got this buddy who used to work there. . . . Harley, you remember Gunner? Dude was my stage manager back in '83. Blitz knows him."

Blitz rolled his eyes while Mike took the credit. Harley looked away.

"Anyway, I tapped Giulia to be a sponsor—"

"You *tapped* her, geeze?" Tank teased as he stabbed a pancake.

Mike gave a wheezy laugh. "Giulia's one smokin' hot broad, alright, but I ain't into workin' that hard no more."

Velvet noticed Mike firing a glance at Blitz, who seemed to seethe just a little. She thought about Blitz's ex, the gorgeous lingerie model who had sent all the wives in his band scrambling for plastic surgeons. She felt a fluttering in her stomach as she waited for Mike to continue. But he just sat there shoveling food into his mouth, scarfing as though he wouldn't be around tomorrow.

"And?" she asked.

Mike leaned in and looked down the table. "Well, Giulia's kinda freaked out about Carlo's reaction if she gets involved. But I told her," Mike roared, "he don't have to know just yet. It's all about creative financin', I've used it my whole life."

Velvet cringed, the words ringing in her ears. Barely two weeks ago she had fallen for that line. They needed seed money to fund the initial concert expenses, but Giulia's friendship was more important.

Mike hacked out a cough. "I said that sponsorin' an epic event like this'll make a big splash for her chocolates in the States—screw that—around the planet. I told her she's gotta jump on it now 'cause this thing's gonna be huge. People'll come from all over the world—"

Gallo gave a disapproving growl.

Mike slugged down several gulps of orange juice. "She's in. Ready to cut me a check to get the Bowl." He pulled a cigarette from his pocket, slid it between his lips, and then nodded to Tank. "Dude, you still got connections at SIR L.A.? . . ."

Velvet gathered up the flatware and absorbed Mike's words—Giulia was in. She bowed her head and suppressed a smile. If he was to be believed, then Mike's ridiculous flirtations had paid off. As she walked to the kitchen, she noticed a bounce in her step. For the first time in weeks—maybe even months—she felt lighter. She twisted the faucet and watched as water filled the sink. The sound of plates clanking onto the counter startled her.

"I can't believe he spent the night with her," said Harley.

"I knew it." Velvet swished soap around the sink and then turned and grinned at Harley. "You're jealous—"

"I'm no such thing," Harley insisted, her eyes wide.

Velvet squinted at her. Harley seemed surprised by the accusation, or maybe she was just shocked to find that she might indeed be jealous. "You definitely have a thing for him," Velvet said, turning to the sink.

"He's . . . an old friend," Harley said in an irritated tone. "Nothing more."

Velvet turned back to her. "You've started smoking again." She waited and then when Harley didn't respond, she said, "You're still in love with him . . . even after all these years—"

"It's not like that," Harley argued as lines formed between her brows.

Forcing a smile, Velvet gently touched Harley's arm and said in a soothing tone, "It's *exactly* like that." Then she turned to the sink. If Harley had such a strong draw to Mike, Velvet figured, she would be drawn into playing the concert. And that just might be enough validation for Vin;

she knew she'd need everyone's participation in order to get Vin's. Velvet plunged a plate under the water and began humming "The Darkest Hour."

When Mike entered the barn, he could see Harley at the other end strapping on her favorite red Yamaha SG. She just stared as he approached, but when he stopped right in front of her, she turned her back.

"Look, doll, instead of lingerin' on the fringe and shoutin' comments from the peanut gallery, why don't ya just join us? You were always hot shit on guitar. It'd be cool to have ya on board."

She stepped forward and flipped on her amp.

"Why do you hang around listenin' to us plan the gig if you ain't gonna join in?"

She just stood there for a minute, clenching and unclenching her fists. When she turned to face him, he thought she might be fixin' to clobber him for some damn reason. But instead she started tuning her axe. "Shame Giulia's funds haven't come through," she fake crooned.

"Yet," Mike stressed. "Ready at my askin'." He wiped the back of his neck. "Real close to gettin' the Bowl."

She snorted.

"What's up with you this past week, Harl?" he asked, shuffling back a step. "You been actin' all weird 'n' shit."

She stared coolly at him. "Nothing at all."

"Bullshit. I can tell by the way the corners of yer mouth drop that yer—" He reached out to her lips but she dipped away from him.

"Right back to your old tricks." She flailed her hands in the air. "Stupid." She stomped her foot as the guitar dangled from her bod. "What was I thinking?"

Mike's gaze darted around the barn.

"Honestly. Giulia?" Harley shook her head. Her lips trembled, and then she shook her head. "You're not one for keeping your cock under wraps, especially with a gorgeous—"

"Giulia?" Mike asked with a raised brow. "Yeah? So what if I did? You fuck Gallo, so what's the problem?"

Harley just stood there, giving him a frozen stare. "That was before . . . and it's just . . . sex."

An awkward silence filled the barn.

"But last week . . . I thought . . ." Harley's voice trailed off as she gave him a brief, flimsy smile. Then she began noodling on the strings. "And now you've gone and nailed her?"

Harley's fingers danced almost angrily across the frets, and Mike recognized the melody: "The Darkest Hour." He squinted, wondering if that was intentional or if she even knew that's what she was noodling.

"I don't know why, but . . ." She dropped her grip on the guitar. "Well . . . it rather hurts." She stood there blinking at him, as if totaled by the sudden urge to snitch on herself.

Mike turned away and glanced around the barn before returning his focus to her.

"Look, I can't explain it." She sighed heavily and bowed her head. "Oh, this is all so confusing." She turned away and then swung around to face him. "But . . . I—"

He took a step backward.

"I just—" Harley said, swallowing hard as she removed the guitar and set it in the stand. "I feel ace around you. We've got this . . . bond. It's like a special, mature . . . well . . . dare I say, love."

Mike stood there rigidly, wondering what the hell he was doing. He'd always felt so different around her—more than just the feeling in his pants that most chicks gave him. He'd wanted her in a bad way since he arrived two weeks ago, and then the fire, and now she'd changed her tune . . . and worst of all, she'd just mentioned the one word that totally freaked him out. His chest tightened and he felt overheated. There was no way, he reasoned with himself. No fuckin' way. His whole life he'd avoided that one thing, in all forms. He couldn't look at her.

"I, uh . . . ah, I dig ya, but . . . this thing . . ." He wagged his finger between them. "It ain't love. That makes people weak 'n' shit. . . . And that ain't me." He glanced over to see her staring at the floor. "This is weird—"

"I've gone mad." She tossed up her hands. "Completely mental. . . .

Forget all this—dunno know what I was thinking." As Harley turned to walk toward the barn door, Mike grabbed her arm.

"Harl, you turned me down twice in like, two days."

"Your cock always comes first."

He tossed his head back and raised a deliberate brow at her. "I gotta, ya know, keep my manhood in check—"

"Player." She shook her head as she sized him up with her eyes. "Always were, always will be. And at the end of the day, who's going to take care of you? You collapsed onstage last summer and you had *nobody*." As she stepped away, he grabbed her arm once more.

"That ain't true." He released his grip when it seemed she'd stay put for another minute. "Last week, on my bed, before the fire . . . I—I didn't even jump yer bones. Know why?" He rubbed his neck.

She just stood there, hands on her hips, waiting.

He reached out and held her arm. "Because yer—"

"Dude!" Blitz hollered as the barn door slammed shut. "Let's do this."

"Player," she said, shaking free from his grasp.

Mike turned to see Blitz and Tank entering the barn, dressed to work on the fire damage.

He grasped Harley's hands and grinned. "C'mon, Harl, play the concert. It'll be like old times."

Her breath caught as she stared at him, an almost hopeful look on her face.

"Look," Mike whispered as he snuck a glance at the approaching guys. "I know yer worried about playin' live again. Me too. That fall in Germany haunts the crap outta me." He hated admitting his fear but he knew Harley'd get it. "I don't even know if my voice'll hold out for a live gig no more. But I'm willin' to take a stab at it—for Velvet and Vin. C'mon, Harl. I fucked up. Help me out here."

Harley slid her hands from his grasp, pressed her lips together, and looked away. "I can't do this," she said, pushing past Tank and Blitz.

Mike watched her walk out of the barn, unsure of just which "this" she meant.

Chapter 28

"**R**eady to rock?" Blitz asked twirling his sticks around the barn like a psychotic dumbass. He seemed awfully eager as he climbed behind the drums.

Mike sneered and turned to Tank. "Why's that dude always so damn peppy?" When Velvet walked in, holding a notepad, Mike glanced around the barn—a drummer, a guitar tech, and a harpist. Since he'd recently been banned from fire damage clean-up, he'd decided to rally the players for the first rehearsal . . . what few players he had.

"How the hell am I gonna rehearse with this buncha mutants?"

"Says the guy who can't even swing a hammer." Velvet rolled her eyes. "You almost killed Tank the other day when you hacked a hole in the roof. You're better off in here. Vin would be so pissed to know you messed with the charred—"

"He belled Gallo this mornin'," Tank blurted out.

"Vin?" Velvet said, her eyes wide and jittery.

"Been ringin' him every day, checkin' in . . ." Tank trailed off when Blitz waved a drumstick, motioning him to shut it.

"He still won't answer my calls . . ." Velvet said, trailing off. "Damn tour." She stared down at her hands. "I wish he'd . . ."

Mike watched Velvet clutch at her necklace and turn with a pained stare. He eyed her blonde hair, which was tied back, with loose strands clinging to the beads of sweat on her face. He could see why Vin had fallen for her . . . when she was younger. Velvet was pretty ballsy, he realized, a take charge kinda chick. She didn't seem to have an off button—but not in a shut-that-bitch-up kinda way . . . in a good way.

"I told ya, I'll get Vin home." Mike didn't know why, but it just seemed the right thing to say. "And on board. Don't worry."

She pressed her lips together. Tank glanced between her and Mike.

"Dude," Mike barked. "I know yer a roadie—"

"Guitar tech," Tank corrected.

Mike glanced toward the barn door. "We ain't got a bass player right now, so ya gotta step up."

"But, geeze—"

"You gonna go out there and convince Gallo to play bass?" Mike said, pointing toward the courtyard. He nodded toward Gallo's vintage Fender P bass in the guitar boat.

Tank half-shrugged and then picked it up. Whacking on the snare drum, Blitz gave a dubious look, as if Tank had just lifted the world's most precious ancient artifact.

"He'll go barmy," Tank said, "if he finds out we're usin' his blastid P bass—"

"Ya played it before."

"Right," Tank reasoned. "But now he's . . ." He shook his head and shuffled back toward the stand. Tank strapped on the red Fender Jazz bass instead, and Blitz launched into a god-awful attempt at the "Rosanna" shuffle.

"Dude," Mike said, shaking his head, "that beat's only for *real* drummers." He looked at Velvet, who'd parked her ass on a bench, and wondered if she too was worried about how the hell they could ever pull this off. He jumped, startled by the submarine dive text message alert, and slid his phone from his pocket. He squinted at the message: *Slave Driver \m/*

"Angelina," he announced and laughed, recognizing the marks as the metal horns salute. "Man, this chick sure digs my tunes," he crowed, grinning as he eyed his phone.

"You're fucking a twenty-something?" Blitz shook his head as he tested the tom toms.

Tank looked up from tuning the bass. "Un-fuckin'-believable."

Velvet stood up and straightened her shirt. "I just don't get how you two communicate."

"She probably recites Coverdale lyrics to him," Blitz said, stressing his joke with a rimshot. "That'd give the old rooster a boner," he sang out and the three of them laughed.

"Fuck off." Mike glanced up and sneered at Blitz and the red streak in his hair that matched his nails. *Moron.*

Velvet gave a shaky sigh and a weak smile. Then, as if sloughing off her funk, she stepped to the little mixing console. "Okay." She grabbed a sheet of paper. "I printed the list of songs and who'll play on what."

Like musketeers unsheathing their swords, Velvet, Tank, and Blitz each whipped out reading glasses from their pockets and gathered around to study her list.

Velvet pointed at the top of the page. "I was thinking today you could start with an easy one." She stole glances at Mike and Blitz. "'Rock My Love Muscle.' Mike, you sing lead on this one—"

"No fuckin' way." Mike stepped back from the group. "I ain't singin' that crap." The hell he'd sing Blitz's trite lyrics, he thought, folding his arms. "Get Harley to sing it."

"It's about a cock." Velvet smirked at him. "Besides, Harley still won't budge."

"When I get Vin on board," Mike crowed, "he can sing it."

Velvet shot him a cutting glance. "Blitz." She turned to him with pleading eyes. "Can't you sing it?"

"With *that* voice?" Mike laughed.

Tank grimaced at Blitz. "Ya sounds like a gleed under a door, geeze."

"Whatever that means." Blitz shrugged. "But, true," he admitted with a shrug. "I can't sing."

"Then we drop the tune," Mike sneered.

Velvet argued, "That was a popular—"

"That was a *lame* tune," Mike snapped, correcting her.

Velvet smirked at him. "The fans would be pissed to see Blitz onstage and not hear 'Rock My Love Muscle.'"

"Then play it on the house music, as people are comin' in."

Blitz glared at Mike and mouthed, "Burn, baby, burn."

Velvet took a deep breath and held it in. Then she looked at Mike. "There's no room for ego—"

"Your voice is perfect for it," Blitz said. Cocking his head like a perky-eared pup, he inched the lyric sheet toward Mike, as if offering an olive branch.

Mike glanced around the barn. Lame-ass song, he thought. . . . It was beneath him. But then, he *was* the reason they were doing all this in the first place. He swallowed a large gulp of pride, snatched the paper from Blitz's hand, and stepped up to the little stage area microphone. "Well, what're ya waitin' for?"

Tank strapped Harley's SG on Mike. As the only guitar player there, he not only had to sing the crappy lyrics, but also jam out the hackneyed three-chord pattern.

Mike adjusted the guitar, looked down at the sheet of shitty lyrics, and rolled his eyes. Then he nodded to Blitz, who counted off the tune. As the first few chords rang out, Mike yelled, "Holy shit!" Cowering at the train wreck of sound, he screeched into the microphone, "Ain't you dudes supposed to be pros?"

Velvet cringed. "Tank's a guitar tech, not a bass player."

"Better than a slap in the face with a wet kipper," Tank said. He gripped the bass, glancing around the barn, and then sighed. "Ah, V's right. Sod this for a lark!" he barked and whipped the bass over his head.

"C'mon, Mike," Velvet said, leaning against the workstation, arms crossed. "He can't do it."

Mike sighed, wishing he was lying on his bed with Harley again instead of stuck in a barn with a half-assed rhythm section. Damn, if only she'd join in, he thought; he'd put *her* on bass. Chick smoked on guitar, and she could play bass a million times better than anybody in the barn. "Harley," he said half-aloud, tapping his finger on his chin. He needed her.

"Tank," Velvet called out as he started for the door.

Mike grinned when it struck him: how he could lure Harley in from the courtyard. He reached down, stretched the strings, and wailed on her guitar—a stirring solo rendition of "The Darkest Hour," a tune he had inspired.

Tank paused and turned around, lips parted. Velvet leaned forward. Blitz stopped twisting the hi-hat clutch. Mike closed his eyes and cut loose, in the zone, moved by the passion of his own playing. When he opened them, he spotted Harley headed toward him—she didn't look happy. Gallo was right behind her, giving him the usual squinty-eyed sourpuss glare. Mike let the notes ring out. Then he left them in a guitar coma as he pulled his phone from his pocket.

"Hey, man," he roared so everyone would hear. "No shit. . . . Cool. Thanks, dude." From the corner of his eye, he scanned their faces. "Yeah, just let me know what else ya need to get rollin'. Killer, dude. Catch ya later." He slipped the phone back into his pocket and announced, "We got a date."

Velvet slowly tilted her head.

"Third Saturday in August," Mike said with a cough. "Hollywood Bowl." He pawed a hand through his hair and looked at Velvet, wide-eyed and clutching her heart. Gallo dropped his grumpy vibe. Harley leaned forward, as if straining to hear.

"Oy," Tank said, stepping closer. "I get to work a big stage again. . . . Me heart's racin' like a blue-arsed fly."

"Mays really did it!" Blitz shook his head and exchanged glances with Velvet. "Crushing!"

"What'd he say?" Gallo asked Harley.

"Hollywood Bowl!" she shouted.

"Ain't that a bit overkill?" Gallo snapped.

"Hell no," Mike boasted. "Only holds . . . like, eighteen thousand."

Gallo cackled. "You'll never fill the place."

"Mark my words," Mike blustered. "People will come. Especially when they find out it's bein' filmed."

"*Filmed,*" Gallo snorted.

The word made Mike a little woozy, so he took a deep breath. "People'll be fightin' over tickets, you'll see. The average Joe can't resist the lure of fame . . . even just ten seconds on celluloid."

"Losin' proposition, dude," Gallo blurted.

"If there's one thing I'm good at, it's gettin' press," Mike said, head held high. "You just wait till all the media hype starts. I got this covered. Sponsors'll foot the bill, they'll look good helpin', and we get the profits—"

"Profits?" Gallo grumbled. "You're gonna *lose* money."

"Brainstorm all you want, Einstein," Mike barked. "But I didn't get us this far by just sittin' on my ass."

Harley took a step closer and gave him a quizzical look. "How'd you do it?"

"Told ya I was gonna track down Gunner. He works the Hollywood Bowl now. Hooked a brutha up." He shrugged at her and then scowled at Gallo. "If you'd been involved from the start ya woulda known all this."

Gallo inched toward the action.

"We better get on with rehearsin'," Mike blustered. He looked at Blitz and then at Velvet. "Yer gonna need to be in top shape for the Bowl."

Harley stared off into space and muttered, "Never played the Hollywood Bowl." Her bottom lip bunched up and then loosened.

Mike shot Velvet a reassuring look. "I'll get Vin locked in—"

"Don't bet on it," Gallo grunted.

"Dude." Mike handed his cell phone to Tank. "Can you open that Skype thing on here?"

"It's in your apps, geeze," Tank said, fiddling with Mike's phone before exchanging it for Harley's guitar. "There. Now ya got a shortcut on your home screen."

Mike wheezed out a laugh. When he glanced down, Tank leaned in and tapped the screen. When the familiar window popped open, Mike touched Brayden's name. Hot damn, the kid was there. The stars were aligning.

"What's shakin'?" Mike asked. He glanced around at the others and could hear Brayden noodling on his guitar in the background. "What's that you're playin', kid?"

"Oh, just a little thing I came up with—"

"Fuckin' 'ell," Tank said with a playful shove to Mike. "It's really happenin', ay?"

"I still don't have harmonics down," the kid said.

"Kid . . ." Mike stalled but then gave a slow, exaggerated, stretch of his arm and decided to run with it, making a point to speak loudly. "Yer gramps is gonna play the Hollywood Bowl . . . big concert in L.A."

As the kid hooted through the phone, Mike noticed Harley twisting her silver bracelet, a pained look on her face.

"Way cool!" the kid said.

Harley shifted her eyes to Mike and then with absolute certainty she announced, "I'm in."

"You're fuckin' kiddin' me," Gallo said, grabbing her arm. "Don't drink the Kool-Aid, Harl."

Mike said into the phone, "Just a minute, kid." He noticed Velvet's mouth had fallen open. Then he looked at Harley. "Huh?"

"I'll play the show," Harley confirmed. "For Velvet." Velvet clapped and then threw her arms around Harley.

"For real?" Mike asked. Harley blinked and nodded. "Fuckin' hell." He grinned and returned to the phone, casting an eye around the barn. "Ya gotta come, kid," he said, puffing out his chest.

"Are you fucking kidding me?" Brayden yelled, as Mike held out the phone so all could hear. "The Hollywood Bowl? I'm so there!"

"It'll be the shit," Mike crowed, noting Gallo's glare. "I'm promotin' this show and—"

"Promoter, my ass," Gallo said to the others. "Only thing Mays promotes is himself."

"But ya gotta come *here*, kid . . . to Italy, to Groove House. Meet all these cats, watch the rehearsals." From the corner of his eye, Mike could see the smirk on Gallo's face, but he just kept on talking. "I'll buy ya a plane ticket. You can hang with me and Harl. You'd dig it. I'll teach ya the ropes, how to play like a *real* pro."

After the call, Mike stood there, grinning as the barn buzzed with chatter. His plan had worked. Gallo turned to split; dude still wasn't buyin' into any of it. Harley stood, skimming her fingertips along her jaw line. Mike motioned to Tank, who brought him Harley's guitar. Then Mike reached it out to her, like a sort of peace offering.

"Don't let me suffer through Blitz's crappy hit tune alone," Mike said with a wink. "You 'n' me, babe."

She glanced at Velvet and then at Mike. Then she gave a long, low sigh and strapped on her guitar.

Leaving Harley to the comfort of her SG, Mike nabbed Gallo's P bass, plugged in, and started pounding out the bass line of Blitz's bullshit song. "See?" He smirked at Tank. "Easy as shit . . . just like this tune."

"Play nice," Harley warned him.

Mike looked up just in time to see lanky Gallo whip around and lunge for his P bass.

"Gimme that thing."

Mike spun away from Gallo's swipe and laughed. "Ya can't hear shit, but from 10 steps away ya could tell I was playin' yer favorite bass?"

Gallo clenched his fists and snarled, "Put it down." His nostrils flared as he glared at Mike. "I ain't kiddin', Mays. Put it down . . . or else."

"You want it back?" Mike teased, holding the bass out toward him and pulling it away. "Come up here and play, then." Mike coughed and goaded Gallo into swiping at his bass with near misses. "Be a man. Play."

Gallo's breathing was heavy and he looked like he might be fixin' to take a swing.

"Mike," Harley called out, and he knew he didn't dare ignore her. She took the bass from him and held it out toward Gallo. "C'mon, Gallo," Harley said with a wink. "Just play this one with us."

"Please, geeze?" Tank pleaded, stepping closer, as if to ensure Gallo would hear him. "My bass playin's rough as a badger's arse."

After straining to read their lips, Gallo patted the cell phone in his pocket, as if reaching for Vin's help.

"He don't make your decisions, man," Mike blustered. He eyed Gallo's expressionless face and noticed his breathing had slowed.

Then Gallo snatched his bass from Harley's grasp, drew back, and narrowed his eyes. "Fuck you, Mays. Don't ever touch my bass again."

Mike laughed. He wanted to snap back, but he just stood there, shoulders set, and watched Gallo leave the barn.

At the door, Gallo stopped and turned back. "I'm watchin' you, Mays," he said, pointing at Mike. "You'll fuck up again, and I'll be there waitin' to catch your lyin' ass."

Chapter 29

Velvet glared at Gallo, sitting there alone in the courtyard, still playing Solitaire. He had always been a selfish prick, she thought, never once returning the Vespa with a full tank. She flashed on the day he'd called *collect* from Redondo Beach after a fifth of Jim Beam; he'd been forced into retirement, like all of them. She glanced at the charred building and then at Gallo; he was practically deaf now, but still a helluva bass player. The concert had to work, she told herself; Harley was in, and now Gallo was the key to getting Vin. Mike had been right—she needed to butch up and lay down some serious demands. She took a breath and tugged on her shirt. He barely lifted his eyes from his hand of cards to acknowledge her as she pulled up a chair and moved in close so he would be sure to catch every word.

"So do you really talk to Vin every day?"

Gallo scratched his stubbled face.

Velvet glanced between him and the barn. "I know Mike's a bullshitter," she said, "but look what he's done so far. I mean, c'mon, the Hollywood Bowl?"

"What makes you so sure?" Gallo sat there wiggling his two false front teeth around with his tongue—a strange quirk.

He looked so gaunt that he seemed helpless, like the scrawny stray dog she'd once taken in. She felt herself wither just a little and gave an uneasy glance around the courtyard. But when her eyes landed on the charred building, she stiffened right up. She leaned in close to his ear and implored him. "Give Mike another chance. For me."

Gallo lifted his hand of cards and then slouched in his seat without even a glance in her direction.

Velvet got up from the table and stared at his deep laugh lines. He seemed like he was always just a bit pissed off to find himself off hard drugs. She took a breath and stood tall. "I don't ask much of you guys—"

He didn't look up.

"Look," she said, brushing the hair from her face. "I know you think this is lame. I hear you every day, mocking Mike, the concert, the olive oil . . . everything—"

"Nobody's hirin' codgers onstage these days," Gallo barked, finally glancing up at her. "It's fuckin' hopeless."

"What about Vin?"

"Got lucky, that's all," Gallo growled. "He's a seasoned axe-slinger. *Some* people still look for talent."

Velvet narrowed her eyes at him. "You've barely gotten off your ass in three weeks."

"What for?" Gallo grumbled. "What the hell do I have to do?"

Velvet glared at him. "Are you fucking kidding me?" She pointed toward the barn. "I need you to get your ass in there . . . right now."

"This ain't got nothin' to do with me," Gallo snapped.

"The hell it doesn't." She turned back and glared at him. "You live here, don't you? You act like you're not part of this household."

"I cook sometimes."

"Why do Harley and I always have to do the dishes? And you leave your laundry for me to deal with." She sighed and then hardened her stare. "I'm not your fucking mother."

Gallo gripped his cards, his eyes searching, as if he might find his ace in the hole.

"You've been hoarding a case of Brunello in Blitz's room for months, yet you won't even buy a tank of gas for the Vespa."

He hunched his shoulders.

"We're supposed to all be in this together. You knew that from the day Vin and I bought your plane ticket to Italy." She paused to take a breath. "You just sit here on your ass all day making demands about your room as if it's *yours*." She pointed to the blackened building. "That room belongs to me and Vin, just like the rest of this property. You live here because of *our* generosity."

"What're you gonna do, kick me out?" Gallo said derisively.

"You know what? I love my husband more than anything. He's all that matters to me. But I don't really give a shit anymore if you're here or not." Velvet pointed to the barn and cringed at the racket emanating from the walls. "My friends are in there busting their asses, doing all they can so I can make things right and we can keep this place. You haven't lifted a goddamn finger." She could feel her nails piercing her palms. "If you won't get in there and do the fucking rehearsals, then, yeah . . . you can just pack your *two* remaining bags, sell those bottles of Brunello, and buy your own goddamn ticket out of here."

Velvet did an about-face and headed toward the barn. As the rehearsal sounds from inside lulled, she placed her hand on the barn door and turned with a final glare. "And don't even bother calling Vin," she blustered. "I'll be sure to tell him about the money I slipped you so you could meet up with that woman in Venice." She opened the barn door. "I'm running this household, and like it or not, Mike Mays is running the show."

When she turned back to the barn door, Mike was standing in the doorway grinning at her. She squeezed her eyes closed for a moment, wishing he hadn't just heard that ego stroke. When she opened them, he was still grinning.

"C'mon, babe," he said. "We got an errand."

He got behind the wheel of the Fiat and they headed into town. Velvet was surprised that Mike even knew what the *Catasto* was, let alone where it was located. As they stepped inside the land register office, Velvet felt her muscles tighten.

"I figure," Mike crowed, "we gotta cut to the chase."

"We?" She looked at him askance. The entire drive he'd refused to give her any indication as to what he had up his sleeve, and that made her nervous. When he escorted her toward Angelina's desk, she held her breath. She turned to Mike and hissed, "What're you doing?" Then she

acknowledged Angelina with a smile. She watched in horror as Mike practically mauled Angelina—in a place of business, no less.

"I been textin' Ange, here," he said. "And I'm gonna fix your tax bill for good." He turned to Angelina and grinned. She returned a smile but Velvet suspected that she also had no clue what Mike was up to.

"Don't fuck this up any more than it already is," Velvet hissed at him.

Angelina plunged her hand into a tote bag as black as her hair and pulled out a clear unlabeled bottle. "For you," she said to Mike in her thick Italian accent. "Grappa. *Fatto in casa.*"

"Homemade," Velvet translated.

Mike sure as hell knew that grappa was booze, and he grinned at Angelina before inspecting the clear bottle. "*You* made this?"

Angelina nodded.

"Fuckin' hell, yer gettin' hotter by the day."

Angelina blinked at him with her big brown eyes.

"Did you just bring me here to be your interpreter?" Velvet asked. "You know I don't speak Italian very well."

"Don't need no interpreter," Mike insisted with a crooked grin. He raised the bottle before setting it on her desk. *"Gracias."*

Velvet rolled her eyes. "That's Spanish."

"Spagnolo." Angelina giggled. "In *italiano . . . grazie . . . grah-tzee-eh.*"

"The only Italian I wanna get to know right now is *you*," Mike said, and started to make a move on her.

Velvet grabbed his arm. "What are we doing here?"

He grinned at her. "Leave this to me, babe." Then he launched into a tirade about the unreasonable increase on Vin and Velvet's property tax bill.

"I've tried this already," Velvet said, taking a step between them. "It's pointless."

Mike was undaunted as he leaned past Velvet, aiming his lecture at Angelina. "From what I gather, either someone's fuckin' around or someone here made a mistake. Maybe there's a glitch in the system. But my friend Velvet here is gettin' fucked over and I need you to—"

"Look at her," said Velvet with a nod to Angelina. "She doesn't understand a thing you're saying."

"If ya just keep talkin' at 'em, they eventually get it."

Velvet rolled her eyes. "You're an ass." In an attempt to explain in rudimentary Italian, as well as apologize for Mike's awkward provocation, she turned to Angelina. "I'm sorry about Mike. . . . *Mi dispiace* . . . he believes there's . . . *un* . . . *errore.*"

Angelina spewed Italian too quickly for Velvet to grasp any familiar words. Then she looked straight at Velvet. *"Non è vero,"* she said sharply. She pointed at her computer, as she had the countless other times Velvet had come into the office. Then she looked sternly at Mike. *"Impossibile!* Is no *errore."*

Velvet turned to Mike. "I've been through this with her so many times. So has Vin." She lowered her voice, "You know I already paid off the tax bill with Carlo's money. What is it you're trying to do here? Get a refund? A blowjob? What?"

He opened his mouth to answer but Velvet plunged ahead.

"The land registry is computerized," she explained to Mike, repeating what she'd learned each time she or Vin tried arguing with Italian bureaucracy. "There are no mistakes. She *personally* enters the data. It's only her and her boss."

Mike cocked his head. "Her boss, Carlo?"

"Carlo?" Angelina hissed and then mock-spat.

Velvet grimaced at him. "He doesn't work for the land registry."

"Ain't they cousins?" Mike asked.

"Distant . . . according to Giulia." Velvet glanced around the office. "Everyone in this village is probably a distant cousin."

"I see," Mike said, slowly nodding.

Velvet recognized the crafty look in his eyes—she'd seen it last month, the night he'd liquored her up at the bar. She narrowed her eyes and warned, "I don't know what you think you're up to, but stop meddling in my life. You've done enough damage already."

"How 'bout a little gratitude for a Good Samaritan, huh?" Mike asked.

He tapped his finger on his chin and stood there grinning. "Why don't you run along now? Go visit yer buddy Giulia or somethin'." Then he turned his grin to Angelina and rocked back on his heels. "I got me a ride home."

Velvet glanced at Angelina and at Mike—yep, it was the blowjob he was after. "You're . . . incorrigible," she charged, and with a sigh, left him alone with his little plaything.

She stood on the main street and glanced down at her phone but Vin hadn't returned any of her calls—not one during the past three miserable weeks since she'd hurt him. She glared up ahead at Giulia's shop and wondered: had Mike been hanging around the shop, sweet-talking *her* friend? Giulia could obviously handle Carlo, but how could anyone be prepared for Mike Mays bulldozing into her life?

She pushed open the shop door. If Giulia was there, maybe she could do a little sleuthing, find out if Mike was indeed taking advantage of her.

The woman behind the counter wrapped candy boxes without so much as a glance toward Velvet—the foreigner.

Velvet stepped up to the display case. *"Mi scusi."*

The woman turned, staring blankly out from under her Fendi gunmetal eyeglasses. *"Prego, signora."* She slid her finger over the jewel-encrusted logo and adjusted her glasses.

Velvet could hear the click-clack of Giulia's heels in the back room and then she emerged, smiling as she skirted the counter.

"Ciao, Velvet," she said, greeting her with a kiss on both cheeks. She gave a pouty smile. *"Carissima,* you must be stress, you coming to my store for *cioccolato."*

She had no idea just how stressed, Velvet thought. "No, I just dropped by to . . . I wanted to formally thank you for agreeing to help fund the concert."

"America." Giulia bounced on her toes and clasped her hands as the bling on her bracelets tinkled. *"La Principessa Cioccolato.* Believe me, I am so happy to be . . . what does Mike say . . . the *sponsor* . . . for the *concerto."*

Velvet smiled at her friend and began, as graciously as she could, to investigate what damage Mike might have done. "What does Carlo think of the concert?"

"Is my business," Giulia replied curtly. "For now, he no needs to know."

Velvet slowly asked, "I've been wondering . . . what exactly has Mike asked you to do?"

Giulia tilted her head. "To pay the money for the Hollywood Bowl . . . to . . ." She looked off as if trying to recall the English word. Then she turned back. "To rent."

"And what has he promised you in return?"

Giulia smoothed her body-hugging skirt. "He give to me the people to call for to *importare* the *cioccolato*."

"I'm just . . . I mean, you've been such a good friend," Velvet began, gently laying a hand on Giulia's arm. "He hasn't asked you to do anything shady, unethical?"

Giulia gave her a quizzical look, and Velvet saw that she didn't understand.

"I just want to be sure he's not taking advantage of you. Let's just say he's not famous for his tact."

Giulia blinked rapidly. "He say he is *very* famous in America—"

Velvet laughed. "No. I mean . . . *tact* . . . it's not the same as famous. And he isn't, by the way. Anymore."

Giulia stared blankly at Velvet. *"Non ho capito."*

Velvet sighed. Giulia really seemed to have Mike up on a pedestal. "Basically . . . he's an ass." She still looked confused, and Velvet realized that Giulia had given her all the evidence she needed: Mike was negotiating a business deal with her, nothing more. "Never mind. It sounds like he's behaved with you." She smiled and put her hand on Giulia's arm. "Truly, I can't thank you enough for helping finance the event." Velvet looked down at her purse and rooted around for her car keys.

"In any moment I can send the money," said Giulia. "To rent. . . . I tell to Mike that I am ready."

Velvet stopped and tilted her head at Giulia. "But I thought . . . you already sent the money, right?"

"No, I am waiting for the words from Mike."

Velvet gripped her keys so tightly she could feel them gouging her flesh. "Wait. You mean—"

"Non c'è problema," Giulia assured her. She smiled and flicked the long, dark hair from her shoulder. "I have the money."

Velvet glanced frantically around the shop, spotting the laptop behind the counter. "Can I use that?"

Giulia handed it to her with a concerned look. "What is it?"

Velvet pulled up the Hollywood Bowl website. "There's got to be something here," she muttered, "promo material, confirmed guest stars." She clicked the link to the calendar page and held her breath. "Please let Gallo be wrong." She blinked at the third Saturday in August and gasped: LOS ANGELES PHILHARMONIC AND THE ANNUAL TCHAIKOVSKY SPECTACULAR WITH FIREWORKS.

"What is it?" Giulia asked.

"Oh my God!" Velvet stepped back from the laptop. A cold chill shivered up her spine. "That sonofabitch doesn't have a venue!"

Chapter 30

Mike grabbed the bottle of grappa off Angelina's desk. Then he lifted a finger and motioned her outside.

"Damn, yer hot." He stood there grinning at her. "Ange, babe." She just stared at him and he figured it'd sink in eventually and she'd get the gist of his words. "I seen you sing—" He gave her a grand operatic *la la la* to get his point across. "Ya got somethin' there. Yer good . . . *bueno*."

"*Buono*," she corrected with a smile.

Mike could tell she was star-struck. He pointed at her. "You. Sing. *La la la*. Good. . . . And ya ain't too shabby on guitar."

"*La chitarra*," she said. "Is my fire and desire."

Mike laughed, which made him cough. "Where'd you learn English, the Blitz Stryker school of lyrics?"

"American rock music."

"Yer shittin' me." Mike widened his stance. "Ya learned English from rock lyrics?"

She smiled and nodded. "Only some words."

"It's yer *passion*, that's what ya say. . . . Music is yer passion."

The timbre of her voice sounded sexy when she repeated his precise words.

"No, *your* passion," he said, pointing a finger at her tits. Then he pounded his chest. "It's my passion too but *you* say, 'music is my passion.'"

"Music is my passion," she repeated in her thick accent. Then she swallowed, as if trying to wash down her fear of speaking English. "I want for to sing . . . and for to play *la chitarra* . . . like you. . . . Also I play . . . before . . . in *Firenze*. You know?"

Mike grinned. "Killer voice *and* yer shit hot," he said. "Winnin' combo. Ya got a demo tape?"

She tilted her head with a blank stare.

"Right, nobody uses cassettes no more," Mike said. "Uh, got a record, recording? CD? What's it kids listen to today? MP3? iPod? *Yer* music?" he asked, making every descriptive hand gesture he could think of. "You. Sing, play. Me hear," he said, strumming an air guitar, and then donning imaginary headphones. "Somethin' to promote yer talent."

Then she latched onto a word. She got it—it was written all over her pretty face. "Promo?" she asked.

Mike nodded. "Yeah, that's it."

"Chee dee?" she asked. When Mike obviously didn't understand, she held up her hands, making a circle. *"Un chee dee promo?"*

"I got *promo*," Mike said. "But I don't know 'bout no tai chi—"

She tapped his arm and then curved her hand to shape the letter *C*, aimed it at him, and said, "Chee," and then, "Dee."

"Fuckin' hell." Mike laughed. "That's how you say CD?"

"My *musica*," she said, shaking her head. "I no have. . . . No chee dee. . . . No emmay-pee-tray," she said, holding up three fingers.

Mike got it. "No MP3 either." He laughed. There wasn't a chick in the world he couldn't get through to. "Cool." He grinned at her. "I got an idea. Vin's got a studio at his pad . . . a barn, really, but he's got all this gear . . . I'm gonna produce a demo for ya."

She wrinkled her cute little brows and shook her head. Then she slid her cell phone from her pocket and held it up to him. "Repeat," she said, with a finger on the translator app that she'd used before.

Mike repeated his proposition and when she read the translation, he could tell she didn't understand some of his lingo. But then when she squealed, it was obvious she got the part about Mike producing her. She smiled at him and clutched his arm, hella excited. He joined the celebration, reaching down to grab her ripe ass.

But then she pushed his hand away and her smile faded. She squinted at him and slowly asked, "Why you do this?" Then she took a step back, glanced around, and whispered, "What you want . . . sex?"

Mike laughed. "Sweetheart, I'd fuck ya in a heartbeat, but that ain't what I got in mind." He grinned and grabbed her phone, speaking into it. "Here's the deal. You investigate Vin's tax records, find out why they skyrocketed, and I'll produce a demo for ya over in Vin's barn."

She took the phone and gave him a puzzled look. "But the computer . . . no lie. . . . I know. . . . Is my work. . . . Is *corretto*, the tax. . . . All the houses, they go—" She pointed a finger up.

Mike reached out and grasped her hand. Then he pressed the app and looked straight at her. "Just check around your office. . . . Dig through records. . . . Look. . . . For me. . . . I can get ya a record deal. I got connections."

Angelina eyed the translation on the phone and gave him another baffled look. She shot a nervous glance back toward her office and then down the street before returning to Mike. "Okay. I do it . . . for you."

Chapter 31

Lydia snuck a furtive glance down the hallway. The deafening guitar noise coming from the living room was great cover as she slipped into Brayden's bedroom for a closer look at the Expedia window on his computer screen. *SFO. FLR.* She gasped: *San Francisco to Florence?* Then she turned and stormed down the hallway, past Brayden playing guitar in the living room, and straight to the kitchen.

"He's looking at flights to Italy," she said to Andrew and pointed toward the hallway. As the guitar volume increased, she folded her arms and scowled. "We've got to do something, Andrew. That hair. . . . I'm going to go in and shave off all that blue dye one night while he's sleeping."

"Is he *looking* at flights or *booking* flights?" Andrew muttered from the kitchen table, without lifting his eyes from his iPad. "If it's the latter, then he has some serious explaining to do."

"He *lives* for that guitar . . . damn thing. And he Skypes Mike . . . and that woman—"

"Harley Yeates," Andrew said, nonchalantly. "Of the *Sex Kittens.*" He nudged his glasses up the bridge of his nose.

Lydia clutched her stomach. Brayden was slipping away, and she wanted nothing more than to take that guitar again—but she wouldn't dare. She bit her lip. "That zero on his math test? That means he didn't even take it. Can you imagine? He must have just sat there." She felt her teeth gritting. "You know, Lisa Dannen's son dropped out of school—"

"He's in rehab," Andrew reminded her. "Thankfully, *our* son's only addicted to guitar."

Lydia rested her hand on the counter and leaned in. Then she looked at Andrew and forced a smile. "I'll give it to him, he's a man of his word. Hasn't touched his homework in—" She tilted her head and listened. The guitar racket had stopped. "Oh, thank God," she sighed.

"Putting him on restriction is useless," Andrew suggested. "He'll just play guitar all day and night like he does now—"

"What more can we do to punish him?" Lydia tossed her hands up. "He's out of control."

"He's a teenager," Andrew asserted as he stood up and moved to her. He leaned toward the hallway and called out. "Brayden? Come here, please." Then he looked back at Lydia.

"He's just a child." Lydia felt her brows squeeze together. She looked up at Andrew and said half-aloud, "I—I just can't take that guitar away from him again." Andrew pulled her close and held her for a few moments before she moved out of the embrace and glanced up at him. "Will *you* do it?"

"God . . . Lydia." Andrew put his hand up and backed away with a shudder. His eyes darted toward the doorway, where Brayden stood, rocking back on his heels.

His juvenile attempt at a Mohawk nauseated her, but she forced herself to look at him.

Brayden rubbed his hand across his hair. "My hawk's gonna be blaze in a few months. Maybe I'll have liberty spikes by the time school starts in September . . . that is, if I decide to even go."

Lydia felt her face flushing. "If you don't get your grades up, mister, you'll be grounded for life."

"The Hollywood Bowl holds like, eighteen-thousand people," Brayden announced.

Lydia glanced between Andrew and Brayden. "The Hollywood Bowl?"

Brayden crossed his arms, all cocksure, just like his grandfather. "Grampa's *huge*." He lunged forward, right into Lydia's face. "He's gonna rock like you've never seen."

Lydia just stood there, blinking at Brayden. She certainly wasn't afraid of her own son.

"Don't talk to your mother that way," Andrew said sharply. He glanced over at Lydia. "Mike says he's playing a gig there."

She took a quiet breath in and looked at Brayden. "Sweetie, your grandfather is always full of big ideas." She feigned a smile. "But trust me, he doesn't follow through—"

"It's the largest natural amphitheater in the United States," Brayden continued. Then he looked at Andrew. "Did you know that Harley Yeates made a Christmas album called 'Bitchmas Eve'?" He gave an arrogant laugh and started to pal up with his father. "Do you own that one, Dad?"

"That's right, 1984," Andrew said with a smile. Lydia glared at him—was he really so proud of his son's newfound love of '80s hard rock music? But then he seemed to recall the reason he had summoned Brayden to the kitchen. "What's that on your computer screen?"

"When I get to Italy, Gramps said—"

"Did he buy you a plane ticket?" Lydia snapped, her jaw clenched. She looked at Andrew and then back at Brayden. "You're grounded—"

"No need. I'm on strike. Only thing I'm doing is ripping on my axe." Brayden rubbed his hand over the pathetic blue spikes on his head. "My chops aren't as good as ol' gramps, but I could give him a run for his money any day of the week."

Lydia squinted at him. He seemed so different, nothing at all like her son. "You sound just like your grandfather." She folded her arms. "You know, normally, one adult calls another about something as extreme as flying a minor to a foreign country. Why hasn't he called me, huh?" she challenged, but Brayden just ignored her and rambled on. It felt like talking to a zombie.

"You can't learn this stuff in school, ya know. This is life-changing . . ."

And that frightened Lydia most. She pursed her lips, sensing her father's bullcrap in there somewhere, between the lines. But she wasn't about to let him get his hands on her son—her most treasured possession.

Brayden stepped toward the doorway. "You know, maybe I'll just quit school." He shot her a nonchalant smile before he turned and headed down the hall.

Lydia gasped. "Andrew?"

Andrew raised his eyebrows. "That was . . . odd." He shuddered, as if to shake off the teenage drama. "He's certainly determined," he said with a grin and then shrugged. "You know my position on the Italy trip. It's one way we'll get him back." He grinned at her. "Looks like our son has finally fallen in love." Without another word, Andrew ambled to the kitchen table and returned to his iPad.

"You mean, with the guitar? With Mike?" Lydia glanced around the kitchen, as if looking for answers. "I'm only trying to protect him." She felt a thickness in her throat. "Can't you see? Mike and his musician friends are a bad influence . . . even six thousand miles away." She turned toward the guitar noise clanging from the other room. 'Lucky Night' again, she thought—damn that song. "The guitar, the Mohawk . . . what's next, drugs?"

"Brayden is not your father. The kid's never even had a beer. I can't exactly see him shooting heroin into his eyeballs when he gets to Italy."

Lydia wheeled around toward Andrew. "*When*? . . . Now *you're* assuming he's going, too?" She wanted to scream. "Why do you keep making me the bad guy?" She glanced at Andrew and he gave her a look. "How much more obsessed can he get?" She shuddered. "I swear, if I hear another word about Groove House and Italy and those geriatric rock stars."

Andrew sighed. "I think we should let him go."

As Lydia stood in the coolness of the kitchen, she felt more alone than she had since her mother died. The person she most loathed had an intoxicating hold on Brayden, and Mike's spell seemed impossible to break. She glanced at Andrew, but he didn't look up from his iPad. She folded her arms and began to formulate a plan. Maybe it was a good idea to allow Brayden to get close to Mike, because Mike would inevitably hurt him, and eventually, Brayden would understand the *real* Mike Mays . . . and then he'd sympathize with her and comprehend why she had banished Mike from their lives years ago. She placed a hand on the counter and steadied herself as the possibilities whirled through her head. Then she stomped her foot. "No," she said quietly and resolutely. Any good mother, she reasoned with herself, would spare her son from imminent peril. And that's exactly why she would never cede anything to Mike. Lydia tugged on the hem of her shirt and stood tall. To hell with Mike Mays. She would find a way to win her son back.

Chapter 32

"That sonofabitch!" Velvet shouted as she pounded the steering wheel and raced the Fiat up the driveway. All the way home her stomach had churned as she considered a hundred different ways to confront Mike, but she hadn't settled on any of them. She took her car out of gear and cut the engine. When she slid from the driver's seat, the harmonious sounds coming from the barn gave her pause. She tilted her head. It sounded . . . really good.

She blasted through the barn door. Once inside, her jaw dropped when she spotted Gallo on bass guitar. "Oh my God."

Mike winked at her and then blustered, "Let's move on to 'Lucky Night.'"

Gallo grumbled, "I ain't playin' a song I shoulda been gettin' royalties for all these years." When he noticed Velvet he softened his stance.

"Can we just run through 'Rock My Love Muscle' once more?" Blitz asked, testing out stick twirls and snare hits.

Velvet approached, dodging Tank, who swung a little handheld video camera past her and shoved it in Gallo's face. When Gallo shooed him away, Tank turned the camera to Velvet. "Bonus material," he said, "for the DVD."

"Turn that off," she ordered him, pushing the camera away. She could feel the tension tightening in her chest as her heartbeat revved. She turned to Mike. "You certainly got your ass back in here in a hurry."

Tank flipped the camera display shut. "V, have a look at the gig site I been workin' on—"

"There's no web page," Velvet snapped, glaring at Mike.

"What you talkin' 'bout?" Tank scrunched up his face. "Already got the domain. . . . Look, www.groove-house.com." He stepped to the workstation and opened a window on the computer screen. "Goin' live with it—"

"That's not what I mean," Velvet said, as she struggled to maintain her composure.

Harley stepped off the stage area and over to the computer. "Groove House Benefit Concert," she read aloud. She leaned in to the monitor, dropping her hands from her guitar. "Why's Blitz's name above mine?" she asked, turning to Velvet.

"Whoa," Mike said, as he stepped from the microphone to the computer. "Ain't no time for diva bullshit."

Velvet stood there, gritting her teeth, and then she thought of the right question, the one that would break the news to them that Mike Mays was all bullshit. "Where's the ticket link?"

Mike ignored her and then stepped in, squinting at the screen. "Yeah, Harley's right." He commanded Tank, "Move her up here—"

"Hey," Blitz argued as he climbed out from behind the drum kit. "Golden Blonde sold more records than she did."

"She had the longer career," Mike retorted.

Velvet scrutinized the screen. "So," she said evenly, forcing a smile. "Where's the ticket link?"

"He ain't gave me that, yet," Tank said, glancing at Mike.

"Shit takes time," Mike crowed.

"Hmm." Velvet glowered at Mike. "In this day and age, *real* promoters have online tickets for sale *instantly*."

"It's comin'," Mike said with a hacking cough as his eyes darted around the barn.

"It's been several weeks now," Velvet said coolly. "You'd think there would be something online about the event . . . on Blabbermouth or any number of music webzines." She motioned to Tank. "Google it. *Groove House, Hollywood Bowl* . . . see what comes up. Or better yet, go to the Hollywood Bowl website."

As Tank reached for the mouse, Mike planted his hand on Tank's.

"No need," he said curtly and then just stood there, staring at Velvet, as if daring her to make the next move.

She folded her arms and glared at him. "I see you managed to get the L.A. Philharmonic to open for us . . . or are we opening for them?" She wanted to pounce on him and beat the lies straight out of him. "You're a royal prick."

"What's she sayin?" Gallo barked, fiddling with his hearing aid.

"I'm saying he's full of shit," Velvet blurted.

"It ain't like that," Mike claimed. "I had trouble reachin' the dude." He steadied himself on the computer desk and wheezed out, "There were some, uh, issues. You don't know all the crap that goes into rentin' a venue as important as the Hollywood Bowl. But I'm gettin' it sorted. I'll have Giulia wire the dough now, cement the Bowl date, and we'll be golden." He stood there, shifting his weight from one foot to the other, and giving them a forced frozen smile as if camera flashes were going off all around him.

"For chrissake, face it," Velvet spat out. "There's no venue, no concert."

Harley, Blitz, and Gallo all turned to stare at her.

"It ain't true." Mike scanned their faces and assured them, "We got a gig, it's just that—"

"How many times are you going to fuck me over?" Velvet yelled.

Mike raised his cell phone and started dialing. "I'm takin' care of it, right now," he blustered as he backed away.

"We've been duped!" Blitz exclaimed.

Velvet felt her muscles tighten.

"Heads are gonna roll," Mike roared into his phone from the other side of the barn. "Get your shit together right now. I don't wanna have to warn ya again. Got it?"

Velvet stared at him, barking into his cell phone, probably talking to a dial tone, she figured.

Gallo pulled the bass off over his head and handed it to Tank. Then he turned to Velvet. "You done now, lettin' this bozo fool you?"

Velvet glanced at Mike, who was shouting orders into the phone. She looked at Gallo and opened her mouth but couldn't think of a word to say.

Gallo shook his head. "Shoulda *never* listened to that swindlin' sonofabitch." Then he stormed out of the barn.

Velvet trailed him outside but went straight for the house. She scowled at Mike's dirty clothes flung about her office. She should've kicked his ass out when Vin left; Mike would've been long gone from Groove House by now, but, like some sort of defiant squatter, he just wouldn't budge. She picked up his mess, shoved his belongings into his duffel bag, and tossed it onto the futon. Then she plopped into the chair and put her head down on the desk. She felt so exhausted. She considered putting on her own fundraiser there in Italy, but she knew Vin would laugh just as hard as he had about Mike getting the Hollywood Bowl.

Aaaoooogah. Mike's text notification outside the window—where was he? She nearly jumped out of the desk chair when he came busting in.

"Houston, we have a problem," he said, motioning outside. "Carlo's bulldozin' the vineyard. . . . Listen."

Velvet tilted her head toward the window and could hear the distant burr of the bulldozer across the way. "Shit, shit, sh-i-i-i-it!" Her heart raced as she fumbled for the car keys. Why now, she wondered. What set him off? Did he find out Mike had stayed out all night with Giulia? Or that he'd been sleeping with Angelina? She trembled for a moment, reflecting on the way that the guys always tagged Carlo as mafia. Then she thought of the land and Vin, and she narrowed her eyes, even more determined.

As she sprinted toward the car, she noticed Mike was tailing her while on his cell phone. Typical, she thought—she was in crisis and he was probably trying to sweet-talk some *italiana* into a blowjob.

He caught up to her and cupped his hand over the phone. "I'm comin' with ya."

"I'm not talking to you!" Velvet said sternly, slinging her purse over her shoulder. "I've packed your shit, now get the hell off of my property . . . *pronto*!"

"I swear, babe," he gloated, shadowing her toward the car. "I got a *real* promoter now—an old-school renegade, who didn't sell out to corporate conglomerates like them other bastard promoters. And Gunner's back from vacation now so I can seal the Bowl deal."

"Your words mean nothing to me." She quickened her pace, hoping to ditch him.

"I'm tellin' ya," he wheezed, as he hustled along beside her. "This is the dude. You gotta believe me."

As Velvet was about to jump into the Fiat, Mike nabbed the keys from her and slid into the driver's seat.

"Let me handle this, doll," he said out the window. "I'll get him to stop. Trust me. Let's go."

Velvet stood there, grinding her teeth, her heartbeat pounding. The audacity of this jerk, she thought. Then she rounded the car and climbed into the passenger seat. She directed Mike on the little roads as he zipped the Fiat down to the vineyard. As the sputtering sound of the bulldozer grew louder, Velvet couldn't help but reach out to steady the steering wheel while Mike furiously punched buttons on his cell phone, cursing as it dipped in and out of service.

She could see Carlo up ahead at the helm of the yellow bulldozer. "Wait!" she yelled out the window as Mike skidded the car beside it. "Stop!" Her eyes widened and she let out a scream when the blade ripped through a section of Vin's grandmother's vines. She vaulted from the passenger seat, waving her arms all the way to the front of the machine. She looked back to see Mike texting as he walked from the car.

Carlo scowled at Mike and throttled the engine to idle. She hoped to hell he wasn't planning to interrogate Mike on his wanton ways. When Mike stepped next to Velvet, she glanced at him and felt a flare of adrenaline; he was about to fuck things up even more royally. Then she saw it—the fully-dozed vineyard. She just stood there, horrified. Her knees buckled and she found herself kneeling among the dirt and vines that Carlo had just scrupulously dozed.

Mike reached out his hand and pulled her up. "Ya gotta stay strong," he preached over the engine's sputter. "Don't let 'em see ya down."

She clutched Mike's arms and steadied herself. Then she sniffled and brushed the dust from her jeans.

Carlo gripped the steering wheel and glared down at her from the cab. Velvet raced to the side of the bulldozer. "Wait," she implored as she grasped a rung and started to hoist herself up toward the cab. Carlo looked down at her hand on his bulldozer, as if she'd just breached a demilitarized zone. She promptly removed her hand and lowered herself to the ground. When she heard Mike's cell phone ring, she glanced back to see him flash an encouraging thumbs up before he turned to answer his phone. She put her shoulders back and glared at Carlo. "You weren't supposed to bulldoze."

"Signora," Carlo bellowed over the engine noise in a sharp, impatient tone. He glowered at her, his eyes flinty. "I pay for the land, I have all the right to bulldozer."

"But I'm buying this land back. . . . You knew that."

Carlo let out a hearty laugh. "And where is your money, eh?" He leaned toward her. *"Boh."*

She glanced back at Mike, coughing, still on the phone. Then she looked up at Carlo. "Please . . . I need the land back . . . I need to . . . save my marriage."

"This *fregatura*," Carlo sneered, pointing a finger at Mike, "everyone know he make the pass on my wife. And he no stay away from my cousin, Angelina. He is a man of the lies."

"Apparently, that's world news." Velvet glowered at Mike.

"I give to you the money," Carlo hollered. "The land is mine."

At the sound of a car, Velvet turned hopefully.

Giulia whisked her Alfa Romeo into the vineyard and parked next to the bulldozer, raising a cloud of dust. Carlo rolled his eyes and cut the engine. The car door flung open and out slid two silky legs. Her petite black stiletto heels dug into the dirt as she stormed over to Carlo, her luscious lips issuing a delicious chainsaw buzz of Italian, her hands assaulting him with a barrage of gestures. Carlo didn't flinch at her words, whatever they were. Instead, he chuckled and retorted something that Velvet couldn't understand.

"The money," he said as he climbed down from the cab. "It is burned—"

"I'll pay you." Velvet knew she sounded urgent. "Just, please, give me back the land."

"I don't want your dirty American dollars." He crossed his thick arms and stood there with a presence so powerful that Velvet could feel herself shriveling. "And how you will pay now? Eh?"

"I . . ." She blinked at him, not wanting to blow Giulia's involvement. "The concert . . . Mike . . . I . . ."

Carlo turned and reached to climb back up the bulldozer.

"We have a plan," Giulia blurted out. She held up her hand, commanding her husband to wait.

Velvet cocked her head, wondering if Giulia was about to reveal her financial support. Then she noticed Giulia's play-along-with me nod. "We do," Velvet said with a sideways glance at her.

Carlo belly-laughed as he released his grip from the rungs and turned to them. "And what do you plan? To sell rock star chocolate bars?" His laughter trailed off as he turned back to the bulldozer.

"No, wait . . . it's . . ." Velvet fished for the right words. She bit her lip and looked at Giulia.

"Is private," Giulia volunteered with confidence.

"So." Carlo muffled his laughter and stared at his wife. "This is how you are, eh? You going to help them . . . buy *my* land from *me*?"

Giulia thought about it for a moment, glanced at Velvet, and then gave her husband an ambivalent nod.

"Well, then." Carlo laughed again. "The price now is three times more."

"Ladro!" Velvet yelled out the word *thief* in Italian, as Carlo's price had just exceeded criminal. Vin must've been right all along, she considered, and Carlo really was mafia.

Carlo pointed a cautionary finger at Giulia. *"Non sputare per aria che ti ricade in testa."*

Velvet caught the words *spit* and *air* and something about *head.*

Then Carlo glanced at his gold wristwatch. *"Allora."* He gripped a rung and began to pull himself up to the cab.

"Carlo!" Giulia demanded. "You will no to do this."

Carlo retreated back down the first rung. He turned to see Giulia stretch a tan, silky leg and plant it toward him. Then she crossed her arms, thrusting her voluptuous breasts forward. Carlo cast a lustful eye down to her bare leg and then up at her breasts.

When her heel wobbled in the dirt, she steadied it and then gave her husband a determined stare. "These are our neighbors, Carlo. They are old," she hissed loud enough for Velvet to hear. "Their house is burn. We must to help."

Carlo ogled his beautiful wife for a moment, as if considering what the cost might be, but then he raised his voice, "I owe them nothing . . . *niente.*"

Giulia spewed rapid-fire Italian at him. Velvet heard her name and Vin's, but she only grasped the words *lost* and *failure.* Whatever Giulia had said to Carlo, it hadn't worked. With a stiff, frustrated smile, Carlo lifted his hand again, reaching for a rung.

"Cool yer jets there, sparky," Mike said, as he swaggered close, cell phone in hand. "The promoter's wirin' money to Italy from the great U.S. of A. as we speak." He pressed on the speaker button and held out the phone. "Yer on, dude."

"Hello. I'm Andrew, from the promoter's office," the voice blasted from the phone. "And I can assure you that we are currently in the process of preparing funds for a wire transfer. As a good faith measure—and because Mr. Mays is such a valued . . . uh, feature . . . of this event that we are so proud to be a part of—we will wire a respectable sum this week."

"Eh?" Carlo said, as lines formed between his brows.

"Should come sometime next week," Mike clarified. Then he gave Velvet a half-shrug. "Takes time to sell tickets 'n' shit."

Velvet gasped and felt a slow smile. "See?" She pointed to Carlo and gave an easy nod to Mike.

"You delay, too long. The land no can wait," Carlo insisted as he looked down his nose at them. "I am prepare . . . for the new vine."

Velvet took a step back. "You're planting a . . . vineyard?"

"*Certo.* What you think, eh, I build a hotel?"

She chewed her lip, knowing that Vin would be even more upset to find out Carlo had ripped out the ancient vines for a vineyard of his own.

Carlo kicked a gnarled vine. "Your husband know nothing about to make the wine."

"Stop plowin', hotshot," Mike blustered as he lowered the phone. "The dough's on its way. You'll have it before July first, dude. You ain't turnin' back now."

Carlo glanced between Mike and Giulia. "Mike Mays," he said with a scowl that looked just as bitter as his tone. *"Uffa."*

"Velvet," Giulia insisted. "Go home. I take care of this and I call you later."

Velvet felt her muscles relax. "Thank you," she whispered to Giulia. Then she glanced at Carlo, who was glowering at her.

"Is now two-hundred and ten thousand Euro you pay to me," he demanded.

Velvet narrowed her eyes. "You heard Mike. You'll get the money. But *triple* the price? Over Anna Maria's dead body!—" she thwarted her rant with a final glare before she headed for the Fiat.

When she reached the driver's side, she looked back to see Giulia pointing at the bulldozer, arguing with Carlo. Velvet glanced at Mike. When he winked at her, she assumed he had called Giulia to the rescue. More than that, he'd finally come through with the concert, and money to help buy back the vineyard. The promoter's voice on the phone—she had heard it herself.

"You." Carlo shouted at Mike. *"Fa i cazzi suoi."*

Mike stared at Velvet from across the Fiat roof. "What'd he say?"

"Something about your dick . . . only it was plural." Velvet shrugged and then slid into the driver's seat.

Mike laughed as he climbed in and slammed the passenger door. "Who the fuck is Anna Maria?"

"Vin's grandmother. You know, the one who owned the land?"

Mike grinned. "We're a good team, doll."

Without even looking in her rearview mirror, Velvet whipped the Fiat up the hill and breathed a sigh of relief. "Thank you," she said, with a glance to Mike. "So where's the promoter wiring the money? Me? Giulia?"

"Ah, I couldn't reach him. That was my son-in-law—"

"What?" Velvet screeched the old Fiat to a stop. "You were bullshitting back there?"

Mike just shrugged.

"Are you for real? This is my life, goddammit, not a fucking game. God!" She pounded the steering wheel. "I need that money . . . my husband . . . I need to fix things. You moron, this is for *all* of us—"

"Relax, I'll get it." He glanced at her and then looked away.

"You are . . . un . . . believable." Velvet felt her hands go limp as she slumped over the steering wheel. "This is it then. It's over," she said, her voice cracking. "My marriage—"

"That ain't gonna happen. We got *loads* of time." Mike shifted his weight in the passenger seat. "Look, Liddy, the promoter, wasn't in his office so I needed a proxy . . . someone to just say what I know the promoter woulda said. It worked, didn't it?"

Velvet lifted her head and stared at him, just sitting there with his crooked grin, in total denial, so impressed with his own bullshitting.

"I got this covered," he boasted. "Trust me. Have I failed you yet?"

Velvet gave him an incredulous stare. "You really want me to answer that?"

He turned and stared out the window.

Her heartbeat thudded dully as she gazed out across the vineyards. Aside from burning her home and all the Euro bills and lying about the Hollywood Bowl, she reasoned, he'd now sworn that he had a real promoter, had pulled it together. She could feel her temples pulsating. Then she let out a quiet sigh. "You realize that my husband isn't even speaking to me? And that's on you, *dude*," she said, giving the last word a derisive twist. "Here's the thing. I've already packed up your shit and I'm about to run you off my property . . . unless . . ." She turned to face him.

"Lay it on me, babe."

"Get Vin to come home. And I mean, *now*."

He grinned. "Easy as—"

"Not another word," she snapped, holding up her hand to shush him. "I want Vin's ass back here. Now. Make it happen." Then she smoothed her shirt, gripped the steering wheel, and pointed the Fiat home.

Mike stared out the window, humming tunelessly.

Velvet looked over at him. "Why'd you insist on coming with me today?"

Mike wheezed out a sigh. "I get it now." Head down, he glanced at her. "How important that vineyard is to you, to Vin."

Velvet drove for a while in silence, and then she softened her grip on the steering wheel. "She texted you, didn't she?" She stole glances at him. "Angelina, about the bulldozer?"

"Let's just say—" Mike grinned like a schoolboy in puppy love. "—I got connections."

Velvet had doubted Mike's *connections*, but this one had paid off. As she drove up the white road, she noticed him clutching his phone. "How do you do it?" she asked as she pulled the car up to the barn. "I don't get how you communicate with her."

Reaching for the door handle, Mike turned back and shot her a crooked grin. "We speak the language of love."

Velvet rolled her eyes. "She barely knows English."

"Don't need no translator. Ya know, I always get what I want." Then he winked and got out of the car.

Velvet stood up and began to walk toward the house, and then she spotted Tank and Blitz heading into the barn. She couldn't face the others just yet, and so she headed to the edge of the courtyard. She stopped and sunk onto a bench near the terraces, and she could hear Mike on the phone down by the pool.

"She told me you'd divorce her if she sold the land. Seriously, she said *no*, but we had that nasty Fernet shit and then a whole bottle of red, maybe two, I don't remember. Dude, ya gotta believe me . . . *I* took her to Carlo's. It was all *me*."

Velvet leaned forward, listening intently.

"Trust me, gettin' out of a tour ain't that hard. Dude, ya gotta come now."

Velvet felt her heart skip. *Vin?* She got up and angled toward the pool. Was Mike actually campaigning to get her husband home?

Chapter 33

"**K**id's turnin' out to be a real rocker," Mike said, glancing at Tank. He tapped his fingers on the desk and stared down at the list of phone numbers he'd collected, or rather, the ones he'd had Tank corral. That dude seemed to know *everybody's* roadies. "Been givin' him a crash course in rock 'n' roll over Skype—"

"Quit pitherin' about, geeze," Tank said, hovering over him. "On yer bike."

Mike coughed and eyeballed the bottle of grappa that Angelina had given him. He considered reaching for it but circled his attention back to Tank.

Tank spotted the bottle stashed under the office futon. "Yeah, nip o' the ol' liquid courage'll do ya." He lunged for the bottle and passed it to Mike. "Take a hit, geeze."

Mike took a swig but the sinking feeling in his stomach had nothing to do with the booze.

"C'mon, geeze," Tank pestered him. "Gotta get yer arse in gear, make this gig happen. If it means grovelin' to blokes holdin' grudges, then that's what you gotta do, geeze. . . . For Vin and Velvet." He picked up the phone and reached it out to Mike. "Time to call in favors."

Mike ran his finger down the list and then slugged down another shot.

"Don't be such a tittybabby. Top of the list." Tank snatched the bottle from him. Then he grabbed the phone and looked down at the list. "Start with that Bertie big bollocks, Bo. He'll come 'round if ya blag on him enough." Tank punched the keys and then grinned at Mike. "Tell him ya stole that mic stand bit," he said, reaching the phone out to Mike.

Mike rolled his eyes at Tank. He downed another swig as the phone rang in his ear. "Hey, dude. It's Mays." He had a sour taste in his mouth and it wasn't the grappa.

"Who?" Bo said.

Mike shook his head and glared at Tank. "Mike Mays. Ya know, the dude you accused of rippin' off yer schtick in the '70s? Ya know, the scarf tied around the mic stand thing?"

"Mays? . . . Haven't heard that name in decades."

Ouch, Mike thought.

"How'd you get my number?"

"Tank—"

"Tank?" Bo laughed. "Fuckin' awesome crew dude. How is that old tea bag?"

Mike looked up at Tank. "Tea bag's right here." As Tank giggled, like a little fanboy, Mike motioned for the bottle.

Bo snorted. "Dude should be knighted for havin' to put up with *your* ass."

Mike smirked. "Look, I just wanted to cop . . . I mean, I uh, I did rip yer bit . . . with the colored scarves, the mic stand—"

Bo cackled into the phone. "Dude—get up off your knees. I'm secure in my place in rock 'n' roll history. Everyone knows *I* was first."

"Yeah, well . . ." Mike grinned. "So there's this other thing—"

Mike went on to explain Groove House and the fire and the fundraiser concert and getting the Hollywood Bowl.

"You lookin' for a handout?" Bo asked.

Mike twisted his shirt. "No. I was just . . ." Mike noticed Tank shaking head. Then he started hopping around making lame-ass hand gestures. "I was, uh, hopin' you'd . . ." Mike waved off Tank and swiveled the chair away from him. "Will ya come out to the gig and jam a tune or two?"

"You got a helluva nerve asking *me* for a favor."

Once the call ended, Mike dropped the phone onto the desk. "Fuck this, I ain't gonna call these cats and confess—"

"You wanna be the one to tell Vin and Velvet there's no gig?" Tank just stared at him, head cocked and arms crossed. "You ain't really got a choice, geeze." Then he dialed the next number and handed Mike the phone.

"Mays?" Dave asked. "Where'd you get my number?"

"Tank—"

"Tank?" Dave laughed. "That's one funny Brit. How the hell is he?"

"Bastard's right here," Mike said, a little annoyed.

"Tell that soppy git he can blow me . . . but *you* . . . well, *you* can just fuck off."

"Look, I just wanted to come clean, let you know . . . back in '80-whatever, sorry I pissed into your convertible when it was parked on Sun—"

"I knew it was you even before you yapped to the press. You're not even smart enough to realize you'd pre-incriminated yourself," Dave said, and then lost himself in a belly laugh.

Tank leaned in close to eavesdrop.

"Hit Parader magazine," Dave charged. "Said you were on a Jack and lemonade kick. My upholstery reeked of Jack, lemonade, and piss, and I just knew it was you."

"Yeah, well," Mike said, motioning for the grappa. "I was thinkin' it'd be cool if you could turn up at the Bowl and jam—"

"Cost me four grand to get your piss stench out. Had to reupholster my classic ride. Why should I do *anything* for you?"

"How 'bout that time," Tank hissed, "he kicked over your guitar at the Starwood?"

"You weren't even there," Mike barked, covering the mouthpiece. "Besides, he was just bein' a cock, seein' how close he could—" He'd been so engrossed in talking with Tank that he hadn't heard the click. "Hello? . . . Motherfucker hung up on me."

Tank let out a lengthy sigh and poured over the list. "How 'bout some of them Left Coast Yanks?"

"I'm done," Mike blustered. "These cats are all losers." As he started to get up, Tank put his hand on Mike's shoulder and pressed him back down into the chair.

"You ain't givin' up that easy, geeze." Tank took a hit of the grappa and shoved the bottle at Mike. Then he dialed the next number and handed him the phone.

Mike snarled at Tank and then focused on the call. "Hey, Jag. It's Mays."

"Mays?" Jag said. "Whoa, who gave you this number?"

Mike rolled his eyes. "Tank."

"How is that little fireplug?" Jag laughed. "Best roadie I ever had—till you snagged him back. Musta been all that blow you kept in your production case."

Mike took a breath. "So, I wanted to square up with you on somethin'. . . . It was me who pulled rank with Atlantic back in '78. Yer second solo album? You were gonna call it *Cruisin' and Boozin'* but that was *my* second album's title, and the label had already gone to press, and rather than scrappin' it and payin' to crank out a whole new album cover, I pushed 'em to make you change your title. . . . I figured, my first album sold more than yours, so it only made sense."

There was a long silence on the other end of the phone. Then Jag laughed. "So you were a prick, but in the end, that's the album that really cemented my solo career. I should thank you, but you know what? . . ."

Jag's long cackle grated on Mike. "This was a bad idea," Mike muttered. "Fuck off and have a nice life." He could still hear Jag's laughter as he hung up the phone. He looked up at Tank and pleaded, "Dude was laughin'. . . . Probably rollin' around in piles of cash—"

"In some warehouse," Tank said, "stacked full of pallets of vodka."

"Dude's worth millions," Mike moaned.

"He ain't worth the steam off my piss." Tank took a swig and studied the list.

Mike shrugged and took the bottle from him. "Never got all the hype about his second LP. Bullshit, if ya ask me."

"Bullshit, geeze," Tank said, humoring him.

Mike took another swig and traded Tank the bottle for the phone.

He caught Chappie as he was checking out of a Miami hotel. "Mays? Wow, is this some sort of time warp?" Chappie asked.

"I, uh, wanted to say . . . look, dude, I fucked Cindy."

"That chick always went for small cocks."

"Fuck you, asshole. I gave her the biggest—"

"Geeze," Tank interrupted, "don't be a lard head." He shoved the bottle at Mike.

"I thought you fucked Tamara—"

Mike took a swig. "Uh . . . the blonde."

"No, that was Cindy, my third wife—"

"Yeah, that's the one—"

"Tamara was my fourth. The redhead."

Mike grinned. "Always felt weird stirrin' your custard—"

"I never forgave you for that, man."

"Yeah, well, sorry. Hey, listen . . ." Mike repeated the same plea he'd made to the others. "Will ya fly down and play the encore?"

"No way, man. I'm tapped—"

"Whaddya mean?" Mike barked. "You got a catalog of multi-platinum records!"

"Ali-fuckin'-mony, man. These chicks are draining me . . ."

Mike nodded. "What if I pay for your travel?"

"I'm on tour, man. Got no time."

"Yeah, well, thanks for nothin'," Mike mumbled as he hung up. He looked up at Tank and motioned for the bottle. "Chalk another one off the list."

Dokken, Martin, Coverdale, they all had the same response—basically, *fuck off.* Mike took another hit of grappa. If he could just get one big name, other stars would be bustin' down his door to get in on the hype.

Chapter 34

Velvet opened her eyes and lay there, listening. She squinted at the stream of morning light beaming through a crack in the shutter. Then she drew the sheet to her chest, rolled to the empty side of her bed, and dismissed it all as just a dream. But when she closed her eyes, the thudding sound resumed. She climbed out of bed and pushed open the shutters. The courtyard was empty and quiet—except for the pounding. When she looked across at the fire damage, she saw nothing. She turned, slipped into her sweats, and headed downstairs.

Gallo's snores sailed from the sofa. She peered through the open office door and noticed Mike's rumpled blanket on the futon. It had been over a month now that they had taken up residency in the main house, the space that she and Vin had previously kept for themselves. As she stepped outside and crossed the courtyard, the pounding grew louder. She inched toward the ladder that leaned against the wall of Gallo's burned quarters. Then she dodged a roof tile, seemingly slung from above.

"Dammit, Mike," she aimed at the roof. "If Vin finds out you messed with this, he'll have a—" Her mouth fell open and then she froze.

He glowered at her from the open window.

"Vin?" Her heart raced, and when she lurched toward him, he backed away. She stood there staring at him. He seemed distant, as if his body had returned home but not his heart. He had deep circles under his eyes, and he looked like he hadn't shaved in a week. She wanted to reach out and unsnarl the tangled hair that fell onto his shoulders.

He tossed two more roof tiles into the courtyard and then gave her a cold, hard stare before disappearing into the room.

She stood there, breathless, her muscles tense. She wondered if she should just come right out with it and tell him that Mike had fucked up again, had lied to all of them about getting the Hollywood Bowl. Or maybe, she considered, she should try repeating some more of the earnest apologies she'd left on his voicemail over the past month. But there was still that chance he might never forgive her.

Vin reappeared and glowered at her as he tossed out another tile.

She moved closer. "Vin, I—"

"Why all the bloody noise at seven-fucking-thirty in the morning?" Harley shouted from next door. "Vin?" She rubbed her eyes and then glanced between Vin and Velvet. "Dahling, you're home . . . and just in time."

Vin glanced at her, frowning. "Olive oil. Chianti."

Velvet swallowed and cautiously added, "And limoncello."

"Limoncello," Vin said, mocking her. "Hollywood Bowl. . . . It's all so lame."

Velvet snuck a glance at Harley, who pressed her lips together. Neither of them dared tell Vin that there was no concert. He reappeared and glanced past her, focusing just over her shoulder. Velvet turned to see Gallo heading toward them.

"Glad you're back," Gallo said as he approached. "Someone's gotta tame that lunatic."

Vin stepped to the window. He stared out over the landscape and shook his head.

"Tank!" Gallo bellowed into the empty courtyard.

Velvet glared at Gallo and wondered if he'd told Vin about the bulldozed vineyard. Maybe Vin had already seen it firsthand. When she turned to him, he would scarcely look at her.

"Nobody gives a shit anymore," Vin said with a distant stare. Then he shifted his focus to Gallo. "What good's a bass player who can't hear?" He glanced at Blitz's quarters. "And drumming's a young dude's gig, anyway . . . like sheetrocking," he muttered before his eyes landed on Harley.

In the uneasy silence, Harley wet her lips. Gallo shifted in place, crossing and uncrossing his arms.

"What you doin' at crack o' sparrow fart, geeze?" Tank hollered, as he crossed the courtyard. "Vin?" He came up to them and just stood there, hands in pockets.

Vin wiped his forehead. "The Internet's full of assholes who jump at the chance to flame any rocker over the age of thirty—"

"Them assholes is wrong, geeze," said Tank. "We'll do it ourselves, find a new—"

"Tank," Velvet interrupted, shushing him with slight shake of her head.

"Point is," Tank said, motioning to the others. "These blokes been practicin' hard. They still got it. Wait'll you see."

Vin lifted the sledgehammer, but then they heard a car coming up the gravel drive, and all heads turned. Velvet recognized Angelina's sporty white *Cinquecento* with the red racing stripe on the side. When Mike stepped out of the car, Velvet squinted and assumed he'd just spent the night with her . . . again.

"Ah," Vin said, staring across the courtyard. "And here comes your ringmaster."

"Looks like someone got a little tiger tail," Harley said half-aloud.

Vin disappeared into the room and then reappeared outside. He skirted the building and rested the sledgehammer against the wall, all the while glaring at Mike, who was strutting across the courtyard.

"Well," Mike crowed as he swaggered close, his arms open. "Look who's back."

Velvet scowled at Mike, so full of bluster. He gave her a wink and a crooked grin. She noticed Harley's tightly pressed lips.

Vin kicked at a pile of rubble and then wheeled around and narrowed his bloodshot eyes squarely at Mike. "I specifically told you not to touch this."

Mike's grin turned into a laugh. "Well, Tank and I—" His laughter evolved into a coughing fit.

He was constantly hacking these days . . . maybe from the stress of them putting him through the ringer, Velvet considered. He spit and then gave her a cocky look, as if taking credit for Vin's return.

"We was just cleanin' up," Tank explained. "That is, till rehearsals begun." He shot Vin a hopeful grin.

Vin brushed a wisp of hair from his eyes. "*I'm* out there. *I* see it." He glared around at each of them. "Trust me, nobody's gonna give a shit about—"

"Did you listen to *any* of my voicemail messages?" Velvet asked.

"Monday," Mike roared. "I been workin' my ass off all night. Check the website." He nodded to Tank. "Hollywood Bowl. Last Monday in August."

Velvet wrinkled her nose. *"Monday?"* She glanced at the others and noticed Tank already working his phone.

Mike shrugged and said with a smug grin, "Gotta take what we can get, babe."

"Everyone knows Mondays are suicide." Vin let out a snide laugh. "Leave it to Mays to pick the worst day of the week for a gig."

"It don't matter," Mike argued. "It's summer. It'll be cool. Wait'll ya see who all I'm workin' to come out and jam."

Tank held out his screen to Velvet and she squinted down at the Hollywood Bowl event page. There it was—the Groove House Benefit Concert. The bastard had really pulled it off. With a slow smile, she shuffled back a step.

"It's gonna be epic," Mike crowed. "Star-studded. . . . I did it all for you cats." He stood there nodding, so cocksure.

"Jesus wept!" Tank glanced up from his phone. "Me Facebook's full as a bingo bus on a Friday night. And I ain't done square root of fuck-all."

"Look at yourselves," Vin barked, glancing among them. "You're like a fucking Mike Mays cult."

"Dude," Gallo growled. "I didn't want nothin' to do with it, but Velvet—" She glared at him and he shut up.

"Pussy," Mike mumbled with a sideways glance at Gallo. "Vin . . . dude, this is gonna be huge. I got it covered."

"This is *my* fucking house," Vin barked.

Velvet could see the tension building—Gallo turned away, glancing over his shoulder; Tank jammed his hands in his pockets; Harley stared at the ground.

"And I'm the man with the plan," Mike boasted with a lopsided grin.

Gallo muttered, "Or the dude who's screwed."

"Out there on the road," Vin said, with a glance at Gallo. "Gallo was my lifeline. Called me every day." He cut his eyes at Mike. "What the hell are *you* still doing on my property, anyway?"

"Vin." Velvet started to reach toward him, but stopped.

Mike shifted his stance. "Ya know, if it wasn't for me—"

"Shut the fuck up." Vin glared at him. "I oughta kick your ass . . . all the way back to California. Or better, call the *carabinieri* and have 'em haul your ass to jail . . . for squatting . . . or maybe arson." Vin kicked a tile into the rubble and then glanced at Harley. "What're you doing, Harl?" he asked, tossing her a nod. "Dicking around with this fuckup again."

"That's preposterous," Harley snapped. Then she fired a look at Gallo. "Why would you say such a thing?"

"Sometimes I wonder if that dude's back on crank," Mike bellowed.

"Fuck off, Mays," Gallo blustered.

"Oh, ya heard that," Mike grumbled.

"I was content out there on the road." Vin announced, sneaking a glance at Velvet. "Even as a hired gun, subbing this summer—especially festivals—even in dingy, little clubs. . . . I'm just . . . happier onstage."

Velvet could feel her eyes smarting and she looked down. Although she knew what Vin meant, his comment still stung.

Vin stood there rubbing at his square jaw. "I don't like what's going on here."

Velvet balled her fists, fighting the urge to reach out to Vin; if he would just hold her, it would make everything that had happened the past six weeks a bit more bearable.

"I'm out there on the road busting my ass," Vin said flatly. "Doing everything I can to try and make ends meet." He shot a flinty glare at Mike. "And you're here swindling the neighbors . . . your stupid-ass concert . . . using my shit." He glanced at the barn and shook his head. "I don't have time for this crap."

Velvet took a slow breath.

Vin pulled off his shirt and threw it to the ground, and Mike took a step back, as if he thought Vin might be preparing to kick his ass. Vin leaned over and picked up the sledgehammer. "I'm tired of people fucking up my shit."

Mike took another step back.

"Vin," Velvet said, stepping toward him.

Vin held up the sledgehammer. "Outta my way. . . . All of you. I've got work to do."

"This is our family," Velvet said sternly. "The only one we've got."

Vin paused a moment, and then he turned to steady the ladder.

"Dudes!" Blitz blasted into the courtyard with Vin's acoustic guitar strapped on. "You gotta hear the tune I just wrote."

Vin glanced at Blitz and then at them all. "Count me out of your little project." He set his foot on the first rung. "I don't want *anything* to do with Mike's little circus act."

Mike cleared his throat and tried herding them away from Vin. When Vin disappeared into the room again, Velvet lowered her head, turned, and straggled across the courtyard. Harley stood at the kitchen door, holding it open for her.

"Don't let Mays rip off your tune," Velvet heard Gallo blurt out. "I'm gonna go help Vin."

"Well, stone the crows!" Tank sang out. "Gallo's offerin' ta get off his arse? Rare as rockin' horse shit. Problem is, ya got fingers like pig's tits. Better for thumpin' bass."

Velvet turned and stole a glance over her shoulder toward the vacant roofline before she and Harley stepped inside. "Jealous?" she asked.

Harley cocked her head.

"Angelina?" Velvet nodded toward the door, even though Angelina had long gone.

"Why would I be jealous?" Harley laughed. "So Grandpa Rooster taps kitten ass. . . . Jolly for him," she said with false cheer.

"Weird that she'd idolize an old fart like him," Velvet said with a laugh. "I still don't get how they communicate." She pursed her lips and reached for bowls and flatware as she listened to Harley's rant. Then she glanced at the kitchen door and back at Harley.

"What the hell is wrong with me?" Harley asked with a weak smile.

"So stop all this hot and cold stuff and just try him on for size."

"Again?" Harley laughed. "You know . . ." She smiled and glanced toward the door. "Mike and I have this deep . . . bond. Dunno how to explain it. He makes me feel things I haven't felt in years."

Velvet got it—the pull of the past, reliving their youth—Mike had a way of bringing it all back. But those two had something more. And now that Velvet had come to know Mike better than she ever cared to, the attraction made sense . . . in an odd way.

"We shouldn't have doubted him," Harley said. "But, well," she sighed. "He's Mike Mays, isn't he?"

"I know," Velvet agreed. "He fucks up but somehow he keeps coming through. It's on the Hollywood Bowl website now, so it must be true . . . right?" She turned to Harley with raised eyebrows.

"He's certainly not technical enough to hack a website."

Velvet looked toward the kitchen door. "I just wish . . ." She chewed her lip and wished she could ask Harley to intervene. "Vin. . . . He'll hardly even look at me."

Chapter 35

Velvet set down the watering can in the courtyard and glanced up at the dripping red geraniums that cascaded from her bedroom window boxes. Then she looked toward the barn, where everyone would soon gather to rehearse—everyone but Vin. Her eyes fell on the empty hammock, where he had slept last night. She'd hoped a good night's sleep might have changed his mind, but no. She could hear Mike's voice blustering in the distance. She grabbed a thick slice of bread and cheese and headed toward the site of the fire damage, where Mike stood talking with Vin.

As she crossed the courtyard, she saw Vin's fleeting glance. Mike swiveled and when he spotted Velvet, he nodded to Vin and then sauntered toward the barn.

"You skipped breakfast," Velvet said cautiously, holding up food. "And lunch."

Vin ignored her and climbed up the ladder.

"What do you suppose Mike's big surprise is for today?" Velvet glanced at the roofline but there was no reaction. She looked down at the food in her hands and then up at the roof again. "Rehearsals have been going," she said with forced enthusiasm, ". . . fairly well."

As a piece of charred wood came crashing down, Velvet set the food on a work table. She hesitated, placed her foot on the first rung of the ladder, and then pulled herself up.

"I was stupid to listen to Mike, I know, but—" She choked out. "I wish I could take it all back, you have no idea." She could feel tears pooling in her eyes as she stretched up another rung. "I'm so sorry, Vin. I'm doing everything I can. . . . It's all for you. . . . God . . . this is all . . . so . . .

exhausting." As tears dripped onto her shirt, she tightened her grip on the ladder and glanced down the courtyard at Tank and Blitz assembling near the barn.

She ducked when Vin pitched another hunk of wood to the ground, but then he suddenly glanced at her and she couldn't help it—her heart fluttered. His doleful brown eyes lingered and she realized she had his attention. She tried to hold his gaze, but he broke away and turned toward the vineyard.

Velvet stared at him and sensed that his bullheadedness wasn't solely aimed at her—it was now partly about Mike. "He could be dethroned, you know," she said. But then he wielded the sledgehammer, knocking down more tiles and burned wood. She stared at him a good long while, shirtless in just his jeans. "Feels like I'm still talking to your voicemail."

She backed down the ladder. On terra firma, she looked toward the barn and noticed Gallo ambling in that direction. Then she glanced back up at the roof before she turned away. Mike was standing solo at the barn door. She could see some visitors had arrived and were collecting camera gear from their van. So she straightened her shirt and headed for the barn.

As she approached, she noticed Mike snuffing his cigarette in the ashtray with a glance at the rooftop. He grinned when he spotted Vin, still at work. She looked back at her husband, who was craning his neck toward the visitors. Great, she thought, Mike was taking over everything, and Vin wouldn't even come down from the friggin' roof in defense—he just stared at them.

"Right this way, gentlemen." Mike held open the barn door and motioned to the British crew—a young cameraman, sound man, and a reporter named Ian, whose grey hair made him look three times everyone else's age. He held the door open for Velvet.

Velvet forced a smile. Then she turned and noticed Harley just steps behind her.

"Remember what I told ya," Mike said to Ian, with a quick glance at Velvet. "Vin don't do interviews. So don't keep askin' 'bout him." Then he led them into the barn.

Velvet trailed them.

"Here's my surprise," Mike gloated to the room. "First interview."

Gallo looked up from where he was squatting at the kick drum, repositioning the mic; Blitz sat frozen behind the drum kit. Tank was at the workstation, looking perplexed. The skeptics all watched as the camera crew scouted the barn. Mike had, Velvet realized, actually come through again.

"You didn't warn us," Harley hissed at Mike.

Velvet watched as Mike pulled Harley aside.

"Look, uh, don't let on 'bout Vin's whereabouts," he said in a soft voice. "I don't wanna have to . . . field a million questions."

Velvet took several slow steps backward and lowered herself onto the old church pew that she and Vin had purchased in Florence years ago. She noticed that Gallo seemed even crankier than usual, and she guessed it was the media presence.

"Mike?" Ian asked from across the room. "Can we move these cases over there, by the instruments?"

"Make yerselves at home," Mike said, laying on the fake charm.

Velvet got up and watched as the camera crew did a quick set up, aligning chairs and the pew into short rows.

"Any chance for a sneak preview?" Ian asked.

Mike laughed. "No chance."

"Can't blame me for asking." Ian shrugged. "Let's give it a go then, shall we?"

As Tank circled around, snapping photos, Mike plopped his ass front and center. Velvet sat to his right and watched Blitz and Gallo scramble to claim their seats as if it were a game of musical chairs. She realized it was the first interview in perhaps two decades for everyone—except for Mike, who surely had done loads of interviews last year, and Blitz, who she recalled seeing years ago on some kind of *Where Are They Now* TV show. She glanced back at Harley and then over at Gallo, who squirmed a little in his seat.

The red camera light blinked and the cameraman signaled Ian.

"Tickets are on sale," Ian directed to Mike. "How does it feel to dust off the old axe and play a charity for yourselves?"

As Mike opened his mouth to answer, Velvet heard the slam of the barn door. All heads turned. It was Vin. She noticed Mike glance over at her, but she sat tall, aiming a hopeful stare at Vin.

"Vin, lovely to see you." Ian smiled and reached out for a handshake. "I interviewed you eons ago for *Kerrang!*... Don't expect you to remember."

"Want some B-roll footage of the fire damage?" Vin asked with a quick, flinty glance at Mike.

"Good idea," Mike roared with a forced grin. "Tug at their heartstrings," he said, squinting up at Vin.

"Sure," said Ian. "After the interview." Ian pointed at the chairs. "Please, have a seat."

Holding firm to his center stage spot, Mike turned and nodded at Blitz to get up. As Blitz moved, relegated to the back, Velvet saw Mike glance at her. When she glared at him, he motioned Vin to the empty spot, but Vin just stood there staring him down. Velvet continued glaring at Mike, daring him to move.

Mike cleared his throat. "Here, Vin." He forced another grin. "Have a seat next to your beautiful wife," he said as he reluctantly shifted left.

When Ian repeated his first interview question, Mike opened his mouth again to answer, but Vin leaned forward.

"Well, I'm the only one here," Vin said with a grin as Ian swung the microphone to him, "who's still out there playing."

"That's really great, Vin," Mike said with a snicker as he leaned toward the mic. "But, of course, *I* was out there last year as a *headliner.*"

"Yes," Ian said with a twinkle in his eye. "And you took quite a tumble—"

"Well, you know," Vin interrupted, "some of us abused our bodies more than others."

Mike glared at Vin, and for a moment, the two sat in a silent standoff. But with Velvet's hard stare, Mike backed down.

Blitz pushed his way to the forefront, nudging himself between Mike and Vin. "This show's gonna blow you away."

Velvet looked at Blitz and couldn't tell if he had jumped in to defuse the tension or if he just craved his own moment on camera.

"Dude," Mike said, turning to Blitz. "You could use another coat of hairspray."

"Blitz is right," Vin said. "This show will kick ass . . . once I whip these guys into shape."

"You?" Mike ground his teeth and glowered at Vin.

"This is gonna be the best shit ever," Blitz interrupted again. "Can I say *shit* on British TV?"

Ian laughed, as if charmed by Blitz's enthusiasm. "This is for Internet. You can swear all you'd like."

Velvet saw Vin shoot Mike a sideways glance, and she figured that it was just dawning on him: an *Internet* interview—they hadn't even made it to television yet.

"This show's gonna be *crushing*," Blitz babbled on. "It's gonna be a better live gig than any date on the 'Pyromania' tour."

Velvet turned to see Harley and Gallo exchanging bewildered glances at Blitz's mention of Def Leppard, but she noticed one good thing—Blitz's energy had seemed to spark conversation, bringing back some of the swagger and banter the musicians had all once had with the press.

"So, Mike," Ian said. "You're in charge of this concert?"

Before Mike could respond, Vin hijacked the microphone again. "*I* am," he declared, head held high. "After all . . . this is my studio. My gear. My house." He smiled into the camera. Then he wrapped his arm around Mike's shoulder. "This bastard right here . . ."

Stuck in a stranglehold, Mike turned limp and succumbed to a coughing fit as Vin gently shook him.

"If it wasn't for him . . ." Vin grinned and shook his head before releasing Mike from his death grip.

Mike coughed and glanced around at the smiling faces. Velvet couldn't contain her own smile as she watched Vin out-Mike Mike. But she couldn't tell if Vin was just yukking it up for the camera, or if he had finally caved.

Mike slithered from his seat and then returned with Vin's blue Ibanez. Even though the guitar wasn't plugged in, he sat there noodling, as if trying to provoke Vin into an on-air confrontation. While Vin talked,

Mike stretched strings and played as loudly as possible, but Vin just kept chattering.

"Got Rod Liddy as promoter," Vin gushed. "Cool dude . . . old school promoter . . . also nabbed a killer PR firm in the States." He paused and then glanced at Velvet. "But, really, it's my wife who's the heart of all this. She's the heart and soul of Groove House, and it's *her* love and generosity that makes this place what it is. You know, the concert was her idea—"

Mike's fingers fumbled on a fret, but then he began playing even louder. Velvet aimed an incredulous stare at her husband.

"It was *her* good friend," Vin continued, "Giulia, the chocolate princess, who gave us the seed money—"

Mike noodled furiously and glared at Vin, but smartly kept his cool. Velvet sat up a little straighter.

Vin reached out and grasped Velvet's hand. He shot her a warm smile. "This woman is my life," he said, and it was as if the camera wasn't even there. "She means the world to me."

Velvet just sat there holding her husband's hand and fighting back tears. She was dimly aware that she was going all reality TV on-camera, but she didn't care.

Then Vin gave Mike a broad smile and reached for the Ibanez. "Thanks, man." He seized his guitar. "My favorite axe," Vin crooned, smiling into the camera.

Mike didn't surrender the guitar very easily, but then he glanced at the camera and loosened his grip, as though he'd decided he might be better off just sitting there looking cool.

"Oh," Vin said, "and don't even ask me about special guests. . . . You wouldn't *believe* who all's climbing up my ass to be on this gig . . ."

Mike just sat there as Vin engaged the interviewer like he owned the place. Well, he actually did own the place, Velvet thought with a smile. She leaned back and watched as Vin stole the show right out from under Mike.

Chapter 36

Rubbing the sleep from his eyes, Mike pushed himself upright on the bench and glanced around the barn.

"Fuckin' 'ell, geeze!" Tank cried out. "Scared the livin' cack outta me."

Mike yawned and scratched his scalp.

"Good afternoon," Tank greeted him. "You sleep here last night, geeze?"

"Gallo's snorin' on the couch kept me up." Mike snaked his tongue around his dry mouth and then swallowed hard.

"Aw, geeze, got a face like a welder's bench." Tank glanced back toward the barn door. "Go wash your donnies, the other geezers'll be here in a flash."

"Had this melody swirlin' in my head. So I came in here and spent all night hashin' it out." Mike stretched and twisted from side to side. "Been strummin' on Vin's acoustic for hours. Guess I musta crashed." He yawned and stretched his arms overhead. "Check it out." Then he lifted the guitar from the floor and spread out a jumble of scribbled notes. As he began playing the melody, he glanced up and noticed that Tank was smiling.

"Fuckin' 'ell, geeze, it's got *hit* written all over it." Tank looked toward the door when he heard voices.

"Just kinda wrote itself," Mike said, working out a few notes on the strings. He heard the barn door close and saw Gallo making his way into the room, with Vin just steps behind him.

Tank couldn't contain himself. "Gather 'round, geezers. . . . Listen."

"This melody haunted me last night." Mike glanced up at the staring faces. "Couldn't sleep so I came in here and—"

"What's on the list for today?" Blitz crowed, twirling drumsticks as he pranced into the barn.

Mike surveyed his KISS Destroyer shirt. "How many of them things do ya own?" He adjusted the acoustic guitar in his lap. Then he spread out his cheat sheets and glanced up again. "It's still rough—"

"New tune?" Blitz asked. "You didn't demo it?"

Mike eyeballed the workstation. "I dunno how to work that shit."

"And that's exactly why I want you to stay *out* of my shit," Vin said as he slipped behind the workstation.

"Yeah, I'm old school," Mike roared. "So you'll just have to listen the old fashioned way. . . . Live."

As Gallo futzed with his ear, Tank turned to him and said, "Get a load of this, geeze." Then he turned to Mike. "Go on, then."

Mike played and sang a few gibberish lyrics since he hadn't written many real ones yet.

"What the hell's he sayin'?" Gallo barked. "Born to be bad?"

"To a dude who can't hear," Blitz said, "it could kinda sound like that."

Mike stopped strumming. "I been strugglin' with a chorus all night." He looked up at Gallo. "*Born to be bad.* . . . Thanks to the dude with the blown eardrums, that's *perfetto*."

"Here we go again," Gallo grumbled.

"You lookin' for royalties on a song title?" Tank smacked Gallo's arm. "I'd be rich as Duke of Cambridge if that were so." Then he nodded to Mike. "Go on, geeze."

Mike played and sang out, toying with a new chorus:

'Cause I was born to be bad, yeah, born to be bad. The long, rough road is the only one I have.

He glanced up to see Tank and Blitz grinning, but Vin just sat there, expressionless. When Mike finished, the kudos piled on.

"*Crushing!*" Blitz exclaimed.

"I originally had it in A minor," Mike explained. "But once I switched to major, then it all just came together."

Gallo picked up his bass and flipped on his amp. "Hey, cockhead," he hollered to Blitz. "Get behind your kit. Got a bass line runnin' through my brain."

At first Vin didn't budge, but then he tapped a finger on his chin. "I'm hearing some parts we could add." He nabbed his green PRS guitar from its stand and plugged in.

A warm glow spread through Mike's body. He suddenly felt as jacked up as the first time he'd worked with Gallo back in the '80s.

"What're you waitin' for?" Gallo growled at Mike. "Plug in."

Mike wiped his eyes, and when Vin offered up the blue Ibanez, he accepted it with a nod.

Vin pointed at Mike. "Play that riff again."

Mike started on the riff and then stopped. "And don't even think about sayin' I ripped off your tune," he roared with a hard stare at Gallo. "You cocksuckers can't even come close to writin' shit this good no more." He glanced at Harley, who walked in with a smile and sat on the bench, as though taking a back seat.

Tank grabbed the camera. "This'll be fab bonus footage for the DVD."

"I was thinking something like this might make the chorus stronger," Vin suggested as he played out his ideas to Mike.

Blitz added, "How about we go into half time on the bridge to make it more interesting?"

"How about one of them Coverdale screeches you like so much," Gallo said and then cackled.

"I'm gonna throw this down," Vin said as he quickly set up to record the new tune.

Mike grinned as each of the players chimed in, sweetening his tune. But he noticed something unexpected. Instead of bullying his way through, he listened and stayed open to their suggestions . . . and it felt good. As they jammed it out, exploring the possibilities, he found himself swept away by the camaraderie. And the hours flew by.

"You worked through dinner," Velvet exclaimed as she walked in holding a plate loaded with sandwiches. She turned to Vin at the workstation. "I can't believe you've already recorded it."

"Just basics," Vin said without looking up from the computer screen. When he reached for a sandwich, he glanced up and gave her an easy smile.

Mike nodded, stoked to see his matchmaking efforts in full swing.

"And scratch tracks," Tank said as he snagged a sandwich off the plate.

"If Mike finishes the vocals," Vin said, "we could knock this sucker out fast."

Mike swallowed hard and reached for a sandwich. The thought of Germany crashed in and zapped the high straight out of him. He'd been so caught up in creating that he hadn't given a thought to actually recording vocals. Sure, he'd just laid down scratch vocals and bullshit filler lyrics to get the song across, he rationalized to himself, but not the real deal. He ran his fingers through his hair.

Vin didn't even look at Mike. Instead, he clicked buttons and started playback. Harley leaned against a chair and listened. A smile played on Vin's lips and Mike realized that he was diggin' the work they'd just whipped out. It was cool to see Vin happy, if only for a moment.

When the tune ended, Vin tapped on the desk. "This could be ideal for promoting the gig," he said. "Finalize the lyrics and add a solo—"

"Is this Wednesday?" Mike asked. "Fuckin' hell. My grandkid'll be here next week. The whole damn family's comin'. . . . Know what?" He nodded. "I'm gonna give the kid this solo." He noticed Vin's smile fade.

"Waste it on a rookie?"

"Wait'll ya hear this kid." Mike grinned. "Dude, he ain't gonna show you up that bad." Mike laughed, which triggered a coughing fit. "Maybe he will, 'cause, I taught him everything he knows—"

"What the hell good is all this, anyway?" Gallo blurted out as he wolfed down a sandwich.

"Whaddya mean?" Mike asked, noticing that all eyes were on Gallo.

"Don't matter how good it is," Gallo growled. "Nobody's gonna play it."

Tank nudged Vin aside and started tapping on the computer keyboard.

"He's got a point," Vin said with a frown. "We all got carried away creating, but now what? Damn near impossible to get airplay these days. . . . Without a major label—"

"This dude." Mike pointed at Blitz. Then he laughed at all the confused faces. "Got a sister who's some Internet star, right?"

Blitz looked as surprised as the rest of them. "Yeah, she has a blog . . . for vegetarian cooking—"

"It don't matter," Mike said. "She can write about anything. People still read that shit and they'll tell other people. Just think what could happen if she put some fire behind it and really hyped the shit outta this thing."

"Yeah," Blitz said "your new tune and the gig."

"*Our* new tune." Mike grinned around the studio.

"It's *your* song, man," Vin insisted. "We just helped bring it to life."

"My Facebook's up to 2,000 friends," Tank said from the computer.

"Why would 2,000 people be interested in you?" Harley asked, chomping on chocolate.

"All those groupies he screwed back in the day," Blitz said as he snatched a piece of chocolate from Harley. "Lookin' for their babies' pappy."

Tank smirked and put his hands on his hips. "Ain't no sheilas never looked me up 'bout no babby." He shook his head. "Not possible. I right nixed that chance long ago, geezers. Li'l snip here, li'l snip there, and Bob's yer uncle."

"And what, love, did all that fame get you?" Harley asked, as she picked up the empty plate.

"Laid," Gallo growled and tossed his cap onto his head. "Tank, you don't even know 2,000 people."

"That's 2,000 more than you got, ya septic," Tank said with a smirk. "Point is, they'll listen and tell their friends."

"All this technology shit." Mike shook his head. "Takes the mystery outta music. But I s'pose we oughta use it to the max." Mike felt his ass vibrating and reached into his pocket. "Probably Ange wantin' to hook up," he bragged and noticed Harley biting her lip. But when he looked down at the phone, the display read *Bruce*. "My former manager," Mike groaned as he stepped away. He answered and rolled his eyes as Bruce blathered through the phone.

"You know," Bruce said, "I've got several up-and-coming acts I'd love to put on the bill. Hollywood Bowl would be a real—"

"Motherfucker." Mike narrowed his eyes. "Why ya callin' me now? Lookin' for a piece of the action."

"Mike, I'm still your manager. I get fifteen percent of everything you do—"

"Uh, not no more ya don't. Last time we talked you said I was a *has-been* . . . your focus is on younger acts, remember?" Mike began pacing the barn. "As far as I'm concerned, that night on the phone you dropped me from your roster. Game over."

"We have a contract—"

"Oh yeah? Try comin' to Italy and suin' me here. You ain't gettin' shit. This is a fundraiser, ya sleazy little prick."

Mike ended the call and slipped the phone into his pocket. When he looked up, they were all staring at him. "He's just lookin' for a cut . . . like every other joker callin' me these days."

"Thievin' bastards," Tank said.

Aaaoooogah. Mike squinted at his cell phone. Then he looked up and grinned around the barn. "Good news, dudes. Dave's in."

Velvet clasped her hands and squealed like an over-amped groupie, and the others began hooting and chattering.

Mike took a step back and glanced down to read the rest of the text message: *But not 4 ur sorry ass. 4 Vin.* He forced a laugh as a burn raced across his cheeks.

"Good on ya, geeze," Tank said as he settled the guitars in their stands for the day.

Aaaoooogah. Mike checked the new text message. "Fuckin' hell. Don's in too."

"Let me see, geeze," Tank said, inching dangerously close to Mike's phone.

Mike turned away from him and read the rest of the message to himself: *V&V r good peeps. Not doin it 4 u.* He glanced up and forced a grin before glancing back at his phone. *And keep the fuck away from me on guitar.*

Tank struggled to pull the phone from Mike's grasp but Mike held firm. "These cats are all comin' around 'cause they wanna play with the best." Then he flashed the phone at Tank long enough for him to see the name.

"It's really him," Tank announced to the others. He giggled as he returned to the guitar tech station on the side of the little stage area.

"Thanks for persisting," Velvet said with a satisfied nod.

Vin didn't look up from the computer workstation except to exchange smirks with Gallo.

Aaaoooogah. "What, is everyone in L.A. havin' a conference?" Mike laughed as he glanced at his phone. "Oh, it's Ange." He looked up and saw Harley glance over at Velvet. He focused back on the phone. *Still nothing,* Angelina had texted. Damn, Mike thought, she still hadn't found any dirt at the land registry.

"Let's call it a day, geezers," Tank said with a yawn.

As they straggled out of the barn, Mike turned back to see Vin still seated at the workstation. When Velvet walked over and placed her hand on Vin's shoulder, he smiled up at her. Mike stared at them, tracking the harmony of their interaction; he could see they belonged together. He turned back and let the barn door hit him in the ass. The land scam, the burned Euros—he'd fucked up royally, he knew that now; he needed to square up with them once and for all.

Chapter 37

Lydia glanced up at the stone barn, studying the worn red brick border that framed the rotting wooden door. No wonder they were planning a fundraiser, she mused; the place could use some work. When Velvet opened the door, Lydia peered inside. As her eyes adjusted, she noticed a few small windows inset in the stone. When she felt Andrew squeeze her hand, she looked at him. He nodded toward Brayden, whose grin was as big as she'd ever seen it. They had double-teamed her into the Italy trip—probably triple, she suspected, as Mike seemed to have beguiled them both.

"Step inside," Velvet whispered. "We'll just stand back here by the door until rehearsal stops."

As Lydia stepped over the threshold, she could hear Mike yelling. "Those bastards put somethin' on the mic. Gimme another fifty-seven . . . a *sterilized* one."

Velvet quietly shut the door behind them. Lydia heard male laughter. She could make out a small stage at the other end, with several figures standing there. A portly, bald man came into view. "God, what is that?" he asked in a British accent. Then he sniffed the microphone and reeled.

She noticed a man sitting behind a drum kit with a powder blue bandana tied over his head. Probably covering up a receding hairline, she thought to herself. Mr. Rock Star wore a yellow shirt and black vest with painted flames that almost matched his orange-tinged fake tan. He laughed and pointed a drumstick at the man with a sour face holding a bass guitar, who then cackled. She glanced up at the rustic wooden beams and imagined all the spiders and critters that had lived up there through the centuries . . . and might still be lurking.

"You blokes clean it," the bald man said, handing the microphone to Rock Star and Sourpuss.

Lydia realized that none of them seemed to notice the group of newcomers. She glanced at the road cases and computer gear scattered around the barn; it was so incongruous to see all the high-tech equipment in such an antiquated structure. She spotted a nice-looking man behind a computer setup and a large mixing board.

Velvet whispered, "We can wait in the house."

Brayden hissed to Lydia, "I wanna stay."

Andrew nodded to her.

"If it's okay," Lydia whispered to Velvet, "we'll wait back here."

As Velvet nodded and put her finger to her lips, Lydia cringed when she heard Mike bellowing. His singing voice sounded raspy and worn—he was certainly no Michael Bublé. She rolled her eyes when she recognized the chorus of "Lucky Night." Then she glanced at Brayden. He still had that grin plastered on his face, and it had now infected Andrew.

"Fu-u-u-uck!" Mike roared. A microphone stand came flying off the little stage and crashed to the floor.

"Would it kill you to show some respect for other people's shit?" snapped the handsome man.

"That's my husband, Vin," Velvet whispered with a smile.

Lydia heard Mike cough. "Voice feels rough," he griped. "Just run through the chorus, then call it a day."

Lydia stood with Andrew and Brayden and listened while the musicians played and Mike sang through coughing fits and a cracking voice. His coughing seemed worse, she thought, wheezier now. After a while, they seemed to be winding down.

"That was *crushing!*" Mr. Rock Star cheered in a high-strung voice.

Lydia nervously repositioned her sandal strap. The stale, warm air of the barn felt suffocating, and she could feel the sweat seeping through her khaki skirt and white tank top. As she watched the scene unfolding before her, she felt immobilized—she had been anxious to get here and yet she felt deeply uncomfortable. The rows of guitars, the rampant swearing, the maleness of it all—the scene brought back uneasy memories of her childhood. It reminded her of the one time Mike had taken her to a recording studio and made her sit for hours, bored to death, while she waited for him. In typical Mike fashion, by the time they reached Marine World, the park had already closed, and he couldn't cope with a crying child. Mike Mays had always had his priorities wrong.

She, Andrew, and Brayden were audience members—detached, watching, momentarily excluded. Finally, Velvet escorted them into the room. As the banter settled, several of the men noticed Lydia. The Brit, now holding a guitar, played a catcall slide.

"We got visitors," hollered the grumpy one. "Who's the broad?"

Lydia turned nervously to Andrew and put a hand on his arm.

"That's my daughter, you fuckin' hosebags," Mike roared.

Lydia stared at Mike. She had hoped he would have gotten a haircut by now, but he looked exactly the same: straggly, shoulder-length hair, rows of studs and hoops in his ears, and all the ugly markings on his arms—what he called his "tats." Her old nausea returned. His face seemed more weathered and he still had bags under his eyes. The slightly larger paunch seemed a good indicator that he had been eating well . . . no doubt drinking, too.

Andrew whispered in her ear, "You know these guys have a rather colorful vocabulary. Breathe. You can handle it." He stood tall and proud, grinning around the barn, as if pleased that these '80s rockers had found her appealing.

Lydia looked at Brayden, who was beaming, as if just being there was totally cool. She watched him stride over to Mike for a hug. But then he looked at all the weathered faces around him and stepped back.

"It's cool to see you again . . . dude," Brayden said to Mike.

Mike lifted his arms and grinned. *"Dude?* I love it!" He laughed as he reached down and ruffled Brayden's hair. "Careful—if ya grow out all that blue ya won't be cool no more." Then, as if he had to ease his way into it, Mike returned the hug and patted Brayden on the back. "I missed ya too, kid."

Mike tried to hide it, but Lydia saw him turn and wipe his eyes. Then he segued into introducing his grandson. Mike and Andrew shook hands and then embraced before Mike glanced uncomfortably at Lydia.

She fought the urge to shudder. Were they supposed to hug? Shake hands? She felt nauseated again, and when she glanced around, the stone walls felt like they were closing in around her.

Mike had noticed his scruffy friends were all staring. "So," he said, as if deflecting the discomfort they both so obviously felt. "This is Lydia." He coughed. "My daughter. . . . She's the one who saved my ass and got me here."

Lydia heard Sourpuss mutter, "Probably couldn't wait to get rid of your ass."

She and Mike took clumsy steps toward each other and then each settled for a civil pat on the back.

"And this is Andrew," Mike gloated. "My badass son-in-law." He and Andrew laughed and exchanged glances.

Lydia squinted. *Badass?*

"Where's Harley?" Brayden asked.

"She flew the coop," Gallo growled.

When Brayden's shoulders slumped, Lydia glared at Mike as if to warn him that he had better not disappoint Brayden again.

"Don't listen to Gallo," Mike instructed Brayden. "He's the poster child for why ya shouldn't do hard drugs. She's comin'. Just had to go take care of some official crap about flyin' to the States."

Lydia glanced around the barn and took mental notes—the portly Brit was Tank; the grumpy one was Gallo; the handsome one was Vin; and Mr. Rock Star was Blitz.

"I got somethin' for ya," Mike announced. He shuffled to a corner of the barn and wiped at his eyes. Then he returned with a bag and handed it to her.

Lydia peeked inside and pulled out one of two bottles of Caparzo La Casa Brunello di Montalcino wine. "Wow. . . . Thanks." She pursed her lips and giggled nervously. Mike winked at her, as if he thought that had squared them up.

"So," Mike said with an uneasy grin. "Lunch's ready, right?"

As Velvet escorted them toward a patio dining table inside an expansive courtyard, Lydia grasped Andrew's arm and pulled back from the others. "What was that all about, anyway?" she hissed.

"Huh?" Andrew looked at her, puzzled.

"That look . . . between you and Mike. When we first arrived." Lydia glanced up at the noisy birds circling overhead. She recognized the forked tails as swallows. *"Badass?"*

"Oh." Andrew laughed. "That." He nudged his glasses up the bridge of his nose. "About six or seven weeks ago," he said with a gleam in his eye, "Mike needed my help with something—"

"Involving money?" she asked, glancing toward Mike, who was meandering across the courtyard with Brayden.

"Well . . . yes . . . but not ours." Andrew gave her a bemused smile. "He needed me to make a phone call, to tell off some jerk. He asked me to play the role of a badass . . . with an actual Mafioso—"

"He made you do *what*?" Lydia glanced at Andrew and then at the others, who were taking seats around the table.

"He didn't *make* me do anything," Andrew said with a smirk that settled into a grin. "Actually, it was rather thrilling." He couldn't stop grinning. "Mike said, 'I know you got it in ya. Remember the time you stood up to that loser from Hayward who said I ain't shit?' I can't believe he remembered that."

"I can't believe you were very convincing in that role." She glanced over at Mike, hamming it up at the table with Brayden. Then she looked at Andrew, who just smiled and shrugged.

"What you haven't figured out yet, my dear," Andrew said as he guided her into the courtyard. "Is that your husband's got some balls."

Lydia gave him a sideways glance and tried to imagine him telling off a thug. When he slipped his arm around her, she gave him a restrained smile. As Andrew strutted toward the table, he was still grinning.

"Lydia," Velvet said, steering them to their places, "you sit across from your father. And Andrew—" She paused long enough to give Mike a look. "You sit over here."

Lydia couldn't quite figure it out, but she thought that maybe Velvet had something on Mike. But what could it be? She glanced at the charred building across the courtyard and thought about Mike's late-night phone call practically begging her for money.

"What's with these fuckin' birds, anyway?" Mike roared to Vin. He coughed and sat down, pointing up at the birds swirling above the courtyard. "Why do they just fly around in circles? Makes me dizzy."

"*Rondini,*" Vin said flatly. "They migrate here every spring from South Africa. And they fly back home in the fall."

As Velvet took a seat next to Vin, Mike shouted, "Is this the world's greatest couple or what?" And then he flashed his grin around the table.

Lydia couldn't take her eyes off Mike. He was sucking down the wine, and she figured that was going to end badly . . . but she had to restrain herself. She breathed in the scent of sage and gorgonzola, and quietly accepted plates of vegetables and a bowl of fettuccine with lemon pepper sauce.

"We don't always eat like this," Velvet explained. "Only when we have company."

"Fill yer boots," Tank said as he handed her a bowl of risotto.

Lydia tried to hide her discomfort, but it didn't help that Brayden was laughing with the others like he belonged there.

"Crash the rocks," Tank blurted out, stretching his neck toward the barn. "Our wench is back."

"Harley . . . babe," Mike called out.

Lydia sat up a little straighter and stared as a silver-haired woman walked into the courtyard. So this was Harley Yeates, she considered. She snuck a glance at Brayden, who sat there grinning at Harley like he had a schoolboy crush. She noticed Andrew had the same expression.

"Dahlings," Harley said in a spirited tone as she approached the table.

Lydia couldn't remember the last time she'd seen an older woman who was so radiant. She watched as Harley first gave Mike an engaging peck on the lips and then greeted the others.

Harley smiled at Lydia. "Lovely to finally meet you." Then she turned to Brayden. "Better keep an eye on this one. Sure to be a heartbreaker like his grandfather."

Lydia swallowed hard and watched Harley tease and hug Brayden as though they were old chums. Then she realized that Vin was involved in telling some off-color story.

"Tank was so drunk—"

"Oh, and which time were that, geeze?" Tank grinned.

Lydia glanced nervously around the table. She didn't think his tale was appropriate at a table of mixed company, especially for a boy as young as Brayden, but it seemed as if she were on her own. She couldn't get Andrew's attention, as he appeared to be enjoying himself immensely.

As Vin spoke, Lydia noticed Velvet paid rapt attention, as if she were smitten. With a faint smile, Lydia hoped that she and Andrew might have that kind of spark after so many decades of marriage.

"Shit the bed!" she heard Tank exclaim. "Grumplestiltskin's usin' his hearin' aid." Gallo gave Tank the finger.

Harley belly-laughed as she squeezed in next to Brayden and tossed a giddy glance in Mike's direction. Lydia noticed Mike's consistent coughing, and his skin looked rather grey.

"You forgot to mention he was stark bollock naked," Harley added. "Bollocks are *balls*," she said, turning to Brayden.

"Had me bloody clothes on," Tank argued.

"How would you know?" Harley said. "You were pissed." She turned to Brayden again. "That means *drunk* . . . not angry, like in America."

Lydia feigned a smile and stifled an urge to whisk her son away from it all. She tuned out the conversation and stared at Brayden, who was sitting there alert and bright-eyed, giggling at every swell of laughter.

"That fuckin' dude," she heard Mike roar.

She looked across the table at him and realized he hadn't been spewing rude remarks or manipulating the conversation. Something had changed, she considered. He seemed softer. She watched his glances at Harley and tried to figure him out.

"It's rubbish, I tell you . . . all rubbish," Tank said with a mouthful of food.

"So, Brayden," Harley asked. "Who's your favorite band?"

Brayden seemed a bit startled, as if surprised to be included in the conversation. He gave a timid glance around the table. When he noticed all eyes on him, he just shrugged. "I dunno . . . AC/DC, Led Zeppelin, Scorpions, Judas Priest." He glanced bashfully at Mike. "Mike Mays."

"Atta boy." Mike grinned.

Harley gave Mike a tender smile and a wink.

"Of course," Vin said with a glance toward Mike, "the ol' dinosaur must've turned you on to the classics like Zeppelin."

Brayden shook his head. "No, the Internet."

"Fuckin' Internet," Mike crowed. "Assholes stealin' our music . . . not you, kid." He glanced proudly around the table. "I taught him to buy, not download."

Gallo groaned. "Not that tired old rant again."

"Years ago," Mike said with his mouth full, "I had a heated discussion with a radio talk show host. This prick felt that all music should be free for anyone to fuckin' download." He guzzled down some wine. "Asked him how he'd like to work at *his* job for a year without pay. Told him that was about how long it took to properly write a record's worth of songs and then go into a studio and record and mix and master. But there was no arguin' with that pompous radio dickhead."

Lydia took a bite of the creamy risotto and wished she was back at the hotel with a good book, sipping a glass of that Brunello.

"Fucker wrote a book later," Mike continued. "Called his ass back and told him I was offerin' his entire book as a *free* Internet download. . . . See how *he* liked losing out on *his* hard-earned dough."

Mike glanced over at Lydia and their eyes met briefly before he tossed her an affectionate wink. She returned an undersized smile. She studied her father as he comfortably interacted with the others—so vibrant, full of life, so obviously in his element—and she wondered if this was the man she knew. It occurred to her that when Brayden was with Mike, he seemed to have that same easy way about him—he was quick to smile and quick to laugh. But then it struck her, and she leaned forward and stared openly at each of them. How could she have missed it all this time? Brayden had a touch of Mike's lopsided grin; she'd always adored her boy's distinctive smile, the way his mouth turned up a little at the corners, but it wasn't until now that she could see a ghost of Mike's smile in Brayden's. She glanced at Andrew to see if he too noticed it, but he was deep in conversation with Vin.

"Look what I scored," Mike boasted, holding up a bottle. "More of that damn good grappa."

Lydia declined as Mike offered pours around the table.

"That's an oxymoron," Velvet claimed, also declining. "There's no such thing as good grappa."

"Damn straight," Gallo growled, fidgeting with his ear. "Mays *is* a moron."

Andrew grinned at Lydia as he accepted the pour.

"Cin-cin!" they cheered, clinking around the table.

"Always blaggin' a free drink," Tank said, turning away from Gallo and toward Blitz, who was inspecting his glass. "You vegan today, geeze? Ya know they make this stuff with all the farm leftovers, bones, fat, skin . . . just like scrumpy."

"Yeah, and I pissed into the whole batch—give it more zing." Blitz grinned as he got up and walked into the house.

Gallo snickered. "Dude's gotta pay for that piss remark. Who's in?" He glanced back at the buildings surrounding the courtyard and then at Tank. "It'll take more than our two sorry asses."

"C'mon," Tank said, tugging Brayden's shirt sleeve.

"Oh, no." Harley laughed and her silver bracelets glinted in the sunlight.

Lydia tensed up as Brayden looked to Mike for permission.

"It's cool," Mike assured her. "Everyone fucks with Blitz." Then he motioned Brayden to join them.

Brayden jogged across the courtyard with Tank and Gallo and they emerged moments later carrying a mattress. Then the two men enlisted Brayden into helping them lob it onto the roof. Blitz's mattress, she presumed. On first try, they missed and it tumbled into the courtyard. The second attempt fell short. On the third try, the mattress stayed parked on the tile roof. Then they laughed their way back to the dining table.

"Aw, you've properly polluted him now." Harley giggled. "The fourth amigo."

Brayden returned to his seat, breathless. "This is the best day *ever*."

Lydia realized that the grin hadn't left his face since they had arrived.

"Hey, kid," Mike said to Brayden. "Got somethin' I wanna show ya."

"Crushing!" Brayden crowed. Then he cocked his head and glanced at Lydia.

She looked across at Mike and then at Brayden. When Mike looked up, Lydia wanted to give him one of her stern, disapproving looks, but she found herself smiling instead.

Chapter 38

Mike led the kid into the barn, plopped himself down at the computer, and then stared at the screen.

"My cheeks hurt so bad from laughing," Brayden said as he took a seat next to Mike.

"Yeah," Mike said. "They're a buncha regular fuckin' clowns." He looked up to see the kid grinning, stoked to be there.

"Um, need help?" he asked, his eyes bright.

"I got it covered."

The kid started tapping his foot. "No," he said, as he leaned forward and pointed at the screen. "Click there."

"I just about got it," Mike said as the kid sat back down. But he had no freakin' clue how to work the goddamn computer. He figured he'd just repeat the moves he saw Vin make over the past few days, but he didn't even know where to start. "So, how're those harmonics comin'," he stalled, fumbling with the workstation. He glanced at Brayden, who shot him an iffy look. "Okay. I got this now."

"Wow, you've come a long way with technology." Brayden laughed. "You're almost geeky now."

"So," Mike asked as he aimlessly poked around the keyboard, "what the hell crawled up yer mom's ass to let you and Andy come to Italy, anyway?" He reeled, a little freaked at the shitloads of windows that started popping up.

The kid cocked his head. Then he stood up, grabbed the mouse, and closed them all. "I can be pretty persuasive when I want." He grinned at Mike and then sat back down.

Mike hit the spacebar but no sound came out. "Huh. . . . Oh, right." He reached over and flipped the switch on the external box. "Digital-to-analog converters," he boasted with a wink and then hit the spacebar again.

Brayden inched his chair closer.

Mike started playback and relaxed into the chair, diggin' the sounds of his new happenin' tune. He looked over at Brayden, knowing he'd be impressed. But instead of rockin' out, the kid sat there with his mouth hangin' open.

Brayden leaned forward and hit the spacebar and the playback stopped.

"What the hell, kid?"

"Grampa," Brayden said, frowning. "That's mine." The kid looked confused.

"I knew you'd dig it," Mike crowed. "Just hit me the other night. Ya get lotsa great song ideas during the three S's—sleepin', showerin', shittin'—"

"No," Brayden said, his voice cracking. "I mean that's *mine*. . . . *I* wrote that."

"Right." Mike scratched his chin. "What're the odds that yer writin' the exact same tune on the other side of the planet?"

"You even asked me what I was noodling when we were Skyping," Brayden argued. "Several times. . . . It's mine. *I* made that up—"

"Never heard it before." He folded his arms. "Like I'd rip off my own goddamn grandkid."

"But you did." The kid was blinking fast and Mike thought he was gonna cry. But then he grabbed Vin's green PRS and began noodling. "See?"

"*My* tune don't sound nothin' like that," Mike squawked. "And that's a *hook*, not a song. You didn't write no *song*."

The kid just glumly stood there with the guitar in his arms.

"I'm tellin' ya," Mike roared, "this tune is a blast of Mays' genius. Late at night. I sat out here and worked it out. Wasn't easy but I stuck with it. Yer gramps ain't no quitter!"

The kid's chin trembled. "How . . . could you?" He gave Mike a long, pained look. Then he stood up and tossed down the guitar with a clang.

"I ain't got E-S-fuckin'-P." Mike got to his feet. "I don't dig what yer insinuatin' here."

The kid stumbled back a step when Mike grabbed his skinny wrist.

"Ya know how many times I've written a melody, only to find out from a bandmate that the idea I just scratched out sounds like some other tune? One I probably heard in the grocery store. Happens to every songwriter. Music's all around us. There ain't no filter for your subconscious."

Brayden shook free from his grasp. He stood there with his arms hanging at his sides and his eyes dull and wet.

"What, ya wanna play on it?" Mike asked, figuring he'd offer up a consolation, even though he knew *that* would only happen over Vin's dead body.

The kid's shoulders started quaking and his lower lip bunched up. "It's . . . mine!" he yelled and then barreled for the door, as if he didn't want Mike to see him cryin' like a baby.

Jesus, Mike realized, the kid was bawlin'. "Fuckin' hell," he said to no one. It was Gallo's snorin' that'd provided the inspiration for the tune—he'd explain it all to the kid, get him to understand.

Chapter 39

Lydia glanced toward the edge of the courtyard. Vin had taken Andrew down to the pool, he had said, to smoke cigars and show him the rest of their property. How fitting for his new "badass" persona, Lydia thought, but it wasn't up to her—what he smoked, or ate, or drank, or thought of this strange pack of riffraff. They all reminded her of Mike. Velvet reappeared and took a seat next to her at the patio table. They both watched as Harley walked across the courtyard.

"I wanted to show you these," Harley said as she took a seat and spread a stack of tattered photographs across the table. "Can't believe I still have them after all these decades."

Lydia shuffled through the faded photos and then stopped at one in particular. *Who were these people?* She studied the photograph and realized it was her, as a child, sitting on Mike's lap. She recognized the yellow pinafore that her grandmother had sewn for her, with the front ruffle and tied shoulder straps; she examined the timeworn photo, guessing that she must have been about five. On closer inspection, she saw that she was laughing as her father kissed her little cherub cheek. His thick brown hair draped his shoulders and his skin looked so smooth and youthful; he held a cigarette between his fingers, as usual. He seemed . . . happy.

"That was a lovely day," Harley recalled.

Confused, Lydia glanced up at her.

"I took this one. Was up from L.A. for the weekend," Harley continued. "Mike had picked you up from your mum's house and the three of us went to Golden Gate Park. See how sunny it was? Not your typical day in San Francisco." She smiled kindly at Lydia. "You had some little stuffed animal your father said you carried everywhere."

And just how would *he* have known? Lydia wondered with a smirk. "Oh my God," she suddenly exclaimed. "My hugging mice! I remember one of them went missing and I cried for weeks. We never did find it. It broke my heart to see the light grey one all alone without the other."

Lydia glanced back at the photograph. The entire episode seemed foreign to her, and yet the exact moment of her father kissing her had been captured on some Instamatic camera. She couldn't recall ever smiling around her father, let alone him ever kissing her cheek. She glanced over at Harley and back down at the photograph. How had Harley remembered about her dear little lone mouse? She hadn't even thought about that in years. She shook her head and handed the photo to Velvet.

"You were the light of his life."

Lydia looked sideways at Harley and wondered what drugs *she* must be on. Mike was barely aware of her existence back then, and he had certainly never shown any affection. She stole another glance at the photo when Velvet set it on the table.

"You know," Harley confided, as if they were new best friends. "That man fucked me over many years ago." Her posture relaxed and she gave a shallow sigh. "I fell in love with him . . . twice . . . but he's a restless soul, that one. Can't be tamed. Not to mention the insatiable urge he had to screw every female he encountered. Christ on a bike, you'd think when a man is with a woman he adores he might manage enough restraint not to drool over every other woman in the room . . . let alone blatantly pick them up and leave you stranded."

Lydia knew the feeling of being abandoned by Mike. She stared at Harley. "How can you even talk to him?"

"We don't choose whom we love," Harley replied with a warm smile. "To this day, Mike and I have this . . . strong connection. Somehow, he's always been there for me in ways that nobody could ever know."

Lydia stared at her. She seemed smitten with Mike, but in some strange, reserved, mature way.

"We're bound together. Don't know how to explain it. . . . It's almost like . . . a complete, unconditional love."

Lydia glanced back down at the photograph on the table, at the loving father adoring his child. *Why couldn't she remember?* She glanced up again and then took a deep breath. "He was never there for me," she said, looking Harley in the eye.

Velvet nodded but Lydia knew she wouldn't understand. Harley, however, gave her a sad smile.

Lydia began to trace the knots on the table with her finger. As Velvet shuffled through the photos on the table, Lydia leaned toward one of Mike holding his guitar. "Oh my God . . . the guitar." She looked up at Harley and Velvet and then back down at the photo. "I'd wedged it into the back of the closet, behind the winter coats and the ironing board . . . I'd completely forgotten about it until now."

"*That* guitar?" Harley asked. "You mean, his Les Paul?"

"Yes." Lydia nodded. "A few weeks ago, this woman dropped it at the house."

"Figures," Harley said and then smirked at Velvet.

"No, it wasn't that way at all," Lydia said. "Mike just showed up on my doorstep one stormy night this past April, with a story that I was certain was bullshit—"

Velvet laughed. "Sorry, it's just that . . . go on."

Lydia nodded at Velvet—no doubt she too had been taken in by Mike's tales. "I vaguely remember some woman dropping him off, but nothing more than that. Anyway, when she came back she told me this story about Mike visiting her husband in the hospital—he spent the whole day there, singing and playing guitar at the man's bedside. Apparently, he was such a huge fan that Mike gave him the guitar at the end of the visit."

Velvet was listening intently and Harley was smiling.

"Well, her husband died . . . and she'd heard about the concert, and she said she knew he would've wanted Mike to have his signature guitar. So she brought the guitar to my house, figuring maybe I could get it to him."

"*You* have the *Black Beauty?*" Harley asked.

Lydia nodded.

"And you forgot about it?"

"I—" Lydia tried to swallow the lump in her throat. "I was angry with him," she said, realizing how defensive that sounded. "He'd—"

Velvet touched her arm and said with a gentle smile, "I completely understand."

Lydia returned the smile. "It's weird . . . holding the guitar that day . . . knowing he'd played it on stages all over the world, I don't know, it felt . . . strange, almost . . . unearthly. . . . But then I got distracted—I mean, this whole Italy trip—and I just shoved the guitar into . . ."

She glanced up and saw Brayden running from the barn toward the terraces. She tensed up when she realized he was crying. "Brayden," she shouted, "come here."

He stopped but didn't turn around.

"Brayden!" she yelled.

He turned and shuffled toward her, his head down. He approached the table and sat on the edge of the bench, his back to Harley and Velvet.

"Mom," he said quietly, "he stole it."

"Who, sweetie? Stole what?" she asked, caressing his hair. She knew something was really wrong because he did not flinch or pull away.

"Mike," he choked out. "He stole my song."

"I don't understand."

He looked up at her and stuttered, "I wrote a song . . . he heard it over Skype, I know he did, he kept asking me about it. And now he says he never heard it. He's lying, Mom. It's *my* song!"

Lydia clenched her jaw. "Where is he?" she snapped, her muscles tensing up. "I'll make him give it back."

Brayden sighed heavily and wiped at his tears. "You don't get it. He already stole it—it's his word against mine. He can't give it back."

Lydia moved toward her son, putting her arm around him. "Sweetie, I'll talk to him, I'll sort this out. He owes you an apology."

"No!" Brayden said, as he put his head down on the table. "Don't say anything. Promise me. It's too late, anyway."

She glanced at Velvet and Harley, who seemed as if they had been stunned into silence. Velvet clutched at her stomach.

"You, too?" Lydia asked, as if they shared the same reaction to Mike. Then she glared toward the barn and embraced Brayden—it felt so good to hold her little boy, to console him again, like when he had skinned his knee after his first attempt at skateboarding.

Maybe she couldn't promise what Brayden had asked—to have the song back. But for so long now she had been waiting for a chance to write her father off, once and for all. She'd had to come all the way to Italy, but at last, this was her moment. Mike had knocked himself off his own pedestal once again.

Andrew came up and gave her a concerned look. As Mike stepped from the barn, Lydia snapped up her family and herded them down the courtyard, as Harley and Velvet followed. Vin, Tank, and Gallo appeared out of nowhere, as if they too had been waiting for this moment.

"How could you?" Lydia glared at Mike as she whisked her family toward their rental car. Brayden wouldn't even look at him. She motioned Andrew and Brayden on and then turned to Mike. "He's a *child*, for heaven's sake. But then that's not your thing, is it? Fatherhood? Being a man to a boy? . . . Your own grandson. He's completely devastated. My God, you're pathetic."

She hustled Brayden into the car, hissing at him, "Now you see his true colors." The others stood there, in spitting distance, just staring at Mike.

"*That's* where I've heard that melody," Harley said, squinting at Mike. With a bitter smile, she slowly shook her head. "Mike, stealing from your own grandson?"

"Rippin' people off is his MO," Gallo growled.

"It was just a hook," Mike barked.

Before Lydia slid behind the wheel, she shot him a final fiery glare that she hoped might burn a hole right through him.

Vin took a step backward. "You're a bigger dick than I ever realized."

"Coverdale would never stoop that low," Blitz snarled as he spun on his red cowboy boot heel.

Lydia slammed the door and struggled to fasten her seatbelt as she watched them all turn and walk away from Mike. He started coughing but nobody even glanced back.

"For fuck's sake," he barked, "we only got twelve notes, eight octaves."

Lydia fishtailed the rental car down the gravel drive, leaving Mike in a cloud of dust.

Chapter 40

"**I** tried to protect you," Lydia said, rolling the rental car to a stop. "But you wouldn't listen." She turned to Brayden in the passenger seat. "Yesterday you were . . ." She wanted to say *in tears*, but she thought better of it. "Are you sure about this?"

Brayden nodded. "Harley invited me to jam today. When will I ever get the chance to be this close to all these cool musicians again? This is *once-in-a-lifetime*, man. I'm not gonna let Mike mess that up for me."

Lydia smiled at her son and reached out to slide a strand of hair from his face. He returned a slight smile and didn't flinch, not even when she stroked his cheek. She suddenly recalled the faded photograph of Mike kissing her own cheek.

"You can pick me up tomorrow," Brayden said as he scooted out of the car.

"Brayden, I really don't—"

"Mom," he said, leaning into the open window. "I'm almost sixteen. I'll be okay."

Lydia watched her son walk away from the car toward the barn. He swung open the barn door and disappeared inside. He had insisted that Andrew couldn't accompany them, as if his own father would be too much of a crutch—he had to go this alone. As she reached toward the ignition, she heard Mike blustering in the courtyard. She glanced up and saw him loitering around the patio, cocksure and crowing, as usual, as Velvet flitted about, clearing breakfast dishes from the patio table. Lydia narrowed her eyes at Mike and then slid from the driver's seat, moving toward the courtyard.

"With all the cats I know?" Mike roared to Velvet. "All the favors I called in? Nobody here's got that kinda clout. When yer rollin' in the dough, just don't forget whose idea this all was. *I'm* the one who made it happen. Got the promoter, the press. Shit, I even got yer ol' man back. He's talkin' to ya again, ain't he? So what's the big deal? Everything's back to normal."

"Minus the vineyard . . . and Gallo's room," Velvet snapped, as she disappeared into the kitchen with an armload of dishes.

Of course, Lydia thought as she inched closer. Mike was always trying to make himself out to be a saint.

"Don't worry 'bout that vineyard," he hollered after her. "Vin said he ain't even interested in settin' foot in that graveyard. I got him buried so deep in the gig, he ain't got time to come up for air—just like I planned. See all I done for you? Ya should be kissin' my ass right about now."

Lydia could hear guitar music coming from the barn and she knew this was her chance to ambush him from behind. Yes, she had promised Brayden, but he was still so innocent and she had to make Mike understand that he couldn't take advantage of him anymore.

He plucked a cigarette from his pack without even realizing she was there.

"He's fifteen, for God's sake," Lydia snapped.

Mike glanced up, dazed, and withdrew the unlit cigarette from his lips.

"When *I* was fifteen, you weren't even there to see me receive my World Language award. Do you realize that no other person in the school was given that award? That was a big deal to me. But you wouldn't have known because you weren't there. You were *never* there. . . . You've had your chance to be there for Brayden . . ." Her voice dropped to a whisper. "But you've failed . . . again."

"I told ya, I didn't rip off the kid," Mike insisted. "It was an honest subconscious grab."

Lydia shuddered. "Only you would use 'honest' and 'subconscious' in the same sentence."

Mike snuck a glance toward the barn. "The kid knows I didn't do it on purpose."

She leaned in to him. "I've tried with all my might to protect that boy from the pain that I *knew* you would inflict. . . . But he idolizes you."

Mike slipped his hands into his pockets and stared at the ground.

"And so you can get away with it. He loves you, Mike. . . . If that means anything at all to you, you should march in there and apologize."

Mike's eyes remained glued to the ground, as he scuffed his foot along the terracotta tiles. Even though he wouldn't look at her, he seemed to be absorbing her words.

She pointed toward the barn. "Don't you dare disappoint him again."

Mike didn't glance up.

"Or I promise you—you'll lose him for good."

Mike inched back a step. The submarine tone blared and he pulled his phone from his pocket and squinted at the text on the screen. "Chick from the village." He glanced up at Lydia. "What?"

She watched as he turned, paused to light the cigarette, and then disappeared down the hillside in a cloud of smoke. Why had she even bothered? With Mike, his *babes* always took precedence.

By the time Mike had had a smoke and circled back to the courtyard, Lydia and her rental car were gone. He stood at the barn door, shooting one last look up at those fuckin' birds doin' circles overhead, chirpin' like goddamn lunatics. Then he blasted into the barn and spotted Brayden on the little stage area yukkin' it up with Harley, Blitz, and Gallo. The kid chunked away on Vin's blue Ibanez as they jammed Free's "All Right Now." Gallo sang as Harley doubled the main lick with the kid, coaching him through. As Harley riffed around him, the kid boldly tossed in a few riffs of his own. Damned impressive, Mike thought as they wound down the tune.

"Does this kid know how to riff, or what?" Mike gloated. "Musta got it from me." He gave them a big grin but all he got were scowls.

Brayden looked over at him, and just like that, the kid lost his smile. The whole lot of them were making an art out of avoiding eye contact. Even Tank turned away. The past 24 hours they all seemed to be givin' him the slip.

Mike could feel his teeth grinding as he stood there and watched the kid smiling at Harley. He cleared his throat. "Kid . . . I, uh . . ." He glanced around at the others, who instantly looked away. "I just wanted to . . . uh."

Harley had pulled her guitar off and was handing it to Tank. "C'mon," she said to the others. "Let's leave them be."

Mike stood there wheezing, his arms hanging at his sides. "Thanks, doll."

Tank relieved the kid of Vin's guitar and set it in the stand. The kid pressed his lips tight as Harley rounded up the guys and corralled them toward the barn door. She looked back and shot Mike a lean smile and an encouraging nod before she headed out the door.

Mike turned toward the kid, who stood uncomfortably rubbing his hands down his pant legs. "Take a seat, kid." Mike cleared his throat again and began pacing the barn.

Brayden lowered himself onto the wooden pew.

"I, uh," Mike said as he pivoted and glanced at the kid. "Well, uh . . . ya see? . . . Here's the thing."

Brayden sat there fidgeting and Mike figured he only had about 30 seconds before the kid grabbed his phone and started surfing.

Mike suddenly felt like puking. He flashed back to his dark days and wondered if maybe he was gettin' the DTs. Feeling dizzy, he staggered forward and gripped the workstation. He could feel his heart pounding. *Shit.* Was this what it felt like when you were sorry? He cleared his throat and glanced at the kid. Then he took a deep breath. "Ya see, in this business . . . people rip each other off all the time."

The kid just sat there like he was doing some angel act—all naive 'n' shit.

Mike swallowed hard and pivoted again. "If *I* had all the royalties due to me," he boasted as he resumed pacing, "I'd be one rich motherfucker.

. . . But that ain't the way it works. . . . Ya know, when you dream shit, it's just . . . well . . . shit's just out there for grabs . . . catch my drift?" He glanced at the kid.

Brayden looked up and blinked innocently. "But . . . it was *my* hook. I don't understand how you could take it from me."

Mike felt his breathing slow. He stopped and stared at the ground. "When music's yer world, and it's all that matters . . . ya tend to put yer career above everything else . . . and sometimes . . . well . . . some people . . . they might get hurt. But it ain't like yer doin' it on purpose."

The kid didn't flinch. "I just want you to admit that you stole my hook."

"Mmm," Mike hesitated, cocking his head. "More like *borrowed* it. You had it all minor 'n' dark 'n' shit. I changed it up, made it more hip."

The kid perked up and stretched forward in the pew. "So you're admitting, it *is* mine."

"Well . . . that ain't really how it works . . . but—"

"This is bullshit," the kid charged, narrowing his eyes. "I'll tell you what." He folded his arms. "If you let me play on the track, we'll call it even."

Mike grinned. Fuckin' little kid had a bit of the devil in him after all.

The kid craned his neck toward the door when he heard the others stepping into the barn.

Mike glanced up and saw Vin headed toward the workstation. "Sorry, dude," Mike wheezed to the kid, "I already tried. I swear. Kid, if it was up to me . . ." It wasn't a bad idea, Mike thought, imagining all the publicity he might be able to squeeze outta havin' this little kid listed as songwriter, even more if he knocked out a few notes on the recording.

"Those are my terms," the kid said as he stood up and stepped over to Harley.

He began to chat up Harley like they were old buds. When Vin rolled his chair up to the workstation and fired a glance at Mike without a word, Mike sighed and walked over to him. He leaned down and whispered, "I kinda promised the kid he could play on 'Born to Be Bad.' "

Vin glanced up. "Then you'll have to *un*-promise—"

"Pipe down, dude," Mike said, shooting a glance at Brayden. "I don't wanna disappoint him again—"

"Not my problem."

"Just a few bars."

"What does he have to do with Groove House? This is about *us*," Vin said through clenched teeth. "I'm not about to let you shanghai it for your own self-serving interests. You're not in charge here, Mays."

Mike straightened up and stared at Vin. Dude had a shitty attitude toward the kid. He watched Brayden clowning around with Harley, and noticed him studying her face as she laughed with Gallo. The kid looked so comfortable, so natural, standing there describing some riff to Harley. He watched the kid air-strumming, and it looked like double picking, a la Randy Rhoads. Mike grinned. That's it—he'd *prove* to Vin just how much the kid could rock.

"Dude, lemme show ya somethin'," Mike said as he stepped toward Brayden. He pointed at the axes in the guitar boat. "If you could play any guitar here, which one would you pick?"

The kid pointed to Harley's red Yamaha SG. Tank bobbed around with the camera, filming everything.

Harley smiled, as if honored he'd selected her guitar. "C'mon, then." She motioned him onto the little stage and grabbed the Yamaha. As Brayden reached for it, Harley stopped him, palm out. "But, I warn you, sire," she said, like some sort of Shakespearean actor. "Behold the power of this guitar." Holding the guitar body, neck outstretched, she knighted Brayden with a tap of the peghead on each shoulder—just like Mike always did, aiming toward the audience at the end of his gigs. "Sir Brayden, I bestow upon you this mighty axe."

The kid grinned and accepted the red beast in his arms. He adjusted the strap and chunked out a test chord. When he glanced at Mike, his grin grew wider, as if maybe he'd put any trace of grudge behind him now. He looked down, crunched out a series of chords and then wailed out several riffs.

"Whoa, dude," Mike roared. "Lookin' at your shoes is so '90s." He grabbed Vin's Ibanez and flipped on an amp. "Ya gotta stand like this—"

"Fuck that posin' bullshit," Gallo growled, strapping on his vintage P bass. "You ain't really cool unless you can do a guitar flip." He tossed the bass over his shoulder in a three-sixty.

"Crushing!" Brayden said, his eyes bright. "Show me how."

"First, you gotta have strap locks," Gallo grumbled. "Of course, Harley does. Then take your stance, lean into it, and swing it around like this." Trying to school the kid on how to swing a guitar, Gallo flung the bass over his shoulder. But instead of a smooth slide, the bass strap loosened, unsnapped, and he ended up lobbing it straight off the stage area—where it landed with a reverberating thud.

Harley cackled. "Oh, please don't do that live."

Gallo grumbled as he snatched his classic bass from the floor and inspected it.

Harley grabbed her gold Gibson Flying V. "Try this," she said and then spun around. "Easy move if you're wireless. Takes some practice when you're wired, though."

Mike grinned as Gallo and Harley posed the kid and tried to enlighten him on rock star swagger. The kid was all smiles, and Mike figured he was in the clear.

Chapter 41

Mike nudged the kid across the dark courtyard, stealthy as a B-2 . . . except for the wheezing. He gave a probing glance behind him before he heaved open the barn door. When he stepped inside, he nearly toppled Tank.

"Bloody Nora, get inside," Tank yelped at full whisper. "Stop actin' the goat, all ninja-like at two a.m." He pulled the kid inside and quietly closed the barn door.

As the three of them snuck to the workstation, Mike glanced at Brayden. He was about to even the score with the kid, but he didn't have the stomach for the Lydia damage control he still had ahead of him. He grinned as Tank lowered Harley's guitar over the kid's head.

"Ready?" Mike asked as Tank rolled the chair up to the workstation.

"As a copper-thievin' pikey on a chapel roof," Tank whispered. "I'll plug the lad in direct and we can all use these." He doled out headphones. Then he pulled up a new track and looked at the kid. "Go on, then. Let's have the bag on Vin."

Mike leaned back in the chair and hoped—he'd be satisfied if all they managed was just ten seconds of the kid playing rhythm. He looked at Brayden and directed, "Listen for the click, then let 'er rip."

Brayden cradled the guitar, his hands poised on the strings as he listened intently through the headphones. After the lead-in click, he crunched out a combination of rhythm chords, single notes, and palm muting.

Mike grinned, impressed with the kid's technique and sense of timing. Suddenly, the kid stopped playing. He stood there with a pinched expression.

"Aw, pull yer biscuit straight," Tank said.

The kid shot him a curious glance and then turned to Mike. "I've played this a million times in my bedroom, but now I feel all rushed and clumsy."

"That's normal, dude," Mike assured him. "Cool thing is, in recordin', you can do as many takes as ya want." He elbowed Tank, who cued up the tune again and nodded to the kid.

Brayden closed his eyes and assumed the pose. He laid down several more tracks, each one more relaxed than the last. Then he boldly asked, "Can I try something on the lead?"

"Vin'll go mental," Tank hissed.

"I told myself, the kid's gonna play on this track if it's the last thing I do. So fuck Vin. It's the kid's tune," Mike said, pausing for effect and then shooting Brayden a knowing glance. The kid broke into a big, satisfied grin. "Go for it, dude."

Tank shrugged, cued up the kid, and let him roll.

As they listened through playback, making selections from all the different takes, Mike reasoned that the riff wasn't something a kid would write; it was a dead-on, signature, melodic Mays riff. Maybe his guitar genius had rubbed off on the kid, or maybe the kid got some fluky gene that had skipped a generation.

"Might can use some of them tasty notes," Tank said to the kid. Then he started comping tracks.

Brayden raked his fingers through his hair and announced, "I'm changing my name. Every rocker needs a cool name like Slash, or Harley, or Blitz Stryker—"

"Stage names are for pussies," Mike roared. "Ya know . . . that's Harley's real name."

"Call me Spike," Brayden said with a nod.

Mike smirked. "I ain't callin' ya that."

The kid soon crashed on the wooden pew while Tank fiddled with the tracks, cutting and pasting and rearranging until he had something usable.

"There ya have it, geeze." Tank pointed to the track on the computer screen. "Sixteen seconds of brilliance."

"It's the kid's riff, gotta be him playin' it, right?" Mike looked at Brayden asleep on the pew and knew he was back in the kid's good graces. He nudged Tank. "Dude, how the hell did ya match the tone?"

"They got these filters," Tank said pointing to the screen. He waved Mike off, knowing high tech wasn't his bag.

Mike snickered. "Vin'll never even know."

"Best. Prank. Ever." Tank tried to shush his own laughter. "Sun's almost up. Get the kid to bed, geeze. I'll finish up here." He shot Mike a campy smile. "Do a quick mix and sync it to that vid I been workin' on. Then load it to YouTube, get the word out, and watch the views roll in."

"Thanks, mate." Mike grinned and got up from the chair. "I'm gonna get some shuteye."

Six hours and a few z's later, Mike ambled into the courtyard and inched open the barn door. Vin was hunched over the workstation, dragging his hands through his hair. Dude looked freaked. Tank snuck up behind Mike and they pussyfooted into the barn.

"What the hell?" Vin muttered. "Who's been fucking with my shit?" When he looked up and saw Tank and Mike, he narrowed his eyes at Mike.

"Geeze," Tank pleaded, "just let me show you. You'll be amazed."

"I don't want to be amazed," Vin said through clenched teeth. "I want to mix this goddamn tune."

Mike tried to curb his wheezy chuckle. When Tank motioned Vin aside, Vin glared at him and then at Mike before giving Tank the controls. Tank took the chair from Vin and hit playback on the version he'd mixed just hours earlier. Vin stood there with his arms crossed.

When the infamous 16 seconds rolled by, he commanded, "Roll that back."

"Killer riffage, huh?" Mike kept on nodding to convince him. "Got a little Jimmy Page in there—"

"I was thinking Clapton," Vin said, taking a closer look at the track onscreen. "Play that back." Vin listened closely and pointed at the screen. "Right there, the passing note . . . that minor bend." He turned to Mike. "You didn't play that."

"Neither did you." Mike grinned. "Or Harley."

"Gotta admit, geeze," Tank said. "Them's some tasty notes."

Vin gave them a sideways glance. "No," he growled and squeezed his eyes shut. "You used my gear, went behind my back?" He opened his eyes and glared at Mike. "I ought to kick your ass. I'm deleting this on principal, if nothing else—"

"Dude." Mike grabbed Vin's arm as he reached for the controls. "I did ya a solid."

Vin gave him a sideways glance.

Tank spun the monitor in his direction and started tapping on the keyboard.

"That, uh, mysterious overcharge on your taxes?" Mike gave him a nod. "So the bill was paid with blood money from Carlo. But ya know you've overpaid. And I can fix it."

"What do you mean, *fix* it?"

"I got connections—"

"You, who doesn't speak Italian?"

"I got my ways." Mike grinned at Vin and pulled his phone from his pocket. "Just one little phone call, and yer problem's solved, yer taxes'll be paid up for the next three years."

"You're so full of shit—"

"Not this time, bud. I'm talkin' *three years* of payments—poof."

"And what do you get out of all this?" Vin softened his glare. "You're not staying here, you know, once the gig's done."

Mike grinned at him. "It's the kid's hook. Leave the 16 seconds."

Vin sighed heavily and glanced around the barn.

"Kid rocked his ass off," Mike crowed. "I taught him everything he knows."

"I doubt that. Sounds more like he's been soaking up videos online."

The three of them turned at the sound of the barn door.

"Do we have a deal?" Mike asked, holding up the phone.

Vin shook his head. "Fuck it."

"Good answer, geeze." Tank leaned around the monitor and shot him a sheepish grin. "I loaded a vid of it to YouTube this mornin'."

Vin's face heated up. "That song's not properly mixed, yet you synced it to video and loaded it to YouTube? What the hell?"

"I mixed it, geeze."

"Like I said, not properly mixed. And now it's out there in the public. Goddamn you!" Vin glared at Mike.

"That one's on me, geeze," Tank said, shielding himself behind the monitor.

Vin glanced in Tank's direction and then at Mike.

"Whoa, geezers!" Tank exclaimed as he stood up and turned the monitor toward them. "Vid's up to 863 views!"

Mike laughed and slapped Tank five. "Ain't even been 12 hours."

Vin buried his head in his hands and let out a long sigh.

Chapter 42

Mike stood at the terrace and eyeballed Harley as she gracefully sliced through the water below. The pool waves shimmered in the sunlight, the water as blue as Harley's eyes. She was the shit, he knew that now, but he'd figured it out too late. He took another swig of grappa and then squinted up at the birds swirling and chirping high above. *Swallows*, Lydia had called them. She'd been gone a week now. He felt a heaviness in his chest. Damn, he realized, he actually missed them.

"Mays, it's been a week!" Mike turned, mid-swig, to see Vin standing there, arms crossed. "I satisfied my part of the bargain. Exactly when do you plan on *fixing* the property taxes, and sorting this *three years* of payments you promised?"

Mike turned back and resumed staring at Harley, still doing laps in the pool below. "Ya know, yer one lucky bastard. Got a chick who loves ya." He took another swig and glanced across the olive grove and the vineyards in the distance, to the house on the neighboring hilltop. "And so does Mr. Mob Boss. . . . Giulia . . . damn, I'd give up all the grapes in Italy to tap that five-star ass every night."

"Really, dude? We've got an American Express commercial to shoot this afternoon and you're getting plastered?" Vin reached for the bottle. "Velvet will be so pissed off."

Mike shielded the grappa and staggered back a step. "Precisely. Only a moron would do AmEx sober." He sized-up Vin and felt a flash of jealousy. Dude had formed some rock-solid bonds through the years—with Velvet, Tank . . . shit, practically everyone he'd ever met. They all looked up to him.

But all Mike had was a trail of burned bridges. He let out a shaky sigh. "So everything's cool now, right? With you 'n' Velvet?"

Vin just stood there, glaring at him.

Mike shrugged, took another swig, and turned back to watch Harley. "Man, chicks sure have some strange power over us, huh? They know how to work a dude over."

"Velvet's not one of those game players," Vin said. "She's . . . purposeful." He sighed heavily. "And, somehow with her I always cave."

"They got us by the balls, man," Mike said, and then turned to Vin. "That's why ya came home, ain't it? You can get a blowjob whenever—"

"You know, you're one shallow motherfucker," Vin said, grabbing the bottle from Mike. "There's more to a marriage than just sex."

Mike thought about the 40-something years Vin and Velvet had been married. Shit, he couldn't even make it through 40 *hours* with the same chick . . . except . . . Harley. He shifted his gaze and focused on her. "That chick down there . . . taught me a lotta shit. . . . I'm such a hard-ass, I didn't even realize . . . but . . . fuck it . . . I think she mighta even taught me about love. . . . Probably the love of my fuckin' life. . . . Only took me my whole fuckin' life to figure that out." He glanced up at the birds overhead and then down at her. "Harl and I . . . we . . . well . . . I guess we shoulda got hitched."

"It's never too late," Vin said.

Mike turned, surprised that Vin hadn't dissed the idea. Dude didn't seem so righteous now, like maybe he was starting to get Mike's vibe. But Mike still couldn't read him. Mike grinned at him. "Shit, maybe I finally got the balls to settle down for once in my life." He sighed as he scanned the property. "This ain't such a bad place."

"Yeah, well, don't get too comfortable here, 'cause you're not staying."

Mike scowled at Vin and then snagged the bottle.

"Don't think I'm just going to let this slide, Mays." Vin gave him a stern glare. "You think you can fix the property taxes? . . . I want proof," he demanded. "Documentation."

"You'll get yer *proof*," Mike snapped, and took another hit off the bottle. *"Pronto."*

Velvet set down the iron and surveyed the clothing spread about her living room. Her dusty old harp stood tall in the corner, draped with scarves and shirts, part wardrobe rack for the day. As she placed a pair of copper-toned jeans on the sofa, she stared for a moment and sighed, relieved that Vin was home for good. She laid the last of the samples from Giulia's designer friends in Milan across the overstuffed chair. Finally, she lifted the mirror that Vin had carried down from their bedroom. She stood there, admiring the clothes that she'd ripped, stitched, redesigned, painted, beaded, rhinestoned and studded, transforming the designer samples into rocked up street gear. As Velvet scanned the room and brushed the dust from her hands, Vin and Harley came through the front door.

"The courtyard looks fab," said Harley, clapping her hands. "Can't believe Richard Curtis is directing *us*—"

"And at our home, no less," said Velvet. "You're due on set in an hour." She turned to Vin. "Time for wardrobe."

"That's my wife," Vin said, glancing at the array of clothing. "So goddamned resourceful." He turned back to Velvet. "You should see Blitz out there—he's acting like it's an episode of 'Unplugged.'"

"At last, he's got an audience," Harley laughed.

The front door opened again and Tank chased Gallo inside, thrusting the video camera at him.

"Outta my face, you limey bastard," Gallo growled and nudged him aside.

"No point in puttin' *you* in the DVD bonus footage," Tank grumbled as he lowered the camera. "Got a face like a bulldog lickin' piss off a nettle." He looked around the room before announcing, "Oy . . . YouTube vid's up to 20,000. That's almost 3,000 hits a day, geezers."

When Velvet looked up, Mike burst into the room with a grin. "Where've you been?" she asked. "Director wants us all in the courtyard in under an hour."

"Surprised you could pull yourself away from muggin' for the camera, Mays," Gallo said.

"Dude," Mike barked. "Why do ya think they're even here? Not for yer ass. They want footage of the guitar legend Mike Mays." Mike took a bow, and then eyeballed a suit jacket. "I ain't wearin' any of that frilly glam bullshit."

Gallo cackled, "You're gonna need that jacket, dumbass, to walk down the aisle." His grin faded when all heads suddenly turned in his direction. "What?" He fiddled with his hearing aid. "Mays is gettin' hitched, so I hear." He glanced at Tank. "That's what Tank said—"

"Vin tole me that Mike tole him—"

"Told him *what*?" Velvet demanded.

Vin just stood there, arms crossed, staring at Mike.

Gallo glanced guiltily at Harley. "He ain't?"

"You told *them* and not *me*?" Velvet asked Vin. She glanced at Harley, who looked at Mike and shuffled back a step. Mike's face flushed and he just stood there, speechless, wetting his lips.

"I, uh . . ." Mike looked down and coughed as he scuffed his foot. "Um . . ." Then he scanned the room before glancing at Harley.

Velvet could see Harley's eyes glistening, and she figured it was what Harley had been wanting.

"Harl?" Mike swallowed hard. Tank nudged him toward her. "Guess now's as good a time as any," he muttered. Mike stepped to her and took her hands in his. "Ya know what an asshole I am."

Gallo snorted, and Tank thrust the video camera in Mike's face.

Mike scowled and ordered Tank, "Turn that shit off." Then he cleared his throat and turned back to Harley. "I . . . we . . . well . . . you 'n' me . . . we been through a lot. And, well . . . I been thinkin' . . . we oughta . . . just . . . tie the fuckin' knot."

Harley stared past Mike, like she was daydreaming. She slid her hands from his, turned away from him, and just stood there for a moment.

Mike coughed and looked at her. "Finally . . . I realized . . . yer the love of my fuckin' life."

"You're about three decades too late," Harley said, releasing a long, drawn-out sigh and glancing uncomfortably around the room. Then she stared straight at Mike. "You know how much I adore you, and we're bonded by this fabulous past . . . Razor's Edge tour, that stormy night in Houston, bottle of Bordeaux at the Eiffel Tower. Oh, the fantastic memories . . . and the *not* so fantastic ones."

Mike glanced down and when he looked up she gave him a sad smile.

"But now, I'm a 60-something woman, and—" She paused and pressed her lips together. "—my future's not with you, Mike."

Mike seemed dazed, and Velvet could see that his chin was trembling.

"Swings and roundabouts," Harley muttered.

Mike said nothing—he just stood there and wheezed. Had he given up? Was he planning a counterattack? He couldn't seem to break his trance.

Harley raked her fingers through her silvery-blonde hair, lifted her chin, and gave a resigned smile.

Mike didn't move or say a word. Their strange duet was painful to watch. Velvet was relieved when Gallo growled, gave a dismissive wave, and started foraging through the clothes.

"You didn't get no leather or spandex, did you?" he snarled. "I don't wanna look ridiculous at my age."

"You already *is* ridiculous," Tank charged as he lifted the camera and aimed it at Gallo.

Angelina appeared in the doorway, a guitar case in one hand and an envelope in the other. Mike's vibe changed as he pushed forward and took the case from her. Velvet recognized it immediately.

Mike swiped at his eyes and coughed. "Dude," he blustered to Tank. "When ya pack up the guitars and pedals for Hollywood, don't forget this one."

Tank lowered the video camera and gave Mike a dubious look. He inched toward the guitar case and set down the camera. Then he slowly opened the case and lifted the black Kramer Baretta. He tilted his head and glanced at Velvet, Angelina, and then Mike.

Mike coughed and shot Velvet a wink—he was revving back up into the old Mike. "Here's one reason I been hangin' with this chick all summer." He snatched the envelope from her grasp and handed it to Vin. "Ange here was key in sortin' yer tax bill. I pushed her till we found there was a glitch in the system. Got a clean bill now." He nodded at the envelope as Vin started to open it. "There's yer *proof.*"

Velvet glanced at Angelina, who smiled.

Vin unfolded the document and studied it. "This for real?" he asked and then he turned to Angelina and spoke in Italian.

Angelina nodded to Vin, and Velvet recognized the word *verità*—truth.

Mike stepped toward Angelina—he couldn't understand what she was saying to Vin and he quite obviously wanted to get the attention focused back on him. "I told Ange how Vin had promised Tank that guitar—"

"Sorry, Tank," Vin said, as he slipped his arm around Velvet's waist. "We needed the money."

"Tryin' to pry it from her's been a real bitch," Mike boasted. "I had to really work it, if ya know what I mean," he said, as he stood behind Angelina and began thrusting his pelvis.

"Since when did getting laid become a sacrifice for you?" Vin said, rolling his eyes.

"Had to charm her into sellin' it back." He gave Angelina a crooked grin. "I can be persuasive when I want. Got a way with chicks, ya know?" Velvet saw him glance at Harley, as if he expected she might contest that last claim.

Angelina just stood there with a naïve smile, and it was clear that she didn't understand a word he had said. She kept looking up at him with adoration, and Velvet realized her glances didn't seem groupie-like at all— they seemed respectful.

"Wasn't suited for her, anyway," Mike insisted. "I got her sorted with a sweet little green PRS." He put his arm on her shoulder. "This chick's got talent. She's gonna be the next big rock star in Italy, mark my words."

Velvet thought back to that evening in the bar when Mike couldn't take his eyes off Angelina; and he was right about her talent—her voice was haunting.

"Thanks, geeze." Tank dabbed at his eyes. "That's about the nicest thing anyone ever done for me."

Mike laughed and slapped him on the back. Then he glanced around the room and crowed, "Got Ange a ticket to L.A. Gonna bring her onstage for the all-star jam."

Vin rolled his eyes. "Leave it to Mays to try to turn this into some rookie talent showcase."

"I promised her I'd—"

"You need to stop making promises you can't keep."

"Oh, like you with the Kramer?" Mike fired back. "C'mon, this bod?" he said ogling Angelina. "Her sexy voice? Trust me, the fans'll dig her—"

"Just because you're fucking some 20-something," Vin said, "doesn't mean you can—"

"Fucking-uh?" Angelina said, taking a step forward and vehemently shaking her head. "Me, Mike-uh, no fucking." She wrinkled her nose and once again began speaking in rapid Italian to Vin. When they finished, she stood there, arms crossed, and it was clear she expected him to translate.

Vin glanced at Velvet and then over at Mike. "Uh," he said, chuckling, "she said that . . ." He trailed off and Velvet could see that he was embarrassed—that, or he didn't want to slam Mike in front of the crowd. She wondered if maybe, just for a moment, he had put himself in Mike's shoes.

Angelina stood there, waiting for Vin, as if she expected he would clear her name. *"Anziano,"* she said firmly.

Velvet knew that meant *old person . . . ancient.* She glanced at Mike, whose face was flushed. But did Mike have any idea what she had said?

Angelina smiled and pointed at the Kramer. *"La chitarra . . .* He teach me . . . guitar. . . . Mike Mays. . . . The best."

Velvet could see the admiration, the conviction in her eyes.

Angelina smiled and fidgeted with the big silver hoop in her ear. She looked uncomfortable, Velvet thought, out of place.

"I wait . . . out," she said before she slipped through the doorway.

Everyone was standing there, as if time had stopped. Harley was sitting on the small harp bench in the corner, like a neglected child. Mike turned suddenly and began to root through the clothes, tossing handfuls onto the couch and the floor.

"Nobody's gonna wear this shit!" he roared.

From across the room, Harley asked, "You really weren't sleeping with her?"

"Hey nineteen." Mike crooned the Steely Dan lyric and laughed. "We got a TV commercial to shoot, dudes," he said as he eyed the wardrobe. "I wouldn't wear these threads to my own funeral."

Tank nabbed Mike's phone from his pocket and plopped onto the overstuffed chair. "Check out this headline," he said, squinting at the screen. "Headbanging Has-Beens Create Commune in Italy." He lifted his eyes. "We ain't a commune."

"That's for hippies and shit," Gallo snapped, as he grabbed a pair of jeans from Velvet.

"Here's another, geezers," Tank continued. "Where Do Washed Up '80s Hair Bands Go? Tuscany—"

"Youch." Velvet cringed.

"God damn," Mike barked. "Will the press ever get over themselves with that '80s hair band bullshit?"

"How conveniently they forget," Harley noted, as if the media people in the courtyard might hear. "Some of us have been around since the '70s."

"How's this?" Vin asked as he buttoned up a blue Florentine patterned shirt.

Velvet smiled. "It goes with this," she said and then helped him into the jacket that she had hand-painted for him.

Mike stood alone at the smaller mirror, scrutinizing, turning left and right. "You *tryin'* to make me look bad?" He held up a voluminous white shirt and examined the copper-toned jeans. "These suck."

"You look naff in that bloody clobber, geeze," Tank said.

Mike turned to face the room and Velvet saw that his eyes were bloodshot and bleary.

"Fuck all of you," he roared. "I lived my goddman life on the road! And ya had to put up with shit on the road . . . bein' stranded at the airport for four fuckin' hours because the promoter's transportation didn't show up . . . or the crappy rented backline . . . or landin' in Barcelona and the airline sent yer guitars to Madrid. I been puttin' up with shit all my life, and it's time all you people start treatin' me with some respect."

Harley got up and moved toward him. "Nobody's disrespecting you, love." She pulled Mike to the mirror. "You look smashing."

Velvet knew those moves so well—Harley was trying to jolly him out of his funk, but Mike seemed lost, like all that mattered now was the glory days.

Velvet snatched up the zippered vest from the overstuffed chair. "Here," she said as she stepped to him. "Try this on."

"Uh, no."

"Dahling, that'll be fab." Harley took the vest from Velvet and encouraged Mike into it.

Tank pranced around the room with the video camera, attempting to catch everything.

"This zipper don't work," Mike bitched as he tried to close the vest.

"That's 'cause you're too fat," Gallo cackled.

"Here." Velvet tugged the vest tighter and tried resetting the zipper.

"When did my ass drop?" Harley asked, twisting in the mirror, smoothing her hands over the back of her jeans. "It's massive as the Sahara."

"That ass is still damn fine, doll." Mike reached down and grabbed it like he owned it. "Sexiest chick I ever known," he said, sizing up Harley.

Velvet noticed the beads of sweat on Mike's forehead and upper lip. He stared at Harley, his breathing quick and shallow.

"Why you wearin' *that* shit, anyway?" he bellowed, jerking his arms away from Velvet. "Dudes wanna see sexy." His lips trembled as he licked them, his breathing shaky. "I miss them skimpy rags ya used to wear."

Harley hooted. "Afraid the days of bustiers and miniskirts are long gone for me, love," she said, boosting her breasts to fill out her top.

When Velvet gently pushed on Mike's paunch and yanked on the zipper, he smacked her hands away and snarled, "Fuck this vest!"

"Do what chicks do with tight jeans," Gallo suggested, pointing to the sofa. "Lay down and suck in that basketball belly. It'll zip up like a charm."

Harley motioned Mike to the sofa. He lowered himself flat while Gallo wrestled up the zipper and then reached out a hand and helped him up.

Velvet looked up at the clock in the living room. "C'mon, guys. We're out of time."

"Remember when your pants split in Chicago?" Harley asked Mike and then giggled. "Dahling, you should have at least worn a jock strap instead of flogging your bollocks around onstage."

Mike gave a weak smile as he inspected himself in the mirror.

"Nobody wants to see your saggy old nutsack now," Gallo growled.

"Fuck this shit!" Mike wheezed, his voice thin and hoarse. "Where's my goddamn Hendrix shirt?"

"How 'bout a Whitesnake shirt?" Gallo snorted.

"Fuck off," Mike snapped, his eyes bulging. "Goddamn stage clothes. Just gimme . . . T-shirt . . ." He seemed so angry that his breath was choked off.

"No need to get so worked up about it," Velvet said with a glance at Vin. "Wear whatever you want." Then she noticed Mike bracing himself against the mirror as Tank whizzed past with the camera.

Harley reached out but Mike held up his hand. "Fuckin' vest," he growled, his chest heaving. "Too tight." He looked panicked as he struggled to pull down the stubborn zipper. "Off," he snapped at Tank, who lowered the camera and immediately applied himself to the task.

Harley and Velvet tried, too, but the zipper seemed welded in place.

Sweat was trickling down Mike's face. "Can't breathe," he eked out. "Whoa, dizzy." Then he toppled into the wall.

Gallo rushed over and he and Vin carted Mike to the sofa, laying him out among the velvet and lace that he had derided.

Harley bent over Mike, who was hyperventilating. "You're shaking."

"I think maybe it's a panic attack," said Velvet.

"It's more than that," Harley said as she vaulted from the sofa.

"Inhaler," Mike eked out between gasps, as he pointed toward the office.

Inhaler? Velvet stared at him sprawled on the sofa, trembling and struggling for air.

As Mike's chest heaved, Vin tugged at the zipper until it finally gave.

Harley rushed the inhaler to Mike. She knelt at his side and steadied it for him while he sucked in. "There you go," she said, caressing his forehead. "You're okay, love. Just breathe."

Velvet glanced up and saw Tank swallow hard. Kneeling next to Mike, Harley whispered in his ear, sweetly consoling him as she dabbed sweat from his face.

"I love you, you foolish old bugger," she whispered as she caressed Mike's cheek. He grasped her hand as he worked to steady his breath. She gave him a faint smile. Then she glanced around the room and announced, "He's got COPD."

"What?" Velvet looked at Mike and then Harley.

"Cardio obstructive pulmonary disease," Harley said evenly, as she hovered near Mike.

Velvet looked down at him. "Why would you keep that from us?"

Mike dropped Harley's hand and shot her a look, but she just shrugged at him.

"He'd better be able to sing," Vin snapped.

"Vin!" Velvet gave him a cutting glance.

"Well . . . our asses are on the line here. . . . *All* of them."

Velvet glanced around at the concerned faces. Then she looked down at Mike gasping on the sofa. She clutched at the tape measure around her neck, knowing that she was thinking the same thing as the others. As much as they all hated to admit it, Mike Mays had the most drawing power. If he couldn't play the gig, would there even be a show?

Chapter 43

The Hollywood Bowl. Clutching a jumble of wardrobe, Velvet shivered as she glanced around the famous backstage. Then she stepped into dressing room B and hung the last of the stage clothes on the wardrobe rack. She turned and scanned the room. Harley leaned into the wall of makeup mirrors, touching up her eyeliner under the silver-caged lights. Vin reviewed the set list on the laptop. Gallo struggled to fasten a stack of bracelets on his wrists. Blitz had decided to go on stage and change the snare and tom heads. Mike was still missing.

Velvet moved to the doorway and snuck a quick peek down the hall before turning back to the room. "Has anyone seen Mike?"

Gallo growled, "Probably off bangin' one of those groupies that were hangin' in the hallway—"

"He doesn't do that before a gig," Harley said tersely. "He's like a fighter."

"I saw him in the downstairs dressing rooms with Dee," said Vin. "He was bragging to anyone in earshot that there were only a handful of tickets left."

Velvet twisted at her hair. "I was just downstairs and I didn't see him."

"Oy!" Tank hollered as he burst into the room, nearly knocking over Velvet. "Song's up to 250,000 views on YouTube. Been floggin' on iTunes . . . like a blind dog in a meat market."

The room exploded in cheers and high-fives. Gallo scrunched up his face and turned down his hearing aid.

"Thirty minutes till show time, geezers," Tank announced, as he disappeared into the hallway.

Vin reached for the pile of freshly inked set lists resting in the printer tray. Tracing a finger down the page, he turned to Velvet and said, "I don't care what Mays says, she's *not* playing."

"It's only at the very end," Velvet said calmly, knowing he meant Angelina. "With so many guests onstage, you won't even notice she's there."

There was still no sign of Mike. The others didn't seem alarmed—after all, Mike was . . . well . . . *Mike*—but she was beginning to worry. She stepped into the hallway and spotted Brayden. Lydia was a few steps behind him, and she was carrying a guitar case. Instinctively, Velvet reached for the case, but Lydia held onto it.

"Were you just with Mike?" Velvet asked.

Lydia glanced at Brayden and then Velvet. "No. We just got here. Traffic was awful."

"He must be with Andrew then."

Brayden grimaced. "The corporate bigwigs summoned Dad to Boston."

"It *is* Monday," said Lydia. "He worked email and phone for days trying to get out of it."

Velvet looked at Brayden and chewed her lip. She didn't want to worry the boy, especially if Mike really was off with some chick. "You know, everyone's getting dressed right now. Why don't we step in here?" She nudged them into another dressing room where a few guests were talking. "Brayden, do you mind waiting here just a minute? I need to borrow your mother."

Brayden shrugged. Lydia gave Velvet an inquisitive glance, but she handed the guitar case to her son and told him she'd be right back.

Velvet motioned Lydia down the hall to the old black and white poster of Hendrix onstage, foot on his wah-wah pedal. "This is weird, but I can't find him, and I thought maybe you—"

"Maybe he's with Tank."

They stepped through the doorway and onto the concrete of the Hollywood Bowl "command central" area, and rounded the counter past the water cooler and control center. Velvet pushed on the double doors that led to stage right, and she spotted the sign: *Water only on stage. No food, soda, coffee, etc. Thank you.* She knew exactly who would ignore it, and he was probably out there right now, downing a Jack and Coke in the wings.

"Huh, I thought for sure—" Velvet stepped over to the guitar tech station. "Have you seen Mike?" she asked Tank, who shook his head. She turned to Lydia. "He's such an attention whore, maybe he's out in the crowd." Velvet forced a smile. "That man treats his fans like they're his best friends. You should've seen him at the airport." She moved to the curtain. "He'll be easy to spot. Just look for the swarm."

Lydia shadowed her and they both peered around the curtain that kept anyone waiting in the wings shielded from audience view. The blistering August day had settled into a warm Hollywood night. Velvet looked up at the lighting catwalk and then out over the terraced amphitheater seating. She waved at Giulia, poised like an Italian beauty queen in her VIP box seat near the front. Among the many sponsor banners flapping gently in the sultry evening breeze, she eyed several for Giulia's *La Principessa Cioccolato* as a steady stream of concertgoers poured in. Some of them held handmade banners, most of them celebrating Mike—*Mike Mays = Guitar God ... Mays Rocks! ... Mike, I could be your "Lucky Night."* But there was no sign of him.

Velvet noticed Lydia staring at the banners. "I had no idea," she said softly. "He's touched so many people."

"Twenty minutes," Tank signaled to Velvet.

"I don't see him anywhere," she said, turning to Lydia. "I *had* been thinking he's just being the usual Mike, you know—"

"Irresponsible?"

Velvet pressed her lips together, wondering if Lydia knew how changed Mike had seemed over the past week. "He's not been ... himself. He's been sleeping a lot, and he tires easily. That's why I'm starting to worry."

Lydia stood there, blinking under the stage lights, and Velvet could see that she hadn't known about Mike's decline. "He'd never miss an opportunity to play the Hollywood Bowl, so there must be something," Lydia said, squinting up at the lighting trusses. "Mike Mays doesn't allow anyone to see him when he's weak. . . . He hides out." Her eyes locked on Velvet's. "So if, let's say, he's not feeling well, he'd be hiding somewhere. We should check every room backstage—"

"I have."

Lydia moved into action. "Closets, bathrooms. Let's look again."

They blasted through the door, back through command central. When they reached the hallway, amidst the chatter pulsating from the different dressing rooms, they both heard it—a faint retching sound coming from dressing room A. It couldn't be Mike, Velvet thought; she had just checked that room fifteen minutes ago.

They stepped inside and Lydia cracked open the bathroom door. Peeking over Lydia's shoulder, Velvet saw Mike crouched on the white tile, his body twisted, his head in the toilet. She scrambled back across the dressing room and closed the door, sparing him from any potential backstage onlookers and rumor-mongers.

"Dad," Lydia said, kneeling next to him. "I think we should call for help."

Mike coughed out a wheezy, "No!" as he reached up and grabbed her hand. "Somethin' I ate," he said weakly. He looked like hell.

"Let me call the staff medics," Velvet suggested. "They'll be here in, like, two minutes—"

"No!" Mike growled. "Ain't . . . nothin' serious."

Velvet spotted his gig bag on the floor. "Should I get your inha—"

"I'm fine," he barked, holding up his palm. "Stop . . . the goddamn panderin'."

He started coughing, and when he grabbed the handicapped rail and shakily pulled himself up, Lydia reached down and tried to steady him. Velvet rushed over to help. They both grasped his arms, hoisted him up, and walked him back a few steps, where they lowered him onto the dressing room couch.

Velvet saw Lydia glance at the half-empty bottle of Jack Daniels on the counter.

"Of course." She dragged over a wastebasket and a chair and sat next to him, putting a hand on his sweaty head. "Just throw it up and you'll feel better."

"Half the bottle?" Velvet charged. "Really?"

"Not me." Mike pointed a shaky finger toward the counter. "Hardly . . . fuckin' . . . drank," he wheezed between breaths. "Couple sips." With a hacking cough, he spewed into the wastebasket.

Velvet leaned in and noticed it wasn't vomit. He was spitting up brown mucus. She looked at Lydia, who said, "I'm going for help—"

"No." He grabbed Lydia's wrist. "Better now . . . somethin' I ate . . . swear." He coughed and feebly pushed himself upright, his breathing shallow, mucus dribbling from his chin. "Pasta withdrawal . . . that's all." Dripping with sweat, he grinned up at Velvet and wheezed before slumping back into the couch.

"Just lie there. Let me get you a towel." Velvet scurried to the bathroom, wetted a folded towel in the sink, and took it to Lydia.

"You're so sweaty," Lydia said as she placed the towel over her father's forehead.

"Sweaty guy." He gave her a soft, crooked grin.

"We should get your inhaler," Lydia insisted. When he scowled at her, she shrugged. "Andrew told me."

His whole body seemed to sag and he struggled to get a deep breath. "Inside pocket," he wheezed.

Velvet rooted around his gig bag and then handed him the inhaler. Mike lifted a shaky hand, took a hit, and then slipped the canister into his pocket. When the door inched open, Velvet lunged toward it, catching Vin and Harley as they peeked inside.

"What's going on?" Vin asked from the doorway.

"You okay, love?" Harley asked as she moved to the couch.

Brayden pushed past Velvet and dropped the guitar case on the floor. "Grampa?"

"You look like hell," said Vin, as Velvet pulled him inside and closed the door.

"Fuck you, too," Mike said with a flimsy laugh.

Harley stepped aside so Brayden could sit on the couch at his grandfather's side. He stared at Mike. "You're going to play, right?"

"Course," Mike wheezed. "Gonna blow these cats away." He shot Vin a crooked grin.

"I *really* think we should call a medic," Lydia declared.

"No," Mike insisted. "Stop makin' . . . such a big deal. . . . Just need . . . a minute."

Vin leaned against the wall and crossed his arms. "He's fucked up," he affirmed, nodding toward the bottle of Jack.

"Ain't," Mike croaked out as he glared at Vin. "Few hits . . . Eddie bogarted the rest."

Vin glanced over at the TV mounted on the dressing room wall. They could now all see Eddie, the MC, onstage firing up the audience. "Shit," said Vin. "We're already 10 minutes behind."

"Go play the show," Velvet said. "We'll tend to Mike."

Mike grunted loudly and struggled to sit up. "I'm fine," he said, as Lydia nudged him back down on the couch.

Velvet eyed Mike—how sick was he? And if it was bad, was he truly in denial? She turned back to see Vin and Harley exchanging nervous glances. Vin glanced at the monitor, at the vacant stage and the restless audience.

"Go," Velvet said to them. "No more delays. We'll get Mike out there once he's feeling better." She turned, forcing a smile at Mike, but she didn't really think he'd be standing up anytime soon.

"Start the show," Mike barked. "Before I . . . kick yer asses."

Velvet hustled Vin and Harley from the dressing room. "I'll take care of him," she assured them.

Brayden stepped from the bathroom carrying a wet towel, which he handed to Lydia. As Velvet watched her gently applying the compress, she realized that these two weren't as estranged as they'd made it seem. Mike's affection for Brayden was obvious, but Velvet hadn't understood *this* relationship, the one between father and daughter. She thought back to their visit to Italy, and the big blowup. Lydia had only done what any mother would have—she protected her son. This ice queen, as Mike had depicted her, didn't seem as cold as Mike had made her out to be. Or maybe she was finally warming to him; and maybe Mike wasn't as tough as he wanted Lydia to believe.

The music started up and Velvet glanced at the TV; Vin and Harley had taken the stage.

"Whoa!" Brayden's eyes locked onto the monitor. "Can I go watch from the stage?"

"Tired." Mike lay back and closed his eyes. "Feels like . . . I just smoked . . . shitload of hash."

Brayden got up and put a hand on Lydia's shoulder, pointing at the guitar case, and Lydia nodded. "Gra—um, Mike . . . we have a surprise. But you'll want to sit up a little." Brayden helped Mike prop himself up.

Velvet sensed that this was a private moment. With a glance at Lydia, she said, "I . . . I should go—"

"Stay," Mike said, tearing his eyes away from the TV. "Yer . . . my lifeline . . . to the stage."

Velvet nodded and lowered herself onto the arm of the couch.

Lydia forced a laugh. "Brayden just couldn't wait." She looked at Mike and swallowed hard. "I have something for you." She lifted the guitar case and set it on her lap with the latches facing Mike, as if it was a sort of peace offering.

"What the—"

Lydia smiled, reached over, and put an arm around her son.

Mike ran his fingers over the road-weary guitar case covered with a patchwork of tour silks from decades past. He unfastened each latch and Lydia helped him push open the lid. His hands trembled as he reached for his Gibson Les Paul Custom "Black Beauty," his chin quivering. He glided his fingers over the body and the fretboard and then breathed in and closed his eyes. "Smells like the road." He breathed in the scent and coughed. "Steely . . . musty . . . ain't nothin' like it."

He looked straight at Lydia. "But . . . how did you? . . ." he asked in a shaky voice as he caressed the guitar.

"The woman who dropped you at my house last April. She brought it back . . . for you. . . . Her husband passed away."

Mike glanced at the guitar and at his daughter before his chin dipped to his chest.

She reached out and placed her hand on his arm. "I'm sorry."

"He was . . . good guy . . . super fan."

"She said he would've wanted you to have your guitar back."

Brayden interrupted, "I can't believe it was in our house all this time and you forgot about it." He turned from his mom to Velvet. "We didn't even know she had it."

Lydia gave a timid shrug.

"When I saw mom with the guitar the other day," Brayden exclaimed to Mike, "she was sitting on the floor—and mom never sits on the floor—and when I asked her to let go of it, she wouldn't. That wasn't like her."

Velvet noticed that Lydia couldn't help but smile—in that moment her son seemed to know her better than she knew herself.

Mike stared at the Les Paul with shining eyes, as if he'd never expected to see it again. When he glanced back at Lydia, they shared a knowing smile. It was as if he were saying to Lydia, *I did the best I could.* It seemed to Velvet that they had reached a truce, or maybe just some kind of compromise. Then Mike gave a manly clearing of his throat, and Velvet figured it was probably his high sign that the old Mike was still kicking.

Brayden placed the guitar in Mike's lap.

"No such thing as . . . too much rehearsal," Mike croaked out, as he noodled a bit.

Brayden stepped up. "Give me that 'Born to Be Bad' riff, you know, how you changed it to start on the upbeat . . ." Brayden began to softly sing: *'Cause I was born to be bad, yeah, born to be bad.* And then he nodded at Mike, who joined in, rasping out between coughs: *The long, rough road is the only one I have. Never playin' safe. Never lookin' back. Always make my own way. 'Cause I was born to be bad.*

As Mike wheezed out the words, he glanced up from the guitar and flashed Velvet that classic crooked grin, and she couldn't help but smile back at him. The lyrics were the Mike Mays credo. Mike, the renegade—he was old and sick, but strumming that guitar and singing that song, especially with his grandson, seemed to transform him.

When Mike broke into a coughing fit, he looked at Velvet. "Ask Tank," he ordered between coughs. "My brew."

Velvet nodded and then turned to Brayden, who was staring eagerly at the TV. "Want to come with me?"

"Hell, yeah!" He glanced over at Lydia and Velvet could see her hesitate, but she didn't try to stop him.

Velvet escorted Brayden to the right wing and deposited him on a road case near Tank's guitar tech station, where he'd have a view of the stage action.

"Mike wants his *brew,*" she explained to Tank.

"How's he?" Tank asked as he handed her the thermos from atop his production case.

She glanced at Brayden and then at Tank and forced a smile. "He'll be . . . fine." She pressed her lips and then asked, "Can Brayden stay here with you for awhile?"

"Fuckin' 'ell, I'm busier than a cucumber in a women's prison." Then he looked at Brayden. "Can you tune a guitar?" When the kid grinned and nodded, Tank grumbled, "Oh, awright. But stay back here."

Velvet positioned herself so that Vin could see her, and then she motioned to him. Chunking out rhythm chords without missing a beat, Vin skipped over to Velvet. "Is Mays playing or not?"

Velvet held up the thermos and hollered, "He's sick—"

"Dude's got an iron constitution. He once snorted Vicodin, downed a bottle of Jack, and walked eight miles from the Cow Palace to North Beach."

"No, he's *really* sick."

"Then call the medics," Vin said and turned back to the band.

"He'll freak out," Velvet yelled out as Vin skipped back across the stage to the front, just in time to burn a solo to the rowdy crowd.

Velvet hurried past all the guests watching the big TVs in command central, to dressing room A. When she pushed open the door, Lydia was sitting right where she had left her, perched on the edge of her chair, fussing over Mike. Velvet handed Mike the thermos and when he opened it, she reeled from the stench.

"My God, what is that—herbs?"

"Some voodoo shit," he muttered and then gulped down the brew and coughed again.

Velvet turned to the monitor, and she could hear Mike take another hit off the inhaler. She turned back to see him reach over and touch a silver charm—a galloping horse—that dangled from Lydia's bracelet.

Lydia shook her head in amazement. "I saw all those signs out there with your name. . . ." She looked blown away, but she paused, as if unsure what to say next. "I saw them and I realized—"

"Fuckin' hell." He reached for her hand and squeezed it. She placed her other hand on his, but she wouldn't meet his bleary eyes. Mike's voice was weak and thin. "Ya got . . . same cute little nose as yer mom."

Lydia pressed her lips together and seemed to be fighting her emotions. After a minute, she let go of his hand and reached down to her purse. She pulled out her wallet and withdrew a tattered photo. "How many women," she asked as she handed it to him, "carry around a photograph of their dad with Jimi Hendrix?"

Mike stared at the photo and grinned. "Berkeley Community Theatre . . . May 30th . . . 1970 . . . fuckin' hell." He ran his finger over the faded picture. "Just inked my first record deal. . . . A&R dude at the label . . . brought me backstage." He lowered the picture and looked at her. "Know who shot this?"

"Mom?"

Velvet glanced at the TV. Vin was singing center stage. Harley and Gallo were headbanging to a raucous audience that had no idea Mike was laid out backstage.

"It's how I met her . . . her old Kodak Brownie camera. . . . Just some random chick backstage . . . with a camera. . . . Timing's everything, huh?"

He handed the photo to Velvet and she stared at the young Mike backstage with Hendrix. "Classic."

Lydia frowned. "She said you met at a concert. I always thought it was yours."

"Nope. Hendrix. . . . Got her number . . . for that shot."

She gave him an anemic smile. "Why did you mail it to me, anyway?"

Mike shrugged. "Just found it . . . in a box . . . thought you oughta have it . . . happiest day of my life." He coughed again.

When Lydia stared into her lap, Velvet imagined that any normal father would have claimed the birth of his child as the happiest day. She handed the photo to Lydia.

Lydia stared at it. "I used to look at this when I was little. I'd imagine you on the road and what we might do the next time you came to visit."

"You know . . . Emily and I . . . we were . . . just . . . havin' fun . . . I had my career—"

"No shit," Lydia said and stood up.

Velvet glanced at the TV again. When the musicians launched into Golden Blonde's "Rock My Love Muscle," Vin took on the lead vocals that Mike had been slated to sing.

Mike growled at the monitor. "Vin's phrasing's all wrong. . . . And Harley's guitar . . . too low in the mix."

Velvet fidgeted with her necklace. "I'll just go . . . check on the stage," she said and headed for the door.

"No," Mike barked. "I'm up next. . . . Help get me ready."

"Dad," Lydia said firmly. "You're in no position to be going anywhere right now."

Velvet exchanged glances with Lydia, hoping she'd grasped the idea of suggesting *anything* that might keep Mike calm. "Just rest up, Mike, and we'll see how you feel in a bit."

Mike tried to sit up and then patted the cushion beside him. "Gimme that," he said and reached for the photo once Lydia sat down. "You . . . actually . . . carry this?"

She sighed and looked at him. "Put it in my very first wallet. I was probably thirteen." She turned away and muttered, "For some reason it . . . got transferred into every wallet since." She looked down and snuck a glance at him. Their eyes met and she glanced away when she caught him smiling at her.

He took a pained breath and then let the force just push it out of him.

"Darlin'," he said, his voice gravelly. "I gotta say." He reached up, as though he might steady his quivering mouth. "Sorry I been . . . such an ass."

"Dad," she said softly and glanced at him.

"I know, I—" He paused to cough. "—sucked at bein' a dad. . . . I, uh." He bit down on his lip. "Well . . . ya . . . scared the shit outta me."

Lydia gave him a puzzled stare but he wouldn't look at her.

"There you were . . . this little kid . . . who made me feel all . . ." He took a wheezy breath and blinked around the room, darting glances at her. "I dunno . . . nervous . . . intense 'n' shit . . . like nothin' I never felt before—"

"It's called *love*, Dad."

"Don't know nothin' 'bout love. . . . But . . . I see . . . you . . . and Brayden."

Lydia just stared at him, her eyes wide.

"Yer . . . a . . . good mom," he wheezed and patted her hand.

Lydia's bottom lip bunched up and Velvet could see her struggling not to cry. "Oh, Dad," she choked out, and then lay her head on his chest.

Mike stiffened and lifted his arms, but then gave a reassuring pat to her head.

Velvet grabbed the towel and quickly stepped into the bathroom, where she stood for a few minutes, listening for an opportune moment to come back into the room.

She heard Lydia take a shaky breath. "When that woman dropped off your guitar . . . and I took it out and held it . . ." She paused and it seemed like minutes before she started speaking again. "I was so sure that playing guitar would . . . destroy him . . . and . . . take him away from me. . . . But . . ."

Velvet moved quietly to the bathroom doorway.

Mike glanced around the room and then met Lydia's eyes, as she took his hand. "Promise . . . for me . . . let him play," he said in a butchered whisper, and then closed his eyes.

Velvet cleared her throat before stepping into the room. "I'm going to get more towels," she announced and walked across the room, but as she put her hand on the dressing room door, Brayden stepped in.

Lydia sprang to her feet and wiped her tears. "I could really use a cup of coffee."

Velvet smiled at her and nodded. "Follow me."

"Don't," Mike growled, "go callin' no bullshit doctor . . . behind my back. . . . I'm cool."

Velvet and Lydia huddled in the hallway.

"That was . . . intense," Velvet said. "I just don't know if I could forgive him like that."

"He's . . . my father," Lydia said with a soft smile. Then, back to business, she straightened her stance. "Do you think we should?"

"You know Mike," said Velvet. "He'll go ballistic if we go against him."

Lydia let out a lengthy sigh. "I'm concerned that if we call the medics, he'll get so upset that he might. . . ." She didn't finish the thought, but Velvet knew what she meant. "But . . . in the final analysis, I'm as bull-headed as he is." She smiled weakly at Velvet. "Do it."

Velvet headed down the hallway to make the call. When she came back, Lydia was standing outside the dressing room door, listening intently. Neither of them meant to eavesdrop, Velvet told herself, but every moment now seemed heightened, as if each word were weighted with history.

"I can't wait to meet DC," Brayden was saying.

"Was hangin' with all those cats . . . for like two hours," Mike boasted. "Ya got here too late."

"Mom wouldn't let me come early," Brayden griped. "Made me miss half of the coolest day ever."

Lydia looked at Velvet and grimaced.

"Don't worry," they heard Mike say before taking another hit off the inhaler. "You'll meet him . . . after."

"Did you hear?" Brayden asked excitedly. "Our song's at number 53 today on iTunes singles. Sanjay's dad did me a real solid over at Apple."

He sounded like his grandfather, Velvet thought.

"Ya wrote," Mike rasped out, "one badass tune."

"Grampa, I've decided—"

"Another lame-ass stage name?" Mike growled.

"I've decided . . . I wanna be a rock star."

Lydia took a deep, shaky breath.

"Nah . . . you don't wanna be no rock star."

"But I can feel it. You said before . . . even Harley said, it's in my blood—"

"Look at me, kid. . . . I got nothin'. . . . Go to college . . . like yer mom wants."

"I know Mom'll have a shit fit."

"Don't be so sure," said Mike.

Velvet exchanged a slight smile with Lydia and then opened the door.

"Brayden," Lydia instructed, all business. "Go take your grandfather's guitar to the stage, where it belongs."

Brayden stopped and looked at her, but Lydia nodded toward the stage.

"It's okay," she said to her son as he picked up the guitar and carried it out of the dressing room.

"Mr. Mays?" a young man asked, poking his head into the room. "I hear you're not feeling so well." The event medic entered and sat down next to Mike.

Mike growled at Lydia and Velvet and flipped them off.

"I'm Doug. You're having trouble breathing?" he asked.

"I'm fine," Mike barked. "Just . . . somethin' I ate."

Doug grinned at him. "You know, my parents are your biggest fans. They got awesome seats, too, 'cause, well, I have a little pull."

"Smart parents," Mike said, as he struggled to take a breath.

"This could be my lucky night," Doug sang out. "Let me just take your blood pressure."

Velvet glanced at the TV. Vin and Harley were trading off lead vocals and lead guitars. Gallo steadied the rhythm section on bass as Blitz shored up the beat behind the drum kit. She looked back to see Doug struggling to put the blood pressure cuff around Mike's arm.

"Let me up," Mike wheezed. "Gonna miss . . . my solo."

"Not yet," Lydia said, placing a firm hand on his chest. "Conserve your strength." She gave Doug a look.

"Bullshit!" Mike growled and feebly tried to push her hand away.

"You're wheezing, out of breath," Velvet said, backing her. "How could you possibly sing? And what if you stumbled out there? Do you really want to see yourself on YouTube, failing in front of 18,000 people?"

Velvet knew it was a low blow, but it served her purpose.

Mike sunk back into the couch, glaring at Velvet. "Who got yer ass here . . . huh?"

"Can everyone please calm down while I take his BP?" The room fell silent while Doug took Mike's vitals. "Sixty over forty," he announced, glancing up at Lydia and then Velvet before looking at Mike. "Is your blood pressure always this low?"

"How the fuck would I know?" Mike barked and then coughed.

"I'm gonna radio my partner, who's on the other side of the venue right now."

Velvet found herself smiling indulgently at Mike. He looked so helpless lying there, as Lydia tended to him, changing out the wet towel and brushing the damp hair from his face. But he had pulled it off—the concert, fixing the property tax fiasco, and fending off Carlo. He was bulletproof and it would not have surprised her if he had risen from the couch and gone out there to play a blistering solo—

There was a tap at the door and Velvet opened it. Vin was standing there, and he beckoned her into the hallway. "Word's out that Mays is down," he hissed.

Velvet could hear Blitz pounding out a drum solo. "Yes," she said, glancing back at the closed door. "But we're . . . managing him, you know, so he doesn't really know. . . ."

"That he doesn't have a chance in hell of playing the Bowl."

Harley came down the hallway and inched open the door. "They're cheering for Mike's set. We've got to move onto the encore." She stepped aside to let the medic out of the room.

"I'm gonna call for an ambulance," Doug said to Velvet. "They're better equipped. Should be here in about 15 minutes. . . . I'll be right back." Then he disappeared down the hall.

Gallo and Blitz blew into the dressing room and they all stared at Mike on the couch.

"Is he dead?" Gallo squawked.

"If I'm dead," Mike growled. "then yer . . . one . . . ugly . . . fuckin' . . . angel."

Vin shook his head. "Not funny, dude."

"Should we get him something?" Blitz asked.

"Weed," Mike joked with a rattly laugh. Then he looked up at the TV and motioned to Vin. "Encore."

"As far as I'm concerned," Vin said, shaking his head, "if you can't make it to the stage, show's over." Then he, Gallo, Blitz, and Harley huddled up. "We should call it," Vin said firmly.

Everyone began chattering at once—Vin, Harley, Blitz, and Gallo debating in the huddle on one side, and Lydia and Velvet on the other. Velvet glanced at the TV, where the audience continued cheering for an encore.

"Put Bobby on my kit," Blitz offered. "And Marco on bass—"

"Dee, David, and Sam are ready to go," Harley argued.

Gallo glanced at Mike on the couch. "That dude just sucked the vibe right outta me."

"Finish," Mike eked out. "For fuck's sake . . . go."

When the audience suddenly roared, they all looked over at the TV. The stage was dark but a single guitar resounded through the Bowl. There stood Brayden, holding up Mike's prized Les Paul, taunting the crowd with the "Born to Be Bad" riff, firing them up to fever pitch.

"You want more?" he crowed into the center stage mic.

Velvet exchanged smiles with Harley as Gallo cackled.

"What the hell is *he* doing up there?" Vin snapped.

"Fuckin' little kid," Mike growled, struggling to sit up. "Lemme—"

"What?" Brayden asked the audience, cupping his hand to his ear. "Those old dudes backstage can't hear you. . . . You're gonna have to scream louder." And they did.

"Goddammit," Vin griped and started for the door.

Velvet grasped her husband's hand. "This is his moment . . . and Mike's," she assured him.

"Little shit disturber," said Gallo. "Just like his gramps."

They all turned as Mike let out a raspy laugh. "Gonna . . . let the kid . . . kick yer asses?"

"C'mon, guys," Harley said. When she reached out her fist, Blitz and

Gallo bumped it, united in the name of rock 'n' roll . . . and Mike Mays. Vin glanced at the TV and held Harley's stare before he turned back, reached out his fist and joined the bump. Then they headed to the stage.

"Fuckers!" Mike barked. "Ain't . . . leavin' me here." He started to push himself up but Lydia helped him back onto the couch.

Doug stuck his head in the door. "The ambulance will be here any minute."

"Fuck off," Mike growled.

"I'm gonna go find my coworker down the hall and meet the ambulance."

Mike pointed at the TV. "That's . . . my grandson," he barked, as if it were news. Lydia hovered near him, and she reached out to readjust the towel, but Mike jerked his arm up to block her. "Just . . . fuckin' help me . . . to the goddamn wing. . . . Get me up there."

Lydia turned to Velvet and when their eyes met, Velvet nodded. She glanced around the room, spotted a desk chair, and rolled it over to the couch. "Hurry!" Lydia steadied the chair while Velvet helped Mike into it.

Velvet steered while Lydia braced her father in the chair. As they rolled Mike through command central and to the right wing, he cackled and grinned throughout the ride.

Velvet flung open the curtain and stepped aside so Mike could see the stage. Lydia clutched her father's hand and watched the musicians all grabbing for their instruments. Velvet glanced up at the set list posted in the wings. *Born to Be Bad*, it read, *all skate*—now, all but Mike. She watched Vin scrambling to recruit guest musicians for an all-star grand finale.

"I think by now you've all heard this next tune," Brayden boasted into the mic, still noodling the riff. "My grampa and I wrote it together."

"Shit!" Vin said, as he tossed on his guitar and turned on his wireless pack. "Who's gonna sing it?"

Velvet pointed to Brayden at center stage.

"No fuckin' way," Vin said, glancing at Mike.

Velvet gently touched his arm. "Just run with it."

Brayden looked to the wings and said, "You know Mike Mays?" When the audience screamed, Brayden swung back around and teased the crowd. "Check out who all he invited to play for you tonight. Dee, Eric, Don, and Sammy are gonna share vocals with me on this one."

Lydia smiled down at Mike and squeezed his hand. He grinned up at her and then back at his grandson onstage.

Brayden took a deep breath. "This is for my grampa."

Tank walked over and gave Velvet a proud nudge. She looked at him and asked, "Did you. . . ?"

"You know as well as I do, the kid can play." Tank winked at her and returned to his tech station.

Brayden yelled, "Hit it!"

They launched into "Born to Be Bad." Brayden sailed through on guitar and shared backing vocals. Vin and Harley wailed alongside him, and Gallo flung his bass, successfully circling it—'80s style—around his gut. Brayden grinned and then launched his own guitar swing with Mike's Les Paul. The audience roared. From the chair in the wing, Mike gave him a shaky thumbs up.

Lydia let go of Mike's hand and clapped feverishly for her son. When Brayden glanced over at his mom in the wings, Velvet saw Lydia mouth, "I love you."

Then Doug was there with his coworker and two paramedics. Mike shoved a wobbly palm toward them and demanded, "Five minutes." He pointed at the stage. "My grandson."

"Please?" Velvet pleaded to the medics, pressing her palms together.

Doug hesitated but then he nodded. "*Two* minutes." He argued with one of the paramedics for a moment, but then the four of them stood back at the rear of the wing.

Vin turned onstage and winked at Velvet. Without skipping a beat, he pointed back at Brayden, and then gave Velvet a conciliatory smile. She returned the smile and watched him relinquish the stage to Brayden and all the guest stars.

Mike leaned forward and Velvet noticed he was weakly fingering the notes in tandem with Brayden, playing along on the encore.

Lydia clutched his hand. "Are you okay?"

"Just . . . emotional," he said.

Velvet could see that the audience was on its feet, rocking out in the aisles and on the seats. As the final notes echoed, she saw Mike's hand slip from Lydia's. She glanced down at him, half-expecting that he might leap onto the stage to steal everyone's thunder and finish the show. But he just sat there, relaxed, his mouth open. She bent down and realized he had stopped breathing.

"Oh my God," Velvet said, looking at Lydia. "I think he's gone."

Lydia bent down to Mike. He was slumped in the chair, his eyes half-open: the last thing he had seen was his grandson, onstage, paying tribute to Mike with his prized Les Paul.

Velvet straightened up and glanced around the wing and then at the stage, but nobody had noticed that Mike Mays had quietly passed away. Over the ear-splitting praise of the audience, the musicians all formed a long line for a bow. Brayden waved to the crowd, and as the line dissolved, still wearing Mike's guitar, he raised the Les Paul and aimed the headstock at the audience, knighting them with it. He turned to aim the headstock at Mike, but Lydia was standing between them. Brayden turned back and gave a final wave to the audience as he stepped up to the mic.

"Thank you, goodnight," he said, as if it was second nature.

Chapter 44

Velvet huddled under her blanket, surveying the hilltop, the Tuscan sky, and the glow of the bonfire, as embers glittered and floated up toward the full moon. Vin tossed more branches into the fire, and Tank stood by his side holding a backstock of twigs. Gallo huddled in a wool sweater and quilted jacket, and Blitz, curled up in a lounge chair, pulled the blanket up to his chin.

"Remember how wigged out Mike was the first time we dragged him up here?" Harley muttered. Then she began softly strumming Vin's acoustic guitar.

At first Velvet thought it was just background music, but when Harley started in on the chorus, she quickly recognized the tune.

'Cause I was born to be bad, yeah . . .

Vin joined in. "The long, rough road is the only one I have. Never playin' safe. Never lookin' back. Always make my own way."

Velvet listened to their perfect harmonies, until Tank interrupted by bursting in, off-key.

'Cause I was born to be bad.

Gallo cringed. "Dude, stick to teching."

"Can't hear shit, geeze, but ya heard that?"

Harley choked through her tears before she stopped strumming altogether. Blitz stood up and moved in to comfort her, but Harley raised her arms, as if to shut everyone out. "Just . . . everyone bugger off." She dropped the guitar and walked to the opposite edge of the plateau.

Gallo scanned the sky. "He's probably banging every hot chick up there."

"Or down there," Blitz added as he settled back into his lounge chair. "I think Mays was the biggest hosebag I ever met."

"Loudest motherfucker I ever met," Gallo growled.

"How would you know if he was loud?" Tank muttered. "Ya mardy git." He shivered and rubbed his hands together. "Jesus sufferin' fuck, the nights have gone parky. Bung me that jacket, geeze."

Gallo snatched the jacket from the ground and tossed it up to Tank, who slipped on another layer.

"Can't believe . . ." Tank glanced at Velvet and Vin. "Just hours before, he was goin' on 'bout some punter in Germany who had a ghostly tattoo of his face above her arse. And then—"

"Fucker never returned my hundred bucks he blew at the Viper Room," Gallo griped.

"I just knew he was sick," said Velvet. "But he kept denying it. How in the hell can someone play with pneumonia?"

"Testament to the true pro he was." Tank sniffled and wiped his nose on the jacket sleeve.

"Can't believe that little kid fucking stole the best lead," Vin said with a slight grin.

"That's exactly what Mays would've done," said Blitz.

"Must admit," Vin said, "it was a rippin' solo."

Gallo cackled. "That was Mays' last fuck you."

"No," Blitz corrected. "His last fuck you was dying before the second encore."

"Thought it was another one of his famous publicity stunts," said Gallo. "I had no idea the dude would pull the ultimate news grab and actually die right there at the Hollywood Bowl."

"And the kid saves the show." Vin shook his head. "Couldn't have written a better Hollywood ending."

"He loved that kid, ya know." Tank pursed his lips. "Was schoolin' him till his last breath."

"Do you think Mike knew he was dying?" Velvet asked.

"Must've sensed it." Tank patted at the pocket under his jacket. "This here paper proves it."

"Just read the fucking letter already," Gallo growled.

"That sonofabitch." Velvet sighed. "He royally fucked things up. But he really did it . . . actually came through. Carlo would've gone to his grave before selling the land back. But Mike . . . he worked some magic with Giulia."

"Got us the money to pay back Carlo," Tank reiterated, "fix the fire damage, and then some. . . . Let's get on with it, then." He withdrew the envelope from one of the layers under his jacket. It tumbled from his grasp and nearly into the fire as he scrambled to spare it from the flames.

"Don't burn the bloody thing before we've even seen it," Harley scolded him, as she returned to the circle.

Tank held up the envelope. "Remember, these is his words, not mine. So don't go shootin' the messenger." Then he slid on his reading glasses and squinted at the envelope. "To be opened only if I croak before you bastards."

"It doesn't say that," Harley snapped.

Tank flashed the envelope in her direction. "Right there's Mike's own scrabble." He smirked at her before carefully opening the flap and removing the paper inside. He unfolded it and read aloud. "Get the boxes now, you limey bastard." He smiled, realizing Mike's words were directed to him. Then he turned to Vin. "Get the bag, geeze."

Vin grabbed the tote bag and stood by Tank.

Velvet knew that Mike had left instructions for Lydia. She listened to Tank, imagining the words in Mike's voice.

"First, and foremost," Tank read, "always at the top of my list, Harley Yeates. My bosom buddy . . . and oh, what bosoms." Tank looked up and grinned before returning to the letter. "My friend, my soulmate, the fuckin' love of my life. . . . I'm sorry."

"Why are you apologizing?" asked Harley.

"No, it says that," Tank explained. He aimed the letter in her direction.

"See? 'I'm sorry.'" He cleared his throat. "Give her the red box, teabag."
Tank laughed. "I think teabag was meant for me, not you, Harl."

Vin rummaged through the tote bag and withdrew a small box
wrapped in red foil. He handed it to Harley, who stepped forward, her
hands trembling as she accepted the box.

Tank nodded. "Bloke was quite busy his last weeks, eh?" He returned
to reading the letter. "Don't worry, Harl, I ain't gonna fuck up again.
I love you—and you, of all people, know how hard those words have
been for me to say. I wanted to do somethin' nice for ya, so I had a little
somethin' made."

"A plaster cast of his cock?" Gallo cackled and pointed to the box. "It'd
just about fit in there—"

"Zip it," Velvet warned him.

As Harley opened the box and lifted out a chain with a pendant, Tank
read on. "Sorry it ain't no precious gem, just an original tuning peg from
my Les Paul. Thought it'd make a cool necklace. I'd be honored to know
that the chick I treasure most is wearing a piece of my favorite axe."

Harley caressed the tuning peg and then held it to her heart and
sobbed.

"Gallo." Tank cleared his throat again. "Gallo, I hope you got that
fuckin' hearin' aid in so you can fully understand what I'm about to tell
ya. Sorry, bud, I honestly had no idea I nicked the 'Lucky Night' riff from
ya back in the day. To show ya I got no hard feelings, I'm giving you 100%
of the publishing and songwriter royalties for 'Lucky Night.' Better late
than never, huh? Okay, so we all know that song ain't worth shit nowadays,
royalty-wise—though the fuckin' record company'll probably reissue all
my tunes the minute I kick the bucket. So to make up for somethin' I didn't
even intentionally do in the first place, I'm givin' you my 50% of 'Born to
Be Bad.' Yep, you heard right. No need to crank up that hearin' aid, dude.
. . . Kid's got his first songwritin' credit, and you two now own that one
outright."

"What the fuck?" Gallo bitched. "I had nothin' to do with that tune."

"Dahling," Harley said. "He was obviously trying to put his house in
order, right all his wrongs his last few weeks."

Velvet looked at Gallo, nervously tonguing at his false front teeth, his gangly legs sprawled out in the lawn chair. "Little fucker," he said in a shaky voice.

Tank glanced up from the letter and wiped his eyes. Then he pushed the reading glasses up the bridge of his nose and continued reading. "Where were I? Oh, yes. Blitz." He traced his finger over the page. "That would be the gold box, you daft Brummie." Tank glanced up and grinned. "Me, again."

Vin handed Blitz a slightly larger box wrapped in gold foil. Gallo moved close to Blitz and watched him unwrap it.

"Blitz," Tank read. "You gotta snort the shit in this box—"

"What the fuck?" Blitz asked, rolling his eyes.

Harley leaned in and cackled. "A handful of his ashes."

"That sick motherfucker," Gallo exclaimed.

"It's a joke, geezers," said Tank. "He knew we'd plant an olive tree in his name, so he's asked that you bury that bit of his ashes in the soil with it." Tank returned to the letter. "Still Blitz. . . . Fuckin' hell. I seriously pissed you off over the years. I can't change what I done, but by having a part of me there in Italy, now you can finally kick my ash." Tank laughed. "Funny." He turned back to the letter. "Seriously, though, you'll get a package in a few days. Sorry I ain't got no spandex left from the '80s, but I do still got my leather jacket. I was gonna give it to the kid, but I think it suits you better. Rock on, dude."

Blitz pressed his lips together and warmed his hands over the fire.

"Tank. . . . Ooh, this one's for me." He looked up and grinned. "I woulda given you a guitar but, sorry man, I sold 'em all last year. I'm sure you want the Les Paul, but no can do, bud. The kid gets that one." Tank glanced up. "Lucky bugger got Mike's prize axe." He turned back to the letter. "So I'm givin' ya that cell phone I made you go buy for me the day we landed in L.A."

Vin handed it to Tank, who accepted it and read on. "Now, since I don't know how to work that shit, I told the kid to plug in some numbers. So the next time ya come back to the States, browse through all the babes in there, drop my name, and have yerself some fun. Yer the best tech I ever had. I'm glad Vin loaned ya to me way back when. I know it was only a few tours, but, dude, yer the shit. Okay, enough sap. Dude, do me a favor and use yer many connections to get my grandkid hooked up. Stay in touch with him and teach him all the technical shit that I never knew. If he can solder his own pickups, he'll be a better man than me. . . . Keep yer pecker up."

Velvet stared at Tank as he just stood there in silence. He wiped his eyes and let out a deep, shaky sigh. Then he looked back down at the letter in his hands.

"Last, but certainly not least," Tank continued. "Vin and Velvet. Talk about a fuckin' match made in heaven. You two really were meant for each other. You got true love—somethin' I think maybe I wish I woulda had. And, man, the heart you got for others? All I can say is, you two are the real deal. Ya let me in when I was down . . . okay, so, I weaseled my way in. Hell, ya took in all our sorry asses when ya coulda just been livin' la dolce vita on yer own. Hey, I'm really sorry I fucked up your pad. And for that, and all the kindness you show others, I give you the rest of my royalties. It ain't much anymore, but the checks should trickle in for a little while longer. Maybe you can help out a few more sad sack rockers."

"He's right, you know," Gallo said. "We're all worth more dead than alive. You can bet your ass his old record label ain't wastin' no time cashin' in on his death. Greedy fuckers."

"There's more," Tank said. "And Vin, you can stop subbin' in shitty clubs. You've always been a killer axe slinger, worth way more than that. I got Krull at Metal Earth Records ready to ink a deal for ya, so give him a call. But just remember, any lick you can play, I could play ten times faster . . . even with arthritis."

"One more thing, dude," Tank continued, flashing a glance at Vin. "I promised Angelina somethin' and ya gotta follow through for me."

Harley tilted her head and listened intently.

Tank read on. "You got way better producer chops than I ever had, so you're the best man for the gig. Chick could probably make it on her smokin' hot tits alone, but she's got the added bonus of a monster voice, plus she's a killer songwriter—the real deal. She shreds today's shitty cookie-cutter chick pop stars."

"She's amazing," Velvet admitted and noticed Harley nodding in agreement.

Tank stared back at the letter. "Dude, record her demo. Then call Giulia. She knows some cats in Milan who can launch Ange all over Italy. Tell 'em yer Angelina's producer, and don't let 'em fuck you outta doin' her record. Ange is a good girl; she'll stick with you."

Velvet reached up to Vin and he smiled down at her, grasping her hand.

"Nearly done," Tank announced. "I wanna thank all you cats . . . for the bad times and the good. It's been a helluva ride. Aren't ya glad ya climbed aboard the Mays train? Fuckin' hell, don't stop now. Keep on rockin' and take that shit on the road. The Groove House Tour . . . can't you see it? I'll sit this one out. Never thought I'd say this, but wherever I am, you can bet I'm missin' you dudes. I'll be keepin' tabs on your sorry asses from the next world. Fuckin' hell, is Harley cryin'? Now stop mopin' around, losers. I know Tank's reading this to all of you up at Forget-Me-Not Forest. Hey, it's all about me, right? So go open some Jack or that killer San-Jo and knock back some good shit for me. Love and blowjobs . . . Mike."

Tank opened a bottle of red and handed a glass to Velvet and then to Vin.

"To Mike," Vin said. "And I never thought I'd say this, but to Carlo. He dropped off this wine earlier."

"Saw that prick chattin' you up in the driveway," Gallo grumbled.

"Shit, I thought he hated Mike, but you know what he said? Muore giovane colui chi al cielo è caro."

"What's it mean, geeze?" asked Tank.

"It's an old saying. . . . Basically . . . those whom the gods love die young."

"He wasn't that young," Gallo growled.

"I'm sure Giulia pushed him into bringing over a Brunello," Vin said with a laugh. "And probably even my wife—"

"I had nothing to do with it," Velvet said, raising her hands. She glanced toward the distant glow that came from Carlo's house on the nearby hill. "Bet Carlo's watching. Just think of all the years he spent loathing us as he glared out his window at our bonfires."

Velvet had brought with her the horrid contract that Carlo had made her sign that night with Mike. She handed her glass to Harley, slid out the folded paper, and tossed it into the bonfire. The embers floated up into the darkness until they dissipated in the cool night air.

Velvet returned to the chaise and snuggled under the blanket. She glanced at Tank, fiddling with his new phone, the light from the display illuminating the grief on his face.

"This app's wicked," Tank exclaimed, tapping until the phone became a flashlight, which he then aimed at Gallo.

"Turn that shit off," Gallo grumbled, using his hand to shield the beam. "You're fuckin' up my eyes."

"Yer old, geeze," Tank teased. "Yer eyes is already fecked up."

Vin was lying back in a lounge chair, staring up at the stars, and Velvet went over and snuggled up to him, reaching under the blanket to take his hand. It was impossible now to imagine anything other than Mike Mays crash-landing at Groove House, setting the place ablaze, and rekindling everyone's spirits. "Hmm." She leaned toward Vin. "Like some raunchy, unlikely guardian angel, Mike Mays actually saved us."

Vin laughed and took another gulp of wine.

"It's good, what we've done here," she whispered to Vin.

"Yep," he said softly. "And it wouldn't work with just anybody. This motley bunch . . . we really give a shit about each other."

Velvet took another gulp. There behind her, crowning the hilltop, Vin's ancestral home stood boldly winking at time. It was much more now than just his grandmother's home—it was the place they had painstakingly renovated, transforming their lives. This was Groove House.

Aaaoooogah. Velvet flinched as the familiar sound jarred her from her thoughts—the text notification on Mike's phone. She turned an incredulous stare toward Harley and Vin, and then to Tank.

"Geezers," Tank blurted out. "Check this out."

Velvet could see Tank tapping the keys. Then Vin stood up and poured Harley more Brunello.

"Nineteen minutes ago Eddie tweeted," Tank reported. "Rick Rousseau just collapsed on stage in Newcastle. . . . Been taken to hospital."

"Rousseau?" Vin asked.

Blitz turned anxiously to Vin and Velvet, and then wagged a finger at them. "Don't even think about it."

"If that dickhead comes here," Gallo growled, "you can bet your ass I'm movin' out."

Velvet pursed her lips and shot Vin a look.

About the Author

Jill Meniketti manages a popular rock band that tours the world annually. She takes pride in belonging to an elite set of women who double as band managers and rock star wives (Sharon Osbourne, Wendy Dio, Denise Martin, Susan Tate, April Malmsteen, to name a few). Jill lives in the San Francisco Bay Area with her rock star husband. *Welcome to Groove House* is her debut novel.

www.JillMeniketti.com

Sign Up
To receive an automatic email when Jill's next novel is released, sign up at www.JillMeniketti.com. You will only be contacted when a new book is released; your address will never be shared, and you can unsubscribe at any time.

Spread the Love

Did you enjoy this book? Tell the world! Please consider posting a review at one of the many online sources, such as Amazon and Goodreads; even just a sentence or two would be much appreciated. Word-of-mouth is vital for any author to succeed. Thanks for your support.

Stay Connected

Jill talks about writing and the music business on her blog and conducts interviews with music business insiders on her feature *Behind the Art*.

Follow Jill online:

www.JillMeniketti.com
www.facebook.com/JillMeniketti
Twitter: @JillMeniketti